Praise for Barney Campbell's first novel, *Rain*

'No better on-the-ground description of Britain's war in Afghanistan will ever be written. *Rain* is what *Chickenhawk* or, more recently, *Matterhorn* was to Vietnam. It's unputdownable, except for when the reader needs to draw breath or battle a lump in the throat.'
EVENING STANDARD

'The best book about the experience of soldiering I've read since Robert Graves's First World War classic *Goodbye to All That* . . . *Rain* is a heartbreaking, brutally truthful first novel written with love and respect for the guys in the frontline.'
SUNDAY TIMES

'*Rain* is not merely good, it's remarkable. Powerful, at times unbearably harrowing, it captures both the fear and exhilaration of men pushed to breaking point.'
JEREMY PAXMAN

'A wonderfully achieved, enthralling and moving novel of war. Its authenticity is as telling as it is terrifying.'
WILLIAM BOYD

'Gripping . . . the ending is genuinely shocking.'
DAILY MAIL

'One of the most powerful and emotional works ever written about British soldiers in battle. Troubling, funny, upsetting, exhilarating and deeply moving. You will never forget it.'
COLONEL RICHARD KEMP

THE FIRES OF GALLIPOLI

BARNEY CAMPBELL

Elliott&Thompson

First published 2025 by
Elliott and Thompson Limited
2 John Street
London WC1N 2ES
www.eandtbooks.com

ISBN (hardback): 978-1-78396-707-0
ISBN (trade paperback): 978-1-78396-901-2

Permissions:
Page vii: 'The Midnight Skaters' from *Selected Poems* by Edmund Blunden
(Carcanet Press), reproduced by permission of David Higham Associates.

Cover imagery © David Osborn / Alamy (plane); © Science History
Images / Alamy (soldiers); Zoonar GmbH / Alamy (sky); © Mrdoomits /
Dreamstime.com (smoke); © Brooks, Ernest (Lieutenant) / IWM.org.uk
(Gallipoli landscape)

9 8 7 6 5 4 3 2 1

A catalogue record for this book is available from
the British Library.

Typesetting: Marie Doherty
Printed by CPI Group (UK) Ltd, Croydon, CR0 4YY

In loving memory of my father,
Andrew Campbell (1954–2021)

Ne Obliviscaris

The Midnight Skaters

The hop-poles stand in cones,
   The icy pond lurks under,
The pole-tops steeple to the thrones
   Of stars, sound gulfs of wonder;
But not the tallest there, 'tis said,
Could fathom to this pond's black bed.

Then is not death at watch
   Within those secret waters?
What wants he but to catch
   Earth's heedless sons and daughters?
With but a crystal parapet
Between, he has his engines set.

Then on, blood shouts, on, on,
   Twirl, wheel and whip above him,
Dance on this ball-floor thin and wan,
   Use him as though you love him;
Court him, elude him, reel and pass,
And let him hate you through the glass.

Edmund Blunden

PART ONE

CHAPTER ONE

Valletta, Malta, May 1915

The bar was packed. Smoke billowed out of the door, creating an inviting fug. Edward Salter and Bruce Haynes-Mattingly looked at each other. Edward shrugged and said, 'Well, I'm game if you are.'

It was appreciably more welcoming than the one they had just come from, full of agreeable chatter rather than shouting, singing and the feeling of a fight about to break out. Edward went to the counter, worming his way through a few kilted Highland regiment officers in full throttle, and ordered a couple of large whiskies.

By the time he got back, Haynes-Mattingly had found a corner table, rickety on its battered and splintered legs. They sat in awkward silence as they worked out what to say; both were too new to the regiment to talk with any real candour and share what they were actually thinking. Edward himself had only completed his training a few weeks ago, having joined the army the previous summer in the war's first frantic days, leaving his job as a solicitor in a firm in Brighton. They began to volley each other dull stories about their platoons, both trying to give the impression that they understood their soldiers far better than the other one did, without appearing to brag. It was a complicated act to keep up and Edward found it exhausting. He looked over Haynes-Mattingly's shoulder to the Highland officers at the bar, envious of their fond camaraderie. After a while they both became increasingly distracted by the activity around one of the billiard tables, gave up talking and went over to investigate.

Shouts went up as one of the players – a bald and ruddy-moustachioed lieutenant from another infantry regiment – potted the black with brio before standing straight and shaking the hand of his opponent. A captain, younger than his comrade and clearly the self-appointed compere, announced to the wider bar, 'That's eight games on the trot for the Snooker Socialist. More pockets than a tinker's jacket. Roll up, roll up, pot's now two quid; five bob buy-in and winner takes all. Any takers?' Behind him the billiards maestro quietly sipped a whisky and then chalked up his cue. As no one else was volunteering, Edward stepped forward on a whim.

He shook his opponent's hand, unable to register his name over the din, and they got down to it. The break wasn't half bad and Edward soon took the upper hand, potting three on the trot. The cue felt good in his hands as he eased through the gears, the whisky burning benignly inside him. The crowd started to show its tension as his challenge grew first more credible and before long inevitable. Then, as he lined up a relatively easy shot to take his final ball off the table with the black perched over a middle pocket, he looked over to catch Haynes-Mattingly's eye and wink at him theatrically.

As he did so he lost his stride. Next to Haynes-Mattingly was a man whom Edward had not seen before and who raised his glass to him in a good-luck gesture, face lit up in an enormous smile. Caught off guard, Edward parried the shot, hitting the cue ball a fraction unsoundly so that the target ball cannoned limply off the sides of the pocket. A sigh went up from the crowd.

He closed his eyes and rubbed his forehead in frustration. His opponent methodically chalked his cue with a fastidious elan, before appraising the tip as though he were inspecting one of his soldiers on muster parade. He swiftly took his own remaining balls off and then firmly potted the black. Cheers went up again. He held his hand out to Edward and said, 'Good game, laddie.

You let me off the hook there. You deserved to win. What did you say your name was again?'

'Salter, Queen Anne's Own. Yours?'

'Attlee. East Lancs.'

'Well, best of luck with the next victim.'

A new challenger having been found, Edward retreated to where Haynes-Mattingly stood with the man who had distracted him. He wondered if this might be the new platoon commander they were due.

The new arrival held out his hand. 'Theodore Thorne. Six Platoon commander. I hear you've got Five.'

Edward looked him up and down, meeting his hand. 'Hello. Pleased to meet you. Edward Salter. Yes, Five are mine, lucky mob that they are.' He grinned self-deprecatingly, hoping he would thus convey a deep sense of familiarity with his men and mask the fact that he barely knew them. Thorne's honest and open face laughed dutifully at his line. Edward liked his confidence.

'Would you like us to call you Theodore?'

'Theo, if you like. Or just Thorne. I'm not really bothered.'

'How old are you, if you don't mind me asking?' From the look of him he could have been any age between eighteen and thirty.

'Twenty-two.' Not so far removed, then, from Edward's twenty-five.

'What were you doing before all this?' He flicked a hand behind him as if to encapsulate not just the bar but the Dardanelles expedition in its carnival entirety.

'Nothing much, pottering round at home really. I'd just come down from Oxford. Preparing to go to the Bar.' He nodded over to the crowd behind him. 'Talking of bars, fancy something?'

Edward smiled and wiped a smear of sweat from the corner of his eye. 'I'd love one. Beer, please. As cold as possible.'

They waited for him to fully disappear into the noise and Edward looked back to the billiard table where he noted with some satisfaction that his successor had been made short work of and the pot had now risen accordingly. He belatedly realised that Haynes-Mattingly was trying to talk to him and leant in closer, cupping his hand to his ear. 'What was that?'

'I said, seems an all right man, doesn't he? Green as hell though, eh?'

Edward paused as he assessed their brief interaction, then replied, 'Yes. He does seem all right. Cocky, maybe. And green, definitely. But then again, we're all green, aren't we?'

Haynes-Mattingly frowned in acknowledgement and downed the rest of his whisky just as Thorne reappeared with the next round.

'How on earth d'you manage that? Crowd's yards deep,' asked Edward, glancing at the barmaid who had been hatchet-faced to everyone else all evening.

Thorne grinned. 'Wink and flash a smile. Usually does the trick. Cheers, anyway. To our poor soldiers.'

Edward laughed and they clinked glasses.

There was a brief disturbance as the recently defeated billiards player bundled past them, slurring to nobody in particular, 'Right, let's get down to these famous whorehouses.'

Haynes-Mattingly smiled as he tottered off. 'Good luck to him. He'll be begging old John Turk to shoot his balls off for him.'

'Eh?' said Edward.

'Come on, man. Port city. It's rammed with sailors at the best of times but roughly a hundred thousand lads have come through here in the last few weeks. Last chance to see some brass. Every bit of skirt in town will be carrying about three dozen diseases. At the very least he'll get a bout of crotch rot.'

'Should we not go and tell him?' asked Thorne.

Haynes-Mattingly lit a cigarette, cupping his hands so that the flame threw yellow and black chiaroscuro over his face. After taking a long first drag, he said, 'Nah. Little shit has to learn somewhere, doesn't he? I would stop him, if he were our mob, but he's not, so I won't.' He tilted his head back to exhale a huge plume of smoke and smiled, the slight gap in his front teeth showing in the dull light.

Thorne looked quizzically at Edward, who raised his eyebrows a little as if to say that this behaviour was typical.

Edward was amused by Haynes-Mattingly's total lack of censoriousness. He wasn't sure he could trust him to have his back, but he had a good sense of where his moral compass pointed, which was in the direction of whichever course of action would be most beneficial to Haynes-Mattingly.

Haynes-Mattingly downed his drink quickly and then made his excuses, saying he was going to bed. Edward rather suspected he had picked up an idea from the young officer who had just staggered past them.

Edward and Thorne stayed in the bar together. The Highland regiment officers started more toasts, including to Ian Hamilton, the general commanding the Mediterranean Expeditionary Force, and finally to Lord Kitchener himself, the secretary of state for war. Edward and Thorne joined in enthusiastically and when the hubbub died down Thorne smiled and said quietly, 'I hope he's got his act together on this one. An awful lot of chaps are going to be in an awful lot of bother if he hasn't. Here, one more time to the old boy. To Lord Kitchener of Khartoum. May Edward Salter and Theodore Thorne be ever at the front of his mind.'

They raised their glasses in a final toast.

CHAPTER TWO

In the following days it became clear that Thorne was indeed a most welcome addition to B Company, whose mix of officers Edward had found to be a little dysfunctional and jarring. Paul Rossi, the company commander, was perfectly pleasant and friendly in his clipped, frank style, but not a great greaser of the wheels of conversation. Haynes-Mattingly tried gallantly if ineffectually to add some humour but always got it slightly wrong with his sharp-elbowedness and bite.

Meanwhile the second in command, David Marks – a bluff, hearty type with a loud voice that clearly grated on Rossi inordinately, although he was too polite to say it – lacked the finesse to bridge the gap between the company commander and his platoon commanders. The other platoon commander, Harold Tufnell, was nineteen if he was a day and, while personable enough, was possessed of such little bearing, made worse by a ratty weak chin and lank hair, that it was amazing that he had been granted a commission at all. Company orders groups and mealtimes together were slow, stop-and-start affairs, with no free flow of conversation. Each man's residual fear of making a fool of himself limited any kind of growth of familiarity, let alone friendship.

Thorne's arrival changed all that in a stroke, bringing them all together from scattered and gritted sprockets into something like a fluently moving unit. Something about him just gave them all a desire to be the best version of themselves. Even Tufnell came out of his shell slightly when Thorne was around. He also somehow tempered the rough edges of Haynes-Mattingly.

The days in Valletta passed in a welter of confusion, impatience, waiting, hurrying up to move somewhere before eventually moving only two hundred yards and then waiting there again, only this time no longer in shade. And everywhere the heat, the bustle, the smells, the Mediterranean patchwork of noise. The huge military presence of British, Australian, New Zealander and French troops mingled in jam-packed proximity with the locals as the city grew into its role as a staging post for troops headed east to the Gallipoli Peninsula – known by all just as 'the Peninsula'. Landings had started there in April and bitter fighting was now well-established as the Allies sought to seize control of the Dardanelles straits and force a way into the sea of Marmara, capture Constantinople and so knock Turkey out of the war.

The expeditionary edge to the air was indescribably exciting. Everywhere around Valletta was activity. Buildings were being hurriedly converted into military hospitals to cope with the pulses of hospital ships that came back daily from the Peninsula. Teams heaved requisitioned beds through the streets as though they were stagehands getting ready for a play. Engineers hauled vast drums of wire to rig up lights in the rooms that were to become wards. Packs of nurses immaculate in their blue and white uniforms thronged the streets, sometimes passing in chaste silence, sometimes chatting and cackling.

Tempers in the battalion frayed as rumour and counter rumour flew backwards and forwards. Were they going to Cape Helles on the Peninsula as they had been told when they had left Southampton? Or would it be Cairo, which now felt an enormous letdown.

One morning, the battalion trooped onto a ship where they were packed into the lower decks and baked in its bowels until evening. It seemed they were finally on their way, although no one knew where exactly to. B Company took up a compartment between two huge bulkheads, a hundred men nearly on top of each other, their hair matted with sweat and many of them topless due to the heat, skin glistening in the low light.

Edward, bored, clambered half-blind over a few of his platoon to get to Thorne, who was deep in conversation with a few of his own men about what each had been up to the previous summer before war had been declared. He noted, not for the first time and with a mix of admiration and envy, how good Thorne was at speaking to soldiers, with the quiet, unshakeable confidence of someone who had been popular all his life and who knew instinctively how to establish an easy communion with anyone.

'Room for a small one?' said Edward as the conversation wound up, and Thorne budged along for Edward to squeeze in next to him, the floor a mess of packs and rifles.

Carrying on the theme of his previous conversation, Thorne turned to Edward and said, 'So what were you doing when Franz Ferdinand got shot?'

'You won't believe it, but I was actually in Russia.'

'Russia?'

'Yup. I was visiting my old governess. My father worked in St Petersburg with his textiles company for a few years; moved there just after I was born. Katarina Kovalyova was my governess. My first true love. I doted on her. Now, sadly, she's Mrs Zubareva. Married a grim engineer from Moscow. Rather like my sister, Cynthia, who married a grim engineer on the railways in India. Dreadful man. Story of my life; both the women I've ever loved stolen from me by engineers. Anyway, I was staying with the Zubarevs on holiday when the news came through. Don't know if I saw what way the wind was blowing exactly, but I pretty soon guessed that I needed to get back home so I cadged a ride on a merchantman back to London. And then the rest of the summer happened as it happened.'

'Do you still speak Russian?'

'Just as a hobby. There was a chap in Brighton, an old boy from Yekaterinburg who repaired pianos. I'd often go and meet him after work and we'd chat away. Quite fun to keep it going.'

Thorne waved his hand to indicate where they were. 'But why all this? Didn't you want to say you spoke it so you could get some intelligence job? Cloak and dagger spy stuff?'

'Not really. Rather fancied just being in the normal army. I'm sure if they really need someone they'll find me.'

Thorne smiled. Edward was about to ask him more about what he had been doing himself but a low murmur started going round the hold. Were they finally to be told where they were headed? Edward was convinced that they were still going to the Peninsula, with Thorne sure that it was Cairo, saying, 'Either way it doesn't really matter. We'll still get a suntan.'

They were quiet for a while in the heavy twilight before Thorne went on. 'You know I've seen the Peninsula before?'

'What? When?'

'A couple of years ago. Summer before my final year at Oxford.'

'What were you doing?'

'Travelling round the Lycian coast, way further south. Just me on my own. It was a great trip. On the way back to Constantinople to get the train home I decided on a whim to stop off at Troy, just to see what it's like.'

Edward smiled. 'To tread in the footsteps of Achilles, eh?'

'Bugger off. I hate that claptrap. All that grandstanding and navel-gazing about us being the heirs to the Trojan war. Never liked the *Iliad* anyway.'

'Heresy!' Edward laughed. 'Or are you being like people who say they hate Mozart, just to stir a reaction?'

'Maybe a little. But for me, it's just a load of loudmouths babbling away about glory and never any mention of their soldiers or the common man. I mean, maybe with the exception of Sarpedon. Look, I'm no bloody socialist but that entire poem is pampered aristos falling over themselves to see who can gain the most honour.'

'Says the pampered aristo.'

'Touché. But, you know, the *Iliad's* still the *Iliad*, so I had to stop and see Troy. I remember quite clearly looking across the water and seeing the Peninsula.'

Edward waited a little as Thorne paused, seemingly serious at last, before saying, 'Go on.'

'Honestly can't say I've seen a more nondescript piece of land in my life. I mean, I bet there are valleys and gullies and high ground and places to bathe in the wine-dark Aegean and watch the rosy-fingered dawn every day and all that rot, but at no point did I ever think, "Oh my, what a signal honour it would be to go there and get my face shot off by a Turk."'

He wound up and said, 'Now, I know I'm the junior platoon commander here, but shall we go and find out what the hell's going on? At least get some fresh air? This place reeks.'

Edward nodded in amusement.

They made to pick their way out of the humidity of the hold, when the burble of low chatter and snores around them stopped and the eyes of the company as one turned to the door. Rossi stood silhouetted there, his nasal voice rising to reach all the men. 'I've just come from the CO. I've got good news and bad news. Good news – we're not going to Egypt; we're going to Helles.'

A weird mix of excited gasps, groans and low cheers reverberated around the metal walls, as though Rossi had his foot on a sustaining piano pedal. 'The bad news is we're not going to get there for a while. We're going to Lemnos, where the battalion is to provide garrison guard at Mudros harbour. But only for a couple of weeks. And then Helles.'

Sensing the downward shift in mood at this delay, he reasoned, 'Cheer up, chaps. It'll be a good opportunity for training—' more groans '—and the Turks aren't going to go away. There'll be enough opportunity for you to all have your fill of scrapping by the time the summer is out. Even you, Baffle.' Laughs went up from everyone and Rossi added, 'One more bit of bad news. This isn't the ship. We're going next week. We've got to be off here in twenty minutes for some other mob. Sergeant Major, carry on.'

The groans multiplied over each other and Rossi left, replaced by Sergeant Major Leyburn barking at them to gather their kit together and get a move on.

Thorne and Edward lay back for a moment to wait until there was space to gather their gear. 'Who's Baffle?' asked Thorne.

'You haven't met Baffle yet? My platoon, one of the lance corporals. Famous regimental character. Should be a sergeant, at least, but he keeps getting busted down for fighting. His nickname's "Three Bar", as he's either propping up the bar, beating people with bars or behind bars. He's quite a character. Charming chap though.'

'Hey, do you reckon we'll get some time to explore Lemnos?'

'I imagine so. Not sure how much goes on there though. Why d'you ask?'

The hold now having largely emptied, Thorne stood up and started to put on all his kit. 'Long story. You'll see.'

CHAPTER THREE

Edward's lungs felt as though they were bruising as they heaved and heaved, trying desperately to get oxygen round his body as he scrambled up what seemed to be the final stretch of the mountain after Thorne. His tunic was dark with sweat and every time he paused a hundred flies – death-black and hateful – descended on him. They were making fast progress, desperate to escape the lee and allow the wind to blow the devils away.

After a series of false summits, the slope finally fell away and he saw Thorne on the top, bent double, hands on knees, smiling back at him, a tossed forelock of his mousey-blond hair drooping down over his face. Edward joined him and they looked down at the spread-out majesty of the island beneath. To their west the enormous quilt of Mudros harbour was studded with battleships and cruisers, smaller destroyers and lighters beetling around them. Around its lip dust was being kicked up from the British and French camps at the shores as the men woke up to another day. A troopship was entering the harbour; impossible to know if it was coming from Britain with fresh men, or from the Peninsula with broken ones, bound for the teeming hospital.

Edward took his water bottle from his haversack and drew heavily from it. The blue of the sea spread all around them was of a kind he had only ever read about before and was fringed in the distance with a creamy, biscuit-yellow line. Turkey. His first glance of it. It was, as he started to rationalise what he was seeing, an extraordinary feeling, taking in not just the here and now of Lemnos's dirt and dust under his feet but of Imbros in the middle distance and then, slightly hiding in a faint haze, the Peninsula. It took him several minutes to try to articulate properly but in the end he just said, simply, 'It's magnificent. I feel like a god up here.'

Thorne wasn't listening to him, intent on looking to the east through his binoculars. Seeming to have found what he wanted, he turned round and surveyed the whole of the island to their west, his top teeth biting into the lower lip in frustration. 'Bugger. Bugger, bugger, bugger. It's impossible.'

Three weeks into their stint of guard duty at Mudros, the battalion was on a rest day. The initial excitement at being closer to the Peninsula – now only fifty miles away and near enough on some nights for them to hear the artillery – had faded into bored contempt once they had realised there was nothing to guard against. All the companies' officers had had their work cut out devising ways to keep the soldiers occupied, there being only so many times one could practise digging or trench routine and only so often one could zero a rifle.

Rossi, a stalwart of the Territorials before the war, and so already well-versed in the management of boredom, was good at encouraging skits and entertainment, with Edward memorably putting in a stint as a pantomime dame and being propositioned by Baffle; for B Company, at least, the Lemnos stay, while dull, had not been unduly tiresome.

They had all been given a Sunday off. Early that morning, as Marks, Haynes-Mattingly and Tufnell snored off hangovers in the tent they all shared, Edward had been shaken awake by Thorne who had whispered, 'Come on, we're going on a secret mission,' before leading him out of the garrison to a Greek with a handsome black horse and a cart.

'Where did you find him?' Edward had asked, still rubbing sleep from his eyes and yawning, not quite understanding why he was up and about.

'Made friends with him a few days ago. A few bob and he's ours for the day. On me, I insist. I love the horse; he's rather like the station one at home.'

As the day had opened up, they'd settled into a lull, sitting on the back of the cart as the horse went on at a comfortably sclerotic pace. Overnight rain had stopped the wheels kicking up any dust, and they'd sat with their legs dangling, looking at the expanse of the harbour growing bigger as they got further away from it.

After an hour or so, the farmer had stopped and pointed to the hills about a mile away, behind scrappy low orchards and olive groves through which the cart would not go. In sign language, and some pidgin ancient Greek, Thorne had seemed to reach an agreement with him that he would meet them back there at four o'clock, and then he went on his way, leaving them surrounded by the hot day and the chatter of crickets.

For the next two hours they had laboured up the hill wordlessly, pausing only to drink water, neither wanting to pre-empt what they knew would be an extraordinary view by turning round to take it in too early.

And now they were at the top. Edward span around, his arms outstretched, marvelling at the absurd omnipotence of being able to see almost the entirety of the key locations of the Mediterranean Expeditionary Force. He felt better than he could remember, as though he was finally enjoying being a young man. He took his shirt off, feeling the sweat on his chest hair chill and noting how absurdly white his torso looked next to his nut-brown forearms.

Thorne was still cursing, alternating between his map and binoculars, now looking out to Turkey and then back over the rest of the island. For the first time Edward noticed the size of his map.

'Where on earth did you get that from?'

Thorne answered absent-mindedly, 'Oh, a pal from school on one of the destroyers. It's great, isn't it? Takes in the whole of this part of the Aegean. Don't worry, it's fine. I'm giving it back to him tonight.'

'What the hell, if you don't mind me asking, are you doing anyway? Just enjoy the view. You're like an umpire fussing over some blades of grass on a wicket.'

With a sigh, Thorne relented, putting the binoculars down. With a child's flexibility he collapsed his leg muscles to sit down cross-legged exactly where he had stood.

'Right,' said Edward. 'Good. Now, what are we doing here?'

The disappointment in Thorne's voice gradually gave way to enthusiasm. 'In Aeschylus's play *Agamemnon*, there's a passage narrated by Agamemnon's wife Clytemnestra in which she says that she knows that Troy has fallen because the beacon chain that goes from Troy all the way across the Aegean to Mycenae has been lit. She lists the names of all the mountains on the way that had a beacon on them. There's about eight or nine or so in all, and there are some lines missing from the passage. But the first part survives intact, and it's quite clear. With a map and a bit of initiative you can have a fair stab at where they would have been. With me so far?'

Edward nodded.

'The beacon starts on Mount Ida,' continued Thorne, 'just behind Troy. That's easy enough – you can see it to the right of the Peninsula.' He jerked his thumb behind him dismissively in its general direction. Edward thought he could make out a low rise in the hazy strip where he thought he ought to be looking. 'But the next bit is why we're here now. The second beacon in the passage is on Hermes' Mount on Lemnos, which is this, here, I think. Well, I can see Ida, fine, but the problem is that the next beacon is on Mount Athos, south of Salonika, and that's what I've been trying to find. We're on the wrong side of the island for it and you can't see it at all for the other damned hills.'

'So the passage is wrong?'

'Not necessarily. I mean, the description makes broad sense.

18

You would go from Ida to Lemnos to Athos, but the thing is you need more than one beacon on Lemnos to do it.'

'Is that so bad?'

Thorne clicked his fingers. 'I mean, not really, but it just loses a bit of its simplicity and elegance. It would have been so good if it had worked. And my old tutor would have absolutely loved it if it had. We always had this thing about how great it would be to one day create the beacon chain again.'

'We could have done all this from a map and trigonometry, surely?'

Thorne's eyes widened as if it was the stupidest question he had ever heard. 'Of course we could. But where would the fun be in that?'

He dug into his pocket for a handkerchief and accidentally brought his wallet out too, spilling it onto the ground, several of its contents caught by the breeze and blowing around the dust.

Thorne swore and scrabbled around on his knees, trying to gather everything up. Edward got down too and intercepted a photograph as it skimmed towards him.

Thorne managed to recover the couple of other loose pieces, looked over at what Edward had done and said, 'Thank Christ for that. Thanks, old chap. Nearly gave me a heart attack.'

Edward gave the photo a reflex glance, more out of instinct than interest. It was of Thorne and a young lady at the piano in evening dress, he sitting and she standing behind him. His hands rested on the keys as he looked back at the camera while she held his shoulders, also caught in mid-turn backwards as though surprised by the photographer. In the background was the curve and sweep of a grand staircase.

Edward reddened and, holding it out, said, 'Sorry – couldn't help it. Nice picture.' Thorne took it and slid it back into his wallet, a natty red leather one. Edward didn't want to say anything more, intrigued though he was. He didn't think Thorne was married. Sister? Fiancée? Perhaps even his mother, if she had had him very young. He knew Haynes-Mattingly would have probed immediately and would already be extemporising fearlessly on some lewd conjecture.

Thorne seemed to read Edward's thoughts. 'Nothing very interesting, I'm afraid. Me and my sister at home. Taken at Easter last year. I've always liked it; makes us look far more musically serious than we actually are. We look like a pair of composers, don't you think?'

They stayed up on the summit for another hour, lying down to bake in the sun before a slight drop in the breeze augured the afternoon getting ready for evening. They dressed and made their way down the hill, meeting the farmer as arranged at the rendezvous. On the way back Thorne, with a Labrador's ease, slept in the back of the wagon while Edward sat, rubbing the dried sweat and salt from his forehead and creases around his eyes, enjoying their tang in his mouth.

The wagon went over a bump and the jolt woke Thorne. He sat up and after a moment, unprompted, said, 'My photograph. You know that was taken the day before old Franz Ferdinand was shot? I'd just come home from playing cricket and as I was getting changed for dinner, Miranda – that's my sister – came into my room with a lemon, an ice bucket, a knife – devilishly sharp – and a bottle of gin. I poured the drinks and, like a surgeon, she sliced off a strip of peel, cut it in two and dropped them in to the glasses at the last moment. We always had this line one of us would say after the first sip, "The only thing better than the first sip of a martini is . . ." and then the other would say ". . . the first sip of the second martini" and we'd down the first one and pour a second. So by the time we went down to dinner we were quite well oiled. And my mother made us pose for the photograph at the piano. Somehow, we both manage to look semi-compos mentis though, don't we?'

He paused and seemed to lose himself in memory for a while. Then he smiled and said, 'And you know, when we had that second martini, I made a toast. "To the summer." And she replied with, "To the summer. And many more like it."' He laughed and said quietly, 'And now this. What a bloody mess.'

After arriving back at the harbour, they walked into camp, the bay ahead of them a huge glittering expanse of metal ships glinting against the setting sun. In the mess tent they found Haynes-Mattingly playing a game of backgammon with a subaltern from A Company, Daniels. He winked at them conspiratorially and mimed to be silent; it became clear he was in the process of destroying his opponent who presently threw in the towel and stormed out, having lost what looked like several pounds. Haynes-Mattingly grinned. 'Nice little earner, this lot. Hook, line and sinker. Bluffed him for a few games that I was a duffer, he fell for it and then I cleaned him out. Four of His Majesty's quid.' His face then fell a little and he added, 'Buggered if I know what to do with it though. Sod all places to spend it. Hang on, what the hell *do* I do with it?'

Edward sat down in a chair opposite him. 'You could send it home.'

'No chance. Bloody wife will only go and spend it. Just have to keep it on my person. Oh well – at least if I cop a shell I'll go out in an explosion of banknotes. Could look rather good. Where have you characters been anyway? Thick as thieves, you two.'

'On some wild goose chase that Thorne invented only to find that the goose wasn't a goose at all. It was a measly old pigeon. All to do with Aeschylus' *Agamemnon* . . .'

Haynes-Mattingly groaned and held out a palm. 'I'll stop you there, old boy. You public school types and your bloody obsession with all that stuff.'

Edward admitted defeat and raised his eyebrows in apologetic acknowledgement.

'Anyway,' Haynes-Mattingly continued, 'from what I hear there'll be precious little chance for you two to carry on all this tomfoolery. Rumour has it the brigade commander wants us out on the Peninsula sharpish.'

Edward stopped and tried to assess what it was that he felt at that moment, surprised at how bloodlessly he reacted. Haynes-Mattingly was a great one for rumours, but the offhand way in which he had relayed this one lent it more authority than his usual utterances. Edward felt his gaze upon him. Knowing that he had to say something that would at least make him not look utterly terrified, he somehow managed, 'Well, I hope the food's a damn sight better than here.' That picked up a quorum of chuckles to show that he had passed the test. Emboldened, he sat down in the chair opposite and added, 'So not long for me to take those four pounds off you and your loaded dice.'

'As if I'd do a thing like that.'

They were indeed not long for Lemnos. The next evening saw the commanding officer address the battalion, all six hundred soldiers sitting on a low sloping bank as he stood before them. Colonel Ackrill was an old Indian Army man who had retired in 1913 only to be mobilised again a year later at the advent of the war to take over the newly formed battalion and whip it into shape. He had done an inordinately good job despite the fact that he looked like someone who would need help whipping cream. Slight and bookish, and lacking the moustache that would have lent him a more military mien, he had the demeanour of a benignly remote academic. His rather uninterested air made him seem to regard the prospect of the battalion fighting like a father regards his son's first proper game of schoolboy cricket – of interest, certainly, but not particularly worth losing sleep over. His first name was Raymond, which seemed to Edward rather apt.

His speech was, to Edward's mind, not exactly a rousing call to arms, something the colonel himself acknowledged, saying, 'I'll keep this simple, gentlemen, I know it's late.' They were to leave in four days for the fighting on Cape Helles at the tip of the Gallipoli Peninsula. There the British and French were trying to sweep the Turks back and so link up with the Australians and New Zealanders established some miles to their north. Holding the whole Peninsula would allow the navy to push through the Dardanelles and so toward Constantinople.

He focused on the necessity of victory to the swift conclusion of the wider war and the difficulty of the terrain they would be fighting on. They were up against a determined and skilful enemy who was fighting in his own country, but they could count on the navy and their allies on the Peninsula, throwing in for good measure: 'Even the French on our right flank are doing a good job, they say.' He couldn't say exactly what they would be doing on Helles but whatever it was he was sure the battalion would acquit itself favourably. He kept it brief and to the point.

Afterwards, as the officers dispersed back to the mess, Haynes-Mattingly said, 'Well, I suppose he obeyed the golden rule of making speeches like a tart's drawers; long enough to cover the essentials but short enough to keep you interested.'

When the day of departure finally came, a succession of lighters were to ferry them out to the ship. An hour before the first one left, the colonel gathered the officers together for a photograph. A camera on a tripod was set up, a nervous-looking lance corporal clerk from HQ Company detailed as photographer.

Edward stood next to Marks and Haynes-Mattingly and behind Rossi, who was in the front row. Thorne and Tufnell, as the youngest officers in the battalion, sat cross-legged before the front row like a pair of schoolboys.

In between the takes, Edward glanced to his left and right and tried to impress the scene into his mind's eye: Thorne with his slightly-too-long hair hanging over his collar; Haynes-Mattingly with his cap tilted artfully in the affected manner with which he tried to achieve maximum rakishness; Rossi fastidious and fussy over his uniform, his tie kept in check by the tiny gold pin that his wife had given him. The colonel himself sat like a tiny sparrow in the middle of them, his worn uniform yellowed by years of foreign sun and comically different to their own ones – issued only months before and still scratchy in their newness.

Edward knew that the law of averages, the law of war and the law of sheer bloody obviousness all demanded that this would be the last time this exact group would ever be together. Still, however, some sprite of a hope jumped in his head that they might all survive unscathed, might all gather in the same arrangement for a second time in a few months.

After several efforts it was deemed that at least one picture would be good enough and the colonel stood up and turned to face them. Taking his cap off to run a hand through his hair, he was silent for a little while, scanning them, thirty-odd in all, with something approaching a hint of sadness. 'Well, gentlemen, I'll see the company commanders on the boat, but for most of the rest of you, I won't see you until we're on the Peninsula. Look after your men, good luck and God speed. Hold fast to your marksmanship principles and look after your rifles. They'll see us through.' He paused as if on the verge of saying something lengthier but held it in, turned, smiled and said to the lance corporal standing nervously behind him, 'That's it. I look forward to seeing the photograph.' He put his cap on again and walked away towards the beach, hands behind his back as he whistled to himself. The group broke up and went to join their men.

A few hours later, the battalion was on its way towards Helles. Edward stood on deck, surprised to be almost alone save for a few of the ship's crew. He waved to the escorting destroyer and then felt rather foolish for doing so, looking round self-consciously to make sure he hadn't been seen. He leant against the railings and watched the ring of hills around the bay as they receded first into the haze and then into the sea behind them. He thought about the photograph and how he should like to see it printed, as though its record of them all together, strong and healthy and safe, would somehow act as a blanket, a memento of a time when everything was all right.

PART TWO

CHAPTER FOUR

Edward rolled over the hump, lay still on his back and looked above him, taking in the gulf of black and diamonds. For a few seconds it seemed that he was the only man on the Peninsula, and then the low shuffling of Baffle and Mason came to him and he felt a hand grasp his ankle. A firm finger tapped twice, meaning it was Baffle; Mason was one tap. He raised his head slightly and could just make their shapes out, darker black against the black enveloping them. Far away, machine gun fire sounded, but so distant and diffracted that to a layman it might have sounded like an unusually loud cricket. Then silence. Edward waited for it to start up again and, when it didn't, rolled back onto his front. Elbow by elbow, painfully slowly and with his nose scraping the dust, he pulled himself along another couple of yards. Then he stopped again, waited for the grab and tap on his ankles, waited some more and carried on.

All three of their faces were caked with boot polish and each had a revolver – Edward his own and the two soldiers having borrowed theirs from Thorne and Marks. 'Ever fired one of these?' Edward had asked them as they'd prepared to leave the trench. Baffle had looked at the weapon with a sneer, replying, 'No, but it can't be fucking hard, can it, sir? Just point it at some cunt's face and pull the trigger, surely?'

Behind them, now some forty yards away, two platoons of the company stood line-abreast, rifles cocked, safety catches off and fingers ghosting pressure on their triggers to lay down a blanket of covering fire if the Turks heard them and they had to run back.

Edward and his tiny patrol were out to try to gauge how far apart the two front lines were from each other in advance of a planned raid on those same trenches on one of the following nights. They had left the trench, worming over the lip of the parapet, at 23:00. It was now 01:20. In the trench Rossi was starting to get nervy, though when he could sense the same impatience in the soldiers, standing in their rictus poses for so long, he realised he had to suppress it. He patted each man he came to on the back, trying to prolong even slightly the adrenaline that had kept them alert for the first couple of hours.

To Edward, out in the scrub, it felt in his blindness as though he had only left the trench ten minutes ago. There was a cord clipped to the rear of his belt that Thorne had been feeding out since he had left. When he got to where he thought the Turkish front trench must be, he was to reach behind him, tug it several times and then unclip it, so that Thorne could then mark exactly how much had been used. The mission had come down from battalion and Rossi had given it to Edward's platoon, his clipped and bloodless orders ostensibly giving Edward perfect liberty to send whichever three of his soldiers he wanted, but with an unspoken inference that there was no circumstance whatsoever under which it would be acceptable for Edward not to lead it himself. Baffle had not been hard to choose, being the most obviously violent of his soldiers, and Mason he chose purely because he was next to Baffle at the time. It helped that Mason was the chalk to Baffle's cheese, quiet and unshowy against the other's constant chirping and chatter.

This was the first action of any note to have been taken by B Company and Edward had felt like a celebrity ever since word had got round the men, though he knew inside that anyone with any experience of real fighting, like the company that they had replaced in the trenches only that morning, would have thought it small beer. After several weeks in the line, their predecessors had managed to seize these new positions in an attack that had 'ironed out' a little salient and thus rationalised the brigade's frontage. It also meant that B Company now looked out over land as yet unspoilt, save for a few shell holes, by the trench fighting which had rendered almost every other part of the line nearly unbearable.

At these other places the line was infused with the stench of bodies in states of decomposition ranging from the newly butchered and still bleeding to bags of bones, which were only kept in some semblance of human shape by their clothing, scraps of meat and tendons hanging off the parts that the birds and rats couldn't get to. And everywhere, layered on top of anything that could ever decompose – skin, blood, flesh, food, vomit, shit, hair – were flies. Millions upon billions of them swarmed and then landed onto their countless others in a sick black impasto, the sight of them already so firmly stuck in Edward's memory that when he closed his eyes and thought of them he felt a pull at the back of his throat.

At least here, however, in this recently taken and unsullied part of the line, they were spared temporarily the wriggling, seething carpets of them that were all over the rest of the Peninsula – covering dead horses, severed limbs, biscuits and backs of necks; finding their way into yawning mouths and bullet wounds; flying from latrines to food to open wounds and then back to the food, dropping larvae, infection and dysentery from their hideous bodies onto everything they touched.

On Edward pressed in his crawl, every pebble felt by his elbows, knowing that every movement he made took him that bit closer to the Turkish line. Every time he paused, he made a conscious effort, for the first time in his life, to try to pump as much blood to his ears and try to get them to be as sensitive as possible. He felt a sharpness and focus, a purity of thought and action, that he had never thought possible before, and he had to stifle a sudden laugh at this newness.

He blinked several times to try to zone back in on the task. And then, just as he tensed to shuffle forward again, he heard a voice, quite clear, speaking a low, easy phrase lilted at the end in a question. Behind him, he sensed Baffle and Mason tensing up too. Then a couple of seconds later a reply came, heavier and grumpier, ending in a little chuckle. Any doubt that he had about his ability to judge distance accurately vanished – he knew exactly how far away the voices were: no more than four yards. A pride at having got so close to the trench was replaced by a horrible tingling through his capillaries to his fingertips, like coolant in an engine, at being so close to the opposite line.

For a moment he lay still, before being seized by the twin imperatives of having to complete the patrol and the knowledge that if he stayed there he was a dead man. Two hands landed on each of his calves – two taps on his right, one tap on his left. Baffle and Mason. In answer he lifted both his legs twice, hinging them at the knee to signal that they were to turn back. Reaching behind his back he unclipped the twine from his belt. Thorne would reel it in once they had got back. He made to worm himself around but stopped himself upon realising how loud it would be, so wriggled backwards instead, feeling the two others do the same until they had covered enough ground to distance themselves and turn around.

When they were set they continued their crawl, faster now and with an abandon growing with every foot they got away from the Turks. Then a scrape of metal that Edward recognised as a rifle being slowly cocked came from his front left, only two yards away. He froze, his mind flicking through thoughts and options. Not Baffle or Mason; they were behind him and, judging from their lack of movement, they had heard it too. They could conceivably have crawled in a circle and be back at the Turkish line where they had already been, but surely not. There was no way it was their own line yet, unless they had crawled at an extraordinarily fast pace.

He reached blindly to his front and side, tracing his fingers over the earth to feel for the twine that he had let go, cursing himself that he had discarded it. Then there was the same low deep voice that he had heard in the Turkish trench, coming from exactly the same direction as the rifle sound. His brain thumped with confusion. He played through what he knew: when he had first heard the voice it was to his ten o'clock. Now, having crawled back in a straight line it was still to his ten o'clock. At the very moment he realised what had happened he felt a body crawl up alongside him, so close that at times it was on top of his. Mason put his mouth to his ear, his moustache scouring Edward's lobe. 'Sap, sir,' he whispered.

His brain cleared. They were crawling parallel to a sentry's sap trench – an advanced listening post – that the Turks had dug out into No Man's Land perpendicular to their main trench. The man they had heard had – presumably – just taken over in the sap. If it hadn't been the same voice that he had heard then the chance of guessing what had happened would have been remote.

Edward figured they had two choices: one, to carry on crawling back to their lines, hoping that they could remain undetected; or, two, crawl towards the sap, drop into it and kill the sentry, assuming there was only one of him. Deciding that discretion was the better part of valour, for this first night at least, he continued on his crawl, shuffling to the right a little to get as far away as possible from the sap. For the first few feet he moved painfully slowly, hoping the others had got the message about heading back – he could just imagine Baffle deciding to take matters into his own hands.

Then, in a chance that made him want to shout with joy, his little finger hooked on the twine that he had let go earlier. Confident now that they were far enough away from the sap to be able to do so, he measured a whisper that he was sure would die almost as soon as it was past their ears and said, 'I've got the route. Let's go.' He turned round to crawl off faster and surer than he had done all evening. It was as though the twine, with Thorne at its end, acted as an umbilical cord, feeding his limbs and muscles with a new invincibility. Faster and faster they crawled, and it was only a change in the scent of the air – a waft of tobacco mixed with sweat hitting his nostrils instead of the usual musty sterility of the dirt – that made him stop and feel forward a little. There it was, the lip of their own parapet.

He bundled himself over and turned back to help Mason and then Baffle into the trench too. They collapsed into its shelter, feeling the sides protecting them like mice burrowing into hay. The low candlelight from the lanterns that hung along the walls of the trench was shockingly bright to Edward's eyes as they panted in great heaves, their lungs desperate to get oxygen round their starved muscles.

'What's the time?' he said to nobody in particular and Rossi replied, standing above him. 'Zero four hundred. How was it out there? Took your time, eh? Thought you were crawling all the way to Constantinople. Patrol report in my dugout in an hour. Zero-five.' With that he melted down the trench away from them and Edward heard Baffle mutter, 'Fucking stuck-up knobhead.'

They stood up and Edward sent them to get as much rest as they could before dawn. Thorne appeared next to them with a rifle. 'Yours, Mr Baffle, I believe?'

'Ar, thanks, sir, was hoping you'd forget about that. Was getting used to the Webley. Don't want to go back to lugging that piece of shite around.' They swapped weapons and Baffle then left, while Edward and Thorne sat back down in the nook of the trench. Silence fell for a while as Thorne let him gather his thoughts.

'Want one?' said Thorne eventually, lighting a couple of cigarettes and putting one straight into Edward's mouth without waiting for a reply.

'Thanks.' Edward took a long draw.

They sat some more, smoking and looking through the gloom

34

as it slowly faded until they could pick out all the details of the side of the trench facing them.

'You know what one of those heirs-to-the-*Iliad* bores would have made of all this, don't you?' said Thorne.

'No, what?'

Thorne nodded over at the remainder of the twine, Edward's lifeline, rolled up round a stake. 'Ariadne's thread.'

They both laughed quietly. Edward said, 'God, can't you just imagine them?'

'Do you want to know how far you went?'

Edward exhaled loudly and shrugged. 'Honestly, it could have been anything from five to five hundred yards. I have no idea.'

'Sixty. With slack bits and tangles I'd say their lines are fifty yards from ours. I've told the OC. Don't worry about all that curtness when you got back – I think he likes to put out this image of him being a cold fish. All the time you were out there he was up and down the men, keeping everyone alert. I must say we thought you lot had been captured at one point you were out so long. It was torture for us back here, so God knows what it was like for you three. How was it?'

Edward couldn't believe he was hearing the words come from his own mouth as he replied, 'It was bloody marvellous.' He paused for a moment more, smiled to himself and got up. 'Right, better go and do the report.' At that moment, veins still flush with the dregs of his adrenaline and buoyed further by being back with Thorne, he felt invincible. Could it somehow stay like that?

CHAPTER FIVE

As it turned out, the raid on the trench was not to take place the following night, but a week afterwards, by which time all of the regard that Edward, Baffle and Mason had enjoyed in the morning after their return had long faded. No one was quite sure of the precise reasons for the delay. They were given various causes such as obfuscation at brigade, rumours of an impending Turkish attack, and even that there was a band of quicksand in No Man's Land.

But the company soon stopped caring about such things as their new line became registered by the Turkish artillery and, for two days straight, breaking only for a few hours either side of midnight, the trenches were shelled in a dreadful, metronomic shriek, a shell a minute beating down upon the company line. Casualties were immediate. The trenches, being recently captured, had not had any of the work put into them that the other trenches in the line had.

Worse, only ten days into their stay on the Peninsula, the men had started to lose their newcomers' immunity to disease. On top of the heatstroke victims – carried down the line, vomiting and in brown-swamped trousers, their shirts ripped off to try to get some breeze onto their torsos – came the dysentery victims, caused by who knew what but aided and abetted by the satanic black clusters of flies. And always, always to the north-east, sat the low rise of Achi Baba, the hill that had been an objective for the first day of the landings but was a mocking prospect now, bathed in the clear and pure light of the sun that was baking the back of their necks livid red and growing in size seemingly every day. Already they had heard chatter from other troops that it had a malevolence about it, that it was an Evil Eye pulsing above the landscape.

Thorne was digging earth to fill spare sandbags when Edward told him this. Thorne burst out laughing and went over to one of the trench periscopes, saying, 'Hang on. Let's have a look at the old blighter. No, looks just like a hill to me. Probably quite a nice stroll up it. I'll say one thing for us Brits – we don't half know how to overblow things do we?' He went back to carry on with his shovel.

They learned an awful lot about how to survive in the line. How to ration each day's sole water bottle. How to unwrap a biscuit in such a way, held right next to the mouth, as to let as few flies as possible onto it. They also enjoyed some success of their own with sniping, finally avenging the dead they had taken on that first morning when, looking back, they had been as clueless and disoriented as children on their first day at school.

They learned about casualties, how to improvise when a wound was too yawning for the issued field dressing. They learned what pain sounded like and how it shifted in tone and pitch according to the type of injury – high, unquenchable screaming for stomach injuries and low, shocked, moans of gibberish for amputations. They learned what bullets did to flesh, what shrapnel did, what blast injuries did. They learned how much bone would fly off from a skull when it was punctured by a bullet. And they learned what the dead looked and smelled like.

After six days in the line the company had taken eight dead and seventeen wounded. Two, Evans and Alton, were killed just behind Edward after they had all finished buttressing a zig-zag in the line to isolate the effects of a shell exploding in the trench. Mason had called him to look at something through a trench periscope, and he had only just gone round the corner when a whoosh and boom threw him to the floor. The buttress, he was amazed to note, had held up and done exactly the job that it was intended to do, but he had to close his eyes for a moment to prepare himself before turning back around the corner to see what lay there. He was too shocked at first to say anything, able only to make a gurgling sound as he stood over what was left of Evans and Alton. Sensing people behind him he turned to see Rossi and the commanding officer, who had come up to the B Company stretch of the line for the first time. The commanding officer put a hand on his shoulder and patted it before carrying on down the trench and stepping over and around the trunks, limbs and odd pieces of flesh and clumps of skull and hair, steaming even in the midday heat. 'Better get this little lot cleaned up, Salter, unless you want every damn fly in Asia Minor to join you.'

It was too late for that. As the platoon shovelled what remained of the two onto a pair of stretchers, trying to keep Evans's more tanned flesh on one and Alton's pale, sallow skin on the other, the volume of flies on them rendered them into pieces of dripping charcoal. They were carried back down the trench on their journey to the rear for the assorted pieces of meat to undergo the solemn administration of being registered as deaths. Baffle vomited as they passed him, causing the flies to scatter before resuming their attack with renewed vigour at this unexpected boon.

In the company dugout that night they didn't talk about it, concentrating instead on admiring the top of Tufnell's ear, that had had a tiny bit, just its top, shot off by a sniper in the afternoon as he had supervised a repair of the lip of the parapet. The wound was very small, no bigger than the nail of a little finger, but was an intriguingly gruesome mix of black and gooey still-forming scab and the purple iodine that had been put on to disinfect it.

Edward didn't say much, playing whist with Rossi as the younger officers led the conversation. Marks sat at the entrance to the dugout writing a letter to his father. It felt good to be transported back, even if by just an approximation, to their time on Lemnos when they had sat together every night after dinner like this. Edward noticed the way that Thorne, Haynes-Mattingly and Tufnell swapped stories. They had all been so close to each other in the previous days, more often than not only dozens of yards away, but in the troglodyte world of the trench, where the blinkered vision to your left and right made it feel like you were in the middle of a telescope, they might as well have been miles away.

Pratt, Rossi's batman and de facto company runner, came in and handed Rossi a note. 'From battalion, sir.'

Rossi took the note and opened it up as everyone looked at him. 'Thanks, Pratt. That will be all.'

Edward knew he was doing this as a way of trying to keep control of the passage of information. Pratt knew too, a little sullen as he left the dugout.

There was a pause until Rossi spoke. 'Well, the raid is finally on. We go tomorrow night. Two platoons, to get as many prisoners as we can. Full orders to follow tomorrow, but Salter and Tufnell, your platoons will be the ones for this. I'll be on it too. Right, gentlemen, tomorrow night is when we stop just sitting here getting whacked and we take the fight to them for a change.'

CHAPTER SIX

In the end, Tufnell was not to go on the raid; he was killed early the next morning helping his platoon with trench repairs. Marks came through to Edward's stretch of line, breathing heavily and sweating profusely, and told him what had happened as Mason and Baffle loitered behind, looking as though they were sorting out ammunition but taking their time over it in order to hear the full story themselves.

'Hell of a business. Not seen anything like that before, I don't mind telling you.' Marks was thirty, but still boyish-looking. Although he liked to take himself quite seriously, and was just a shade away from pomposity a lot of the time, he always treated Edward as an equal. 'I went to go and give him the time for the O Group for tonight. Oh, by the way, that's why I came here too; it's at midday in the OC's dugout. Anyway, I arrive at Seven Platoon, and there's Tufnell, standing on the firestep and hauling sandbags up to the parapet. At first I'm impressed – you know how tiny he was–' the past tense hit Edward and he wanted to be sick '–but then I see his face and he's got this manic look, and saw he was totally away with the fairies. And I think: Christ, we can't send him out tonight – he's just not with it after that near miss yesterday.

'And he stoops down to take another sandbag and stands up again, but he misjudges it. And then there's two shots – must be a couple of snipers working together – or maybe they had no idea the other one was firing too; God knows – and he gets whirled around as he's hit in the shoulder first and then a split second afterwards his jaw flies off as he's hit in the face. And he stands there, looking straight at me and I swear his eyes are still carrying a smile of greeting but there's just this maw beneath his nose where his lower face should be. And then his eyes shift to this animal look and he collapses, falls off the firestep and there's a crack as his leg breaks, literally snaps and lies there crooked, his knee folded the wrong way. And he's on the floor of the trench, his eyes looking up, sometimes fixed on me and sometimes flicking up to the sky, and his tongue is snaking around as if he's trying to say something, but it's covered in blood and I could see the hole of his throat brimming over with it, so he can't get any noise out. And the men are all just watching. There are his teeth scattered around him and when I step forward to kneel down to him I tread on one and feel it go into the dirt.'

The sangfroid Marks had managed to summon at the start of the conversation had disintegrated, his act of nonchalant phlegm evaporated entirely. Edward let him carry on and get this stream of consciousness out. He looked aside for a second from Marks' fixed, unblinking gaze and saw Baffle and Mason behind him, their initial prurient interest at wanting to hear about the casualty now overtaken by shock at Marks' state. There was still no stopping him.

'And I don't know what to do. I just don't know what to do. His eyes are getting bigger and I don't know what he's screaming for, if he wants me to cradle him, or he wants me to fix him, or if he thinks I'm his mother or something or if he wants to be told he's going to be all right. And still the men do nothing. So I just panic. I reach for my revolver and decide the only way out is to shoot him but I'm fumbling with the buckle and I can't get to it. And then his hand comes up to mine and takes it away, and he's scrabbling around and his gurgling starts to get high-pitched and little bits of screams come out and I don't know if he wants me to shoot him or if he wants me to try to treat him.

'And then his body starts spasming and shuddering and I see his top lip has got these tiny little stubble hairs on it and I realise that he hasn't shaved that morning and I think to myself that the OC is going to give him a rocket when he sees that and then I remember that I don't think he's really ever shaved properly because he's so young. Then I get dragged away and it's Sergeant Meade and the bearer party are there. And one of them gets this dressing out and just shoves it over the entire gap and I think how painful that must be and then there's another massive judder and he dies. And the bearer party stop and we all just sit there until I snap to it and get a blanket and lay it over him and he gets taken back down the line. The OC appears and tells me to come and see you. And everyone just goes about what they were doing before. I should think the parapet's looking perfect by now.'

Edward put his hand out and held Marks' shoulder, gesturing to the firestep. Baffle had reappeared with a mug of tea. 'Sit down, there you go. Corporal Baffle's made some tea for you, David.' He mouthed a silent thank you at Baffle who shrugged and then melted away again as Marks sat there rocking back and forth, sipping his tea.

When he finished it, he stood up. 'Thanks, Salter. Damn fine char that. Midday at the OC's dugout, then? I forgot to say, now that Tufnell's gone, it's going to be Haynes-Mattingly that goes with you, I should think.'

'All right. Not Thorne?'

'No. Not this time. He'll be in reserve, though, in case you lot get into trouble.'

Edward felt disappointed for Thorne – he could just imagine his shoulders slumping when he heard – but something in him was relieved that he wasn't coming out with them. And Haynes-Mattingly was competent; it would be easier with him than it would have been with poor old Tufnell. He nodded and said, 'I'll be there.'

*

Later that night, Edward arrived at Company HQ with his squad of nine men. Rossi had decided in the end that two full platoons would be unwieldy in the dark but wanted officers and good men on the raid with him so both Edward and Haynes-Mattingly were going out, leaving their sergeants but taking the pick of their men. Edward looked at them: Baffle and Mason had selected themselves on account of the previous recce; and then the best of the rest, or at least as far as he could work out who would be the best in their as yet unblooded state.

Edward went down the line of men. Baffle, his second in command for the raid, accompanied him, tightening straps on the men's kit, checking the fit of their magazines, making sure they all already had the top round chambered, feeling the pins in their Mills bombs were firmly set, rubbing more boot polish into their faces or evening out the streaks that they had put on like a make-up artist giving a dance troupe the final once-over before they trotted out on stage. Down the line they went – Mason, Curtis, Ewart, Harry, Albyn, Cradley, Sefton, and Rosslyn. At Albyn and Sefton, Baffle reached into a haversack and handed them both hideous wooden batons studded with nails and old puttees wrapped round the bottom as a handle. Edward frowned at him when he saw them.

'Makes sense, sir,' Baffle replied. 'When we get into those trenches the rifles are going to be fuck all use; too long. It's revolvers and clubs we want in there, trust me. Want mine? Swap it for your revolver?' He opened the bag to reveal an evil-looking knife with jagged serrations, its handle fashioned behind a set of brass knuckles.

'Thanks, Baffle, but I'll do just fine.'

Rossi gave them a final pep talk. The plan was straightforward. Edward's section and Rossi were to crawl out to the Turkish sap. They would drop into it, clear it – in the military euphemism – and then Haynes-Mattingly's group would rush forward and jump into the trench proper, clear that and then get back in the confusion. Meanwhile Marks on the left flank with Tufnell's old platoon would be firing machine guns to keep the Turks' heads down in the rest of the line. Thorne would be in reserve and would come forward if he heard any of the three officers' whistles be blown. All told the raid should last, from Edward's soldiers dropping into the sap to everyone being back in the trench, ten minutes.

Rossi wound it up. 'All right, chaps, nothing more to add. Salter, Haynes-Mattingly, it's going to be violent out there; short, sharp, when we're in their lines kill whoever we see, take a prisoner if you can, then get back here. Thorne, you hear a whistle, get over and give us a hand. Marks, keep that fire coming. Raise hell with it. We do this well, we send a clear message to them that we own this line and we own them. And next time we kick them all the way back behind Achi Baba. Clear?'

Each of them echoed it back to him, Edward not sure if his was audible, sounding more like a croak.

Rossi added one final note. 'You all know what happened to poor old Tufnell earlier. If you don't manage to get any prisoners it's no great shame. Salter, Haynes-Mattingly, I'll see you back here at H-15.' He left them in the now almost total blackness, taking Marks with him into his dugout.

Thorne said, 'Good luck, you two. We'll be with you the moment you need us. Don't hesitate to blow those whistles.'

Edward could sense Haynes-Mattingly straighten in his preening fashion as he said coolly and patronisingly, 'We'll be all right. Piece of cake. Just make sure there's a nice cup of tea waiting for us when we get back in.'

'Oh bugger off,' Thorne replied irritably and the conversation ended awkwardly, Haynes-Mattingly going back to his men as if in a silent boast that he was taking soldiers out that night and Thorne wasn't.

Down the line came a hiss, 'Shut up, everyone!' Edward recognised CSM Leyburn's voice. 'What's that, lad?'

Another voice, disembodied in the dark, came through clearer this time after the movement in the trenches stopped, the attack squads standing still amidst their adjustments and preparations. 'Don't know, sir, I'm sure I heard something out in front. Metal on metal.'

A stab of fear went from Edward's neck down his arms, his ears filling with blood.

The waiting went on for only a couple more seconds and then the night was zipped undone. Three flares shot up, blinding in their light, and across the whole line a scream rose up from scores of voices as at the very lip of the trench Turks now appeared in their dozens.

Leyburn pitched forward, a bullet in his throat, and started scrabbling at it on the floor of the trench, his boots kicking at the back of Edward's shins as he instinctively drew his revolver, flicked the safety catch with practised ease, and emptied three rounds into a figure hurling itself at him from the top of the trench. He missed with two but on the third caught the man full in the stomach.

A second figure leapt at him and Edward shifted to his left so that he landed full against the back of the trench and fell down onto Leyburn, who was still gargling out his life. Edward emptied the rest of the revolver into the Turk's back and Leyburn went silent too. Kneeling down to pick up Leyburn's rifle, he took his bayonet as well and fixed it, drawing breath for the first time and cursing as he did so, fumbling and missing the right thread until he heard the click as it hit its housing, begging that no one would go for him as he did so.

He stood up and next to him saw Thorne bringing down a spade again and again onto a Turk lying on the ground, sometimes hitting his throat, sometimes his jaw and sometimes his upper chest as the sound of splintering ribs managed to pierce the all-consuming chaos erupting around them. Another Turk jumped down onto Thorne, knocking him over so that they both lay sprawled on the trench floor. Before either of them could move again Edward lifted the rifle to his shoulder and blew the back of the Turk's head off. Turning as more flares went up, he saw some of the men were throwing grenades into No Man's Land. One went off in the trench to an eruption of screaming. A Turk sat astride an unknown figure, bringing a box of ammunition repeatedly down onto their face. Edward ran forward, not cocking his rifle to chamber another round, but instead thrusting his bayonet through the back of the Turk's neck, pitching the man forward onto his victim. Putting his foot down, he pulled the bayonet out, just like they had been taught at training, the form beneath him juddering and shaking. A pistol at his side indicated it was an officer. Edward unholstered it from him and shot twice into the back of his head to finish him off. Pulling the body aside he saw that the man had killed Rosslyn from his platoon. Rosslyn's face lay open as a mix of bone, pink gums and blood.

Everywhere was screaming and vicious, animal grunting. Edward seemed for a moment to have been put there artificially, a spectator to some alien carnage, enclosed entirely by the night and cut off from everything outside. He had no idea who else was alive, where Rossi was, if the battalion understood what was happening, on how wide a frontage the Turkish assault was. Then there was a gap in the flares going up and for ten seconds the trench seethed in complete darkness, no one knowing what on earth they were shooting or hacking at before another one came up and the sickly light resumed.

Edward could hear Thorne's voice through the din. 'Keep at it, men! Keep at it! Man the line, man the line, stand to, stand to!' he screamed, shoving men up to the firestep. He reached down to one prostrate figure, shouting, 'Get up, man, get up there or I'll kill you myself,' and then, realising he was dead, dropped him to the floor.

Edward started to follow his lead, realising that the immediate danger was over and the first Turkish attack had withered. Now they had to ensure a second one wouldn't get nearly as close. He peered over the parapet, the first time he had dared to do so, seeing the yellow lights of the dropping flares swirling in the interplay with the darkness. In the trench the screams of the fight started to give way to shouts of military order, instructions being barked, ammunition being called for.

And then the Turks came again.

The night passed. It passed in hideous technicolour, it passed in clinical, anodyne black and white. It passed in unearthly screams, tense silence, tears of grief and primal howls. It passed in calm commands, stentorian bellows and soft whispers into ears urging the dying to go well. Tracers bouncing off rocks faded like shooting stars into the sky and over Achi Baba. Bullets flew, sometimes dully into sandbags and sometimes ricocheting angrily off metal or bone. Shrieks of artillery covered first a Turkish withdrawal and then set the foundations for a new attack at midnight, throwing earth up in great plumes, bursting eardrums and shredding nerves.

Splintered images heaped up in Edward's brain, his blinks a camera shutter that burned the scenes onto his mind. A Turk thrown bodily in the air by a shell to land, impaled, on a barbed wire post. Marks appearing down the line, his arm hanging shredded by his side, to tell Edward matter-of-factly that Rossi had been killed, shot in the chest, in the first wave of the assault, before he, in turn, collapsed. Baffle on the firestep firing round after round into each new wave. A wounded Turk on the floor of the trench striking a grenade as Cradley tried to stem the bleeding from his chest, its blast riddling him with metal slivers as he died in blinded screams some glacial minutes later. Thorne walking up the line with his revolver, encouraging the men on. Haynes-Mattingly white and in shock after taking a bullet in the calf and his hand livid with a burn from the barrel of a Turkish rifle which he had grabbed to push away from him before shooting his attacker. He would be out for weeks with those wounds, Edward thought dispassionately.

The fighting finally ceased at around three o'clock. At the arrival of the grainy half-light before dawn, the true scale of the night was laid bare for them all to see: dead men looking as though they were sleeping and those left alive moving as if they were dead.

CHAPTER SEVEN

When dawn did appear, cruel and cold in its lateness, the men shrank down from the firestep and out of view of the Turkish snipers, back into their subterranean world. B Company's trench was a bog of dead men, strewn kit, the glint of spent rounds, improvised clubs bent and distorted from impact on skulls, brown cloying earth where blood had recently run freely.

At a wider part of the trench Edward sat down and held his head in his hands. He massaged his temples with his thumbs and brought them inwards round the edges of his eye sockets to the bridge of his nose, as if trying to test if he were fully intact. His forehead was a film of sweat and dust and blood. He had a pang to be clean, a longing to wash, shave and to blink cleanly. He wanted to rub away the night as though it were only a stain on a surface that could be got rid of in a moment.

Opposite him lay a Turk, his throat shot out and his foot wrenched inside at an awful angle. He was huge, with a bushy moustache and a confident, bullish air that made it seem impossible he was dead. Edward sat looking at him for fully half a minute, as the flies woke up and started first to scout him and then to accrete on his throat and eyes. A thought came into his mind, turning straightaway into a conviction, that the dead Turk was the one whose voice he had heard in the trench and the sap that night. He knew that it was sheer conjecture, but somehow it meant a lot to him and he felt at that moment – his muscles starting to stiffen and his dehydrated head starting to throb – that a chapter in his life had closed.

He thought about mentioning it to Baffle and Mason, to see if they thought the same as him but then he thought better of it; it would be too childish, too crowing, macabre. Ghoulish to look at a dead man and wonder if he was the owner of a voice you once heard. And besides, it struck him, Mason was now dead too anyway.

They were taken out of the line that afternoon, the battalion deemed too mauled to be combat effective. Their life as a fighting unit had been short – a week – but 65 out of 600 were dead with 190 wounded. Every man was grateful for the comforts of the rear: a shave, copious water in troughs to wipe away the filth, and the breeze on the shoreline of the cape that neutered the threat of the flies.

The following morning found B Company lying on unshelled ground in the lee of the wind that came over from mainland Turkey, with a milk-blue sky above them pitted with cotton wool clouds. The battalion reorganised itself with remarkable rapidity. D Company on the far right had essentially ceased to exist so its thirty remaining soldiers were folded into B Company who, Edward and Thorne were amazed to learn, had been the company that had emerged from the night the 'least denuded'. That was how the commanding officer had put it in the morning upon appraising the devastation. So they inherited D Company's surviving soldiers and two of its officers: Sinden and Hurst.

Edward barely knew either of them but they seemed inoffensive enough. Thorne said that Hurst, whom he had run some ranges with while on Lemnos, seemed a good man, cheerful and sanguine. Sinden, a burly, diffident type, seemed more withdrawn, but was friendly enough and Edward liked that he took notes of everything into a small jotter – no guarantee of competence but at least a sign of trying to be effective, which he supposed was better than nothing.

The biggest change of all, to Edward's mind at least, was that with Rossi dead and Marks wounded he was now the B Company commander and had been promoted to acting captain. That afternoon he was called to see the commanding officer, who had taken residence in a dugout overlooking the vast depot at the tip of the Peninsula with its hordes of stores and *materiel* piled up over the previous weeks. The commanding officer looked immaculate, his Sam Browne shining in a deep nutty brown and its brasses glinting. He looked as though he was preparing for a lunch in the mess after seeing to the final details for a parade, squinting over some papers and rubbing his spectacles with a red handkerchief as he did so. Yet in the night attack he had been in the thick of the fighting, coming up the line to A Company's trench for the first half hour, his adjutant Lloyd-Jones being killed next to him, before withdrawing back to the supply trenches to coordinate the deployment of reserves to weak points.

He looked up as Edward entered. 'Ah, Salter, come in.' He smiled in the manner of a friendly bank manager and motioned him to the map board so that they stood opposite each other. 'Well, congratulations on your command. Damned bad circumstances, clearly, but that's this business for you, I'm afraid. Rossi was a good man. I liked him a lot. Enormously capable, and only a Territorial too. Damned impressive. I'd have liked to have seen him go regular when all this is over. I daresay you'll be a worthy successor to him, though. He said you were doing a decent job.'

Behind the commanding officer Edward saw a print of the photograph that had been taken of the officers on Lemnos on the evening that they had left for the Peninsula. 'Sir, do you mind if I . . .?'

'Oh, of course not, please do. Have a look. My runner managed to get it developed by some of those RNAS aerial reconnaissance types on Imbros. God knows how he managed to convince them to do it; he wouldn't say. He's a marvel. Still, no names, no pack drill eh? He'll make a brilliant quartermaster sergeant one day. It's rather good, isn't it?'

Edward held it and looked into its newness, all the fresh faces in it, the confidence mixed with happy ignorance and unspoken insecurities. Also on the dresser was a small shaving mirror, smartly edged by a thin line of highly polished brass, and he looked into it, comparing himself to his likeness in the photograph. He looked exactly the same. They all did; it had been taken barely three weeks earlier. He could still remember adjusting his cap a second before the first photo in case it was askew. But counting the faces in it, he realised that at least a third of them were now killed or wounded.

'Are you all right, Salter?'

'Yes, sir.' He looked up and into the CO's face, lined and tanned tree-bark deep, the mark of having spent nearly all his adult life abroad.

The CO came forward and put a hand on his shoulder. 'You'll be fine. Command of a company is deceptive; in some ways it's easier than platoon command where things are rather more intimate. You have more time to think, more distance between you and the action, intellectually and physically. Just always deal in threes. One platoon moving, one platoon supporting the move, one platoon in reserve. Well, doesn't work so well in this infernal trench warfare, but if we ever do get into the open, then that's how you do it. Here's a tip: keep your best platoon in reserve. They'll hate it, naturally, just as you'll hate it whenever I put you in reserve or I get annoyed when the brigade commander puts us in reserve, but take it as a compliment.'

He took his hand away again, as if embarrassed by the momentary and unaccustomed closeness, and drew himself up to all of his five foot seven, his tiny sparrow frame immaculately unsoldierly. As though remembering the distance between them in experience, masked now by Edward's sudden promotion to one of his four immediate subordinates, he made his way back to the map board. It was an unspoken instruction that that was Edward's time up and he was to leave the tent, but he looked back up for a final word.

'Oh yes, one more thing. I know you're close to Thorne. He's a fine man. Cocky, like you all are, but that's not a crime. And he stays on the right side of the line, unlike that ghastly Haynes-Mattingly.' This made Edward smile. 'Still, brave chap, though. He'll be back soon enough, I should hope. Anyway, Thorne. I know it's tempting to make him your second in command, but I'd resist that. Keep him as a platoon commander. He'll be disappointed at first but he'll get over it. It's just always good to have one platoon commander you can trust implicitly, who knows the men. That said, frankly it's your choice what you do. But that's my advice. Well, that and go for a swim tonight. The water's marvellous. Any other questions?' He smiled in his slightly frowning, upside-down way, the rest of his face remaining taut and inelastic, and Edward thought how wrong the saying was about not trusting someone whose smile doesn't reach their eyes. The CO's smile got nowhere near his cheeks, let alone his eyes, but he instinctively felt an innate goodness and decency in him that was just hidden behind the stiffness of a military hierarchy.

Before Edward could respond, the CO started suddenly, looking past him through the entry to the dugout over to the depot behind.

'Well, I bloody never,' he said. Hearing even that mild expletive from the colonel's mouth was somehow more shocking than the thousand worse curses that were heard on an hourly basis amongst B Company.

Edward looked out the dugout too, blinking at the light as the colonel sidled past him to open the flaps a little more and peered out. 'What's that, sir?'

The colonel kept watching for a few moments and said, 'Christ, he's coming this way. I'm going to go and say hello. Pass me my cap, would you, Salter?' The CO inspected himself in the mirror Edward had used a minute beforehand, appearing to check his shaving and then his collar rim. Duly satisfied, he strolled out of the dugout and Edward heard him holler, 'Good evening, General! Come along, Salter. Think you might enjoy this.'

At the foot of the hill were some officers all peering into the centre of their group where a tall, rake-thin and stooped man bent over a map while those closest to him gesticulated excitedly and those on the fringe stood at a remove as if too timid to weigh in with their own opinions. Edward knew the profile immediately; as famous as Lord Kitchener himself. General Sir Ian Hamilton, the commander of the entire expeditionary force, one of the Empire's greatest soldiers. And here he was, barrelling down the hill with the CO towards him as though off to accost a friend in the street. As they approached, the phalanx around him bristled at the sight of the CO approaching, and one of the outer circle, presumably one of the General's ADCs, started forward as if to try to apprehend the introduction. Just before he was able to, Hamilton looked up, smiled and said, 'Good God! Well, I never. Raymond Ackrill!'

Edward stood to attention, throwing up what he hoped was a semi-acceptable salute. It was returned rather stylishly by Hamilton who then started chatting away with the CO, completely ignoring his entourage who all turned to look at Edward in accusation that they had been interrupted. One of them, a major general, asked him amusedly, 'And who might you be?'

'Captain Salter, sir, B Company commander, Queen Anne's Own.' Edward found it came quite easily from his tongue despite being all of six hours into the role.

The CO interrupted and led Hamilton over to Edward. 'One of my best men, General. Salter here was in the thick of it a couple of nights ago.'

'Were you, eh? Good show, young man. Bad business, that,

but you held 'em. And we'll hold 'em again and again until the time we turn it back on them and roll the entire Peninsula up.' He fixed Edward in his gaze and smiled, his eyes sad and friendly, and Edward was struck for a second by the enormity of command pressing in around his head. Everything around them, the fighting, the flies, the gore to the north and the vastness of the scene around them behind the lines, now came down onto this man.

'What were you doing when the war started, laddie?' Hamilton asked. It seemed absurd to Edward that such a man could even take a minute out to think about anything else but then he thought, why the hell not, the man has to have a bit of a rest.

'I was a lawyer, sir. Not terribly interesting. To be honest, I think this has rather been the making of me. Actually, I was in St Petersburg on holiday when it all looked like kicking off. Had to make best speed back.'

'Russia, eh? Speak it, do you?'

'Yes, as a matter of fact. I wouldn't volunteer to translate Chekhov, but I can get by. I had a governess growing up who taught it to me.'

'Interesting. Very interesting.' Hamilton turned to the major general. 'Keep young Salter in mind, Walter. Never know when he might prove useful.' The general nodded to one of the ADCs on the outer circle of the group, all of whom seemed to Edward a little resentful that one of their rank was getting such attention from Sir Ian himself.

Hamilton finished up with the CO. 'Well, Raymond, take care. Keep the men in good spirits, keep pushing on. God willing, and with some more artillery and more men, we'll crack this nut, but it's going to be a damnable business. Think you can do it?'

'Don't worry about us, sir. We'll get there in the end. Some artillery wouldn't go amiss though, as you say.'

Hamilton winced. 'Don't get me started, old chap. It's what Walter and I spend our entire lives trying to sort out with London. Anyway, best get going.' They all saluted their farewells to each other. Hamilton turned and the party went on its way, leaving Edward and the colonel to walk back up the hill to the dugout.

'Well,' the colonel said, 'not every day that happens, is it? Speak Russian do you, Salter? Kept that under your hat. With that up your sleeve why didn't you go for an intelligence job? Cushy number in Whitehall, that kind of thing.'

'I don't know, sir; I suppose I was scared that if I did say I could speak it I wouldn't get the chance to come to the front.'

The answer was evidently the one the colonel was looking for. 'That's the spirit.'

Given their new intimacy, Edward decided to ask. 'Two things, sir. How do you know the general, and who was Walter?'

'South Africa. Long time ago. Served under him at Ladysmith. A great man, Sir Ian. Bit of a dilettante, terrible social climber, but hard, damned hard with it. I dare say he's bitten off more than he can chew with this show, but it won't be for want of trying. Us old Empire soldiers you see. Same as K and Roberts. Being in the ulu is exactly where we like to be. Doesn't mean we'll win, but at least this is our metier, far from home, in the heat, with the men, where we were as young platoon commanders and where we'll wish we were when we're long retired and tending the hostas on our lawns.'

'Who was Walter?'

'That's Braithwaite. His chief of staff. Yes, don't really know him. Bit of a prig, they say, but nice enough. That was his son who he told to take a note of you. His ADC. All a bit too hugger-mugger for my liking, frankly. Sir Ian would have been better served by his previous one, chap called Ellison. But none of that's really for me to say, what? I've said far too much, Salter; yesterday you were a mere platoon commander and here we are gabbing away like we're a pair of fishwives.'

Edward took his cue and saluted his departure.

CHAPTER EIGHT

Later that evening, the battalion was at the beach and B Company were in the water, having waited their turn behind the other companies to go swimming. On the southernmost tip of the Peninsula, to their left as they looked out to sea, stood the great hulk of the beached SS *River Clyde*, a dull shine from it reflecting the setting sun. It had been used on the first day on the landings back in April, crammed with soldiers and rammed straight into the sand to disgorge them onto the beach. Now it stood incongruous and awkward, like an altar to an abandoned god.

Most of the men were naked, those who could swim pushing far out into the deepest water and those who couldn't staying in the shallows, some sitting down and ladling water over themselves, others tackling each other and play fighting. The rumble of fighting rolled down the western side of the Peninsula from Anzac.

Thorne, treading water in the deep, got Edward's attention, gesturing to the *River Clyde*. 'Like Ozymandias, isn't it? "Look upon my works, ye mighty and despair." Seems like it will be there forever. Well, at least we'll leave some monument to our efforts, I suppose.' Thorne was completely naked and Edward in his underpants envied him his freeness. His sandy hair and light-brown skin were funny to see on top of his alabaster body and Edward looked down at his own, not quite as firm in the places where Thorne's was rock hard but still, retaining a pleasing compactness.

He was about to reply when, down the beach a quarter of a mile or so away, two spumes of water kicked up near each other and the screeches of the shells that made them followed in maenadic orison. They were a couple of shots from 'Asiatic Annie', the Turkish gun on the Asian side of the straits that sometimes registered the beachhead to disrupt the rear area. They landed in the centre of a group of soldiers from another regiment and all of B Company looked over at the screams and shrieks as a mass of white figures, as naked as they were, coalesced around broken bodies and then moved to the shore, the whole scene far enough away to render the individuals unrecognisable.

No more shells came, the Turks content with just a brace of shots, having no idea what damage they had done. B Company carried on swimming in their own patch of sea as over at the other one already the liver spots of red diffused into nothingness and small pieces of flesh and bone were eaten by fish and creatures on the seabed.

For ten further minutes they swam, expiating their bodies of the blood of two nights before. Edward fussed over the cuticles of his nails and the ridges of his ear lobes to make sure that every single bit of grime was gone. He felt eyes on him and turned to see Thorne looking at him in fond, affected bemusement. A moment hung between them, the fading evening to the west behind Thorne silhouetting him in the last of its gold as night came on, before he snapped into command mode.

'We'd better go ashore,' he said and then shouted across the water to the rest of the company, 'Come on, chaps, that's our number up. In we go.'

Company Sergeant Major Jeffcoat and the platoon sergeants took over, cajoling and shepherding the men back onto the shore and into their uniforms while Edward and Thorne stayed out at sea, treading water as the night rushed in to envelop them. Several of the huge ships in the waters off the Peninsula started to fade into the black and sprinkles of stars that would become their blanket appeared above them. They were far enough from the shore not to be able to hear the men and it seemed for a moment absurd that on the three miles of Cape Helles in front of them were hundreds of thousands of men. Not one of them would sleep tonight on a normal bed, most of them were probably going about their individual evening routine while some others lay dying or maimed and others wondered if they would even survive the night. They swam in silence while Edward contemplated this awesome sense of their cosmic irrelevance, as able to influence events as ants in a wildflower meadow.

'You know I met Sir Ian Hamilton earlier?' he said. 'With the CO. Turns out they know each other from the Boer War. Funny really; they were chatting like a pair of subalterns.'

'What did you say to him?'

'The usual tongue-tied formalities. Seemed nice enough. He was interested in me speaking Russian but I daresay he's already forgotten it. It was odd, meeting him. When you've heard so much about someone, when you actually then meet them and see his grubby Sam Browne and the look of tiredness in his eyes – goodness he looked tired – all the mystique around him melts away and you feel a little let down. I was brought up on people like him, Kitchener, Roberts and the rest of them.'

After a pause, Thorne replied flatly, 'I don't buy any of that stuff. All that great-man bilge. You know when they write histories of this, all they'll do is talk about Hamilton, about bloody Winston, about those narcissists in the RND and the VC winners and all that lot. But the whole thing about the Peninsula is that it's not the bigwigs with all their staff and hangers-on around them laughing at all their awful jokes who count; it's Baffle, it's Tufnell, it's you and me not having a clue but somehow managing to muddle through. And then the shooting stops and we survive and the war's over and we leave our uniforms behind us. And the regimental histories are written by the chaps who want to make a career out of it so they pull their punches with the criticism of the commanders and beef up the role they actually played. When instead, when it comes down to it, it all boils down to a million incidents of people like Bruce grabbing a red-hot rifle barrel with one hand and shoving a bayonet into the eye of the John Turk who's built like Mount Ararat with the other. Ha – can't imagine what he's going to do after all of this. It'll be something fast, whatever it is.'

'Oh God, I don't think I could ever go back to my previous career after all of this. Makes you think, doesn't it?'

'What do you think you'll do?'

'No bloody idea. At the moment I'm trying to get through the next week. Come on, let's go in.' Then, as an afterthought, he said, 'But I can't see myself going back to that kind of life. It'd be, I don't know, like a horse deciding to go back to a life wearing blinkers.' He pushed out to go back to the shore.

They swam in, their eyes adjusted to the sky's dark purple and the sea's swell swinging them up and down in their strokes, as they both started to swim faster and then, at an unspoken impulse, breaking into a race. Thorne pulled away, eventually winning by a clear three lengths and stood, panting knee-deep in the tiny surf lapping at his calves as they reunited at the shoreline.

The rest of the company were almost dressed and starting to form up into their four platoons so they pulled their clothes on quickly. Putting on their uniforms provided a sudden barrier between them; while in the sea and in their nakedness they had been the friends they had always been, now the gap was made clear by the visible reality of their different commands and Edward's three captain's pips to Thorne's one. They wound down their chatter, Edward grateful that Thorne was adept at this and happy to play ball until the next time they could be themselves together out of sight of the men. Thinking about this he felt a nasty lightness in his stomach, a fear that one day their friendship would come in the way of a difficult command decision, hoping that he would neither prejudice Thorne's reputation by showing excessive partiality for him nor his safety by going too far the opposite way. He pulled on his helmet, enjoying its reassuring tightness on his forehead, and adjusted his belt. He felt ready to go, energised and fresh. Most of all he was looking forward to several nights' sleep behind the line.

Thorne left to go to his platoon and in his place appeared CSM Jeffcoat, a short, reserved, flinty man who wore the permanently pained expression of a man who had just caught himself in his fly. 'Right, Sergeant Major,' said Edward. 'Up to the camp please, carry on.'

'Yessir.' Jeffcoat saluted, turned to the men and yapped, 'Right, B Company, look sharp.' He brought them up to attention, set them off and they softly went up the bluff to their billets, their trousers swishing and the crunch of gravel beneath their boots. Edward buzzed around the company, sometimes at the front, sometimes the rear, listening to their low chuntering, joking and gripes and looking at their mass, nigh on a hundred men that he now essentially had complete ownership of. He found himself smiling. No, he said to himself as he thought back to Thorne's question in the sea; he couldn't see himself ever going back to before.

CHAPTER NINE

As the summer dragged on, Edward came to marvel at Thorne's innate ease and elan, his debonair swagger. There was something about his gaze that gave Edward a sense of calm, and a courage that fizzed through his bones. He could so clearly see its effect not only on himself but on the others in the company; with just a chirped good morning he would visibly lift those he passed in the trench.

One night Thorne went out with Gill and Beck into No Man's Land to retrieve the headless, armless torso of Goyle, who had been blown out of the trench by a shell that afternoon. Edward watched Thorne speak with them when they got back in, slowly bringing Gill down from his stammering hysteria and coaxing the deathly silent Beck into shy smiles and then finally back into speech, both of them leaving the scene restored and repaired. Not that it mattered much in the end for Beck, whose head flashed over the parapet for too long the next evening and was blown half off by a sniper. He lay at the bottom of the trench as Thorne, the first on the scene, cradled him in his lap, whispering to him as his life drained away and his warm, sticky blood drenched Thorne's legs. Finally, a bearer party took him away and Thorne resumed his business down the rest of the trench, with a plaintive 'Anyone got a spare pair of trousers? I've had a bit of an accident with these ones,' getting a few laughs in response.

Edward himself had a pit pony-like ability to just keep going, his brain shouldering more burdens every day. Command was his making but was also visibly undoing his body. He was wasting away even as his eyes flashed defiance and a nervous hardiness. If Thorne himself relied on words and easy, unruffled patter to bolster those around him, Edward achieved the same just through his presence. He never exuded a palpable courage; it was, however, the visible suppression of his fear that was most inspirational for the men and the example he set to them all that they, too, could manage to operate the same way if they were so minded.

Edward noticed that while his friendship with Thorne was founded on a real and deep fondness, it was strengthened immeasurably by a criterion that had never been a consideration in any of his other relationships: respect for the other's competence. The feeling came hand in hand with an intolerance for those who didn't have it. Before this, it had never seemed to matter, but here in the stark air of the line, where a basic mistake could bring disaster upon oneself or – worse – others, those whom Edward and Thorne deemed not effective were soon hated and ostracised. They were lucky in B Company that the platoon commanders and NCOs managed by and large not to drop beneath a basic level of effectiveness, but some of those in other companies they soon grew not just to resent but actively despise.

A thousand things occupied Edward between the orders, the rotation of the platoons and the attempt to share jobs equally among them – the trench fortifications, the state of the wire, the eternal jigsaw of managing men ravaged by illness and the fear of being torn apart by shell or splintered by bullets. But the task he found most difficult was the letters that he was required to write to the families of the killed. It was not just the fact that he was having to engage with the hateful matter in the first place but also that he had only a mere side or two of paper to do so that just seemed horribly inadequate. 'A bad job that can only ever be done badly,' he once complained to Thorne about it.

Thorne often asked if he needed any help with them but always received a firm refusal, as though each letter was a sacrament he could never give up. But one day, when Mitchell and both the Wilsons – unrelated to each other but who had become close friends – were killed when a wiring party had been caught in the open, Thorne went away to his dugout and hurriedly wrote out the letters of condolence. He had proofread enough of Edward's other letters to know his style and tone and he knew even the white lie of his forged signature. He arrived at Edward's dugout with them at midday, the line around them dead as both British and Turk sought any shelter from the heat, finding Edward alone and in the pose he sometimes adopted when there was no one around – sitting down, elbows on his knees and his head in his hands, fingers massaging the rims of his eye sockets. It was as though he was either trying to squeeze sights out of his mind or knead them further into his brain.

Edward looked up as Thorne handed him the letters. 'I took the liberty of doing these for you. I think I got your tone. I won't take any offence if you don't like them, shouldn't care a stitch, but if you do approve of them I hope I've saved you a little time.'

Edward's body stiffened in the way that it always did when confronted by something he didn't like. But he took them and read them. Then he read them again and looked up and smiled. 'Thank you. Yes, these'll do. Nice to have that hour back, I must say. I'll go and visit the chaps in the sap.'

As he got up to go, Thorne, knowing he was overstepping the mark but taking a punt, reached forward and firmly stayed him by the shoulder. 'No you don't. Get some sleep. Just an hour. I promise you it will help.'

Again anger flashed across Edward's brow but abated again. He staggered over to the recess in the dugout that made for his bed, a couple of blankets matted with dirt and sweat on top of some pallets they had scrounged from the supply depot.

Like a puppet with its strings cut he crumpled and went straight to sleep, only briefly registering Thorne's handkerchief soaked in cool water wiping his forehead.

CHAPTER TEN

Even while they sought to hunker in the shade, the summer's heat sapped any strength that the illness that ravaged the battalion might spare. Edward was struck down like the rest of them but got off relatively lightly and did not have to be taken back from the line. Thorne succumbed terribly, his drained, papery form carried down the trench by a group of sickness-drunk men who were not in much of a better state than him. He was out of the line for two weeks, and Edward missed him badly.

One day, Edward was in his dugout censoring some of the men's letters during the lull that came over the entire Peninsula at midday. Along the trench he heard himself being asked for and peered out to see a runner from Regimental HQ who handed him an envelope and said, 'From the CO, sir. I'm to take it back the moment you've finished with it.' Opening it, he was surprised to see that it was from the ADC to Braithwaite, whom he had met the day after he had taken command of the company; coming down from the adrenaline of the night battle at the time, he had all but forgotten the encounter.

In florid, slanting green ink it said, '*Salter. Need to know to what extent you can speak Russian. Scale of one to ten please, if one is hello/thank you and ten is that it's your first language.*'

He lit a cigarette and sat forward on his stool of three ammunition crates lashed together. On the one hand he didn't want to lie but he also didn't want to get some job that would see him removed from company command. He decided he would score himself as an eight but just as he put pen to the bottom half of the paper, oddly stark in its cream stiffness against the dirt and dust of the dugout, he downgraded the mark to a six, and followed it with, *Good enough to maintain a social conversation but not good enough to understand technical intricacies of banking, industry, military matters, politics or suchlike.*

He folded the paper again and handed it to the runner who saluted and left him. Only a minute later another one appeared, a smiling little bundle of breathlessness who looked far, far too young to be a soldier. Even the eighteen-year-olds in the company at least looked as though they had grown to fit their faces; this one seemingly hadn't even progressed into adolescence yet. He reminded him of a drummer boy in Napoleonic times. 'Message for you sir,' he said proudly, 'from the commanding officer.'

Edward took it with a smile, friendlier and less business-like than he had been with the previous runner, trying to make the boy feel at ease. He motioned him to take a seat, as he looked as though he had sprinted the whole way.

He opened the note, the spidery writing thin and scratched in comparison to the affected, smart rococo of the note from the ADC. It was spare and sparse, just like its writer.

'*Salter. Well done B Company these past days. Parade at my dugout at 23:00 with the other company commanders for orders. We are to leave the line, destination unknown, timings unknown.*'

Edward looked at the runner. 'Thank you. Tell the colonel I'll be there. What's your name, by the way?'

'Preston, sir.'

'How old are you, Mr Preston?'

'Eighteen, sir,' he said, in a bluff, dismissive way as though this was a question he had become thoroughly bored of.

'Come on, Preston, I wasn't born yesterday. Although you clearly were. Look—' he lowered his voice '—you're not going to get in trouble with me. If you want to be here it's your damned choice. I'm not going to shop you.'

'I'm fourteen, sir. Fifteen next week.'

His sudden candour took Edward aback. He thought he would be sixteen at least; definitely not as young as fourteen. That was positively barbaric. He could understand people lying about their age but couldn't see how the army had let this so visibly underage specimen slip through.

'How on earth did they let you in? I don't want to seem rude, but while I can see a recruiting sergeant turn a blind eye to an unusually tall lad now and again, you, with the best will in the world, are a different kettle of fish.'

The boy looked affronted and tilted his chin up in defiance. 'Well, sir, they let me in. I wanted to get amongst it and I'm here now so I might as well make myself useful.'

Edward had to admit that he had a point. 'What did you do before the war?'

'I was a paper boy. In Northampton. Would hold all the papers out for people to buy. Anyway, when it all started last year so many people took papers from me and went straight to the recruiting station to join up I felt as though I should join too. I thought in a way that they were going to get shot at because of me, so I went to join them. And I thought it would beat the hell out of staying in a street holding out a bit of paper for the rest of the war. Though that's exactly all I do here anyway.' He glanced at the CO's message in Edward's hand. 'Takes the piss.'

Edward couldn't help but be beguiled by the boy's brio. 'Well, Preston, for God's sake look after yourself.'

'Is that all, sir?'

'Yes, thanks. Oh, want one of these?' He held out the packet of cigarettes.

'Don't mind if I do. Thanks, sir.' He took one, thought for a moment and took a second one with a grin and put it in his tunic pocket. 'One for the road.' He saluted and scampered away down the trench, sliding past the company sergeant major just as a handful of shells landed around them, not apparently perturbed as all the other men ducked, shrank and covered their heads out of long-ingrained habit. Edward watched him go and laughed a little to himself. He went back into the dugout where Jeffcoat was waiting, his shiny domed forehead split by his widow's peak, a little faint stubble underneath his greying temples, the antithesis of the tatterdemalion figure who had been there moments before. He grunted thanks as Edward gave him a cigarette and lit it for him, immediately regretting it as at this rate he'd be out of them by nightfall. Jeffcoat blew out a few puffs and then leant back against the dugout wall.

'Who was that then, Oliver bloody Twist? Looked as though he was ten.' Jeffcoat smiled, his white and perfect teeth sitting oddly in his weathered and sallow face. 'Still, good lad. I wonder how many of those kind of cases old John Turko has.' He nodded dismissively in the direction of the Turkish lines. 'Anyway, sir, what's the juice? Duty rumour is that we're coming off the line.'

Edward was always amazed at how the rumour mill would invariably outstrip any official communication of news. 'Looks like it. Pretty soon too by the sound of it. I wonder what they've got planned for us.'

'Another push somewhere? Salonika? Maybe Egypt for some leave? I've always fancied seeing the pyramids, me.'

'Goodness knows.' The most extraordinary feeling struck him at that moment, of impending regret at leaving the Peninsula. He couldn't work out why – in his every waking and sane moment he recognised the situation for exactly what it was: rankness and horror with the maiming, the exposed and rotting flesh, the heat, the dehydration, the flies, the held breath at every explosion or rifle crack at expecting to have metal rip through your bone and organs. But there was something beyond that, that came only occasionally, at odd, unexpected moments. It was the feeling of hanging on to the edge of the world by your fingernails and refusing to be pushed back so much as a yard. The feeling of complete unity of purpose that he had never had before.

'You all right there, sir? Looks as though you're having a funny turn.'

He caught himself, realising he must have just been staring blankly into space for the last few moments and it came upon him that he felt very tired. 'Oh, it's all right, Sergeant Major. Just thinking about how odd it's going to be not to be here. Gets under your skin a bit, if that makes sense.'

CHAPTER ELEVEN

They were taken out of the line to be put into the order of battle for the new phase of the campaign, the attack to the north-west of the Peninsula at Suvla Bay that was planned to support a breakout from Anzac and so crack the summer stalemate that had strangled momentum and initiative. The battalion was to be on the right flank of the battlefield, part of the effort to seize the high ground around the bay. After being shipped away from Helles, they spent ten days on Imbros preparing for it and then arrived on Suvla the day after the main landings. The scene on the beach was chaotic as they stumbled into the surf and were eventually corralled into a holding area, where they were to stay indefinitely until a mission became apparent for them.

That evening, Edward was in what purported to be B Company HQ, a shallow dip in the ground that was a far cry from the relative comfort of the subterranean world on Helles, when an excited Thorne came over to him, bursting through the scrub, running in the crouched way they all did due to the sporadic shellfire that raked the landing area. He grinned, the brim of his too-large helmet tipping over his eyes. The sight of it stabbed Edward with a momentary sadness at how young he was, as though he was just a boy playing at being soldiers.

'You'll never guess what. I've just had the most fascinating encounter on the beach. Sapper chap called Moseley. We got talking and it turns out he was some kind of bigwig scientist before the war. He was pretty modest about it but he was so evasive that I think he was probably something quite special. Anyway, turns out he was the absolute last word in signals. I told him about the beacon chain and he said . . .'

Edward was struggling to catch up with this blizzard of information. 'Hang on, the beacon chain?'

'You remember, on Lemnos. The beacons from Troy to Greece. From the *Agamemnon*.' Thorne looked affronted that it wasn't at the forefront of his brain and Edward smiled. 'Gosh, yes, I'd completely forgotten. Anyway, you were saying; this chap, what's his name, Moss . . .'

'Moseley. The beacons. I was banging on at him about it and he said all you really need is a heliograph. And there was me thinking that we had to do it with the real fires again, that maybe we should all meet up after the war and have a battalion reunion. You know, you take command of one beacon, Bruce one. Even dull old Sinden can have one. Baffle, the sergeant major. I get to do the final one, obviously. Maybe get the colonel to do one. I'm sure he'd be keen.'

They ended up staying for four more days in the rear, baked by the heat and given no let-up in the windless and fly-clawed air, their mouths parched and heads throbbing from lack of water. Finally, they were given their mission. In a couple of days the battalion was to go up to relieve one of the units that had been mauled in the first days of the attack and to press on with its unfinished task, to seize the topmost ridge of a convex slope that maddeningly was sculpted in a way that gave it very many false summits. Edward knew it had the potential to be a massacre.

The day before they were due to move, Edward and Thorne sat in the shallow scrape, now reassuringly augmented by sandbags. They looked up at the same time as the sound of scurrying footsteps came through the shrub and then the pixie-like figure of Preston, the colonel's runner, appeared, slid into the scrape and helped himself to one of the cigarettes from the packet that Edward had left on the side. 'Don't mind if I do, sir.' Then there was the noise of panting and heavier steps that came through the bushes as someone who neither would have guessed at all appeared.

Haynes-Mattingly.

'Well, I bloody never.' Haynes-Mattingly collapsed clumsily down next to them; he'd put on weight. Preston was already curled up like a cat, having learned quickly the imperative of getting sleep whenever possible. Haynes-Mattingly grinned from ear to ear and said, 'Well, here I am. Someone said I'd find you two here.' He looked down at Edward's sleeves, adorned with his captain's pips. 'Congratulations, old boy. Handing those out with the rations, I'd heard.'

He waited just long enough to see that he had pricked Edward's indignation and then retracted with another of his infuriating smiles. 'Sorry, sorry. I overstepped. Look, I'll toe the line. You're the boss. I promise you.'

'I should bloody well hope so,' Edward snapped back. 'Speak to me like that again and you're on a charge.' He was surprised at himself – and quite impressed – at the amount of venom he managed to inject into the words. He noted to himself that if Haynes-Mattingly did step out of line like that, he would come down on him like a ton of bricks. 'Well, it's good to have you back.'

'How the hell did you get here, anyway?' asked Thorne, lightening the fragile atmosphere. 'We thought you weren't due out for another month.'

'I wasn't, but I busted out of hospital. Ghastly place, Lemnos. They wouldn't move me to Malta, worse luck, despite all my begging. Can you imagine how much fun I'd have had there? Anyway, I got bored and escaped a couple of days ago. Managed to hitch a lift on a French destroyer to Imbros, found out there where the battalion was and then jumped on a boat here. Bloody lucky to find you. Marvellous not to be back on Helles, I have to say. What a godforsaken pit of misery.'

'I'm afraid this isn't much better,' said Thorne.

'How's the hand?' Edward asked.

Haynes-Mattingly took off a white cotton glove to reveal his palm, livid with twisted skin and purple like a tattoo. 'Well, it looks worse than it is. I can move everything fine now but only quite recently. Lost all feeling in the palm though. Nerve endings all dead. Still, not too bad. It'll make me a champion at fives, I reckon. And the ribs are holding up. Leg's now fine. Honestly, I just got bored. And I thought that the company needed at least one good officer.' He winked. 'The old man agreed with me. Saw him on the beach just now and he said, "Ah, Haynes-Mattingly, how good of you to join us," as though he was welcoming me into a drinks party. He sent me off up here with this little scamp.' He nodded down to Preston, who was now fast asleep. 'So, do I get Seven Platoon back?'

This was not a problem that Edward had expected to have, but having too many officers wasn't a bad one in the circumstances. He thought for a moment. 'No, Bruce, I'm afraid Hurst has your old lot. Sinden's got Five. Be nice to them, will you? They're a fragile pair. You can be my second in command for a while.' He pretended not to notice Haynes-Mattingly roll his eyes at Thorne, who stifled a laugh.

They were interrupted by Baffle who ambled over to the scrape. 'Sorry, sirs. There's just been a post run. Not much in it but a letter for you, sir.' He handed a letter to Edward, who took it, puzzled. He didn't recognise the writing and in any case the only letters he got were occasional ones from his aunt.

Baffle looked at Haynes-Mattingly. 'Welcome back to you, sir. Couldn't keep you away I see.' Edward could tell, as the two exchanged pleasantries, that Baffle didn't like Haynes-Mattingly at all. He was perfectly polite but there was a coldness, a stiltedness that he didn't show around others. It was funny: they were the two most obviously violent characters in the company, but there was something that Baffle, who had time for everyone, young or old, bold or timid, didn't find right about Haynes-Mattingly. Baffle's love of fighting didn't seem to be personal in any way. He undertook it with a sort of happy nihilism that didn't really intrude on his normal life. But with Haynes-Mattingly there was no such barrier, the poison of his time in the line at Helles quickly and visibly having oozed into his day-to-day thoughts and dealings. Edward wondered how he was going to cope now; whether he would worsen or revert to the engaging – though bumptious and infuriating – character he had made friends with before. More than that he wondered how having him back would affect the rest of the company.

Once Edward was alone he eyed the letter Preston had brought him again and opened it.

High Hedges
Leighton

Dear Edward (if I may),

I hope that this finds you well. It feels funny opening like that, as though I am writing to a school pen pal, but I don't really know how else to begin. I should introduce myself. I am Miranda Thorne, the sister of your friend Theo. He writes very fondly of you in his letters to us here. I don't know; one feels so helpless that it seems like the only thing I can do is to write to you to ask that you watch out for him. There, I've said it, you may think this is the most frightful bunk but from what Theo says about you I don't think you will. We pray every hour for your safe return and I hope very much that your own family are delivered you safe and sound. I also hope that we might meet some day. It would be good at any rate to have someone there to tell us which of Pip's stories are real and those which aren't.

You will note the handwriting on the front; I asked the postmaster to do it for me as I didn't want Theo to somehow see my writing on the envelope. He would think it most unusual me writing to you and get in a frightful bate.

Yours sincerely, and with my most earnest prayers and good wishes,

Miranda Thorne

He frowned. Thank goodness she had done that trick with the handwriting as the way the letter had been handed to him meant Thorne had seen it clearly. There were several things to consider. She had let slip that he was called Pip. Why? Second, Thorne clearly considered him as great a friend as he did him. Miranda hadn't been addressing him in his capacity as Thorne's company commander but in a far more intimate role. He thought about how he should handle all these pieces of information and then realised that the easiest thing to do would be to say nothing at all to Thorne.

Deciding there was no time like the present, he took out a postcard from his pocket and scrawled on it.

Dear Miranda,

I have just received your letter. Thank you very much for writing. Apologies for the haste of this; I wanted to get something off to you as soon as possible. I'm not sure how to reply without promising something that I couldn't – and shouldn't – possibly guarantee. But I will say that your brother has become a very good friend of mine out here and that we look out for each other. We are in excellent hands in our battalion; we have a first-rate commanding officer and are lucky to have some of the finest soldiers in the army with us – although don't tell them that! We are up against it, certainly, with the Turks, but we hope to prevail shortly. I must say we are all rather looking forward to some British weather as it is terribly hot out here. The food could also do with an improvement too – bully beef and biscuits start to get rather monotonous after a while.

I should very much like to meet when back home. In any case, should you have any concerns about your brother's welfare please write again.

I remain yours, faithfully,

Edward Salter

Lacking an envelope, he repurposed the one she had sent him, crossing out his own address and writing hers in its place, keeping the letter in by folding the unstuck flap into its body. Then he shook Preston awake. 'Come on, old chap. You'd best be off.' Preston got up fresh and alert. 'I say, you couldn't pop this in the post, could you?'

Preston shrugged and stuffed the letter unceremoniously in his pocket. 'Sure thing, sir.' He nodded farewell before scampering away through the scrub back to battalion.

For a few minutes Edward sat contented, pleased to have struck up such an unexpected correspondence. Then, though, he started to think of the note he had just written with an embarrassed doubt. Had his tone been overly schoolmasterly? She had written solely asking for him to look after Thorne and he had merely brushed her off to her in effect that that wasn't anything he could guarantee. True, maybe, but hardly in the spirit of things. He wished he hadn't been in such a hurry to reply, that he had done so in a slower, more considered fashion. He was on the verge of leaving his HQ and following Preston back to intercept it and write another. But a salvo from the Turkish guns then started to fall a few hundred yards away and kept him in. When it had finished he decided it was pointless. 'Bugger,' he said out loud. He would just have to hope that she didn't think that he was a total prig.

81

CHAPTER TWELVE

A few days later, the battalion having now been moved to the bottom of the hill in readiness for relieving the unit on the heights above, B Company were getting some rest at midday. The sun was at its zenith, making the men's shadows tiny and turning the six feet above the ground into an invisible furnace that sapped every drop from them; in such conditions men could do nothing.

B Company's officers were all at Edward's HQ, a ruined old shepherd's hut. All the timber from the roof had been removed but enough of the walls remained to enable a tarpaulin to be drawn over it, providing some shade.

Edward was content to doze as the others, led by Thorne, took it in turns to detail the special mantra or daydream each had to get them through the nights, or the dull moments, or the fear of action. Edward noted how innocent they all were; mothers, fathers, games of tennis, drinks with friends. None of the salaciousness that he had expected. The last to go was Sinden, who had remained a puzzle to them all thus far. Quiet, reserved and, for such an athletic and well-built man, almost painfully shy, he was possessed of a witheringly inadequate moustache that clung to his lip as though with an apology for being too fair and not founded on enough follicles to be properly bushy. Edward imagined that his daydream would be something about fishing on a favourite river or golfing a particular course. He wasn't ready for what followed.

Sinden started nervously and then found his feet, speaking in a clinical monotone with a flat, accentless voice, as though his version of English was the blandest, least nuanced in existence. He was from the outskirts of Hertford and before the war had been managing the sales division of a company that sold cleaning products.

'I start off with me sitting by the fire in my daughter's nursery at home, feeding her a bottle of milk in the early evening as the sun is setting. That then changes though to a scene many years in the future and she's a grandmother, in the same house, the same room, at the same time of day feeding milk to her own grandson, her youngest one. The year must be what, I don't know, nineteen eighty-five or something. Can you imagine?' He laughed a little and Edward liked the sound of it. 'And I switch between those two visions, one of me feeding her, all of six months old and feeling her tiny shoulder blades in the crook of my elbow and then one of her as an old and frail lady, with everything about her tired and aged apart from those eyes that used to look up at me – you know how they say that a person's eyes never get old? And I sometimes wonder if that grandchild of hers will ever even know my name, or if he does, then if he'll know at all what I did and how I used to cradle his own grandmother in the same way that she's cradling him. I used to hope that he would but now I think that I don't really care – why should he bother; as long as he's alive and is having a good time; I suppose that's all that really matters, isn't it? And I spend a few minutes like this.' He smiled. 'It's nice. And then I shake it off and I carry on with what I'm doing. I first had it on the ship out to Malta. And then every night since. Most hours actually, if I'm being honest. Each time I close my eyes for longer than a blink.'

Silence settled on them and, as Edward lifted the cap from his eyes, he saw Sinden looking as contented as he had yet seen him;

in the place of his nerves and diffidence there was a collected and considered calmness.

It was then that he realised that all the other eyes of the group were looking to him for his own memory. He knew exactly what it was. Sitting next to his aunt and uncle on the terrace outside their drawing room on an Indian summer's evening, talking about his late parents and how they had met, with a feeling of contentment buzzing down his spine. But the mundanity of the memory made him reluctant to share it. He might tell Thorne, perhaps, but not the others.

Instead he brought their gathering to an end, telling them to parade there again at dusk and dismissed them, walking out of the shelter with them to stretch his legs. Just as they all set off in their various directions, they heard the soft booms of Turkish guns begin a midday show to their north. They knew that this salvo was for them and dived onto the ground as the projectiles came crashing down, six of them in all that Edward counted by burying his eyelids even deeper into the dust with each one. He felt a weight on the back of his knee and, after the dust from the sixth one had settled, he looked to see that it was Sinden, lying perpendicular to him. He smiled, though he didn't know how or why, at the fond proximity engendered by such events. Ten yards away he saw Thorne kneel up from where he had thrown himself and dust himself down with a piqued air, full of disdain at an enemy who had made him untidy. He looked over and seemed about to give him a wink when his face fell and he stood still. Haynes-Mattingly too was now up and looking over at him as though he was about to be sick.

For a second he thought it was because he was hideously wounded, although he felt no pain, nor any sensation at all other than the dead weight of Sinden's leg on his. Then as he lifted himself up onto his elbows and twisted his body to shake Sinden off he looked back down and saw the maw of pulp that ate away more than half of the head and the dark red streams that spooled around it. Of the rest of Sinden's head there was no sign.

He got to his feet and appraised the sight, repulsive but at the same time weirdly, anatomically fascinating. The others drew around him. Haynes-Mattingly lit a cigarette and Thorne took it from him for a large drag. Edward hoped that no one would break the silence as the seconds lapsed and he pre-empted one of them making an off-colour line by saying quietly, 'Back to your platoons, please. I'll deal with this.'

He knelt over Sinden. He could hear one of the sergeants shout over for a bearer party and he wished that he could have longer with him, his skin now white and the enormous scoop into his head already the focus of several hundred flies. Edward thought back five minutes previously and hoped that the last thing Sinden saw was the dream with his daughter. He frisked his pockets for maps, classified material and personal effects and took from them the usual sundries: a compass, an old tourist map of the Hellespont, a blue and white spotted silk handkerchief, a leather folded frame of photographs of Sinden's wife and parents, a pocket diary, cigarettes and lighter, a smart red wallet and a couple of letters bound in a ribbon. He put them in his haversack and turned to greet the bearer party, who were no more shocked by the sight of Sinden than they were by any of the hundreds of other excrescences they had witnessed, assessing the body with a reassuringly professional eye as opposed to a human one. 'Lighter at the head end – you go there, John.' Edward watched as they took him back down to the clearing station, one of the khaki puttees from the leg that had lain on his now loose and trailing at the side of the stretcher.

Back in his empty HQ, he looked longingly at a whisky bottle that Haynes-Mattingly had brought with him from Mudros but thought better of it. He laid Sinden's possessions out in front of him and began to catalogue them before their journey home – the blood on the bundle of letters ensuring part of Sinden at least would be returning to Hertford. He shouldn't have read the letters but his guilt at not getting to know the man better prevailed.

There were three of them in the neatly tied green ribbon. One was from his brother who was in the navy, talking of the drudgery of minesweeping patrols around Orkney and complaining about the cold. Edward couldn't imagine Sinden having much sympathy for his brother's plight there. The second letter was from his wife.

My Darling Keith,

It is nice weather here at the moment although Mother says that will change and we are in for a blustery few weeks. She is now sleeping in the day bed in your study as the stairs are getting tricky and I said of course you wouldn't mind. Reverend Simpson mentioned the Dardanelles in his sermon yesterday and he said that his younger brother is serving on one of the ships there. I do think it would be funny if you met him.

I saw Doctor Consett this morning and I am afraid that he doesn't think that I will be able to bear children. It was the strain of the miscarriage that did it. I don't know quite what to say but I wanted to write to you and tell you it in these spare words before I started to think too much about it. To put it in plain English as it were. I will write further about it when I have thought more on it. Mother doesn't know although I suspect she saw me coming back today looking disheartened and will soon start asking questions, no doubt – you know how she is.

I am so very sorry, Keith. I don't know what else we can do.

I remain your loving wife, longing for your return,

Charlotte

It was almost too much to take in and he decided to try to blot out ever having read it. He turned to the third letter. It was on smarter writing paper and was far different in tone from the second. Far more flowing, far more emotional, far more sexually explicit. The only trouble was that it was also in different handwriting and from a lady who lived in Bishop's Stortford. He held the letters in his hand and thought for a moment, before tying up in the green ribbon the first and the second and then using his cigarette lighter to burn the third. There was no need for anyone to learn of its existence, he reasoned. As he was doing so, looking at the flames licking up and curling the letter into black and gold, he heard the crunch of footsteps and looked up to see Thorne. 'Room for a wee one?'

Edward shifted backwards into the nook of the wall. 'Hop in.'

Thorne slid down next to him and looked at the stub of the burned letter in Edward's hand. 'Burning secret documents?'

'Something like that. A letter I found in Sinden's things that was probably best for all if it didn't see the light of day. The other stuff I'll get back to his widow.' He then added, hoping to deter any further enquiry, 'You can have his cigarettes if you want, though. No point them going to waste.' He held them out and Thorne took them saying, 'Oh great, can I? Thanks.' and looking as pleased at this fillip as a child finding an unexpected sixpence in his pocket. He seemed to understand. 'Sinden, eh? Poor bugger. At least it was quick. I was going to make a joke as we were all standing around him wondering about the last thing going through his head being that piece of shell but thought better of it.' Edward looked at him sternly at this and then started laughing, both of them then descending into stomach-bursting giggles for a minute. They broke off and fell into silence again before Thorne said, 'Strange, that. Just after we were all talking about our dreams. I hope he was thinking of that one with his baby when it happened.'

Edward thought of telling him about what he had learned from the wife's letter but decided not to. If Sinden's futile wish could survive in some form, even in the back of Thorne's mind, to be plucked from memory only once or twice in the future then that constituted, he supposed, a tiny victory of sorts.

Thorne went on. 'I didn't really tell mine properly.'

'What do you mean?'

'You know, with everyone saying theirs. How I said mine was playing tennis with my sister. I mean it's true, partly, but not entirely.'

Edward didn't say anything, fearing that he would put Thorne off.

'The tennis definitely forms part of it but the real dream, that I have every day – like Sinden said almost every time I close my eyes – is much more detailed. Every time we come home from London, the gardener, Jacobs, wonderful man, meets us at the station. But the thing is it's fifteen miles away and a hell of a journey for him. And he's growing old. And it's a hassle with the horses et cetera. Blah blah blah. I always felt quite guilty getting him to come out. So for the past few years, as long as it's not an absolute monsoon, I walk home from the station, even in the winter. Almost prefer it in winter, to be honest. There's a chain of bridleways and footpaths that make a good-enough straightish line and that deliver you to the village, and then we're just a few hundred yards or so outside it.'

'How long does it take?'

'Rain or shine, light or dark, four and a half hours on the nose. I know the route like it's a part of me. Every stile, every change in gradient, every way that the height of the crops in the fields will change. Every bank of dull grass that in the spring bursts into cow parsley. Every fold and every dip. I must have done that route fifty times. And every time I see something different, something new in it. And then when I get back home, I stand at the bottom of the drive, look up at the house and walk over the lawn to it, so that I don't make a noise. Sometimes in the cold you can hear my feet as they break the frost on the grass so then I walk on the gravel, which is so frozen together it doesn't make a noise.

And I let myself in the front door and go over to the piano in the hall. I sit at it, open the lid – it's always shut – close my eyes and then all I do is play a C major broken chord – CEG – four times. I close the lid and go to find whoever's around. And more often than not about half an hour later I'm playing tennis with Miranda; that's the part that was true. Well, in the summer at least. But the core of the dream, the thing I play through in my mind at every point I want to escape from here, is the journey from the station to the piano and to that broken chord. I can do the entire walk in a second sometimes, as though the whole thing's happening at the speed of light. And if I want to concentrate on just one aspect of the dream then it's the chord. At the piano, in the cool of the hall that seems to be the same temperature in June or December, and those three notes. Every time. And it gets me away, even just for a moment.'

'But that's a great memory. Why did you not say all that?'

'Because I didn't want to; I just wanted to give them something bland. I didn't want them to own that proper piece of me, that precious memory. It's like if they knew that then there was nothing left for them to discover of me. And then, if I died, they would think that they at least had got to see all of me. But if I didn't say it then there's still something of me to discover. It's why when I heard Sinden talk about his daughter I sort of knew that he was done for. It was such a window into his soul that I felt that here was someone who I knew all about.'

He paused.

'Sounds pretty awful that, doesn't it?'

Edward smiled, trying to show understanding in his eyes. 'My only concern is what you might do when you find out all about me. Leave me to rot in No Man's Land because I hold no further interest for you.'

Thorne smiled. 'Don't worry, Wise Owl. You'll always be a source of fascination for me. Anyway, you never told us your dream.'

'Quite.' They both grinned. 'But you've now told me yours.'

'But you don't count.'

'Why's that?'

'I don't know. You just don't.'

They fell into another silence, Thorne taking out his revolver to clean and Edward finishing up going through Sinden's wallet to sanitise it of any other mementoes of Bishop's Stortford that might be lurking inside as a surprise to his widow.

'Always C major?'

'Always.'

'Why?'

'Just because. C major's the simplest key. The purest, I think. Stupid, isn't it?'

'Not at all. I think it's, I don't know, very . . .'

'What?'

Edward smiled. 'I don't think there's a word for it. But I like it. It's the kind of thing that the Germans would have a word for, probably. About fifty letters long. Something that combines a sense of purity with a sense of nostalgia with a sense of being anchored in oneself. Christ knows what that would be though.'

CHAPTER THIRTEEN

It finally became clear what was planned for B Company as they moved closer to the line in the following days and eventually took over a stretch of it. The orders were clear: at 04:30 the next day, just before dawn, the battalion would rush forward and seize the enemy trenches ahead of them, while to their left flank a battalion of the King's Light Infantry would attack at the same time against the trenches on the higher ground. Diversionary attacks would be mounted at other points in the line. Haynes-Mattingly summed it up well enough for all of them when he said, 'I feel sorry for the poor buggers who are going to be killed on this one. Bleakest patch of earth I've ever seen.' B Company were to be held in reserve for the attack, to be led by A and C Companies on a double frontage, which pleased Edward on two counts; firstly that there was a chance they may not be needed, and secondly, it was an implicit compliment from the commanding officer. He remembered their chat back on Helles – you always kept your best outfit in reserve, the CO had said.

That night the battalion went about its battle preparation, five hundred men in shoddily dug trenches, barely more than thigh-deep furrows in some places. Their position on the lower reaches of the ridge gave them a good view over the entire Suvla battlefield with the plain and its salt lake unfurled before them, and the stud of Imbros in the sea beyond that faded into the sky as the night came on.

Edward's Company HQ, shared with Jeffcoat and his runner Hogan, was next to Battalion HQ, who were themselves squeezed into the stretch of the trench that Thorne's Four Platoon were in. He looked around him and realised that he was surrounded by the people in the battalion he was fondest of – Thorne, the company sergeant major, the colonel and little Preston. Only Baffle was missing but he had seen him earlier in the evening as he had done the rounds of the company.

With Sinden dead, Haynes-Mattingly had taken back his old platoon with tangible delight and while this left Edward without a second in command, he was glad that Seven Platoon were in good hands. He had spent five minutes with Baffle as he was cleaning his rifle, Edward oiling the firing pin for him while Baffle pulled through the barrel with a craftsman's pride, frowning as he looked down it at the setting sun for specks of dust. 'What do you reckon about this one then, sir?'

The patrol they had done together when they were first on the Peninsula had made an umbilical between them that allowed Edward to speak with Baffle in a way that he never did with the other men. 'I don't know,' he replied. 'It all depends on those ridges and how far the final rush has to be. God knows how many of them are waiting there. I imagine it's going to be a hell of a show.'

'Aye, sir. Hope you've got a good supply of ink.'

'Eh?'

'Because I bet you'll be writing a fair few letters after this little lot, if you get me.'

Edward grimaced. 'I daresay you're right.'

Baffle laughed in his honest, open, totally blood-thirsty way. 'Don't worry about me, sir. It'll be good. I'm looking forward to it. Good job of work.'

Edward went on his way. He knew that as the night dragged on few men in the company would sleep properly. Maybe Baffle and Haynes-Mattingly would manage to get something approaching solid sleep, but most of them would be like him; whatever rest they were able to get was merely them gaining momentary mastery of a fraction of the night and the swells of sickness in their stomachs.

He carried on down the line and came to Company HQ, dug into the front of the trench wall and lit by a single candle glued to an upturned ammunition box by its own wax, its flame standing still and true, unmoved by any breeze in the still night. He slid down next to Thorne and felt a little respite from his sickness.

'All OK, Wise Owl?'

'Ready as we'll ever be, I suppose.'

'It's going to be a massacre tomorrow, isn't it?'

Edward was so taken aback by this matter-of-factness that he didn't reply, his silence giving his concurrence.

Thorne went on. 'Ho-hum. If you can't take the joke you shouldn't have joined, I suppose. This is the worst one so far, though, isn't it? I can't believe I thought it would get better as you went on.'

'Funny you say that. I was thinking exactly the same thing. I feel it in my stomach. You?'

'I don't really know. All over, strangely. It changes. Sometimes it's a prickling in my fingers and toes, sometimes in the back of my throat with a dry mouth. Sometimes my heart just goes like a steam train. And then it fades. Look, you couldn't look after this for me, could you? Make sure it gets to my family.' He took a slip of paper from his tunic and passed it to Edward. Without thinking, Edward unfolded it and then realised what it was, and closed it up, apologising for doing so. All he had seen were the final words of it, 'Your ever-loving Pip. I'll see you soon enough.' He handed it back to Thorne. 'I'm not taking this.'

Thorne shook his head. 'No, please. Just in case. Look, if I do make it then you can just give it back to me, all right?'

Edward thought a moment. 'All right. But you'll have this back tomorrow evening.'

'Thanks, Wise Owl. Annoyed I don't have an envelope for it.'

Edward took out his notebook and put it gingerly between some blank pages at its rear. 'Well, you know it's here; if I get hit then you know where you can find it.'

'Oh, you'll be all right, Wise Owl. You're indestructible.'

Edward changed the subject and asked, 'Pip eh? Is that a nickname?'

There was a tiny delay in Thorne's reply. Edward immediately regretted asking. He was about to say that he didn't have to answer but before he could Thorne said, 'Oh, it's just something my mother does. She always calls me Pip, from *Great Expectations*. Been my name at home ever since I was a boy. Silly, really.'

He seemed embarrassed and Edward remembered what he had said about Sinden, about being scared to give too much of himself away and he wished he hadn't asked it. He just smiled and felt a deep sadness that he wasn't able to protect his friend as he reached over and squeezed his shoulder, its muscles as firm as a horse's and he nearly gasped at how something so strong could be so completely vulnerable as it would be under the lottery of flying metal in a few hours' time.

The rest of the night passed in fractured moments of conversation and eyelids settling in heavy blinks to become tiny scraps of sleep. Edward said a silent prayer for Thorne, although he didn't know who to address it to in the godless empty plain, overlooked by the faint, apathetic stars and their sound gulfs of indifference.

Presently the battalion stirred itself into its positions and the men silently went through their well-oiled gears to take post ready to launch. The land was still in night's hand but its grip was weakening, black yielding to a dark grey as men up and down the trenches adjusted straps, tightened puttees, kissed keepsakes. The need for surprise meant that it was all done with tiny whispers, the only interactions between men who were otherwise lost in their own thoughts, their own imagination of what the morning ahead might hold, their own conception of what it might feel like to have metal smash bone or rip through flesh. Brains flicked back through images of home, of families, of friends, of mud-rich fields or puddle-specked pavements, of church bells or horses' hooves on busy streets, of jostling in crowds, of panic over missing collar studs, of hands dirty with the ink from newspapers, of crisp sheets, of autumn evenings and clean Atlantic winds winding through a park's trees resplendent in their pomp, not like the hunched and shrivelled husks that purported to be trees around them now, offering nothing save the most token shelter from the unblinking furnace suspended above them.

Edward counted down the minutes on his pocket watch, its hands pleasingly luminous and a reminder of a civilisation and benign industrialisation. For the final minute he counted every one of the seconds, trying to see if he could taste them, somehow actually taste time. He was struck with a desperate longing to stay here forever, on the two square feet of fried and crumbling earth covered by his legs and the side of his buttocks, forearm resting on the lip of the trench.

The hand hit H-Hour and in front of B Company a portion of the night shifted, seeming to create a fractured prism, as the inchoate forms of A and C Companies got out of their trenches and moved forward. Edward hissed, hoping it was loud enough to carry to both his left and right, 'That's us. Let's go,' and, as one, the company crested the trench, in a movement so firm and full that he gained an extraordinary confidence, his mood changing at once from fear to a bullish buoyancy. He was part of a wave that could not be stopped. No more anticipation. You can't dread what you're in.

He found that he was smiling and gone was the knot in his stomach as he welcomed back the sharp and metal tang to his gums and his pulse started to ramp up, flooding his capillaries with blood and beating his brain inside his skull. Within moments they were at the trenches that the others had just left. B Company skipped over them – a few grunts and muffled cries came from either side of him as some soldiers fell into it, the others ignoring them and sweeping on up the hill. The night was melting away quickly and to Edward's two o'clock a film of bluey-white, like the spume of a wave, bled across the sky to announce dawn just behind it. There was a clear delineation now between the gunmetal grey of the scrubby ground and the imperial purple sky above, as they slowed their pace and they came into the last stretch of dead ground before the final piece of the advance, where they were to remain until called forward.

A and C Companies were now over the ridge, out of sight and in the open. Edward called the company to a halt, all the men instinctively going down to a knee. There was a moment's silence, just long enough for him to imagine that the Turkish lines ahead had been taken without opposition, that they had been vacated over the night and the battalion had got through the mission scot-free, the task over before it had begun. And then the world over the ridge erupted.

CHAPTER FOURTEEN

B Company sat beneath the ridge as the light show danced above them with its appalling wall of noise. Tracers darted over their heads, probably a dozen yards or so above but seeming close enough to reach up and touch. In the gaps between the sounds he could make out screams and shouts. The Company remained on its knees, awed by the hidden chaos above them. A blurred shape emerged over the slope and then a shout, 'Mr Salter?'

'Here!' Edward replied.

It was Preston, coming back from the CO. He skidded in next to Edward and shouted into his ear. 'Colonel wants you. A Company are in pieces. Follow me.'

Edward went with him, shouting behind him for the company to stay where they were. He crested the ridge, seeing that ten yards ahead there was another one, the tracers above far closer now. Some of A Company lay on the lip of the ridge, dead, while others were being tended to by the medics. The colonel's HQ group, with Hardcastle the adjutant studying the progress of the attack to their left higher up the hill through a pair of field glasses, were at the lip looking out over the fighting. The colonel looked back and said cheerily, 'Ah Salter, glad you could join us. Come up here. Thank you, Preston.'

Edward joined them and the colonel said, 'C Company are doing all right. Purcell and A are taking a hell of a beating though.

I need you to get up and reinforce him. Get your men and push out there now. Understood?'

'Yes, sir.' Edward went back down the hill and spoke to his platoon commanders. 'Right. A Company are having trouble. We need to get in there. Get back to your platoons, watch me and when I say go, we go. Above this there's another little rise; that's where Battalion HQ is. Don't stop for them, just go over and then hell for leather. See you in the Turkish lines. Understood?'

They all nodded and went back to their platoons. Edward gave them a little time to brief them, impatiently flicking the inside of his lip with his tongue. Unable to wait any longer, he stood up so he would be seen and ran forward. He came over the lip where he was greeted by the colonel again. 'Well done, B Company. Good hunting.'

He didn't even break step, throwing himself up over the final ridge and into the new land above it. Immediately he appraised the battlefield, taking it in in a split second and distilling all he saw into parcels of reason. It was a gentler incline to the crest of the hill, over a hundred yards with undergrowth becoming thicker lower down the slope which explained, presumably, how C Company had managed to take the lines.

The dead, dying and wounded of A Company were studded all around him. He sprinted over the ground, glances to his sides reassuring him that the company were with him, some of them now ahead, their rifles held out in front of them, one of their bayonets suddenly glinting despite the sun still not being up. It struck him that the light must have been made by a bullet hitting it. Invisible bullets and glowing tracers hummed with crack and woosh all around. He felt one pass his neck and saw out of the corner of his eye another take the man next to him full in the chin, whipping his head back so violently he heard his neck crack. He leapt over a form in his path, recognising him as Adams, one of A Company's platoon commanders, who had one of his cheeks flensed off and hinging up over his nose like a piece of apple peel while his torso lay ragged with bullet holes beneath. Ahead he saw Purcell, A Company's commander, in a low fold of ground, screaming and clutching his knee, blood oozing through his knuckles and face white with shock. He thought then, bizarrely, that maybe this could be a chance for Haynes-Mattingly or Thorne to step up and command a company. He pressed on. There was no way he could make it. He could see fighting in the trench ahead. He held his revolver out straight and fired all six rounds at one of the Turks, knowing there was next to no chance of hitting him but at least enjoying the sensation of doing something to try to kill the enemy.

He tripped and fell, landing on a small shrub. Its dry and brittle shoots tore his face. He picked himself up and carried on, dozens of the soldiers now jumping into the trench ahead of him. Tracers came at them from the left, whipping two men round. Edward locked his eyes onto one of them, a look of childlike fear on a face that could have been no older than eighteen – one of Thorne's platoon, a new arrival who he recognised but couldn't name.

The ground whizzed under his feet and there was the Turkish trench, empty at the point that he had come to. He jumped in and came down heavily on his ankle, yelping in pain. All along the line the company was jumping in, bayoneting Turks on the floor, clubbing them with rifle butts or kneeling on top of them repeatedly knifing any flesh they could. He stood up, reloaded his revolver, amazed at his deftness and speed, and looked over the back of the Turkish trench to see if there were any depth positions. There were none he could see. The shallow reverse slope went down a good two hundred yards to a nullah and dead ground, before rising again to a hill about the same height as them, maybe a fraction lower. There would be Turks on that, he had no doubt. He needed to get a grip on what the company was doing in the context of the wider battle so went along the trench downhill and towards C Company, coming to a mass of fighting, a dozen people at least locked in combat. He saw Baffle stamping again and again on the head of a Turk, his face breaking and squelching with every drive of the boot.

Edward held his revolver out, Baffle stepped away and he blew the man's brains out. Baffle looked to him and smiled and then crumpled, his head cracked forward by a shot behind him. In reflex, Edward thrust out his revolver and squeezed the trigger, hitting a Turk in the throat. The man dropped his rifle in shock and collapsed, blood spurting all over him and spasms of coughing suggesting that his voice box had been blown away and that he would drown in his own blood. Edward stood over him and for the second time that minute shot the contents of a man's cranium out the back of his skull like it was the most normal thing in the world. Blood blew back and sprayed him in the face.

He looked at Baffle who lay face down in the trench. Dead. For several seconds he just stood there, unable to factor in the most heinous loss to the company, before regaining himself. Henderson and Lidgate from his old platoon also lay dead on the floor, both on top of the corpse of a Turk whose head had been sliced nearly clean off by a spade that was still stuck in his neck like an axe resting in a block. All along the line men were locked in the fight. Edward realised he had to tell the commanding officer what was going on and put his head above the parapet to look back at the ground they had just covered. He was surprised to be immediately met by the cheerful Preston, 'There you are, sir, was wondering if you'd made it.'

'Get the hell in here, Preston.' Edward grabbed him by the shoulders and dragged him down into the trench even as a burst of machine gun fire coming from God knew where kicked up dirt where the boy had just been. They looked at each other in the bottom of the trench and Preston smiled. 'Thanks, sir.' He looked up and down the trench, frowning theatrically at the carnage piled up around them. 'Nice place you've got here. Colonel wants to know if you can hold this. It's going to shit on the left flank with those scousers. They haven't taken their line yet which means you might be exposed here. If they break then you have to fall back too. The colonel doesn't like it but it's the only way. Whole day will have been a fucking joke.'

'Tell the commanding officer I understand and that we can hold here for as long as necessary. B Company have the line.'

'Got it, sir. Right, I'm out of here.'

With that he vaulted back out of the trench. Edward needed to get a grip of what strength the company was. Men were firing over the back of the trench and he put his head over it to see Turks beginning to launch a counterattack from the nullah. Either their reserve was there or they had sent some men back upon seeing the first assault for precisely this moment. At least we're the ones on the high ground, he thought. He picked his way along the company up the slope to understand the state of his own left flank. B Company men were interspersed with those from A Company who had survived their initial insane charge. 'That's it, men. Pour it on them, pour it on them!' he shouted.

He stepped over the dead Hearne from his old platoon and then one of A Company's lance corporals, breathing shallowly, gut-shot and surely about to go. Stretcher bearers weren't going to get to them for hours yet if at all, and the thought flashed through him that he should just shoot him and put the wretched man out of his misery. The CO probably would have, as would Haynes-Mattingly. But not him. He knelt, took the man's water bottle and with fumbling hands unscrewed the cap and held it to his lips, prompting a grunt of relief as the liquid silked his mouth and gave his brain one final pleasure. Edward felt like he was ministering communion. 'Go well. Go well. Go well,' he said, over and again like an incantation until the man at last died, his tobacco-stained front teeth biting gently, mouse-like, on his lower lip. Edward retched, until the bile lancing up his throat woke him up and he snapped back into command mode.

He drained the remainder of the bottle himself, slurping greedily to slake his awful thirst. The bottle empty, he felt a sudden shame at giving into his animal impulses and laid it on the man's chest like a knight's blazon, just above the blood-black and sodden mess spreading over his tunic.

He continued up the trench, men around him shouting encouragement to each other, spurts of dirt flinging up and the tin toy whine of ricochets squirting into the sky against the sharp bangs of the rifle fire slamming against his eardrums. Edward ducked and weaved through the men, relishing the clean, pleasing sound of new magazines being pushed home into their housing. Here he saw one of the sergeants give clear and precise fire control orders, there one of the corporals, Williamson, lay collapsed and jabbering away in garbled tics having soiled himself, plaintively holding his shattered wrist with his good hand, his face alabaster white. Edward stood up over the parapet and fired his revolver until empty again. If it keeps someone's head down for a while it will have done at least some good, he reasoned. Then he saw Haynes-Mattingly who had got hold of a Turkish Maxim gun and was in the process of directing some of his men as they hauled it up to fire back at its previous owners down the hill. Haynes-Mattingly turned, his face spattered in blood, a wide, evil smile giving him a callous, vulpine look.

'Salter! Hell of a scrap. Any word from above?'

The machine gun started firing so loudly that Edward had to pull him down to the floor of the trench and shout into his ear to make himself heard. 'I'm trying to get stock of how we are. Have you seen any of the others?'

'Yes. Hurst's dead. Through the chest, two bullets. Wham-bam. Thorne's to my left, I think. Saw him jump into the trench but Christ knows how he is now. He made it across the ground, though. We're in good shape. Not A Company though, they got minced.'

Edward lost himself a little in a panic about how Thorne was but then broke out of it and patted Haynes-Mattingly on the back. 'Good man. Keep this fire up.'

'How long are they going to keep coming at us?'

'As long as there's any of them left, I imagine. Mighty angry, aren't they?'

As he continued on his way, Edward looked back to see Haynes-Mattingly drag the cowering Williamson up and scream at him to get up and fire his rifle with his one good hand. Almost immediately Williamson's head evaporated in a grey fog as a bullet took the side of it off, Haynes-Mattingly still holding him by the shoulder. He looked at him with disgust and let go, pushing the juddering corpse down to the floor again. 'Waste of fucking flesh,' Edward heard him say.

He carried on and suddenly found himself surrounded by quiet.

Puzzled, he looked over the trench lip and saw that the crest of the hill was now hidden from the bottom of the valley beyond them by a convex slope that meant that they were out of sight. He heard a familiar voice shout up and down the line, 'Well done, lads, keep your eyes peeled. Watch and shoot, watch and shoot.'

Five captured Turks eyed him as he passed, guarded by old Cromlix, one of Thorne's corporals. One of the prisoners, with dark and austere hooded eyes, stood pointedly at a distance from the others, presumably to mark himself out as an officer. Bully for him, Edward thought; he's damned lucky he doesn't have a bullet in his skull. The beat of machine gun fire still came from Haynes-Mattingly's platoon and Edward realised the danger Thorne's platoon was in despite the appearances of quiet. At that moment he came to Thorne, who had none of Haynes-Mattingly's nonchalance; he was in it, focused and with no time to waste on pleasantries.

'Hello, Salter. We're all right. Four dead, eight wounded. Nothing like those poor buggers in A Company. My main worry is this blind slope. I have no idea how close they are down it. I don't know if we put picquets out on it but if we do they'll be exposed as hell.'

As if in response, shrieks of artillery came screaming in, the dreadful anticipation of their explosions bringing out their old habits of involuntarily crouching and grimacing so that teeth were bared by rictus faces all along the line. 'Here we go,' Thorne said grimly, with none of the ease that he had in previous fights.

For five minutes – it felt like hours but Edward's watch told him differently – the crest of the hill was raked by artillery fire, the ferocity of which they had not seen even a half of in their time on Helles. He didn't look up, curling himself into his ball and only glancing sideways to see Thorne do the same. Crash after crash after crash came in, the sides of the trench shedding sheets of dust and grit with every one. Edward could feel grains fall down the back of his neck. He lay with the side of his face scraping the ground, begging that one wouldn't land on them. Then a rapid whoosh, and they were both thrown against the other wall of the trench.

Edward thought they were gone. He smacked his head against the wall and blacked out for a moment, before getting up on his knees and, a few yards away, seeing two legs sticking out of a mound of earth where the trench had collapsed. They crawled over, clawing at the dirt to get the man into the air, their hands sliced and mauled. Finally they pulled out Grennan. Dead. Were there more men beneath him? They would never know.

A new smell hit his nostrils: burning. The bombardment stopped and the shooting began again, men getting up to pour fire down the hill to stop whatever nascent attack the bombardment might have preceded. The smell grew, and Edward looked over the rear of the trench to see a grey haze where shell fire had lit up the grass and shrubs, the occasional, indifferent breeze bringing it sometimes towards them and relenting at others to send it straight into the sky. If communication was hard before, it was going to be nigh on impossible now. Edward called in the information from the company to get a rough battle state. Around seventy rifles, meaning that thirty or forty were dead, wounded or unaccounted for. They had taken fifteen prisoners and killed perhaps triple that, to judge from the pile of bodies.

The smoke at their rear was getting thicker now, the wind keeping it away from them for the moment, pushing it up the hill to their left. With a new kick in the stomach Edward heard the cries and screams that came up the other side of the ridgeline – the Turks were attacking the high ground and using the smoke as cover. The boys along the line realised it too and looked to him, the weight of their gazes shooting right through him. If the Turks took the high ground they would be able to enfilade onto them. It would be a massacre. He looked away and his eyes were drawn somehow to those of the Turkish officer who he had seen beforehand, who sat smiling with malevolent eyes and a knowing sneer on his face seeing exactly the position that Edward was in.

A moment of utter inadequacy settled on him. Everyone was looking to him and all he wanted was someone to whom he could pass responsibility. Then he saw the act that removed all his doubt. On the ridge line first one, then two khaki figures, then dozens of them started streaming back down the hill. The line had been broken. They were next. There was only one way to act.

'Thorne, stay here. Cover the withdrawal.' He grabbed a pair who had commandeered another Maxim gun, threw them into position and pointed up the hill. 'That's your target. Cover the company.' He seized another man and said to him, almost conversationally, 'Get down the line and tell everyone you meet to withdraw. Now. Tell them to leave the position immediately and get out. When you get to C Company tell them the left flank has collapsed. We have to get off this hill.'

The soldier looked at him; not one that he recognised. Tall and slight, a reed of an individual, he wore glasses with one lens cracked, a last smattering of teenage freckles behind them.

'Understood?'

'Yes, sir.'

'Good man. Go, go. Get everyone out.'

The boy ran down the trench and as though carving off a slice of ham as he went down the trench the men heard him, got up out of the back and started running down the open ground before the ridge folded down to dead ground.

Thorne and his platoon were now firing up the hill, some of them over each other's heads, desperately trying to lay down some cover for the rest as they withdrew. Through the smoke Edward could see the Turks on the crest of the hill crumple under the wave of bullets, while back down the line C Company soldiers were leaving the trench. For a moment he thought about what he had done, unzipping the entire frontage and wilfully giving up their hard-won prize, but he had to do it; the fall of the left flank had made the entire thing untenable. But then he just felt relief that the message had got through. 'Right. That's us. Let's go. Party's over, chaps. Withdraw. Go, go, go!'

Edward blew his whistle as all those around him got up and made pell-mell down the hill. All he was able to do was scream, 'Fall back! Fall back!' Bullets pierced the blankets of smoke that enveloped them with whipped vortices hanging in the air. One of the men to his front crumpled, shot twice in the back with a thud-thud of bullets that sang just past Edward's shoulder. He stopped, turned and fired his revolver back up the hill, the enemy now invisible save for muzzle flashes studding the smoke. The fallen man was still alive, screaming in pain. Edward saw it was Thurlow, from Thorne's platoon, and he dragged him by his epaulettes until they ripped off and he fell back, jarring his coccyx. Rounds flayed the air around them. And then out of the smoke came Thorne. 'Hello Wise Owl, want a hand?'

They both took hold of Thurlow and started to pull him away together. The bush beneath them lay in charred stumps, black claws reaching out of the ground where the fire had gone through it; the smoke stung their eyes and filled their throats and lungs, leaving them heaving and hacking. They passed a body whose face was a mash of burned flesh, the stench rising to mix with the smoke. Then another bullet ripped out of the haze, hitting Thurlow in the hip. He collapsed from their grip, dead.

They started again down the hill. The smoke was so thick that Edward had no idea how far away the false summit and safety was. Still the crack of bullets all around fenced them in, crushing any sense of hope. Each bullet was the sound of inevitability, a nasty, spitting crowing that one of its successors would hit home. They ran over two other bodies. Guts lay black and charred next to warped limbs, an arm shaped in such a way that the man had to have been alive while the fire consumed him. Another bullet whizzed through Edward's legs and pinged off a rock in front of them. Then the ground fell away and they both tripped up, tumbling down the hill. Edward landed on a smouldering bush and gasped in pain as the branches broke against his body. But it didn't matter. They had made it.

They picked themselves up into a sitting position and laughed with incredulity for a full minute. Then they stood up and trotted down the hill to the trench, the smouldering vegetation underneath the smoke giving way to open hillside and clean, water-like air. For a moment Edward feared that they would be shot by their own men who stood in the trench, rifles set and pointed up the hill, daring the Turks to try their luck. But no bullets came. They slid into the trench and someone passed Edward a water bottle and he heaved up his lungs trying to get rid of the clinging grime the smoke had left in them. He looked at his watch; it was ten o'clock. It felt like they had only been out for ten minutes.

At dusk, as a dull, cloudy evening turned into night, Edward took from his pocket the list that he had made of all those in the company either known to be dead or still unaccounted for. Over the afternoon various wounded had crawled back in dribs and drabs, some on the very edge of death, others crying from the smoke, hair singed off and faces raw-pink and livid from the fires. All told, the company had twenty-eight dead or missing and thirty wounded out of a dawn total of one hundred and eight.

He read the dead or missing list for the twentieth time that day, the paper already thin and its folds weak and fraying from his fingers and thumbs.

Hurst, Jeffcoat, Grennan, Williamson, Meath, Rosen, Thurlow, Ruvigny, Pym, Fletcher, Yerbury, Devitt, Jones, Relf, Sackett, Woolley, Freeston, Guilly, Tinnion, Davidowitz, Hughes, Hearne, Smith, Brockbank, McGinn, Henderson, Lidgate. And the final name. Baffle.

It was that name that always caught him. It was as though the thread running through the company had been unravelled, with the afternoon passing in a flat and defeated tone that would have been expected given the failure of the day's operation but made somehow starker now that their talisman was gone. Every man felt that he personally had been robbed of his guardian angel by Baffle's death. The one person in the whole Dardanelles who had seemed truly invincible was now no longer there to protect his comrades.

They settled into their uneasy night-time routine, in their purgatory of the ground beneath the ridges, not knowing if the Turks were massing for a rush down the hill, a third of the company's rifles still on the firestep in case they did. They would hold like this for the night and get reinforced the next morning.

Edward folded the paper away and sat down in the trench, grateful for the dark, not sure what his face was doing. He kept thinking of three things: Baffle being hit; the wounded Williamson being dragged back up to the parapet only to be killed; and the moments he had leant over the A Company lance corporal, giving him water as he slipped away. He couldn't believe that he hadn't held his hand. It felt an awful dereliction that he had not. He wondered where his body was now. Dumped over the rear of the trench, most likely, and kicked and rolled far enough away to fester, bloat and rupture over the days ahead.

He closed his eyes, willing sleep on and surprised at his

descent into it when a commotion from further down the trench brought him back, his senses suddenly buzzing, tingling with new adrenaline. Muffled shouts for a medic came down the trench and then, 'Get the company commander here now!'

Edward ran, stumbling occasionally as he picked his way over the legs of sleeping men. He rounded a bend and there, framed in a burst of flame to light a cigarette that showed his face black and matted with blood and a snarling wound, glinting with exposed flesh, running straight across the side of a head that he knew so well and whose presence was already lifting the company, his name spilling down the trench and injecting their veins with quicksilver to make their hearts thud a little lighter. Baffle.

Baffle was alive.

He sat back, hidden in the darkness as he heard Baffle's nasal, amused voice. 'So I go down, and it all goes black. I swear I actually was dead for a bit; I can't remember a thing. But then I come to, and my head feels like it's got a thousand horses in it, and I look up and all I know is that you lot have all fucked off. And there's Johnny everywhere. So I lie doggo and then get up, grab this pistol off this officer and he looks at me like he's caught me with his wife and I shoot him and three other fuckers next to him. But then the fucking thing runs out of ammo, so I fuck off out of the trench and run down the hill into all the smoke. And they're all shooting at me and one of them skims the top of my shoulder and I fall down into this dead ground, just a little pocket. But I'm still sort of in their view, and they spend all fucking afternoon sniping at me. Still can't believe they didn't just come out at me and grenade me. Anyway, I wait until dark and then come down the hill. And look—' he lifted his hand up to show the broom handle Mauser '—hell of a souvenir.' At that moment he saw Edward and stood up. Edward had never been one to show emotion in front of the men but he lurched forward and hugged him.

CHAPTER FIFTEEN

They were out of the line and the battalion had been reorganised. Haynes-Mattingly had been given command of A Company to replace the wounded Purcell, which he had accepted with an unbecoming delight. Edward still had B Company, but Thorne was now his company second in command and the platoons were commanded by three replacement second lieutenants, Alderville, Linver and Cortayne. In the troops there were also promotions: Baffle became sergeant of Three Platoon ('I give it a couple of weeks before I'm busted down again,' he had said to the CO at the time. 'Judging from your previous history, I'd say it will be more like one, Mr Baffle,' the CO had replied).

In terms of the general situation, the lines had crystallised across the whole semi-circle of the Suvla position, especially in their sector, and so it had been decided by division that the blind crests, as they had come to be known, were simply not worth the difficulty of gaining, the position not actually giving enough of a view of the bay to warrant trying to take it. Instead, the line could be held and fortified so that the Turks too would decide that to press in that sector was pointless.

One afternoon, when they were in the rear, Edward was swimming in the sea when a shout from the shore made him look back. It was Preston. 'Got to come and get you, sir. Some bigwig from HQ wants to see you.' He waded ashore and got dressed, walking with Preston as he did up his Sam Browne and checked his revolver in his holster. 'Any clue from the colonel what this is all about?'

'None at all, sir. Just told me to make it snappy.'

'What rank was this chap?'

'Only a lieutenant. Strutted around as if he owned the place though. Wouldn't have minded seeing him up on the blind crests the other day; that would have got rid of the carrot from his arse.'

Presently Preston delivered Edward to the colonel's dugout, a sandbag construction half dug into the ground and half built above. As befitted an old campaigner, the colonel had endeavoured to make it as habitable as possible – 'Any fool can be uncomfortable, Salter' – and somehow he, or more likely Preston, had scrounged bits of kit to make it a little more homely, including a couple of canvas chairs and a rather smart little wooden table with a faded chessboard lacquer on its top. Edward looked at it and then quizzically at Preston, who shrugged like a cherub as if denying all knowledge of it. The colonel and his visitor looked up from the map board.

'Ah, Salter. You'll remember Valentine Braithwaite?'

A serious-looking young man held out his hand, tight brows above an open face. His britches were the widest Edward had ever seen. Above his breast sat the ribbon of the Military Cross, the white faded and yellowed. It was the son of Ian Hamilton's chief of staff.

'Hello, Salter. Good to finally meet you properly.' His voice was friendlier than he looked, but still Edward remained stiff and reserved with him in his own reply, trying to work through in his head what on earth Braithwaite wanted with him. His youth was disconcerting; he looked about twenty yet here he was, Edward's junior in rank but unofficially far superior to him in influence.

Braithwaite turned towards the colonel. 'Ah, Colonel, you wouldn't mind . . . ?'

The colonel looked absent-minded before getting the message.

'Eh? Oh, I see, yes of course, better go and see the QM anyway.' He left them in the dugout together, quite unoffended by essentially having just been turfed out of his own HQ by a boy less than half his age.

Braithwaite waited a moment before beginning, not wasting any time with small talk. Edward wondered if he was a little self-conscious as a member of the staff and a little intimidated by those in the line, but then remembered the MC ribbon and thought probably not. There were chairs available but Braithwaite remained standing.

'You elaborated on how well you speak Russian in the note you sent. We've got a job for you. Nothing overly onerous but we'd appreciate your help.'

Edward thought back to the message that he had given Preston weeks ago. So this was what all that was about. He didn't want to give away anything and so stayed silent, Braithwaite finally blinking from the pause and carrying on.

'There's a delegation from the Russian Army visiting us in two days. All above board. All totally straightforward.' Adding that final bit made it sound anything but. 'They're visiting Imbros, Helles, Anzac, Suvla. Dinner with Sir Ian, et cetera. Fatted calf wheeled out for them. Need to show we're doing all we can for them here so they get breathing room from the Turks. But it's a visit. A visit is a visit. All they'll really see is what we want them to see. And we want to find out things from them without them finding out that we're doing so. Hush-hush, nudge-nudge; you get the picture. The trouble is that we're providing interpreters for them but they won't be idiots and will likely watch what they say at all points. We really need to get them around someone who speaks Russian but without them knowing he does. Which is where you come into it, if you'd like to help us.'

Edward couldn't deny that the young man had an authority about him and felt that he was having any autonomy slowly squeezed away from him. He had been around the army long enough by now to know that whatever people like Braithwaite had planned for him they would dress it up as a request for a favour when in fact he had absolutely no free will in the matter whatsoever.

Braithwaite went on. 'What we'd like to do is that when they're at Suvla we offer them the chance to see a quiet bit of the line. There's no way they can refuse without looking like cowards. Which is where you and the blind crests come in. We'd like you to meet them and take them up to the line, introduce them to a few of the men, I don't know, lob a few grenades into No Man's Land if you want, spin them some lines about the fight last week and then bring them back for a cup of tea. Officially, it'll be a valuable part of the visit, a chance to see the British Tommy doing what he does best. Tick, tick, very good. Everyone then goes home. But hopefully, in the couple of hours or so you've got them for they might say something interesting, unguarded, showing what they really think about us. But for God's sake don't get them killed. GHQ has enough paperwork going on as it is without some kind of diplomatic incident adding to it.'

It took Edward a moment to realise that Braithwaite was trying to be funny, and he laughed. The mission itself seemed utterly absurd but one that also, given the terrain of the blind crests, would be safe enough. But he decided to play it a little coyly.

'I don't suppose I've got any choice, do I?'

'No.'

He had to admire Braithwaite's directness. 'OK. Well, of course I'll do it.'

Braithwaite smiled. 'Good man. We'll bring them up to you at midday or so in two days. All you need to do is a couple of hours with them. Introduce them to the men, give them some bully, sing Tipperary, that kind of thing. We don't really care what you do. Just tell us if anything happens in the margins.'

Edward thought for a moment. He couldn't believe how he had managed to get caught up in this scheme but supposed that at least it had novelty value. 'Understood. I'll do it. But I bet you all I'll pick up from them is how much they hate the flies.'

'That's just fine, old chap. It's just on the off-chance anyway.' Braithwaite slackened his stance and reached into his pocket for a cigarette packet. 'Fancy a smoke? I'm dying for one.'

CHAPTER SIXTEEN

By the day of the visit, the battalion was back at the blind crests. Edward and his runner, Hogan, were down at the beachhead among the vast towers of stores, having left the company in Thorne's hands. A hundred yards away a party of staff officers were talking to the Russian delegation, a group of four men dressed as British sailors for secrecy.

The day was a relatively nice one, a gentle breeze adding some freshness and, crucially, keeping the worst of the flies at bay. Sporadic shellfire harried the western part of the bay like a fat, bored Pasha occasionally deigning to try to swat a fly.

'Look sharp, Hogan,' said Edward, as a gaggle of eight broke away from the group and headed towards them. He gave a quiet 'Up' and they both saluted Colonel Waite from GHQ who was leading the visit. The colonel made an introduction to the Russians.

'Salter, this is Colonel Voronov.'

Edward saluted a short, tubby red-faced man with a stiff collar amusingly poking up underneath his British rating's uniform.

Then introductions to the three others – Major Yeryomin, a gaunt, unshaven man with a glowering face over thin jowls and then Captains Lipin and Borov. Edward smiled at them in greeting. They looked as bewildered as he felt.

Edward tried to maintain a fixed expression of impassivity and humility as Colonel Waite went on to make some fairly exaggerated claims about the battle of the blind crests. He shifted his eyes unobtrusively over the Russians. They were sunburnt and bored, incongruous in their naval uniforms.

'Well, gentlemen,' the colonel wound up, 'Major Salter is your guide for the next couple of hours. He's going to take you up to the front line. But not to worry, it's a quiet sector, and I've already told him that if anything happens to you he's going for a swim in the sea with a couple of shells tied to his feet.' The Russians laughed politely.

'Well, gentlemen, Salter's got you now. I'll see you back here at seventeen hundred hours.'

Colonel Voronov spoke up in stiff but excellent English. 'Thank you, but I regret to say that we will not all be going to the front line. It would, how does one say, not look very good if something were to happen to us. I think this is a trip for you, Misha, and you, Boris,' he said, indicating the two younger officers, Lipin and Borov. This was clearly news to Borov, who looked as though he wanted to be sick.

Colonel Waite nodded and turned to Edward. 'Happy with that, Salter? Should be a bit more manageable, what?'

Edward had to admit that this was now a lot easier than having to shepherd the four of them through the complexities of the trench system. 'Yes, sir, absolutely. All right, shall we go? Colonel Voronov, we'll be back here at seventeen hundred hours. I promise you they won't come to any harm.'

Voronov waved his hand in a manner that seemed to suggest he didn't really mind either way, and the group of senior officers then faded away back to the beach and Edward appraised his new charges. 'Well, gentlemen, first things first, please call me Edward. Second, can I assume that you both speak good English? I'm afraid my Russian, is, er, non-existent. Well, "*da*" and "*nyet*", I suppose. And "*Tovarich*". The great failing of Great Britain, I'm afraid to say. Very good at attacking other countries, but never any good at bothering to learn any languages.'

He was gratified to see Lipin, at least, laugh at this. He was handsome, lean and elegant, very clean-looking even in his tatty British uniform, with classic high Slavic cheekbones underneath fair hair, a button nose giving him a benign, friendly look. Borov was less prepossessing, with lank long hair spilling over his collar and a shifty, greedy look in his eyes. Their body language suggested that Lipin was de facto the decision maker of the pair .

Then, in Russian and with a vicious leer that threw Edward completely off balance, Lipin said jovially, 'You're lying, you cocksucker son of a whore. You speak perfectly good Russian and you know it. Don't treat us like a pair of fucking clowns.'

A fear unlike anything he had experienced in any battle ran down Edward's spine. He felt his pores open and skin tingle. He hoped that he hadn't missed a beat when he replied, 'I'm sorry, what does that mean?'

For a moment he was convinced that his bluff hadn't been good enough and that he had failed before he had really begun. But Lipin smiled enchantingly and said, 'My apologies, just a traditional Russian greeting. We are lucky to be here and to have you as our guide and may the wind always be at your back.' Behind him Borov nodded inanely and offered an ingratiating smile that did little to redress Edward's impression of him as a simpering idiot. Edward felt a little confidence seep back that he had managed not to fold. It had been a damned near thing though.

He cursed Braithwaite and his stupid plan while outwardly maintaining his breezy jauntiness. 'Right. Well. No time like the present. Follow me. It's a ten-minute walk to the trenches and slower going after that. It'll take us half an hour to get to the front.'

They set off up to the line, Edward leading with Lipin behind him, then Borov and Hogan bringing up the rear. They passed through the scrub and head-high trees giving some shade from the sun, now and again passing a shell crater that had been punched into the earth. The sound of the Turkish artillery was soft and muzzy in the background, softened by the trees and the crickets. Edward heard Lipin and Borov muttering to each other, but could only catch snippets of it, Lipin berating Borov now and again for being unfit.

Edward halted and said, 'Anything wrong?'

'Nothing,' Lipin replied cheerfully, 'we are just complaining about the heat.' Borov nodded in agreement. A hundred yards further on their conversation started again, this time clearly audible as Lipin laid into his companion. 'You'll damn well come up, you fat bastard. What are these British going to think if we have to leave you here. It's totally safe, they're not going to risk one of us getting hurt. If you don't come it will be a complete humiliation for us.'

'But Misha, my blisters are hurting.'

'Rubbish, you don't have any blisters at all, you pathetic weasel.'

They came to a low wall, ancient sheep droppings in its lee and rays of sunlight dancing on the leaves above in the breeze. As they sat down to take a drink Lipin said, 'I am sorry, Edward, but I'm afraid we must leave my comrade here. He has very bad blisters and will be a burden to us as we continue.' Borov nodded and winced apologetically, looking sadly at his feet by way of explanation.

Edward thought for a moment. Part of him was thankful he would only now have to shepherd the clearly quite competent Lipin, but it did mean that with only one Russian the entire point of the charade, to overhear their conversation, was now rendered completely impossible. Well, it was out of his hands. Bugger Braithwaite. 'That's quite all right. Hogan, look after the captain, make him comfortable, will you? I'm sorry about his blisters. I'm sure we could get the doctor to have a look at them if he'd like.'

A look of horror swept over Borov's face. 'No, no, that will be quite unnecessary, I assure you.' Edward saw Lipin's lips turn a tiny grin. Edward had to admire Borov in a way. In all the last months he had seen scores of scared soldiers, screaming and out of their minds, and he had seen shirkers and potential deserters who were only denied leaving by being physically stuck between rocks and the sea. But he had not yet seen someone so brazenly wretched. He couldn't bring himself to try to embarrass him any further. 'Wait here and we'll be back in a couple of hours. Hogan, over to you.'

'No problem, sir.' Hogan led Borov away to shelter in the shade of an ammunition dump dug into the side of the hill and Edward heard him quell any protest: 'Oh, don't worry, Russki, if anything hits us here we won't have a clue about it.'

Lipin turned to Edward and said, 'I'm sorry about that. He's a bloody coward, disgrace to the uniform. He's only on this mission because his uncle is one of the generals fighting the Turks in the Caucasus. A Georgian too.' He spat theatrically on the ground. 'Brigands and rapists. Anyway, we'll have a lot more fun without him.' He seemed delighted by the turn of events and as they entered the trench system he began to whistle away to himself.

The tour of the line passed initially without incident. Edward found Lipin to be a highly entertaining companion who clearly loved the art and craft of soldiering. First they visited Battalion HQ where Lipin got a ground brief from Hardcastle, the adjutant, and had a conversation with the commanding officer, mostly about orchids after the colonel discovered that he was keen on them too. As they left, the colonel gave Edward a stage wink that almost made him laugh, clearly not weighing GHQ's plan with much credence himself and recognising like Edward that it was now completely futile. Then they went on to the front line, to the trenches they had surged forward from those weeks before that were now unrecognisable having been titivated and fortified with all manner of saps, rows of wire and machine gun positions.

Lipin appeared to enjoy meeting the men and had an especially long conversation with Baffle about the design of the new weapon that he'd had made. He had somehow convinced one of the naval bods who shuttled back and forth from the supply ships to the Suvla beaches to get a technician to weld a bayonet onto a pair of brass knuckles, the blade's front keen, razor-sharp and whetted on a daily basis by its owner and its back notched by a series of gruesome serrations. Lipin looked delighted by it and made a show of trying to take it away from Baffle, who laughed and said, 'I wouldn't, sir. I'd gut you if you tried to do that. And your Tsar.' Lipin laughed politely, if a little nervously.

Edward managed to glean from Lipin that he was from Petrograd and had learned his immaculate, mannered and remarkably idiomatic English from a lady from Cambridge whom his parents had hired to teach him the piano. Lipin had joined the army in 1912 having grown bored of studying to be an architect and in the first months of the war had seen action at the great battle of Tannenberg where, he said ruefully, he had been one of only ten in his company to survive. He had spent the next months in a series of frantic rearguards as the Germans pushed the Russians ever further back, before being plucked from the front just before Christmas to become the aide to the father of an old school friend who was a general on the staff. His knowledge of English had made him a natural choice to send with the delegation here.

Edward noticed that Lipin and Thorne struck up an immediate affinity with each other, sharing an easy manner and the sangfroid that made Thorne such a byword for morale. Within minutes of meeting each other they were laughing and joking. Lipin's courage was put to the test unexpectedly when towards the end of the tour the Turkish guns gave the line a two-minute hammering. He didn't so much as flinch as the other men hunched instinctively at the hideous whoomp and crunch of the shells landing on the slopes above them, sending rocks and clods of earth flying down the hill onto them and kicking off hundreds of trickles of dust and sand down the walls of the trench. Edward looked up to see Lipin's face, finding his expression of utter calm uncanny; it was as though he was in a trance. His blank eyes only snapped back into their engaging glint and verve when the shells eased off. He patted the man next to him on the back saying, 'And you men have to do this without vodka. I take my hat off to you!' and everyone around laughed.

'So,' Edward said after they had bid farewell to B Company, 'how do you think we're doing?'

'Do you want the answer I'll give to your general or the one I'll give to mine?'

Edward chuckled at his frankness. 'Both.'

'To your general I will say that your men are heroes and that the work they are doing is vital to protect our southern flank while we try to concentrate on the Germans and Austro-Hungarians to our west'.

'And to yours?'

'I'll say that you're being butchered for no good reason. You don't have the ground, you don't have the men, you're operating at the limit of your supply chain and you should leave next week, if you had any sense.' He paused for a moment and added, 'But your men are very good. They are excellent fighters, that is clear. You must be very proud of them.'

Edward was silent for a while as every moment he could recall in the trenches flashed through his brain. 'Thank you. Yes. Yes, I am. They're marvels. Don't tell them I said that, though.' He felt a little embarrassed and changed the subject. 'How is it with you, in Russia?'

'Oh, the usual. Everything threatening to explode at any moment. But we will be all right, we will come through. Like I'll say to your general, if you can stay here and soak up the Turks, then we will be all right and we'll push the Germans right back beyond Berlin and crush them against the anvil of the French.' His tone was light but Edward could tell that he was not really joking. 'But the tragedy is that we will do this with or without you being here.'

Edward didn't know whether or not to be offended by Lipin implying that they were wasting their time but decided to let it rest. At least he was being honest, he supposed.

Eventually they got back down to the nick of the slope where they met Borov and Hogan. They trooped back to the shore where, on the dot of 17:00, they met the rest of the Russian delegation. Surrounded now by senior officers the informality disappeared and both Edward and Lipin reverted to the stiff stiltedness of when they had first met. 'Well,' said Colonel Waite, 'glad to see you returned our friends in one piece, Salter.'

The Russian colonel leant in, hugged Edward and kissed him on both cheeks. He could see Lipin smirking at this and smiled back.

Further pleasantries were swapped before Edward was dismissed by Colonel Waite. He went to shake Borov's hand who returned it with a friendly smile and an arm on his shoulder as though he and Edward were great friends. Escaping Borov, he went to Lipin, who pulled him into an embrace and whispered, 'Thank you, my friend. Take care. Please don't let anything happen to you. God speed.' And then the Russians left, the absurd caravan of the visit moving on. Edward watched them go back along the shore to boats that would take them to GHQ at Imbros. He couldn't fathom Lipin. There was something unnerving about him. Not just the spitting violence with which he had tested Edward's Russian at the start but his strange detachment during the bombardment.

As Edward made to set off, Braithwaite appeared from behind one of the ammunition dumps, clearly having hidden there while the Russians had been making their farewells. He looked excited and it struck Edward again how young he was, belying the heft of his role.

'Well, any luck?'

'Not really. They didn't really talk much to each other about anything.' He was about to mention that fact that Borov's flakiness had put paid to any hopes at all of the plan working when Braithwaite looked at his watch. 'Damn, I've got to go. I need to be on the boat with them back to GHQ and it goes in five minutes. Nothing at all?'

'There was one thing. Lipin said that while he would tell us officially that what we're doing here is helping them, in reality he thinks it's a complete waste of time and that we're pouring blood and treasure away for no end whatsoever.'

'Did he now? That is interesting. Very good, Salter, very good indeed.' A shell then landed a couple of hundred yards away, the first one in the sector almost all afternoon, perhaps presaging a more general bombardment creeping closer to them. 'Right, I really must go.'

That evening, as the sun shafts shifted on the sea, their gold streaks stitching together the grey layers of cloud above and sea below, here catching a destroyer, there a lighter in the net of dapples, the gloom drew in and for the first time since leaving Southampton, Edward felt something new: not a chill as such, rather an absence of the customary heat. If he had known that that slight thinning of the air, which seemed to herald the end of the summer's trial, was in fact the baleful first scout for the autumn and winter that would follow, he would not have welcomed it as he did, smiling at having at least got through one more season. Baffle appeared next to him. 'Why are you smiling, sir?'

'No special reason, Baffle. A nice evening, that's all.'

Baffle, unusually for him, didn't respond. In silence, they looked out over the plain spread out before them and the fleet beyond it while night came on.

CHAPTER SEVENTEEN

Summer lapsed into autumn and the heat fell out of the effort across the entire Suvla Bay area. Any gains achieved – a ridgeline, a piece of commanding ground, an ironing out of a chink or nick in the line – were shown almost immediately to be puny in the context of the vast bowl that enveloped them. Still they kept trying, as though they could take the Peninsula bite by bite, but the game, Edward realised, was up when Ian Hamilton was removed as Commander in Chief in October. Almost every man in the force had had occasion to lay eyes on Hamilton in the months since April and his personal bravery was never in doubt, a constant demonstration to the callow young that it was possible to grow so familiar with shot and shell so as to be apparently oblivious to them when in action. Hamilton's removal felt like a personal insult to the men to whose lives he had been bound so inextricably. That also meant the departure of his chief of staff Braithwaite and his son, a move, Edward reflected, that put paid to the comical charade of his tasking with the Russians. Edward asked the CO, accepting a cigarette from him in his dugout on an overcast, humid morning, whether he was sad that Sir Ian had been replaced.

'Gosh, not really, Salter. You'll see when you grow up—' Edward liked the fact that he continued to treat him as though he was still in his teens '—how little these things matter in the grand scheme of things. Comes with the job. You get into any kind of position in this man's army and the whole thing becomes political. That's why the honours system is there, why they all end up festooned with Orders and Knighthoods and Grand Commands of the Bathwater pursuivant to banana-bending and all the rest of it. It's not in recognition of anything they've done or achieved, per se, but the currency the system has invented to assuage the egos of the people that inevitably have to get given the boot when they get into the rarefied airs of senior command. A peerage flung this way or that can be an awfully good tonic to relieve the sting of a sacking. Sir Ian will have had his enemies knifing him back in London from the day he left. A shame; you should have seen him in his pomp. He was magnificent. In any case, now that he's gone I shouldn't expect we'll be hanging around here much longer. Ho-hum. Way of the world, dear boy. All we need to do is keep killing the Turk until we get told to leave. Easy.' He looked at Edward and tutted at his gloomy expression. 'Cheer up. If you can't take the joke you shouldn't have joined.' He looked down at his papers, his signal that he considered their meeting closed and Edward saluted him and left.

He made his way to his own dugout to join Thorne, who was reading a novel, tapping his feet in their field boots rhythmically up and down as though he was playing the pedals on a piano. He put the book down and asked, 'So? Any idea where all this is going?'

Edward took his helmet off and ran a hand through his short, tufted hair. 'He thinks we'll be gone any time soon. I daresay he's right. Don't know how it's going to go down with the men though. After all they've done.' He couldn't bring himself to mention the greater truth, which was all the people who'd been killed.

'Oh, I wouldn't worry about that. They'll get it. As long as we win this in the end it will have been worth it. Soldiers are clever like that. They don't think that just because you attack somewhere then withdraw from it, that that per se has been a waste of effort, as long as in the end you're on the winning side. I think they will be a little shocked at first though. Baffle would remain here for another sixty years if you told him at the end of it he'd get to knife the Sultan in Constantinople.'

'Still, don't tell anyone, for God's sake. We can't let them drop their effort for one minute.'

Thorne grinned at Edward's compulsive tic, always having to remember that he was meant to be setting an example. 'I know, I know, Wise Owl. You know your face purses up when you remember that you have to reassert your command. Like you've just eaten a lemon. You don't need to worry. You know how much the men adore you.'

Edward was rescued from this flattery by the arrival of the young platoon commanders. 'Ah, come in, chaps,' he said, ushering them in. He and Thorne exchanged glances at how new they still looked in their uniforms. They were all seemingly about sixteen years old and seemed to all intents and purposes exactly the same as each other.

As the Orders for that night's patrols into No Man's Land broke up, Preston appeared at the dugout breathless and flushed, his red cheeks visible even in the gloom.

'Sorry, sir. From the colonel.'

'Yes, Preston. Come in, for God's sake. Calm down. Have you run all the way here?'

'Yes, sir. The adjutant's just been killed by a shell. Hell of a mess. Colonel asks if he can borrow Lieutenant Thorne as his replacement.'

Edward felt as though he had just had a dagger slice beneath his navel. Losing Thorne like this, even though he would still be all of a quarter of a mile away from him, meant that for the first time in months he felt a different type of fear. Not the adrenaline-filled type that accompanied combat but instead an orphan's or widow's one, an overwhelming loneliness. But he tried to muster what he hoped came across to the other officers as a wry nonchalance. 'Well, of course he can, Mr Preston. He'll be down with you in the morning.'

''Fraid not, sir,' Preston said with his irreverent assertiveness, 'I'm to take him straight down. The colonel needs him for a plan.'

'Does he, now? Well, Thorne, happy to exchange your revolver for a pen?'

Thorne was deathly pale, as if he was a staff officer being told he was to go up to the front. But he knew the CO as well as Edward and said, blankly, 'Very well, Mr Preston. Just give me five minutes.'

Edward dismissed the platoon commanders and Thorne got his things together. Edward looked at him bereft, utterly incapable of finding any words to match what he was feeling.

Thorne cleared his sundry things from the nook he had dug into the wall of the HQ: a haversack, a couple of books, his field glasses and a battered old pack of cards. He picked up a bag of liquorice from Fortnum & Mason and tossed it to Edward. 'Here, have this. I kept it from the CSM's clutches.' He patted down his pockets to check he had everything, double-checked his haversack and revolver and put his helmet on, an instant divide between them. 'Adjutant, eh? I'll try to get the company all the cushy jobs.' He paused. 'This won't be forever.' Another pause. 'I hope.' Neither of them wanted to reach over and shake the other's hand as that would make everything final and settled. So they stood looking at each other for a couple of seconds and then Edward broke it off. 'Right, off you go then. Off for your pink gins and sandwiches.'

Thorne smiled weakly. He turned, kicked the dormant Preston, and made his way out. 'Come on, urchin. Off we go.' And then the dugout was silent. Edward sat alone and gazed aimlessly around. He stayed there for a few minutes, then he got himself together and went out to the trench to put on a brave show to the men. An immaculate sunset fired arcs of gold over the line. He felt empty.

*

That night, Edward went back to his dugout and lit the small candle in the nook, like a church's aumbrey in the wall, where Thorne's kit had been kept. He sunk down onto his stool and took in the new silence, the palpable absence of his friend, and again felt newly afraid. The tiny flickering yellow of the flame shook its light over the walls and he saw, lying flush to the floor beneath the nook, a brown book that matched the colour of the earth and must have been missed by Thorne. He stretched over and picked it up, a collection of detective stories. The spine was still pristine and the pages in unthumbed cohesion. He opened the book up, carefully so as not to damage it, and in the inside cover was a stamp, ornate like a wrought-iron gate around an oval in which was written '*Ex Libris Miranda Thorne*'.

As he gently flicked the pages he came to an obstacle near the book's end, an envelope placed in it. Unthinkingly he took it out, opened the letter and started to read the single piece of folded white paper inside, seeing the words, '*My Dear Wise Owl*' and then he froze and his pulsed raced, blurring his eyes immediately so that he didn't read any more.

Scalded, he put the paper back in the envelope and back in the book and returned it to the nook as though he was about to be caught stealing something. What on earth was Thorne doing writing to him? Was it a letter to him in the event of his death? Was it a joke he was going to write for him? Or something else? He stared at the book on its shelf wondering if he should look at it again. Several times he reached over to it but something stayed him every time, not wanting to dare to see what was in the letter, wondering if his brain would be able to understand it. What business was it of his anyway to look at it? This was Thorne's private work and surely to read it now would be the gravest breach of trust. Eventually he calmed down and was firm with himself; he would keep the book with him and return it to Thorne without a word next time he saw him. But still his head swam.

CHAPTER EIGHTEEN

A couple of weeks later, Edward went into Battalion HQ to find Thorne and the CO over a map. Both of them looked up when he came in and the CO flicked with his pen to him to sit down. Edward sat on one of the wooden crates that passed as furniture and felt as though he was perching on the club fender of a grand drawing room, looking at the spread of magazines and books on a low table with uneven legs. He helped himself to a yellowed copy of *The Gallipoli Times* and leant back against the wall of the dugout, flicking through it absent-mindedly and enjoying being able to defuse his brain for a little while. He was worried about the onset of winter. They were holding up so far, but without any proper supply of winter clothing the colder nights were starting to become awful ordeals. Uniforms that had been unbearably hot in the summer were now cursed for being about as good as newspaper at keeping out the cold. The men were wearing two tunics, even two pairs of trousers, beseeching wives and mothers in their letters to send gloves and socks.

Edward spotted the photograph of the mess that the CO had had taken back on Lemnos and reached over to look at it. He had to catch his breath. Of the thirty or so men in the picture only six now remained, and Edward could hardly recognise them. Haynes-Mattingly had lost all of his buoyancy, his cynical and infectious humour rubbed and picked away to reveal a nasty, pitted husk at his core. Edward hadn't seen much of him at all lately apart from at Battalion Orders groups, where he would needlingly compete with Edward and Addison, the C Company commander, to get A Company out of any tasks he didn't fancy, or make cutting remarks about their performance. Thorne had probably changed the most physically; in the photo he still had the faint vestiges of teenage puppy fat round his cheeks and jowls, his chest puffed out as if trying to bust his tunic. Now his physique had been so ravaged by dysentery that his uniform hung off him. He seemed to have aged a decade in these few months. Only his eyes retained their youth and flash. On most of the other faces Edward saw a tiny cross drawn just underneath them – the ones who had been killed or so badly wounded they were unlikely to ever return. He vowed that whatever happened neither he nor Thorne were going to end up with a black cross on their ties.

He put the picture back on the table and stood up as the Colonel said, 'Ah, B Company. Sorry to keep you waiting.'

'Not at all, sir.'

'I must say I'm grateful, Salter, for your giving me young Thorne here.' The colonel looked at Thorne in the manner of a schoolmaster appraising his star batsman. 'Not doing too bad a job at all. Still a bit rough around the edges, but we'll get there in the end. Still getting used to being a rear area paper-pushing paperclip wallah, aren't ye, Thorne?'

'Um, yes sir.' Edward could tell that Thorne found it as odd as he did that the colonel referred to any area that wasn't the absolute front of the front line as being in the rear even when they were only a hundred yards away from it.

'Well, just thought I'd get you here to tell you you're on another one of your tour guide stints tomorrow. We've got a visitor. Brigade won't say who it is but it's clearly someone damned important – they're in a deuce of a flap about it. I suppose it might be General Monro. Or perhaps some chap from London: Churchill, or that ghastly charlatan Lloyd George, maybe. Anyway, whoever he is, he's coming tomorrow and wants to see the front. I told them that with your success with that Russian chap you were just the man. Should be arriving here around eleven hundred. They'll come here and then we'll take the party up to you. Prime some of the men to be as charming as possible, will you? And whatever you do let's not get whoever he is killed, there's a good chap. The admin farrago would be disastrous.' He gave a shudder that Edward thought was only half in jest, before changing subject. 'How are that new lot of yours?'

'The platoon commanders? Oh, they're all right. Green as anything but they'll be fine. It's more the cold that's worrying me.' He noticed the corner of Thorne's eye twitch at this; clearly he had struck a nerve.

The colonel went on. 'Tell me about it. There's a frantic bloody effort to get proper clothing out to the men, but between us three it's not going to work. Beg, borrow or steal, I'm afraid, Salter.' Edward was expecting him to go on, but he stopped there, a look in his eyes deeply apologetic. 'It's what I'm most afraid of as well. I fear we're going to become damned miserable damned quickly.'

He left his words there and was quiet for a little moment, before turning away back to his maps. 'Well, carry on. Thorne will see you out.'

They took their leave and walked up the communication trench away from Battalion HQ, to the fork that would take Edward to B Company, ducking at exposed parts, their bodies knowing instinctively now how deep a trench actually was and jinking past the constant traffic of trench life coming down: men carrying water, letters, food, vast bundles of new wire, timber, fresh stretchers, accompanied by a stream of greetings and irritation – 'You all right, Cyril? You better not have touched any of that bully'; 'Oi, mind yerselves! Oh, beg your pardon, sirs'; 'Get that mule fucking moving!'; 'Letter for you, John. From your wife. And one for me from her too.'

They paused at a wider part of the trench to let the chaos pass and Thorne lit them both a cigarette, his thumb working the roll of the lighter with quick ease.

'Missing me, then?' he said.

Edward feigned nonchalance. 'Honestly? Not really. Don't think many of the chaps knew who you were in the first place.'

'Bugger off.'

'How is it anyway, working for the old man?'

'Dreadful. You should see the blisters I have from lifting all the boxes of paperclips. And I had far too much foie gras and port at dinner the other night, too.' He grinned, but Edward could tell that there was a lingering – insane really – embarrassment that he wasn't at the very sharp end. 'No, actually, it's jolly interesting. Learning a heck of a lot. He's an utter demon of a mind. Constantly whirring. Barely sleeps a wink. Such a nice man, though. You notice that behind everything, all his clipped brusqueness, there's a sort of deeply paternal concern about us all. He's got terribly sad eyes, you know. You don't really see them when his glasses are on but when he takes them off there's a look he has when he thinks no one is watching. It's heartbreaking really. But anyway, how are they?'

'Fine. They do miss you, I promise. Baffle's almost bereft.' He wanted to add how much he himself was missing him but couldn't immediately find the right formulation of words to do so and the moment passed. They carried on smoking, enjoying just being together again.

'Oh, before I forget.' Edward took out the detective stories book from his tunic pocket. 'You forgot this in your haste to leave us real soldiers.'

Thorne's eyes lit up. 'Oh, great. Thanks. I haven't started it yet.'

Edward reddened as he saw Thorne flick through the pages and find the letter hidden in it. He said, 'That was in it too. Don't worry, I didn't read it. Your secret correspondence with a Turkish spy is safe.' This seemed to mollify Thorne and he relaxed a little and tried to keep the joke up. 'Thanks. Just a quick *billet doux* to the Kaiser.'

Edward smiled but he knew that something was bothering Thorne and decided it was best to move on. 'I'm afraid I did see that it was your sister's book. You get her permission?'

Thorne grinned. 'Probably not.' He paused, as if weighing something up. 'You know, when this little lot is over, would you like to come and stay at home?'

Edward was taken by surprise but was delighted, Suddenly the world opened up a little at being allowed to think of something that wasn't the Peninsula. 'Gosh. Yes, I'd love to. Thanks.'

'Nothing special, I'm afraid. We can play cribbage, bridge, that sort of thing. Raid the cellar. Bore everyone silly with stories about this patch of earth.'

They smiled at each other, like a couple of boys who had decided that they would be best friends.

Edward then dropped the stub of his cigarette on the ground and stamped it out. 'I meant what I said to the colonel. We're going to get hammered by the weather any day now. Can we get anything up to us?'

'I'll do my best. The QM's on it but it's hen's teeth at the moment. How are the men?'

'The same. Deeply sceptical of the new bunch, but then I daresay they thought we were a pair of clowns when we turned up. Right, better get back to the nursery.'

CHAPTER NINETEEN

The next morning, Edward had B Company ready for the visit, which had elicited the usual torrent of moaning from the men. They were ready, shaved and in position, CSM Broomhouse getting amongst their general tidiness and Edward making sure that exactly the soldiers he wanted were going to be on the circuit of the line he had planned. At the apex of the route he had positioned Baffle at the head of the sap they had dug out into No Man's Land, reasoning that whoever was coming up here at least deserved to hear the unvarnished truth of what was going on.

At ten to eleven he was back outside the HQ dugout with Broomhouse, counting down the minutes and seconds on his watch, and almost exactly on the stroke of eleven he felt an electricity come up the communication trench from the battalion rear area, rumours cascading upwards. There was a ripple of men standing sharper, men who were habitually and showily unimpressed by anything suddenly craning their necks and straightening their backs.

Twenty yards away, Thorne appeared round a corner, in the van of the group coming up the line. He caught Edward's eye and winked at him, then turned back to walk in the odd sideways-backwards way people do when they are escorting someone as part of a group. And then there he was. Not General Monro. Not Churchill, nor Lloyd George nor even the prime minister. A clear head taller than everyone around him was the secretary of state for war himself, the physical embodiment of the Empire, surely one of the most famous men in the world, Field Marshal Earl Kitchener.

Edward gulped. He knew all about how the mere physical presence of someone was enough to lift the morale of those around him, but he had never seen it pulled off so naturally, how someone's presence visibly – almost literally – lifted the men in the trench as Kitchener's did. He was treading in huge strides, head bowed as he listened to the CO and the brigade commander in his wake. Sometimes he broke off to speak to one of the men lining the route, smiling at them like an uncle and leaving them completely struck dumb by the encounter.

Next to Edward, Broomhouse muttered, 'Jesus Christ, sir, what in fuck's name is he doing here?'

'If something happens to him while he's with us we're all buggered,' said Edward, dry-mouthed.

The frisson continued up the trench and passed through them so that even the men at the front line, well out of sight, were standing to attention. And then from somewhere a low cheer came up that grew and grew until it filled the whole trench as Kitchener and the entourage pressed on up it. By the time they arrived at Edward it had grown into a full-throated, almost primal, roar of defiance that despite having everything thrown at them by the armies of an entire continent they would not be moved. Having the warlord come right up to the front line to recognise them seemed to release in them all a savage bark. In that moment, if asked, the men would have stormed out of the trench foaming with bloodlust and rolled the Turks all the way off the Peninsula.

Kitchener himself was clearly in his element, grinning benevolently beneath his huge, straggly moustache, as the group stopped at Company HQ. Edward appraised him as the brigade commander and the CO paused, neither sure of who was going to make the introduction. Edward's first thought was how old he looked, the eyes nothing like the ones he remembered so clearly from the famous poster that they had all seen, sharp and direct, but instead puffy and soft, glazed with an old man's kindness. The cheeks and jowls were sagging but still, despite that, the man was utterly magnificent, his huge frame giving him a bearing that he had seen in no one else before, a cross between an Old Testament prophet and a prize fighter. Even the King himself would not have had such an impact on the men.

The CO broke the deadlock. 'Well, my Lord, this is B Company. Major Salter and Company Sergeant Major Broomhouse.'

Kitchener nodded his approval and looked Edward and Broomhouse up and down. 'Very good. Thank you. Very nice to meet you, gentlemen. So this is where you've been holding the Turk, eh? Let me tell you, the job you've done here is tremendous. The Cabinet aren't going to believe their ears when I tell them of what I've seen. God, it's good to be round soldiers again instead of damned politicians. Bunch of snakes, I tell ye. Right, let's take a look at the line then, shall we?'

'Yes, sir.' Edward hoped to God that the Turks hadn't got some snipers on the ridges as there was no way that Kitchener's frame would remain beneath the parapet all the way up. He led him up, tingling with the atmosphere pulsing along the trench as the men stood for them. Even in their ravaged, pestilential state after the months of everything that had endured – the bullets, the heat, the sores, dysentery, lice and shells, the screams, the filth, the cold and the flies – he saw now how heroic they must have appeared to Kitchener. Their sinewy, tough bodies, their skin as weathered as their rifles' bolts were oiled and clean, their soldiering immaculate. Behind him Kitchener said, 'Fine body of men you have here, Samuels,' and even as he smiled at being called the wrong name, his heart swelled.

They threaded their way up to the base of the sap, Kitchener littering their progress with grunts of acknowledgement and little words or sentences. 'Hello, lad.' 'There's a good man.' 'Wager that Vickers has seen a few Turks fall before it, what?' 'Well done, men.

We'll get them, don't you worry.' 'Good morning, gentlemen, thought I'd drop in and see how you are.'

They came to the base of the sap and Edward turned to Kitchener. The brigade commander and the CO were still with them and again the feeling came of the most inordinate risk being taken and he almost laughed at how absurd it all was. He collected himself and said, 'Well, sir, this is it. We've got a listening sap out with some men in it now. It's where we usually send out our wiring parties and patrols. Would you like to come and meet them?' Behind Kitchener the brigade commander went white but, before either he or the CO could discourage the idea, Kitchener said, 'Don't see why not. Rather fun.'

'Follow me then, sir. You'll have to stoop, I'm afraid.'

They went down the sap, Edward hunching exaggeratedly to encourage Kitchener to do the same. Ahead of them, Baffle and Ewart, another old dependable, were crouched at the head of the sap.

Baffle glanced back at Edward and grinned easily. Edward, surprised at how relaxed he was looking, realised that he probably still had no idea who had arrived in the trench – it would have been just the style of the company not to tell Baffle. The head of the sap widened out from the narrow route up to it into a space big enough to hold half a patrol or so. As they arrived he saw Baffle and Kitchener's eyes meet. He winced as he waited for Baffle to say something inappropriate.

'At last, now they send us a good quality recruit,' said Baffle without a pause, and Kitchener let out a guffaw so loud that Edward wondered whether the Turks would hear it.

They settled in the sap in a crouch. Edward watched the most powerful man in Britain talk freely with Baffle about the tactical situation, of both the immediate one in front of them and the wider Suvla beachhead, as easily as might an engine designer and that engine's mechanic, both intimately acquainted with the subject matter but coming at it from entirely different ends.

It was with regret that he looked down the sap to see the colonel tapping his watch.

'I'm afraid, sir, that I'm going to have to take you back,' he said.

'What? Shame. Would rather be in this sap with you chaps than round some infernal bloody conference table.' He gave a mock shiver, 'Oh well, off we go, excellent to have met you, gentlemen. Keep up the sterling work.' Then his guard seemed to drop, his face falling momentarily and for an awful second Edward thought that he was on the verge of tears. 'We'll get you out of here. I promise you that,' he said quietly, and it was like a punch to the gut, taking Edward's breath away.

If it hit Baffle too he didn't show it. 'Thank you, sir. God speed. Oh, sir, if I may ask one thing?'

Edward flinched as he thought of the galaxy of inappropriateness that Baffle could topple into now and he said, 'Is it true that you invented the stitch in our socks? Chap in our QM's said that you had designed a new stitch that means that there's no ridge in the seam at the front of the toes, like.'

If Kitchener was surprised by the question he didn't show it.

'Ah. Funny you say that, young man. I know the stitch you mean, though technically it's not a stitch, it's a seam. But much as though I'd love to take the credit, I believe that might be some rather generous spirited fellows putting my name to it.'

'Or ladies, sir.' Kitchener actually seemed to blush a little at this, Edward was amazed, and a little horrified, to see. Baffle quickly went on. 'You know the Archbishop of Canterbury has said that women are now allowed to knit during services? My dad told me. Said it was like a blooming tap-dancing hall in those churches now.'

Kitchener barked a laugh at this, 'It's a fine activity, knitting, y'know. Good for passing the time. I've done it since I was a boy; had a nanny who taught me.'

Baffle gave a grunt of acknowledgement that Edward knew

translated as him being quite impressed. 'Well, you never know, I might take it up if old John Turko gives us a second or two.' They made to leave and Baffle and Ewart both threw up salutes as smartly as the confines of the sap allowed. Edward led Kitchener back down to the trench, by comparison with where they had been now feeling like a bastion of safety. They were received back, the visit party still slack-jawed at having had Kitchener become one of the most exposed men in the whole battlefield under their watch. Kitchener saw the look in the brigade commander's eyes and admonished him cheerfully. 'Do stop looking so worried, Alan. Nothing I haven't done a thousand times before. Perfectly safe with those two fine chaps and young Samson here.'

The commanding officer coughed a correction, 'Salter, sir.'

'Eh? Yes, Salter. Good man. Thank you very much.'

Edward smiled proudly and was about to speak when the commanding officer said, 'He's an old hand at trench visits, my Lord. Took a Russian delegation on a tour of the line here in the summer.'

Kitchener narrowed his eyes. 'Russians, eh? Speak it, do ye?'

'Um, yes, sir. Not absolutely fluently but—'

'Well, if you can host some of them then that seems to suggest you're good enough. I may have a use for you, laddie. Fitz, take the details please.' He nodded over to a lieutenant colonel on the fringes of the group, weak-chinned and with prominent ears, who smiled in a friendly manner at Edward. 'Well, young man,' Kitchener said, tying up the loose ends of his visit to B Company, 'jolly good to meet you. Keep it up.' He turned to the wider trench to address the rest of the soldiers. 'Well done, men. We'll get there in the end.' Then he turned to go, the visit party shuffling off back down the communication trench to the rear.

Edward didn't notice initially the lieutenant colonel whom Kitchener had mentioned sidle over to him, smoothly taking a card from a silver box and then shaking his hand with it, rather like he was a *maître d'* in a smart London restaurant. Easy urbanity oozed from him. 'Give me a ring when you get out of here and we'll have a talk.'

Edward looked at the card, an immaculate and incongruous reminder of the accoutrements of a lifetime ago, cream-coloured, thick and with the details picked out in smart dark-blue lettering. 'Lt Col OAG Fitzgerald' and then a Whitehall telephone number.

Edward replied, 'If I get out of here.'

Fitzgerald smirked in a soldier's recognition. 'Quite. Cigarette?' He held out a different case and Edward accepted. 'Thank you for that. The old boy will have loved it. I haven't seen him on this good form for months.'

'No problem, sir. I'm just glad we didn't get him killed.'

Fitzgerald laughed again. 'Don't joke. Should think a lot of the Cabinet would have been absolutely thrilled by that. Right, Salter, I'd best be off. Don't want to miss the boat out of this hellhole. Get in touch, I mean that. Oh, and don't be offended by his getting your name wrong. Old habit of his. Sometimes I think he does it on purpose to see how people react.'

He held out his hand and Edward took it, surprised that so reedy a frame could have such a strong grip, and then he left.

Edward looked at the card again, flicked it a couple of times and then put it in his breast pocket. He went back into the dugout to sort through what needed to be done with the line over the course of the day, the men in the trench back at their tasks, whistling and chuntering, or back at their rest, snoring and laughing, as though the visit had never happened as they resumed the vigil on their bare hillside at the end of the world.

CHAPTER TWENTY

Autumn turned into winter. The battalion moved a mile to the north-west of the blind crests to relieve a unit that was deemed combat ineffective following the twin heads of a failed attack and a virulent strain of dysentery that had torn through it.

Progress up to the line was appallingly slow, rivulets of loose earth and rocks running down the trench walls to line the bottoms with obstacles. To Edward, sleep-deprived and hallucinating in the cold, it was as though he was a giant treading through a twilit valley, the countless little landslips becoming mighty waterfalls tumbling down the sides into the plain below. His feet – as they stumbled on the pebbles and stones – were great hammers that crushed houses and villages. He realised he was grinning and that the sounds that punctuated his progress were his own short bursts of laughter. He took several gulps of air to snap out of it and hoped that no one had noticed him in that state.

The next day, the men got used to the tiny strip of ground that was now their home, titivating the line and getting to grips with the lie of their land.

And then came the evening. The normal weather of the daytime, no different from the hundred that had preceded it save for winter's siphoning away its daily ration of heat, passed into a squally, adolescent late afternoon with fast-moving clouds scudding across the sky before a vast grey blanket was pulled across it.

At seven o'clock the first drops spattered down onto them, tiny pinpricks to start but growing soon to fat droplets that sounded like sleet as they hit helmets and hands clenched round rifles. They kicked up sand round the rims of the tiny craters they bored in the ground, soldiers craning their necks back to let them fall onto parched tongues. Within ten minutes, the rain had whipped up to a tempo that would not drop for three days, skin, uniform and ground all now equally saturated and the men sitting there like cattle, morale and discipline melting away.

After half an hour, Edward had never seen the men so low, so visibly deflated, so *defeated*. The wind picked up and up, each gust bringing waves of freezing rain onto their scant, thin uniforms. They started to shiver uncontrollably, some lucky ones seeking shelter under the flimsiest tarpaulins. Those who couldn't sat in the bottom of trenches that had quickly become swamps, hands thrust into pockets, their necks bent forward over their chests as rifles were cast into the mud, sentry duties abandoned, anything military forgotten about. Each minute rammed home that the biggest threat to their survival now came not from the Turks but from the weather.

The darkness was total, with the moon entirely obscured. The mud grew into an ooze that sucked in anything that fell on it, a slick, slippy filth that afforded no purchase for their boots, the leather already sodden and chafing. Edward held off from looking at his watch for as long as he could, but eventually broke and saw its luminous hands tell him it was only nine o'clock; it felt like four in the morning. He was so cold that he knew that to sit and sleep might be fatal; he had to keep moving, so he began a lonely plod up and down the trench, slipping and sliding, cutting himself a dozen times, anything to keep moving, anything to encourage the men.

All through the next hours he did this, joints rigid with cold, teeth chattering, his fingers reduced to bones, all deftness taken away from them. All along were men in various stages of uselessness. Not one man, not even Baffle, was in a state to operate, let alone to fight. He would find a group of four or five men, clinging to each other for warmth, and tell them to get up and to swing their arms around them and to jump up and down, a useless errand in the ooze of the hillside. At one point he collapsed himself, and when he came to – he didn't know how long later – he wet himself, providing a fleeting semblance of warmth on at least a part of his body. The only blessing was that the Turks would be suffering as much as them.

As the rain hardened to sleet, Edward sank into the bottom of the trench, wanting to die. Something though, a tiny animal kick in the base of his brain, sparked in him and he got up again to labour on, a skeleton in the rain. The only things that felt as though they were working were his heart, beating so frantically that sometimes he could feel his carotid artery pumping, and his jaw that ground his staccato teeth; everything else – his muscles, his bowels, his marrow – devoid of energy and life.

Forms appeared as he moved along the trench, mouthless and lifeless, their pale faces the only things not entirely swallowed by the swirling, drenching dark. He came to one shape and shook it by the shoulder only for it to fall away to one side without any movement of limbs and he realised the man had frozen to death. He was too cold to try to work out who it was. The next man too was a corpse. This one didn't collapse. It remained there, rock-like as though it would always be there, the once supple, yielding flesh now hard and frozen. He felt over its face, its mouth open and rictus, with a thick moustache on the top lip, and he thought of the men it could be. Jenson? Dexter? Rogers? He moved on. The next lump he came to was a couple, huddled together for warmth. Albyn and Ewart. They, at least, were alive; perhaps it was only the three of them in the entire line.

Edward stuttered, 'Come on, chaps, let's sing. Come on.' He led them in a husky, gibbering round of *For He's a Jolly Good Fellow* feeling ridiculous trying to shout the words out and managing only a croak. He felt a nudge beside him. Who was it? 'Scott, sir. Thought I'd come and join you.'

He didn't know for how long they sat, chanting the song like a mantra, their brains not having to think about the words, their muscles learning the movement and running through them like automatons. But it was keeping them alive, Edward knew. He thought of all the other men across the Peninsula who would be suffering like them. It seemed hard to believe at first, as if only B Company could be experiencing this, as if they alone had been selected for one night to be the object of a divine wrath.

Dawn did not so much break as melt over them in a painfully slow release that revealed the devastation of the night. Entire parts of the trench had collapsed in the torrents of mud that had bowled down the hill, bringing with it long-dead bodies from No Man's Land, bones and rotting flesh now piled at various points.

Some men wandered in a trance along the line to feed blood into wasting limbs, their heads clearly visible over the parapet but with no bullets coming to break them as an unspoken truce seemed to hold sway. Others lay gibbering at the bottom, with hardier men going round trying to smack life into the most desperate, shouting and screaming at them to clean the mud from the bolts of their now useless rifles, slapping them in the face to get some life going. Edward gathered the officers around him and bade them to just keep their men alive, their cowed and beaten faces pinched and sallow, scabbed with sores, snot running unhindered from their noses. He noted that Alderville had soiled himself and with flecks of vomit still on his tunic was barely able to hold himself upright.

Still the rain came, flung at their virtually naked forms by a wind that just kept on getting stronger, visibility reduced to fifty yards. At midday, he was surprised to see the imp-like figure of Preston appear next to him. He looked around him with distaste and as though the entire shambles, the filthy slaughterhouse floor, was Edward's fault. 'Fucking hell, sir. What have you done to the place?'

'Hello, Preston. How the hell did you get up here?'

'Colonel wanted me to, sir. Let him know what state the line is in.'

'Tell him we're not going anywhere. We'll hold it, but if the weather gets any worse things might start to fall apart elsewhere.'

'Tell me about it, sir. You should see the state of the other companies. And if you think this is bad, you should see the rear. It's chaos. The piers on the beach have been washed away.'

Edward felt a dart of ice down his back even in his freezing state. If the piers were gone they were cut off from supplies. A few weeks ago he would have received the news and given Preston a sober acknowledgement; now though the storm had blown away any pretence at keeping the integrity of chain of command. 'Well, that's us fucked, isn't it?'

Preston said, 'Jesus Christ, sir, that's the first time I've ever heard you swear.'

He smiled. 'Don't tell anyone, will you? Don't want to let my mask drop.'

'The adjutant wanted me to give you this, sir.' He dug into his tunic and pulled out a pristine piece of folded white paper, miraculously dry but immediately dampening in the rain. Edward bent over and used Preston as a shelter so that he could read it before the rain washed away the scrawled handwriting.

'Iliad Book 21. The river Scamander on the plain of Troy comes alive and chases Achilles. Not a million miles away from us really, is it? Those Homeric bores might have had a point, you know. Chin up. Hope the men are doing OK. Bloody grim. One day we'll look upon this with fondness, I suppose.'

Edward put the paper in his tunic pocket. There was no way that it would survive intact but he hoped that maybe a shred of it would. 'Tell the adjutant many thanks. Tell the colonel we'll be fine. And stay out of trouble yourself. Understood?'

'Trouble, sir? Don't know the meaning of it.' He grinned and scampered away down the trench, the only man on the battlefield who seemed to be enjoying himself.

The afternoon dragged on even wetter and muddier. Their uniforms were caked in the slick of dirt, their armpits and crotches clogged up by the silty, grainy mud. Broken men sat on the parapet staring blankly ahead of them. One of the younger men, Arkwright, who only needed to shave once a week, sat crying into his palms, his hands covered by socks. In a new burst of energy, from God knew where, Edward again went up and down the line, cajoling and encouraging. Day ceded to night once more and the rain became sleety for a while and then transformed into snow. By midnight it was inches deep across the line.

Dawn came at last but brought no respite as the temperature dropped yet further. The rain on their bodies had become ice overnight; even those who had managed to find some kind of shelter were now in as bad a state as those who had been in the open all night long. Edward watched as another three men who had frozen to death in the night had their clothes stripped off them to give others extra layers. He noticed the body of Dexter lying filthy in a coat of mud at the bottom of the trench, naked save for his underpants. Even his socks had been taken off to be used as gloves. He realised that this was the body with the moustache he had come across the previous night. Somehow this corpse caused him more revulsion than any of the ones he had seen ripped into shreds of meat and bone over the year.

In the middle of the morning, they were shelled by a few salvos, earth and snow spitting up from the ground and shrapnel singing more cleanly than it usually did through the brittle air. The very first of the shells landed full in the trench, obliterating Lyon and Wright and ripping the legs off Thomson, one of which cartwheeled backwards into Scott, who was asleep on the floor, the jagged femur tearing his face open, his shredded cheek studded with teeth and his glistening tongue ripped at its base, pumping blood over the snow.

The bombardment ended after five minutes and the guns fell silent again. Edward thought that the Turks had only done it to provide their gunners with hot barrels and shell casings to warm themselves on. He ate some frozen bully beef and then some mouthfuls of snow. His urine was treacle-coloured and he felt wizened inside, so starving that it felt like his body was feeding on itself.

Time lost any sense of linearity, the present somehow now a fusion of night and day, wake and sleep, made bearable only by the command Edward wielded that forced him to step out of his own personal misery to try to consider the wider tactical situation, to encourage the men, to rotate the sentries, to try to keep the company in even just the barest semblance of cohesion as a fighting unit. He was amazed that the young soldiers, with nothing to do other than consider their own sorry state, did not just turn their rifles on themselves, surprised that there was not a self-inflicted wound occurring every quarter of an hour. But somehow the men held on, through the day and into the night, the temperature plunging again.

The morning finally came and with it the thaw. All down the line came a low hum of cheer and laughter as a weak low sun gained in strength and started to feed their skin and unlock them from the storm's grip. But that soon brought new problems. The snow melted so quickly that again the line was a morass, entire stretches of the topsoil of the slope sliding down the hill and through the trench, buckling the few shelters that had managed to survive that far. But relief was to come – Preston appearing as fresh as he had been all campaign, puckish and grinning, tanned and supple amidst the rest of them who were pinched, saturated, white, withdrawn, broken. They were to be relieved that evening by the same unit that they had taken the line from just before the storm. The rest of the day they tried in vain to shore up the trench, but it was no use. None of them had any strength. Any embarrassment that Edward might previously have felt about handing over the line in such a parlous state was nothing compared to the hatred he felt for those who had not been in the line freezing and bleeding with them.

B Company made its way down the slope that evening, slipping and sliding in the knee-deep mud, picking their way through pieces of wood and bodies that here and there studded the surface of the filth. At the bottom of the hill they found that the rear was in just as bad a state, but eventually they found some kind of shelter, the Quartermaster having moved heaven and earth to try to get them some.

Edward went into the tiny dugout that had been made for the B Company officers and lit a candle, looking at the others who were not so much asleep as plain unconscious. He inspected his hands in the friendly light of the flame. His fingers were as creased as they would have been after a hot bath, the skin in some places already looking as though it might start to rot and the grooves matted with dirt. He ran his hand over his face and felt four-day-old stubble. More shells screamed down onto the beachhead in a final vindictive salvo from the Turks, as though the war itself was angry that it had not managed to claim him. But the shells were far enough away not to be his problem. He slumped in the corner, head resting on a rolled-up sandbag and passed out.

When he woke up, shivering uncontrollably in his damp clothes, the reedy dawn came through a gap in the hessian hung over the dugout entrance onto the face of Alderville, who looked as peaceful as a young boy sleeping in his nursery. Edward watched him for a few moments before realising that there was no rise and fall of his chest. He got onto his knees and checked him. He was dead, colder than the rock and grit that he lay on. His body was taken out and buried in an old shell hole.

CHAPTER TWENTY-ONE

When the end came it was surprisingly swift.

In mid-December Edward left Company HQ, now near the beach, summoned by Preston to the commanding officer.

'I'm afraid, Salter, that we have received orders that we are to resile from the beachhead, the whole of the Suvla force. Anzac, too, I believe. Well, they said "withdraw", but I prefer to use "resile". Sounds rather more dignified, doesn't it? Brandy?' He held out a battered flask, a silver lozenge shape that looked like it had had a rolling pin taken to it and Edward gratefully took it. Ackrill smiled in his purse-lipped fashion. 'It's not the end of the world; all it means is that we just have to make a slightly better, more authoritative argument next time against our next opposition. And if in that argument I'm still backed up by Baffle and Preston then more to the good.'

Edward was caught off guard only by the order's timing, the decision to leave the only logical way out of the hideous impasse they were at with the Turks. Even then the surprise lasted only for the time it took him to have a first swig of the brandy and then, the colonel looking away momentarily, another one. He asked the question that he had wanted to ask for weeks now. 'What do you think it was, sir? Why couldn't we do it?'

The colonel laughed and replied straight away, as though the answer was entirely obvious. 'Oh, it's a conventional enough military disaster, Salter. All the ingredients. Poor tactical position, not enough men, half-baked leadership. Not remotely surprising. If you only have two of those, then you can win, sometimes. But all three? Not a chance.'

'And you knew that all along?'

'Yes. Why do you look so shocked, man? What was I meant to do – complain? Resign? What good would that have done? Well, I suspected it after the attack on the blind crests. But when we were then sentenced to be surrounded by the high ground I knew from there that it was just a question of time. We should have withdrawn, sorry, resiled, then. Poor old Sir Ian just got obsessed by it. Like a man who has been rebuffed by a lady thinking that just asking again and again will make her change her mind. Time to move on to another target. I fancy Mesopotamia; don't know about you.'

'Do you think that it mattered that the Turks are fighting for their homeland?'

'Not really. We are too, in a way. Never underestimate the capacity for men to transfer their concept of home from houses and fields and family onto their comrades. Seen it again and again. The North-West frontier, South Africa and here in damned spades. Just look at the things that the men have done for each other over these months. Home isn't just bricks, Salter. Look at me, for instance. I'm forty-seven years old and I've spent, what, fifteen of those in Britain.'

They were silent for a while.

Edward's throat was dry and he decided to close up the meeting and get back to the company.

'Well, sir, that's me. I'd best be off to the chaps.'

The colonel looked at him, his age showing more than it had all year. He brightened and smiled as though he were an elderly man recognising someone again after initially being confused as to who they were, as he snapped out of personal memories and back to the day.

'Yes. Yes, well done, Salter. Well done, B Company. Not long to go now. I'll tell you more as and when. Going to be a hell of a show, getting us all out of here. Just make sure we don't lose any more.'

Edward saluted and left the dugout, tightening the knot of his tie against his neck at the wet wind. He felt a flick on his ear and he turned, irritated, only to break into a huge smile upon seeing that it was Thorne. 'Hello, old boy. Just back from a briefing at brigade.' He jerked a thumb in the direction of the dugout. 'Has he told you? Looks like our Mediterranean holiday's drawing to a close.'

'Yes. Can't say I'd recommend it, if I'm being honest. The weather's dire.'

'And the locals. *Terribly* rude.'

'I'll say.' Edward had so much in his head that he wanted to elucidate but in the end was just able to smile, happy to be back in Thorne's orbit if only for a moment.

Thorne went on, speaking as if to himself. 'I've been trying to think what it's like. Us having to leave. Is it like seeing a girl you love be taken away to be married to some complete wretch? No, not really. More like a funeral, I reckon. For someone who you wished you'd known better and you feel guilty that you never now will. Maybe. I don't know. What do you think?'

Edward tried to get his brain to find some words, sort through his hopelessly jumbled thoughts, but couldn't. He felt drained. 'I have no idea. Perhaps one day. For now all I want is to get off this beach with everyone intact.'

Thorne answered in a teasing, fond manner. 'There we go. My Wise Owl. It's your leadership that has got the boys this far, you know. Pure and simple.' Edward couldn't help noticing a furtive look to Thorne as he said it, as though he still hadn't forgiven himself for as he saw it – ridiculously, to Edward's mind – deserting B Company. He wanted to say something but at that moment the CO barked from inside, 'Adjutant, will you stop nattering like a fishwife and come in here, please.'

They shook hands and parted.

Edward stood alone and looked around. On the beach stretching along the bay were low-slung tents, the blocks of mules in their pens, little towers of stores, the men beetling round them, a strange little piece of Britain clinging on to this empty, pointless wasteland, and all now about to be gone. He thought of his and Thorne's jokes earlier in the year, mocking all those officers who had dreamt of the campaign as a second Troy. They were idiotic, but at least the place back then had had an undeniable grandeur, a sense of majesty and import. Now Edward couldn't summon the barest flicker of excitement for the low hills and broad, flat pan around him, randomly plucked out of obscurity to be a graveyard. And then what? No one was going to build a city here. It would go back to being a land roamed by sheep. He sighed audibly. Was that so bad, he supposed. There were worse fates. He turned his back to the beach and the wind and made his way over to the B Company lines.

CHAPTER TWENTY-TWO

Ten days later, on the final evening of the evacuation, B Company were in the line. Shells came whirring over their heads as the artillery, key to the deception that they were still on Suvla in force, slammed round upon round up onto the ridges and the Turkish positions. All through the day, the artillery had fired, and B Company had made an extra effort in the line with their activity, now occupying a stretch with A Company that only the day before had been held by the full battalion.

Over the past five nights, thousands of troops had been taken away by boat, thinning out the forces to such a degree that now the entire Suvla battlefield was held by four thousand men instead of twenty. It had worked phenomenally well so far, to everyone's surprise, with each man left in the line working like half a section in their whirl of activity and those in the rear of the beachhead also making it look as though normal activity was underway, helped by the fact that all the vast stores were still in place, unable to be moved. But even so Edward could not help thinking that the Turks must be onto them. If they attacked now they would overrun the entire battlefield in a matter of hours. It was the greatest confidence trick any of them had ever seen pulled; Baffle described it as playing a game of poker with a hand of a two, a three, a six and a pair of jokers.

The tension ratcheted up with the onset of evening. To minimise the noise of their departure from the line, all the men had empty sandbags and strips of cloth wound tightly around their boots. Any spare rations in the trench were pierced with bayonets to render them useless to the Turks. In the Company HQ dugout Baffle was administering to a crude booby trap. He had filled an ammunition case with earth packed tightly around a candle. At the rim of the tin he had anchored a piece of twine that led diagonally up, crossing the body of the candle, to loop over one of the struts holding up the dugout roof. The other end of the twine was attached to a brick-sized rock that hung in the air above three shells that he had managed to cajole from the artillery and somehow get brought up from the rear, and then convinced some sappers to rig up a trigger mechanism for.

'You see, sir? Simple as you like. When we leave the trench I light the candle, it gutters down and then after a couple of hours the flame reaches the twine, snaps it, rock falls on the trigger and then,' he gestured to the three shells as though they were a famous circus act, 'these boys do their stuff. Just a shame we won't be around to see it.'

Edward nodded in approval. The barrage that the Turks had sent over during the storm, which had killed Lyon and Wright, maimed Thomson and mutilated Scott, had been judged so unsporting, so against the run of play in the miserable shared experience of the weather, that the men had hardened their attitude to the Turks. Edward patted Baffle on the back and said, 'Well for God's sake don't let anything touch that trigger until then,' and walked out to inspect the line for the tenth time that day.

C Company had left the line the previous night, leaving A and B Companies and a skeleton staff from Battalion HQ including Thorne and the CO, who was set on being the last of them all off the beach. A Company under Haynes-Mattingly held the trenches to their left; they would leave the line at 22:00. B Company would be the last to collapse their position, at midnight.

At twilight, as shapes and faces were still just visible, on the verge of melting into each other, Edward looked down the trench at the men. Despite their overt keenness and taut bodies, they all shared a look of exhaustion, their eyes hanging almost dead in their sockets with no sparkle, just a deep, abacinated gaze. They had only hours of strength left in them. They had to get off the beach tonight.

Midnight came and, beside Edward, Broomhouse said, 'It's time, sir. Off we go.' They heard Seven Platoon start to move out, slowly feeling their way back through the communication trench. Then Six Platoon went until it was just Edward, Broomhouse and Five Platoon. From the side of the trench there was a brief flash and then Baffle came out of his dugout.

'Candle's lit, sir. Looking forward to the fireworks.' Edward was the last to vacate the line. It felt extraordinary leaving it empty and deserted. He did not, in the end, turn to look back for one last time at No Man's Land. He had a child's fear of not wanting to look under the bed, a shiver at the thought of what was behind him. For a few moments he felt the dead of the last months all around him. He had never seen a ghost before but in those seconds he was alone in the trench he realised that it would forever be made of a thicker air, pregnant with the silken presence of those who had died there and their unborn children. He followed after his men.

Progress down was slow, but not overly so. At the very point that the scrub of the plain gave way to the reeds and open sand of the beach the line halted as the front of the column reached the marshalling area.

Edward looked around, seeing nothing in the dark but feeling the vast emptiness of the plain press against his face. B Company were called forward, the men ahead rising from their crouches and slowly, uncertainly shuffling in a chain onward onto the beach to then get onto the lighters that would take them out to the bigger ships.

The commanding officer and Thorne were doing the rounds,

quietly reassuring the men. Then up on the ridge to their north came a huge explosion, horribly loud in the silence and larger than most shells.

He heard Baffle mutter from somewhere ahead of him, 'That's my baby. Hope she got one of them.' A muted cheer went up from the men before it was hissed quiet by others.

They were called forward into the surf and pulled their legs through the cold water, each man then dragged up onto the lighter by the others already on board.

Edward made sure all the men were on the lighter and went back the ten yards to the beach. He wanted to be with Thorne for this and he found him with the CO, standing together watchfully on the water's edge.

'Come on, sir. Room for us three still.'

Neither replied and they all stood still for a moment. Then they walked out into the water, Edward and Thorne abreast of each other with the CO bringing up the rear.

There was only one person who he wanted to do this with and he felt a warming glow go through him despite the cold night, a shiver at the aptness of it. Edward and Thorne had arrived with each other and now they were leaving together. Neither felt the need to say anything as they waded. Edward helped the younger man up into the lighter and then strong arms reached down to lift him up too, as his feet lifted from the shingle and he was, finally, no longer part of the Peninsula.

PART THREE

CHAPTER TWENTY-THREE

London, February 1916

Edward was leaving Victoria station to walk up to Green Park, where he was due to meet Miranda for the first time. He turned a corner and quite literally bumped into Valentine Braithwaite, who was wearing his service dress and carrying a kit bag. After an immediate torrent of apologies, although it had been neither of their faults, they recognised each other.

Braithwaite was quicker off the mark with a greeting. 'I say, Salter! Damned good to see you. Almost didn't clock you in your civvies. So you made it off, did you? I say, I'm parched and I'm a little early for my train. Time for a cup of char?'

They ended up in a cafe a hundred yards from the entrance to the station, empty and cold in the dull February day. A waitress plonked two mugs and a pot of some questionable tea in front of them, as Braithwaite lit a cigarette and, instead of any kind of small talk to ease into the conversation, took Edward by surprise by saying directly, 'Damned funny business with the Russians that, wasn't it? Did anything come of it?'

'Goodness me, I don't think so. Do you know, I haven't even thought about it since. Although Kitchener mentioned it when he came out to visit.'

'You met K? What did you make of him?'

'Don't know really. He looked as though he was out of his depth a little. Well, not so much out of his depth but more as though he was yesterday's man. As if the world had moved on from him and he wasn't able to understand it. I don't know, like a master calligrapher looking at a printing press.'

'What did you make of his ADC? He's a good man. Oswald Fitzgerald. Fitz. I presume he was there too?'

'Funny you say that. He told me to get in touch with him when I got home. I think they rather enjoyed the visit that we put on for them. We ended up sending K up into a sap about a grenade's throw from Jacko. He couldn't have been less fazed about it. Meanwhile Brigade were having kittens. Bloody funny, really.'

'So have you spoken to him since?'

Edward looked a bit sheepish. 'Well, he gave me a paper with his details on it but it got completely destroyed in a storm we had. Turned to mush.'

'I heard about that.'

'Honestly, I think that was the worst bit.'

'Worse than the flies?'

'Much. It was just the absence of hope more than anything, as though you were the only person there and that the rest of the world had forgotten about you. At least with the bloody flies you knew you weren't alone.'

They both took a sip of their tea. Edward wondered if Braithwaite had as much trouble as he did trying to accurately recall what it had all been like. He could remember sights, but his brain was incapable of recreating the sound or the feel of the Peninsula. He hoped that he would one day be able to. Lots of the others had said that the sooner they forgot about it the better but Edward wanted to remember every bit of it, to help him try to comprehend exactly what had happened to him. To know that you have changed without being able to understand the catalyst felt to him like trying to understand a painting without knowing the type of brushstroke the painter had used.

Braithwaite brightened and said, 'You needn't worry about getting in touch with Fitz. My father'll do it. I'm seeing him tonight and I'll mention you to him. I've heard they're looking for someone. Right up your street, chum. I imagine if you want it the job's as good as yours.'

'But I've barely met the man.'

Braithwaite waved in impatient dismissal; it amused Edward how worldly he was despite his youth. 'Oh, forget all that. You've met him once, in the bloody line, that's enough. And the important thing is Dad getting involved. That's how it all works up there, amigo. Not what you know, it's who you know.'

Edward, completely bewildered now, admitted defeat. 'Well, that's jolly kind. Thank you.' Then he thought for a moment, 'But—?'

Braithwaite pre-empted him. '"But do I really want that?" Not having any of it. Look, my friend. War isn't just fought by men with bayonets. Everyone plays a part. Did I feel guilty about not fighting in Gallipoli? No, because I knew my time would come again, and it has; off to join the old mob now after leave. And I knew that at the end of a staff officer's pencil is a soldier's life, so what I was doing for Dad was vital work. The army's about a damned sight more than digging holes and shooting people in the face. You've got a brain, man. Put it to use. The war isn't going anywhere any time soon. A year doing a job in London would be fascinating. And besides, you haven't got anything to prove to anyone.' He looked at his watch. 'Christ, that's almost my train.'

Braithwaite withdrew from the cafe, nodding a grinning thanks at the waitress and then running full tilt down the street to the station. Edward sat at the table alone and drank the rest of his tea, rather wishing it was something stronger to help take the edge off his nervousness about meeting Miranda.

He left and started out again for Green Park.

When they had got home after the long voyage back, the battalion had been given three weeks' leave. Thorne had invited him to High Hedges for as much of it as he wanted. 'We'll have the run of the place. Miranda's rattling round it, keeping things running. Mum and Dad are off in America for one of Dad's finance summits, raising bonds off pensioners in the Midwest or something, way over my head. So it won't exactly be buzzing with activity. I could use the help, if I'm honest. Hell of a lot of jobs to do around the place with all the staff gone. It'll be just like keeping on top of the line. Home from home. Come. Please.'

Edward had accepted at once. Now he was to get a lift in the car from Miranda, who was going to be driving home from a party the night before.

'How will I know her? How will she know me?'

'This isn't a spy novel. No need for code words. It'll be pretty obvious, I should say. Single girl driving a car. Bloke looking for one. Time, location, that should do it.'

They had agreed to meet at midday sharp at the corner of Clarges Street and Piccadilly. Still, though, Edward felt completely unprepared, far preferring to meet Thorne's sister for the first time in a more conventional setting. He had no clue what he would talk about. He laughed to himself; if there was one thing that he had become a master at on the Peninsula it was filling time with conversation. Now he was terrified of not knowing what to say. In the field he could be supremely self-confident, but back here he still found room to be completely at sea when faced with the simple proposition of meeting a girl at a given time and place.

In the event he needn't have worried; it was all very easy. The car was already there, an Austin with its hood up. Next to it was a streak of black – a figure wrapped in a coat underneath a wide-brimmed hat. Brown hair, darker than Thorne's, and with the same honest, guileless face. A breeze of a smile.

She said, as if a doctor summoning a patient from a waiting room, 'Edward Salter? My Oriental correspondent. Wonderful to finally put a face to a name. You're far more cheery-looking than I thought you'd be. Bang on time, too. Hop in.' She threw open the driver's door and motioned him in. 'Now look, you'll think me awfully rude, but I've got a head like someone sunk a ship in it and I think that I am very possibly still drunk.' She winced in over-exaggerated embarrassment. 'You don't fancy driving, do you? Terribly easy; head north to Bedford, then wake me up for the directions for the final bit. Couple of hours' sleep is all I need.'

Before he had the chance to consider, she smiled and said, 'You're a brick, thank you so much. Knew you were a star.' She promptly opened the rear door and slid in, bunching up her coat and some other furs around her like a cocoon.

Edward, stumped, limply followed her instructions. He put his valise in the boot and got into the front. He spent a few moments gingerly getting himself accustomed to the seat and pedals. Just before he set off a voice came from the back, disembodied of the pile of material she was enmeshed in: 'One thing; there's been a power cut at home. Dreadful storm a couple of nights ago. We're cut off for God knows how long, all the village too. Theo's holding the fort, running about like nobody's business repairing all the damage. Please feel entirely free to drop out now if hanging round a gloomy cold house with just us floating around like ghouls with candles sounds like the worst thing. But it might be quite fun. Yes or no?'

Edward started the car and said, he hoped with the nonchalance that he wasn't feeling, 'Wouldn't miss it for the world. Northwards then.'

No further sound came.

He enjoyed the miles to Bedford, losing himself in the almost empty road and the white noise of the engine. After the two hours she had predicted, she stirred and then directed him with occasional curt instructions – 'left', 'right here'; 'the turning after the church'; 'this road now for a couple of miles' – as the roads became narrower, his driving slower and the sense of imminent arrival ever stronger.

They came to the tall wrought-iron gates of the entrance to High Hedges at the edge of the village of Leighton, the estate seemingly entirely enclosed by its eponymous beech hedges that the road had skirted for several hundred yards before. The long drive was flanked by woods devoid of colour and straggly with storm damage. The house itself, that they approached at an oblique angle and slightly from behind, catching glimpses of it through the trees, was covered with so much ivy it was impossible to tell if it was made of stone or brick.

As they came round the side of the house to its front, he gasped. The ground fell away down a gentle slope to present before them a countryside of miles and miles to its front in a glorious bowl, the scene drinking up light even on that grey day. He swept the car raffishly onto the gravel. It was magnificent. This side of the house was a classical rectangle, with two main storeys and then some attic windows in the roof. The ground floor windows stretched to the ground; he could only imagine the height of the ceilings. The ivy, intimidating and eerie at the rear, here made it look as though the house had grown out of the landscape itself, as though the low hill on which it stood had always had its foundations etched into it. Immaculate box hedges lined a path on the slope down to a body of water too big to be called a pond but not large enough to be a lake, the wildness of the plants around it contrasting with the immaculate grass that led down to it.

'Well, here we are,' she said, stretching her arms up in the air. 'Welcome to Bedlam. No idea where Theo is. Come inside and have a cup of tea. I'm sorry I've been such a bore. Give me a few more hours and I'll be right as rain for this evening.'

'What do we say about our letter writing?' He couldn't help but say it in such an awkward way that it made it sound far more surreptitious and illicit than it had been.

She laughed. 'Well, I won't tell if you won't. You make it sound as though we were conducting an affair, Mr Salter,' and Edward immediately blushed. He stammered an offer to carry her bag from the boot but she declined with, 'Oh, don't bother with all that here,' and strode off into the house. Edward got his own bag and followed her.

The hall was vast, huge rugs strewn over a smooth wooden floor with about a dozen candles lighting its gloom. It was cold, barely warmer than outside. A round table sat in front of the entrance, a simple vase of fresh snowdrops at its centre incongruously tiny in the context of the space. In the corner an umbrella stand held a cricket bat and a few tennis racquets. A wide, shallow staircase with a blue carpet led the eye upwards through the atrium to a large skylight. Underneath the staircase was the piano. It felt odd to finally see it when he had so many times imagined Thorne standing there, playing his roll of chords. The scene didn't look hugely different to what had been in his mind's eye, just with less wood panelling than he had thought and with unexpected *trompe l'oeil* murals of birds and classical vistas on the walls.

Miranda flicked through some post on a side table and said absent-mindedly, 'Sorry about the dark. Tonnes of candles all over though and most of the rooms have a fire. One sec, let me just look through this. Nothing. Right, Mrs Gavin should have put some tea out for us in the kitchen. Stay here and I'll go and get it, then I'll show you your room and things. Trust my brother not to be here for the big arrival.'

A tiny floorboard creak came from behind him and her eyes lost their fix on his and looked beyond him.

'There you are! What on earth are you doing there, you skulker?'

Edward turned to see Thorne move into the hall. He must have been waiting round the corner.

'Salter! Damned good to see you,' he exclaimed, but without the easy, immediate charm that he had known so well on the Peninsula. It hit Edward then how foreign this was, how artificial a restart to their friendship.

For several moments they took each other in. Edward had

never seen him like this before; gone was the ebullient, sanguine soldier. Instead he was presented with an art student, tweed waistcoat on a collarless linen shirt atop billowing corduroy trousers and a pair of velvet slippers. It was as if he was dressed as a lovelorn Parisian poet, about to go off upstairs and die of tuberculosis in a garret.

They had only been off the Peninsula for a few weeks and while Edward often felt that he was still on it and only in some kind of a dream, Thorne looked utterly removed, as if he had never been there. The awkward pause lingered until Miranda interrupted. 'Quite remarkable. You're like a pair of schoolboys.' She marched over to Thorne, grabbed his wrist and led him to Edward, where she made them shake hands. They both grinned.

'Good to have you here, Salter.'

'Thank you, Thorne. It's great to be here.'

Miranda rolled her eyes. 'Oh, leave all that claptrap, will you? Theo and Edward. I don't want to hear you call each other anything else. Now, come on, Mrs Gavin's tea. Go to the drawing room and I'll bring it. Do get a move on.' And with that she left them alone in the hall. Again silence. Thorne chewed his lip slightly.

Edward said, 'Well . . .'

And then they both dissolved into laughter, for two minutes unable to draw breath.

CHAPTER TWENTY-FOUR

Edward quickly realised that his expectation of his stay at High Hedges being the scene of dilettante bliss in a rural idyll was misguided. The parkland surrounding the house looked as though it could attain Poussin levels of beauty in many weathers, but not in this limp February, which had rendered it brown and grey.

The house itself was glorious but the power cut made it feel like a building abandoned. Candles gave it a solemn, funerary air and only the fires gave out any warmth. The three of them clothed all day long in thick jerseys on top of jerseys as they set about trying to clear the storm damage. Fallen branches were to be cleared and heaped into piles, loose tiles on the house and all its outbuildings to be found. When they weren't working they would gather in the drawing room to play cards, read if the light allowed, or eat the sandwiches provided by Mrs Gavin, the only member of staff who had stayed in service at the house.

The butler, gardener, groom and odd man were all now in the army, and the cook had gone after suffering a breakdown over the death of her brother in the navy. A brisk, stern woman who lurked in the nether regions of the house, Mrs Gavin took a shine to Edward that surprised him given her demeanour. He was given a room on the second floor, snug and friendly, contrasting with the grand bedrooms on the first floor whose tall windows looked over the parkland. He liked it and would often lie on his bed soaking in the gloom and the silence, the only sound his breathing as he tried to empty his brain.

For the first couple of days Miranda remained a little away from him, watching on amused and aloof as he and Thorne chatted away or squabbled over cards. She would go to bed before them and preferred to work on her jobs alone while the two men often did theirs as a pair. The longer it went on, the more Edward came to want to break the ice with her but could never quite find the right time or situation to do so, Thorne himself remaining amusingly oblivious to the impasse.

He had his chance on the third morning. He was up on the roof, hands freezing from cleaning out the mulchy slop of leaves and twigs that had been blocking one of the gutters. A cold wind blew through light, silky rain as he lay on his front and crawled along the lip of the roof to reach down with his arm into the gutter a couple of feet below. He would scoop out a foot or so of gutter and flick it over the side onto the ground below, a blackish streak on the gravel evidence of his handiwork. Hearing a sound behind him he levered himself up to see Miranda stepping deftly out onto the roof from an attic window, carrying a tea tray.

'Gosh, that's kind,' said Edward, getting onto his knees, shuffling away from the edge and hauling himself up. He gave his hands a cursory wash in a shallow puddle and looked at them apologetically.

'I wouldn't mind about that,' she said, handing over a steaming china cup. He held it with both hands to get some warmth back into them as she unwrapped a paper packet to reveal two slices of fruit cake. 'Left over from Christmas. Still fresh though. So much brandy in it that it'll probably last five years.' They both ate in silence at first, Edward delighted to be with her like this.

'Are you not terrified doing this? It's a hell of a way down,' she said, brushing her hands together to get rid of crumbs and with her mouth still full of the last of the cake.

Edward smiled. 'It's not too bad. You just blur your eyes.'

'It would be dreadful to get you all the way here just for you to meet your fate falling off our roof.'

'Or the perfect murder.'

She laughed full-throatedly and delight ran through him.

'You know, this has really given me a new outlook on things, having you here.'

'On what, the war?'

'Well, ish. No, more on my experience as a sibling. I've been an older sister for what – how old is he? Twenty-two years now. And yet since you've been here, and seeing how you are together, you're in so many ways like his older brother. Which, in a funny sort of way, has given me a window into what it would be like to be a middle child between you both, free of all the burdens of being the oldest.' She grinned. 'I know that sounds odd. But I quite like it; I now know what it is I've been missing out on.'

A little sadly, he thought, she went on. 'It's only ever been us two. I don't think Mummy and Daddy ever wanted more. Or at least if they did they never said. You're one of two, aren't you?'

'My sister Cynthia is five years older than me. Haven't seen her since 1908 though. Went off to India to marry some railway wallah. Odd chap. Quiet, remote. I'd love to see her soon, I miss her dreadfully. She was – is – just very, very funny. But I can't imagine when that will be. I wonder if she'd even recognise me sometimes.'

She tilted her head a little and drew the sparkle from her eyes, making them matt and sincere. 'Was it terribly bad there?'

He smiled. 'Oh, I don't mean that. Just that by the time we do ever meet again it will be so long I'll have to have changed; she left when I was sixteen. I was still in shorts really.' He paused, realising that her question had politely, obliquely, given him the chance to talk about the Peninsula. He decided that he actually quite wanted to.

He changed gear, quickly trying to work out how to explain it all. 'But yes, on the Peninsula, you're right, it was appalling.

By any yardstick it was the most awful, brutal, dreadful place on earth. I'd call it satanic at times.'

She recognised his intonation and said softly, her mouth in the ghost of a smile, 'But—'

He smiled back. 'Well, there you go. But.' He wondered how he could explain what it was about the place, but before he could she said, 'Don't worry. I think I understand. Sort of. I can see it in him sometimes. It makes me feel, I don't know, somehow envious of what it was that happened. It's the look he gets around you, of seeing him with an older brother. Or is that too presumptuous?'

'No. I don't think so.'

They fell back into silence. She finished her tea over-theatrically to draw the conversation to its close, and he took the hint and said, 'Right, best crack on, this sludge isn't going to remove itself.' They went their ways, he back to the edge and she back up the steps. He felt guilty though and said, 'You do know that I'll look after him whatever happens, don't you—'

She interrupted him. 'Please, none of that. I'd never hold you to a promise that you can't in a million years guarantee. Understand?'

'Understood.' He went back to his gutter.

CHAPTER TWENTY-FIVE

'I'm afraid this must be terribly boring for you,' she said after dinner a couple of evenings later.

Edward shook his head. 'Good Lord, no. It's great fun.'

'Well, tomorrow we'll liven things up a bit.' Mischief glinted in her candlelit eye.

'No. No way. Miranda, no. Absolutely not,' said Thorne.

'What?' said Edward.

'Just a little bit of fun. I'm going to go for a ride tomorrow; do you want to come?'

Before he could answer, she added, 'Have you ever ridden?'

'No. Well, a few times when I was about six.'

She smiled. 'Marvellous. I can be your teacher. I've got Eagle for you. She's an absolute dream.'

Thorne tried to dissuade her, only half-jokingly. 'Look, Edward's a vital cog of His Majesty's war machine. You can't have him being carted off over hedge and field and then thrown to break his neck when he's just survived the bloody Peninsula. I won't have it.' He got up to get some more wine and Miranda looked at Edward and mouthed, 'We will have it.'

They wound up ten minutes later, went up to bed and gave each other a brief goodnight on the landing to get out of the cold as quickly as possible.

Once in his room, Edward placed his candle on the chest of drawers, changed briskly into his pyjamas and got into bed, feeling the heavy damp of the bedclothes slowly being warmed by his body. As he slipped into the twilight before sleep it wasn't a noise that startled him but the slight guttering of the candle. He sat up, spooked, and saw that the door had been pushed ajar. He stood up as a voice came. 'Are you decent? It's only me.' Before he could reply, Miranda poked her head around the door and giggled at him. 'You look like Wee Willie Winkie.'

He shrugged, trying not to appear as nonplussed as he was, unnerved but a little thrilled too.

'I know old misery guts down there said that I wasn't to take you riding tomorrow, but for heaven's sake. You'll love it. He won't be up until nine, so we can be out and back by the time he's at breakfast. Easier to ask for forgiveness than permission. What do you say?' She spoke almost seductively, beneath her entirely guileless smile of schoolgirl enthusiasm.

He blustered his way through a reply of ums and ahs before she stopped him.

'Good, I knew you would. Meet you at the piano at seven sharp. Wear these.' She stole into the room, laid out a pair of britches on the chaise longue at the bottom of his bed and withdrew again to the door. She was wearing a short silk dressing gown over a longer frilly white night-dress. Edward gulped, unable to work out where to look. 'I took them from his wardrobe when I went out earlier. Should be a rough fit. There are some boots in the tack room. Shirt and jersey on top. Or jacket, whatever you fancy. It'll be fun. Promise you.'

'If you hadn't said you promise, I'd be more inclined to believe that.'

She threw her head back and stifled a cackle. 'See you at seven.' She brought her hand down from the door and seemed to brush her lips as though she was blowing him a kiss but before he could work it out the door was silently shut as she left him in the candlelight.

He stepped over, opened it again and poked his head into the black corridor. She was gone. He stood in the dark for a minute listening for a trace of her but there was nothing.

He got back to his bed and lay there as the candle dwindled down, trying to work out what he felt about her, before finally drifting off.

He woke at a quarter to seven and shaved quickly, feeling a bolt of excitement at the knowledge that this was a chance he might not have again. He dressed, clumsy and hurried, the britches a little small for him but a tolerable fit. He walked softly downstairs and went to the piano; no one there. He wondered briefly if the whole thing had been a joke and then he saw her in the doorframe of the corridor that led to the back of the house.

'Bang on time. I'd expect nothing less, Captain Salter. Come on,' she whispered.

He followed her as they went through the maze of the kitchens and servants' rooms and left out the back door of the house, crossing the ivy-covered courtyard to the stable block. The day was misty and damp, malign low cloud threatening rain. The warm, acid smell of urine-damp hay hit him as they came to the stables, where her magnificent black hunter Falcon whinnied at seeing her.

Edward stopped suddenly, transported in an instant back to a day on the Peninsula where he had seen a horse near an ammunition dump at the beach, as big and beautiful as this one, cut clean in half by a shell, its entrails lying in a vast heap, steaming like autumn compost and even just seconds after the explosion swarming with a broiling mass of flies. It was as though he was right back there, remembering even now the sweat on his neck, the dust in his eyes. His pulse quickened and his brain swam.

'Are you all right?' asked Miranda, sensing his oddness.

He snapped out of it. 'Yes, just a little nervous, that's all.'

'Don't worry about Falcon, she's mine. You've got Eagle. And it's probably just a hangover you've got; you and Theo do put it away, you know. Still, no better cure than a quick gallop.'

He blanched further and she grinned. 'Only kidding. Nothing more than a trot.'

She brought Falcon out, tied her to an iron ring set into the wall and then went into the adjacent stable.

Edward looked in as she roused Eagle, a comatose grey, smaller than Falcon and with dopey eyes and a hangdog manner. 'Wake up, sleepyhead.' Eventually the horse complied and allowed her to take her to stand next to Falcon. Edward couldn't help but think that the horses were mismatched in the same way as those two Russians had been; Lipin and Borov. The one sleek and graceful and the other dumpy and rather comedic.

Miranda went over to the tack room, brought out a huge weight of kit, and deftly got the horses ready. She motioned him over to the mounting block in a corner of the yard. He felt faintly ridiculous as he stood waiting for her to lead Eagle over to him. He had his heart in his mouth and got on, feeling very unsteady. Luckily Eagle seemed to read his mood and loped around the yard helping him to get the hang of her as Miranda eschewed the mounting block and just pulled herself up onto Falcon in one superlatively lithe movement. She smiled at him. 'Shall we?' And they set off out of the yard and onto the drive.

They headed out into the fields, the earth split into three round them: the dark-green grass; the brown spindles of the barren trees; and the blank slate grey of the sky. It seemed that they were the only things moving in it. They were silent at first, Miranda letting Edward get the hang of Eagle, who he found to be sure and steady, with a pleasing heaviness helping to ease him into the ride. Now and again she would let Falcon loose into a canter and petalled around their route and the axis that the lumpen Eagle made, unperturbed by her more glamorous companion's restlessness.

A little wind picked up and brought the mist in thicker grey gossamer strips flitting over the ground. It hid her as she rode away from him for some moments, reappearing elsewhere, never where he expected her to be.

'It's like being in a dream, isn't it?' she said as she came back to join him, face flushed red.

Edward didn't know what to think, his brain was so addled by competing thoughts. In one moment he would think of the smoke from the bush fires on the Peninsula, how Thorne had used it to escape the Turkish counterattack on the blind crests. At another moment, an eye's blink on, he would think of how atmospheric and freighted the whole scene was, how he wished the morning would never end and that their safe, mist-shrouded cocoon would protect them for the whole day. He would think of how he still didn't know how to play her, with her newness and spring that were just like her brother's but so different somehow. More knowing? More wry? He found himself smiling, alive and full with the mist leaving tiny pinpricks of water over his hands and the reins. Before he knew it Eagle's hooves flicked over in a new rhythm as she picked up a slow canter, he now settling comfortably into the beat and instinctively squeezing her flanks with his thighs to drive her on.

'That's it! Well done!' came her cry as he glided on, giggling at the joy of movement. She appeared out of the mist to his nine o'clock as she drove Falcon next to him. She reached out and clapped him on the shoulder. 'I told you you could do it. Come on, up a little more?' It was as though she was talking to Eagle and not to him as she brought Falcon up to a gallop and Eagle followed suit, the soft metronome of the canter ceding to a manic staccato as the two horses pounded forward. He laughed uncontrollably, a joyful terror seizing him as they raced over the field and into the grey. He wished it could last forever. Presently though, Eagle ran out of steam and slowed quickly to a sweating, panting heap as her age and stomach caught up with her. Miranda drew Falcon up and looked back at Eagle fondly. 'Poor old girl. She's still got it when she decides she has it.'

'Amazing. Amazing. You just feel . . .'

'What?'

'I don't know. Invincible. Like nothing can stop you.'

'That can't be so unusual for you. You're here without a scratch. Both of you.'

Edward thought for a while. It wasn't strictly true; his body had been pitted by scrapes, burns and cuts, but yes, he and Thorne had emerged extraordinarily unscathed. Without knowing what he wanted to tell her he found that he just went for it. He had no idea if she would understand but thought that he might as well try.

'It's funny. I always thought there were two types of people, two routes to take. One was my approach, where you convince yourself that you are as good as dead anyway. That you're all in the hands of some higher power. God or fate or random luck or whatever you want to call it. For me it was a kind of resigned agnosticism. I used to think it sometimes when I looked up at the stars, that you were this tiny collection of cells on a rock in space and whatever happened to you didn't matter one jot in the grand scheme of things. A kind of cosmic irrelevance. Quite comforting really once you come to terms with it. It doesn't mean you're not scared – I was terrified most of the time – but it means that you can function without this kind of existential dread hovering over you. You die, that's it, you're gone, you lost, the world moves on, bang. You have no control over what happens to you so you might as well play along with it, try to enjoy yourself where you can and if you get hit then bad luck, there was absolutely nothing you could have done about it.'

He broke off, before picking up again.

'And then there was the other type. They were the lot I envied. The ones who ditched my passive approach and just grabbed the situation by the throat. They decided that they were the master of their surroundings, that nothing could ever happen to them. It was inconceivable to them that they would not survive. Whereas I and the others resigned ourselves to being at the mercy of some higher power somewhere, this other lot saw themselves *as* that higher power. I had – have – a soldier like that, a sergeant called Baffle. And there's a brother officer of ours, chap called Bruce Haynes-Mattingly, who was like that too. It didn't mean they didn't get hit; it just meant that on the battlefield they had a sort of aura, could operate under this mantle of invincibility. I had it once or twice myself, but only for an hour or so. And it was intoxicating, amazing. But it was also dreadful.'

'And Theo?'

'He was the only person I knew who seemed to operate under both points of view at the same time. He could be so funny, so dry, with his fatalist point of view. But then when you saw him in action, or about to go into action, it was breathtaking. This kind of primal fierceness, as if daring bullets to come and pierce him. But then afterwards there would be none of it, all that violence, that kind of teeth-baring savagery that the others had melting away in a flash and he'd be picking a flower to press into his notebook or checking his men's feet for blisters and sharing some chocolate with them.'

She didn't reply at first and he thought he had overstepped. She didn't need to know all this. He regretted unburdening himself like that, throwing out thoughts that he had never said to anyone else.

Through the mist the house appeared in front of them a couple of hundred yards away. She had brought them expertly back in a great circle round the parkland. 'Well, that's quite some trick,' he said. 'How did you do that?'

'Just knowing this place. And the horses know it too. Eagle's hunger is better at pointing the way to her stable than any compass.'

They walked back up the hill to the house and the stable, Edward suddenly allowing himself to imagine for a moment that he lived at High Hedges with her and that they were husband and wife returning from a morning ride before going to greet their children at breakfast. He felt a satisfaction, deep-seated in him, that then gave way to a knot of nervousness that he would never get to realise it. It left him tongue-tied, unable to say anything as they wound their way back, for fear of saying the wrong thing. He knew now that whatever he said to her would be said in that dry-mouthed way of wondering how every utterance sounded.

They came to the stable block, Eagle whinnying loudly at the prospect of food and rest. He reached forward and stroked her neck.

As Miranda got off Falcon, a boy cycled into the yard carrying a large bag on his shoulder and smiled as he greeted her, 'Good morning, Miss Thorne.' He looked at Edward and doffed his cap, a little resentfully, he thought, at Miranda not being alone. His insouciance was just like Preston's. He reached into his satchel and took out a newspaper. 'This morning's offering, Miss. Already had a read, nothing special.'

Miranda said, 'Good morning, Mr Tyson. Hang on, hands full here; just leave it on the mounting block, will you?'

Then it happened, in slow motion and with unerring predictability. The boy Tyson walked over to the mounting block and placed the paper on it at the exact moment when a gust of wind ruffled its loose corners for a couple of seconds before then picking the whole thing up and sending the sheaf of loose pages flying everywhere.

The previously imperturbable Eagle immediately took fright and she reared up with a brutal surge that had Edward stand upright in his stirrups. His nose banged against the back of her head before she crashed back down onto the cobbles, sending him scrabbling for her reins and neck but twisting off and smashing down shoulder-first onto the ground. A thud and a clean snapping sound broke the air.

He must have been knocked out for a moment as the next thing he saw was Miranda and Tyson, who he wanted to punch, looking over him. A wounded vanity forced him to try to stand up. His right arm was useless and he struggled up using his left side, angrily spurning their offers of help. He could feel hot wetness above his lip; his nose was bleeding.

Eagle was looking sheepish in a corner of the yard. He had a pretty good idea what had happened, his arm hanging limp beside him and his shoulder slouched forward; he had broken his collar bone.

Wearily, as though he had been awake for a day rather than an hour and half, he walked over to the mounting block and sat down on it, feeling faint and pathetic. He couldn't believe that it had taken such a banal accident to finally wound him. He thought how funny the mess would find it. He thought how angry the CO would be. He looked over to the pair of them.

'Do either of you have a cigarette?' he said. 'I'd kill for one.'

CHAPTER TWENTY-SIX

As the local doctor had long since gone to the army, the only recourse they had in the immediate area to help Edward was the vet in a nearby village. Thorne drove him over in the Austin, still livid. Edward wasn't sure what concerned him more, the gnawing, throbbing pain of his shoulder or Thorne's studied coolness as he drove deliberately fast, throwing the car into corners as Edward winced with the speed and bumps.

They arrived at the surgery, a smart Georgian house at the heart of the village, and had to sit in the waiting room as the vet finished dealing with a cocker spaniel who had been sick after eating chocolate.

Thorne flicked through a newspaper ostentatiously, as though to visibly mock Edward for the cause of his injury. He tried to break the ice. 'Well, this is pretty humiliating, isn't it? Hardly very Iliadic.'

Thorne didn't even look up. 'It's not funny. Do you know how badly this is going to go down with the men? Good luck explaining this to the old man, is all I'll say.'

It hit Edward that he hadn't yet mentioned to Thorne that he had bumped into Valentine Braithwaite in London and what he had said about linking him up with Fitzgerald. Before he could work out how to broach it, the spaniel's owner walked out through the room, carrying the wretched dog, the weight of the world on its shoulders, and Thorne raised his eyebrows as though he was likening it to Edward. The first flicker of a smile appeared; a sign of him maybe starting to melt.

The vet was called Claremont, a rake-thin man in his fifties or sixties with a greying toothbrush moustache who seemed unperturbed that his new patient had two legs instead of four. He greeted Thorne and ignored Edward.

'Good morning, Theo.'

'Hello, Mr Claremont. Good to see you again.'

There was a fondness and relief in Claremont's eye that were hidden by his rather gruff manner. 'We've got you back from the Turk, I see. Are you keeping well?'

'Yes, thanks.'

'I imagine it must have been . . . rather challenging.'

Thorne smiled. 'Yes. Yes, it was a little.'

There was a heavy pause before Claremont said, 'Well, as I said, good to see you again, young man.' He turned to Edward holding his arm up across his chest and said, 'Now look, I've got to be quick, I'm afraid. I have an appointment with Mr Farley's cows in Great Heyford. What happened? Shoulder?'

His matter-of-factness and lack of bedside manner were quite comforting in their own way and Edward said, 'Fell off a horse, sir. An hour ago. Landed on my shoulder. I think the collar bone's gone.'

'Dear me. Can't move it, can you?'

'Not at all. Hurts like hell.'

Claremont took out an enormous pair of tailor's scissors from his drawer, went behind Edward and cut straight up his shirt and jersey. He came round the front and felt along Edward's chest and clavicle with his heavy, weathered hands. Halfway along, Edward jumped back.

'All right, all right,' said Claremont, soothing as if talking to an animal. 'Sit down, old chap. Get your breath back.'

Thorne helped Edward over to a chair and he sat down, feeling as though he was about to pass out.

Claremont went behind his desk to a cupboard and dug out several large bandages and a box that he gave to Thorne. He looked at Edward. 'Yes, you've broken it all right, I daresay a proper human doctor would be a good idea at some point but there's not much they'll tell you beyond that. There's nothing you can really do with collar bones; just try to keep it stable, sleep on your back and it'll fuse together, surprisingly soon in fact. Rest for a couple of days and then you can get walking. Just don't give it another shock. Mind that you do see a sawbones at some point though. Use those bandages. Keep the arm high across your chest in a sling. Start moving your arm as and when you feel it can be used, but don't overdo it, for God's sake. It'll be two months, I should think, before it's back to normal. In the box are a few phials of morphine for the pain. Add to some water and drink. Don't go mad with it.'

Edward nodded.

Claremont smiled. 'Sorry about your shirt. Rather a smart one. Still, needs must. Take a blanket from my stable on the way out for the journey back. I'll pick it up when I next go to see Falcon and Eagle. Which was it, by the way?'

'Eagle.'

'Dear me. And such a gentle little thing. Dare I ask, were you in the Dardanelles too?'

Edward nodded.

'Well. Well done. It's very good to have you back. Thank you.'

They got up to go and Edward thanked him. Thorne said, 'Please pass on my best to Veronica.'

Claremont's eyebrows raised in an old man's expression of gratitude and Edward saw a sudden frailty in him. 'I will do. Take care, the pair of you. Now come on, chop-chop. The war effort needs milk and Farley's cows are a damned sight more useful on that front than you two are.'

He ushered them out and soon they were back in the car, Edward shivering with the pain and cold but at least now under the thick blanket. 'He seemed a good man. I quite liked how unfazed he was.'

Thorne, driving now in more sympathetic fashion, replied, 'The best. Such a nice man. You know he lost his son at Le Cateau. Paul. A sapper. Missing, never been seen since. Trawled through the Red Cross and the camps but not a trace of him. He was a couple of years older than me. Fine cricketer.'

'Christ. No clue at all?'

'Nothing. Must have been a shell. Just pieces of him, probably.'

Edward looked out the window. Somehow that story hit him harder than anything he had seen on the Peninsula. He realised that that was the first time he had ever met the parent of someone who had been killed. They had become so accustomed to seeing the dead and dying but had never yet seen the effect of that death away from the battlefield. And it hadn't even been mentioned.

Thorne seemed to be having exactly the same thoughts as him. 'It kills you, doesn't it?'

There was silence for a while, until Edward broke it: 'You know, I bumped into Valentine Braithwaite in London? You remember, the son of Hamilton's chief of staff. In the Somersets. Chap behind all that Russian stuff I had to do.'

Thorne didn't answer, as if keeping his powder dry.

Edward went on. 'Seemed to think I should press on with that offer of going onto Kitchener's staff. I'd forgotten all about it.'

'So had I,' said Thorne, an edge to his voice. 'Well, you might as well.'

Edward didn't like his tone. 'What do you mean by that?'

'Nothing. Just that, with you now crocked, you're not going to be much use at battalion, are you?' He said it in such a sullen, spoilt manner that Edward was immediately riled.

'Look, I didn't ask for this bloody injury.'

'I know you didn't. But I warned you explicitly against it. But oh no, off you go, just go for a ride when you barely know one end of a horse from the other.'

'It was a freak accident. It could have happened to anyone.'

'But it didn't, did it? What the hell are we going to tell the men? Sorry, chaps, B Company commander's not going to come over to France with us because he was arsing around with a horse. Still, that's OK; off you go, enjoy it.'

'Don't be so bloody obtuse. There's a thousand jobs I could do. You heard him. Two months and I'll be back.'

'But don't worry, lads,' Thorne carried on, 'Mr Salter's now back in London, drinking pink gins and fluffing pillows for Lord fucking Kitchener.'

Edward didn't reply. They completed the journey in silence. Edward couldn't understand how his friend was so angry.

When they got back to High Hedges, Thorne grudgingly opened the door for him and helped him out, before stalking off into the house, saying, 'I'll find Miranda. She'll bloody look after you. No doubt you've probably already arranged something with her.'

Edward, exasperated and stung, walked into the house after him. He was exhausted. The grandfather clock told him it was only just eleven o'clock. He climbed the stairs to his room, using the banister to pull himself up to rest at each step. Thinking that he might as well just leave, he managed to get most of his possessions into the bag but then wondered how on earth he was going to get dressed on his own. He couldn't go wearing just the blanket. He stood the pillows against the headboard in an upside-down V to allow him to sit almost upright, then gingerly got into the bed. A little sleep would sort things. He hadn't had any of the morphine yet but his brain was managing to quell the worst sharp tugs into a dull ache. The sling Thorne had tied outside the surgery was nice and tight. He closed his eyes and fell fast asleep.

When he opened his eyes the room was different. Gone was the gloomy, damp air; instead warm light spilled from the two bedside lamps. The curtains were drawn and Miranda was smiling at him from the chair.

He felt totally compromised, naked. He wiped away dribble from his chin. 'God, I'm so sorry. What time is it?' he said.

'Shh. Lie down, it's fine. It's six in the evening. You've had a good sleep. That's all. And behold—' she smiled '—we have light! Finally. Came on at teatime. Thank goodness for that. What a complete palaver.'

He had an overwhelming urge to urinate and said, trying to hide his embarrassment, 'I'm terribly sorry but I think I need to go to the lavatory.' She came over wordlessly and helped him up out of bed, leading him out of the room and to the bathroom. His head hurt and his arm was in agony anew. Managing to lean down to the basin he clamped his mouth round the cold tap and drank and drank until he could take no more. Outside the bathroom she led him back again to the room, her touch light on his elbow, and then propped him back up in bed. Next to her chair was a plate of sandwiches that she brought over. 'Ham and cheese.'

'Gosh, thanks. I think that Theo's terribly annoyed with me . . .'

She waved her hand dismissively. 'Oh, don't worry about him. He'll have forgiven us before you know it.'

The way she said it made Edward think that she thought Thorne was still annoyed with them just for going out riding and that he hadn't mentioned the argument they had had in the car to her.

'I've never seen him like that before.'

'Really? Oh, he could be a proper little terror growing up. Sweetness and light most of the time but would throw the occasional huge tantrum. They never last though. I used to think they were like April showers. You think the world's about to end when you're in one but before you know it it's over and the sun's out again. You almost become quite fond of them. Now come on, eat up. And drink this. He gave me the morphine. I only put a couple of drops in.'

She came over and held a tumbler to his lips.

He ate the sandwiches ravenously as she looked on.

He didn't feel anything yet and didn't want to be sent back to sleep, wishing they could keep on talking. 'How is my nemesis?'

She laughed. 'Eagle? Oh, fine. Right as rain. Young Tyson was mortified though.'

'It's fine. Accident. But you couldn't make it up, could you?'

They chatted away for a few more minutes. Gradually the drug started to worm its way through his limbs, his eyelids drooping longer and heavier with each blink. The last thing he noticed before he fell back to sleep was her coming over to him, pulling the blanket up his chest a little and then sitting back in the chair, singing softly as he landed back into nothingness.

CHAPTER TWENTY-SEVEN

He woke late into the following morning, a bright winter's sun creating a glow behind the curtains and Thorne now in the chair where his sister had been. Before Edward could say anything Thorne began, 'Morning. Look, before I ask you how you are and how you slept and any of that I just want to apologise for yesterday.'

Edward wished he wasn't doing this, but nothing was stopping him.

'It's just that I was annoyed that having got yourself through whatever the hell it was we've just had happen to us that you then get clobbered by some stupid accident, like something out of some damned farce. I was thinking how it would be that we would have to go to France without you, how the men would hate that. And then when you said the stuff about the Kitchener job it just exacerbated it. Look, I'm sorry, I went way, way too far. Unacceptable. If that job comes up you have to take it, you need to take it. Just come back to us once it's done.'

'It was just a chance meeting with Braithwaite; he probably forgot all about it.'

Thorne nodded, but his eyes looked as though they didn't believe him.

'And if I do get it I don't have to take it.'

'Don't be so bloody stupid. Of course you do. It's the army, not the Fabians. And you have to do it for our sakes anyway. If we can get you at that level, making sure all that lot understand what's going on, understand what decisions made in Whitehall eventually translate into once they've made their way to the line and what someone shoving a bayonet into someone's eye socket actually feels like then all to the good. I promise you. You must do it.' He burned with an intensity, a righteousness that Edward had rarely seen in him before.

Edward mulled it over, wondering what he should do. Then Thorne made the decision for him. 'You know Baffle would tell you to do it. And the CO.'

That sealed it. 'All right. I'll do it. If it comes that is.'

'And if you don't then I'll bloody well apply for it.' Thorne was softening now, the rain passing as Miranda said it would. 'I'd kill for the chance to do that job. In on all the big decisions. Who knows, maybe you can have a hand in preventing the next big P. T. Barnum's travelling circus of freaks and horrors like the Peninsula.'

Edward's shoulder throbbed badly but even as he reached for another of the painkillers on his bedside table the relief that he felt at having assuaged Thorne eclipsed any discomfort his injury could give him.

They talked through the plan for the next few days. Edward would stay for another three nights and then get a train back to London and thence to his aunt and uncle, by that time able to travel and – hopefully – able to put at least a shirt on. In the meantime he would rest in bed. Thorne got up to go; a leak had appeared in the cellar and he was trying to find out where it was from. 'I hope to high heaven it's easy to find. Plumbers are hen's teeth at the moment. This kind of thing was so much easier before all of this. About five chaps on the staff who would have dealt with it before Dad or I would have even found out it had been a problem in the first place.'

Edward raised an eyebrow. 'Yes, the war really has destroyed civilisation as we know it, hasn't it? That horrible rotten Kaiser. What next; having to reuse napkins?'

'Bugger off.' He grinned, went to the door and left.

CHAPTER TWENTY-EIGHT

For Edward's last evening, and his first dinner downstairs since the accident, the stops were pulled out. He had regained enough movement in the rest of his arm to walk comfortably, or at least now knew what would and wouldn't dig a spur into the break. He was in trousers and a loose shirt while Thorne and Miranda had got themselves up in evening dress – 'To dine you out, old chap', as Thorne put it.

The drawing room at drinks before dinner was awash with the reds and golds of the sofas and curtains underlit by a dozen lampshades. Thorne was immaculate in a stiff collar and shirt that forced his posture even straighter than usual. Miranda came in as they were mixing gin and tonics. Her black velvet dress showed the top of her arms and Edward found himself unable to speak for a while. Thorne slapped him round his good shoulder. 'Buck up, this is the same gorgon who got you thrown off your horse. Look at her too hard and you'll turn to stone.'

Edward laughed as he mumbled some inadequate, strained compliment.

Dinner was pheasant and then a tarte tatin and, Mrs Gavin having taken the plates away, they remained in the dining room smoking and drinking. Miranda looked at Edward, puckish and piercing. 'Quite the time we've had with you here. I hope you've enjoyed it as much as we have.'

'I don't know what to say. I can't thank you enough. It's been . . . I don't know . . . It's been the tonic that I never knew I needed.'

'That you both needed,' she corrected him, looking at Thorne pointedly, who shrugged and just said, 'Not me, don't know what you're talking about. Walk in the park, the Peninsula,' and then started laughing. He got up. 'I'll go and stoke the fire in the drawing room. Come through in a minute.'

Once he had left, Miranda fixed Edward again and said, 'Do you know what I think of you?'

Edward tried to look as cool as possible in the face of her directness. 'No.'

'Do you want to know?'

'I might. Go on.'

She took a sip of her wine before she replied. 'You have this twin approach to things. For you, life is like a chess match that you want to win, but it's also a feast that you never want to end. If that makes any kind of sense.'

He tried to reply instantly but couldn't come up with anything, and the longer he stalled the more he thought about it. Was that true? He took another swig of his brandy, the pain in his shoulder now gone and a warm numbness filling him. At last he said, 'Is that a good or bad thing?'

'It depends. Too much of the former and you won't get to enjoy your feast. Too much of the latter and you won't win your chess match. But there's a balance in there somewhere. I'm sure you'll find it. I hope you find it.'

All the previous days, the repressed thoughts and flirtations they had shared condensed for him into that moment. Right now was the right moment to say something. But what? Before he could decide she stood up, crossed over to his side of the table, put her hands gently on the back of his chair and leant down to whisper into his ear. 'I'm off to bed, I'm afraid. I hate goodbyes, so I won't be standing outside waving you off like some chump tomorrow morning. But don't be a stranger. I'd like to see you again very soon.'

She inched closer and kissed him lightly just beneath where his sideburn ended, seeming to breathe in a little as she did so. Edward sat frozen, not knowing what to do and wishing that it could go on, but then it ended, her skin left his and she went out of the room and up the stairs. A minute later Thorne came in, bluff and hearty. 'Where the hell did she go? More for us, I suppose. Come on, old chap.' They went through to the drawing room and had more brandy there.

In bed that night, Edward lay awake wondering if she would come again to him like she had done the night before the ride. Eventually, hours later, he fell asleep. In the morning though he noticed that the door – shut by him when he had got into bed – was now ajar and the cushion on the chair facing the bed had been sat on. At least he thought it looked as though it had been.

He packed and went down to the hall to meet Thorne who was to drive him to the station. It was an icy, clear morning and they had a quick cup of tea before they went out of the front door to the car. As Thorne turned the engine on and tried to get the ice off the windscreen, Edward turned back to look at the house, its friendly yellow stone greyed a tinge by the frost. He looked up to Miranda's window and thought he saw the fraction of a movement in the curtains. He smiled and brought a hand up a little in an awkward, schoolboyish wave, wondering if she could see him. He would be back, that much he knew for sure.

'Come on.' Thorne tooted the horn behind him. 'All aboard.'

He got in and the car swept away down the drive, the cold binding together the gravel so that it made barely a sound.

CHAPTER TWENTY-NINE

Less than two weeks later, Edward arrived at the War Office, propelled there by a telegram that had been handed to him by the commanding officer back at battalion, summoning him for an interview. 'Can't imagine it's an interview that you'll flunk, my boy,' the CO had said, no trace of the expected disappointment on his face. 'Off you go. Best pack your bags. Chop-chop.'

And now here he was, being shown to Fitzgerald's office and greeted in a friendly, if quite perfunctory, fashion. It was as though he knew Edward of old instead merely from their brief chat on the Peninsula. He poured him a cup of tea, sat behind his own desk and got straight to the point, not bothering with any pleasantries. 'What we'd like from you, Salter, is to be the field marshal's eyes and ears in the army. You won't be his ADC as such, but you'll have his authority.'

Edward suppressed a surging panic at being ripped so suddenly from everything he had grown so accustomed to at battalion. He swallowed, he hoped not visibly, and tried to keep his answer cool. 'OK, sir, but why me?'

'Because you've got recent combat experience. The perfect man. Get amongst the New Army battalions. Tell us what you think their weaknesses are. Get amongst the units of the Old Army. Tell us what you think their weaknesses are. And get amongst the Territorials. He's particularly sniffy about them.'

'But all I know is the Peninsula . . .'

Fitzgerald cut him off. 'Don't give me any of that balls. Being under fire is being under fire, doesn't matter two hoots if it's in France or Flanders or Falmouth. You know soldiering, you know men, you know what good leadership looks like and I daresay you know what bad leadership looks like. Get around. Get amongst the men. Go to Amiens, go up to Ypres, get as close as you bloody want to the line. Go to Montreuil, have a look-see at what Haig and his mob are up to. Have a look at Aldershot, the Plain, any garrison town you want. And come and tell us everything after each trip.'

'Right, sir. But I was under the impression that I was here because I speak Russian.'

'That you are. But we don't need you for that quite yet. Not for a couple of months at any rate. We do, however, need to get a grip on what is going on. It's going to be a hell of a year in France. And this New Army is going to lose its newness damned quickly. Don't know where and don't know when, but it's going to be a damnable test. Less than two years ago these boys didn't know one end of a rifle from another and we're about to ask them to break the German Army. We need to know exactly, *exactly*, the state of it, the unvarnished truth.' He paused, got up from his chair and went over to the window, where he continued as though he was now talking to himself.

'The problem K has, you see, is that no one ever tells him the truth. Everyone's so keen to impress him and to get in his good books that they inflate success or deflate bad news. So when the poor chap goes to Cabinet and presents to those shysters, he's often batting on a wicket he doesn't honestly know is true or not. It's a hell of a problem. They are out for his blood, believe you me, and he's a lot weaker than you think he might be. He's not made for this, you see. He's a superb general, but a politician he isn't. OK, I'm not saying they're all ghastly. Some are all right; AJB's sound, Haldane was damned fine before he got the chop, Grey's a good man, the PM himself isn't too bad, when he eventually makes a decision. Winston's heart was in the right place. But it's a completely different mindset to a soldier's and K just can't work out how to play it. It's like putting a hunter onto the flat. It's everything I can do to keep his head above water; I desperately need some help.'

There was a knock at the door and a clerk put her head round. 'He's on his way, sir. Just coming up the stairs now. Not looking best pleased.'

'Oh dear. Thank you, Jean.' Fitzgerald looked at Edward. 'I'm not quite sure whether to tell you to leave or tell you to hide. Nothing for it, I suppose. Brace yourself.'

The door opened and Kitchener strode into the room, almost throwing a load of papers and files down onto the desk. 'Well, that was bloody awful. That wretched scoundrel Lloyd George just runs rings around me at every bloody meeting. Revels in making me look small in front of those other spineless windbags.'

Fitzgerald coughed a little and looked at Edward, 'Sir, may I reintroduce you to Captain Salter. I told you about him joining us . . .'

If Kitchener was chastened at having let his guard down in front of Edward he didn't show it. 'Ah. Slater.'

Edward saluted with his left hand for a second time – feeling utterly ridiculous while doing so – having already done one unnoticed when the field marshal had burst in. Fitzgerald coughed a correction. 'Salter, sir.'

'Yes, I mean Salter. That's right. My new spy. Jolly good. You were my guide at Suvla, weren't you?' Kitchener's face had changed completely upon seeing Edward, swiftly reassembling itself from the scattered jigsaw it had been upon entering.

'That's right, sir.'

'Amusing sergeant of yours I met. Asked me about my knitting.'

'Yes, sir. Baffle. Just picked up his colour sergeant's crown. And an MM to go with it.'

Kitchener looked delighted. 'Jolly good. Send my congratulations when you see him next, will you?'

'Yes, sir.'

Kitchener eyed his bandage. 'Turk get you, eh? Hope not too badly.'

'Um, no, sir. A riding injury during leave.'

'Really? Silly bugger. Still, good to know we can't keep you away from the thrill of things.'

Kitchener clearly thought that Edward had fallen at great speed and was something of a daredevil. He decided it would be best not to disabuse him of the notion and so just nodded meekly.

Kitchener frowned at him approvingly and then looked to the vast mounds of papers that he had dumped on the desk, saying to Fitzgerald, 'Right, let's get all this bumph sorted out. I want to get down to Broome by dinner,' and went to sit in Fitz's chair, the cue for the end of the meeting.

Fitzgerald escorted Edward out. 'Don't worry. That's just him, I'm afraid; never a great one for small talk. You'll get used to it. Broome is Broome Park, his house in Kent. Goes there every weekend. Honestly, I don't know what he would do without that place. It's the only thing that gives him any release from all of this. This is to be your office.' He knocked at a door and without waiting for a response went straight in to find a Grenadier Guards major sitting at a desk with his shirt tucked out and halfway through eating an iced bun. 'Morning, Anderson, here's your new roommate. Salter, by way of Gallipoli. He's survived that, so try not to bore him to death with stories about parade grounds.'

Anderson smiled and held a hand over his desk for a vigorous shake. 'Pleased to meet you. My parade ground stories, I'll have you know, are a lot more amusing than his ones about ironing the old man's pyjamas.' He remained seated and explained apologetically, 'Boche got my leg, I'm afraid. On the Marne. The whistle had only just gone, as well. Bastards.' He nodded to the corner next to a wire wastepaper bin at a long crutch, the type that supported the armpit.

'Well, I'll leave you two bluffers to crack on with it,' said Fitzgerald. He slinked out the door, closing it softly behind him.

Perplexed, Edward bounded back across the room, opened the door and said down the corridor, 'But sir, I haven't even had an interview.'

Fitzgerald turned, having already made it halfway back to the office. 'Yes, you have. And you passed. You passed in Gallipoli, old chap. This was just the final confirmation that you could get yourself dressed and turn up at the right place at the right time. Make yourself at home, have a good weekend and see you on Monday.'

Edward went back to the office, an odd mix of deflation and apprehension beginning to come over him. He looked absent-mindedly out of the window over the street below, at the city starting to shake off winter and the sun eking out its light a little longer into the late afternoon. He wondered what he was going to feel when it fully dawned on him that he wasn't going back to the battalion.

He wondered what Thorne was doing now. A sense of helplessness, of both of them being at the mercy of events incalculably greater than themselves, threatened to overwhelm him. This had never happened on the Peninsula, when, despite everything, they had always had each other. It was a yawning, gaping terror that soaked through his limbs and seemed to swell his brain. Behind him though he heard a drawer opening and the chink of glasses. Anderson had taken a bottle of whisky and a couple of tumblers from his desk. 'This is the drawer for my "secret papers". Entry is strictly *verboten*. Quick snifter? Must be six o'clock somewhere.'

CHAPTER THIRTY

That had been Edward's introduction to life at the War Office, although in truth he barely spent any time there at all over the next weeks. When he was there, his interactions with Kitchener, as it turned out, were very limited. The great man was so busy, so pulled from pillar to post, that he was hardly ever in London. Nearly all Edward's dealings were with Fitzgerald, who he came to like enormously. When Kitchener was there he kept to his office. From their fleeting interactions, Edward had the same impression he had formed of him at Suvla: that this was a man who knew that his time had probably passed. He knew he was a behemoth, but a behemoth of an age whose light was dipping below the horizon. You could see it in his bearish, lumbering gait and the large, empty eyes in the face sagging down into its jowls.

Edward's visits took him all over France and Belgium. By the end of April he had already been on half a dozen trips, travelling all around formations and units. He found that he was able to tell a good unit from a bad unit very quickly; there was not, in the end, any real nuance to it. The character and performance of a brigade, battalion, company or platoon was dictated almost solely by the character of its commander. If the leadership was good, the soldiers would be good. If the leadership was bad then, unless there were some unusually superb subordinates, the soldiers would be bad. Wherever he went, all the talk was of the big offensive and the fighting going on in Verdun. The trips lasted for a week or so at a time and then he would come back over the Channel to London and be debriefed by Fitzgerald. It was satisfying, peripatetic work that Edward found extremely rewarding.

The tension across Whitehall was turning up that spring, things coming to a head all at once. Kitchener himself often seemed a seething, schizophrenic mess. All through the spring, rumours were swirling, always with him at the centre or at the immediate periphery.

It was an open secret that at some point in the summer, before the big offensive, when all eyes would be on France, Kitchener was to be sent to Russia on a mission to meet the Tsar and to see what could be done to support the Russians against the Germans in the east. Edward was desperate to be included on it, but no one had told him any concrete details about it at all. It was all very confusing. He wondered if he had somehow inadvertently made some huge blunder in his work, or in his manner, that had deemed him unsuitable.

One morning at the very end of April, he bounded up the stairs in a sprightly manner, having jauntily returned the salutes of the guards at the entrance and swapped 'good mornings' with a few of the secretaries. He knew they had been gossiping about him ever since he had arrived, as they did about every officer in the building who they ascertained was not married. Anderson was already at his desk, as he usually was, doing *The Times* crossword and looking unusually smart and fresh, which meant he was hungover. He didn't look up from chewing his pen, just nodded over to his desk and said, 'Letter for you, old man. Looks like it's from one of your old amigos.'

Edward immediately recognised Thorne's writing. He opened it, fearing for a second it was going to be telling him about the death of either the CO or Baffle. He wasn't sure he could cope with either piece of news, but any relief that he had at that not being the case was replaced quickly by a tugging, knotting nausea that wormed down from the bottom of his craw through into his gut.

Wise Owl,

Some news you should know. I've just taken over B Company from Haynes-Mattingly, who has been arrested and is in the hands of the French police. Details hazy but the short of it is that he is accused of murdering a prostitute. The old man and I went to see him in jail yesterday. He is completely broken. I've never seen someone like it. He didn't look up at us and sat on his chair with his head bobbing up and down, mumbling to himself about the Peninsula, the flies, the line, Jacko etc. CO out of nowhere barked at him to snap out of it and he suddenly focused and explained, clear as day and with no emotion, that he was in the room with her and there was this large fly buzzing at the window, trying to get out. He couldn't stand it and so broke a chair to try to hit it, the girl tried to stop him and he just went at her. Beat her to death and only realised what he'd done when she was dead – he said he thought he was just swatting a fly. The madam arrived with some goons but it was too late. They did him over and handed him to the police, he was none too tidy I have to say, nose broken, both eyes black. But he didn't appear to be in any pain, or indeed to have any remorse. The only thing he said as we left was, 'She was a pretty little thing, I must say,' and then shot me a sly grin, as though he was just shooting a line in the mess. It still gives me shivers now. I knew he had changed over those months but didn't know how, I don't know, 'mutated' seems to be the only word, he had been by it. Or maybe he was always like this and the Peninsula just stripped away the veneer. Maybe we are all like that. I don't know. I don't really want to think about it.

So I've now got B. Unlucky sods. New chap called Deering is now adjutant; good egg thankfully. The old man is on good form, l'affaire Haynes-Mattingly notwithstanding. I think he'll swing, surely? Come and see us on one of your trips. We all miss you. Rumour is that we're going to move south soon for the big show. It's the only thing anyone can talk about. No idea where exactly but do us a favour and ask old K of Chaos to tell you so you can then tell us. And write to us. Precious little else to read here.

Theo

'Anything interesting?' asked Anderson. Edward folded the letter and put it in his drawer, taking a moment to get his thoughts in order. He smiled back. 'Not really, just an update on the chaps.'

Anderson leant back, put his leg up onto his desk and lit his pipe. 'Shame. Looking for some juicy news from the front.'

Edward's temples started to throb and his mouth was dry. 'I say, I couldn't trouble you for some of that scotch, could I?'

Anderson inspected his watch theatrically. 'Well, I suppose it's six o'clock somewhere, isn't it? Good idea.' He poured them both a generous slug and Edward, hands trembling slightly, drank it gratefully.

For the rest of the week, the letter continued to needle Edward. He desperately wanted to write back to Thorne, guilty that he hadn't done so already and had had to wait for him to make the first move, but as the hours after reading the letter turned to days, so the days turned into a couple of weeks so quickly that suddenly the chance to reply naturally was missed. The same reticence held him back from inviting himself to High Hedges too, though he knew he could, instead remaining in the mess in London over the weekends that he was in town.

He constantly agonised about what it was that compelled him to stay his hand with both siblings. When he was with them, in their immediate presence, everything was so simple and he was presented with the most generous licence to friendship that he had ever been granted. But now he was apart from them, he found himself meekly accepting the barrier of distance and shirking from trying to overcome it. Inaction was safer than action, he supposed. A dozen times a week he thought about writing to Miranda, always stepping back at the last moment from doing so. It appalled him to think that the friendships that he had worked so hard to forge would wither due to common neglect, but still he was never strong enough to address that and it ate away at him.

And then, unbearably, another letter came from Thorne a week or so later. He read it with eyes unblinking in shame at his inertia, his throat dry with embarrassment and skin tingling in the knowledge of his dereliction. Its ostensibly jocular tone was the barest veil, he knew, to deep-seated hurt, even as he laughed while reading it, imagining so clearly Thorne's face as he wrote.

To the gallant Major Salter's secretary/ boot polisher/ toast butterer/ peach peeler/ punkah wallah/ Passepartout/ drinks cabinet Ganymede,

Now look, I know he's __terribly__ busy what with meetings with the PM, champagne tastings at the Ritz, trips to the tailor to have some jolly smart red tabs sewn on to his Service Dress, that kind of thing. However, when his diary does display even so much as a chink of spare time, might you prevail upon His Excellency to deign to toss even some barest scraps of news the way of his erstwhile comrades, slogging it out amidst the grime and grey of the particularly insalubrious part of France that they infest currently. All his former partners in crime are well; we want to know that he is too, lowly of station though we are. And we want to hear about London food as a break from our rations (goodness me the rations). So come, Ganymede, unhand the decanter, strip him of his cigar, remove him from the lady's salon and thrust a pen into his idle hands if you will. We await news.

Yours, etc,

Boring old Capt. T. Thorne, 1st Bn Queen Anne's Own, Adjutant, dogsbody, misser of his pal.

Edward stood for an age, grateful that he was alone in the office. And then, unforgivably, he put the letter into his desk drawer and closed it. He just didn't know what to do, what to write, what to think.

CHAPTER THIRTY-ONE

Edward's cloying sclerosis was brought into terrible relief one evening early in May. He was in Amiens. The city was, as ever, full of British soldiers, it having become in the years since 1914 as familiar to them as any large town that most of them had known in Britain. He was in the outside seating area of a busy bar having a drink with a major from the staff who he had been briefed by earlier. He was an amusing, wry type called Emerson, keen to demonstrate his knowledge of the surrounding area in the context of British military adventurism. Edward was half listening, nodding and hmm-ing in all the right places as he scanned around the masses of soldiers in the square, wondering idly if he would see anyone that he recognised.

Emerson was rabbiting on. 'You see, you blur your eyes and this could all be another time. Chaps from Cornwall, chaps from Caithness, Carlisle, scrapping here centuries ago. Just better weapons now and probably a better class of prostitute. Well, that's debatable. The point is, all Albion ever does is scrap over this piece of land. Waterloo. Crecy. Even bloody Agincourt's not a million miles away. Basically, any time it kicks off in Europe, the French and Belgians lay out the welcome mat on this sodding piece of earth and say, "Come one, come all and have a ding-dong." And here we are back again. *Plus ça change.*'

Edward, feeling that he needed to give back something a little more substantive to the conversation, added, '*Plus c'est la même chose,*' and they both laughed archly, enjoying each other's erudition.

Then he saw him, about thirty yards away. Thorne. Or was it him? Could it be? Through the square walked a major – as he knew Thorne now was – flanked by a pair of chattering subalterns. They were walking not particularly quickly nor with any sense of urgency or direction, on the same evening meander that a hundred others were taking. Could it really be him? He knew that the battalion and its higher brigade weren't far from Amiens and that most officers took any chance they could to get away into town for drinks and dinner when off the line.

His mind flashed back to the Peninsula and how they would have killed for such a chance of respite from the front. As they came closer Edward recognised the collar dogs of Queen Anne's Own on their uniforms. It *was* Thorne. It felt remarkable seeing him like this, so close but at a remove, as a silent spectator. At one split second it seemed an appalling invasion of his privacy, at another it felt as though Edward was his invisible guardian, looking on his beloved friend with a god's benign watchfulness.

He ignored whatever Emerson was talking about, fixing his eyes on Thorne, not wanting to look away and desperate to get up and say hello. His brain couldn't even begin to compute the emotions pulsing through it in those freighted, tortured seconds. He was hurt at how natural and at ease Thorne looked without him. Where was he off to? Drinks or dinner? Who were his new companions? They must be from the tranche who had joined the battalion only recently, before they set off to France. How had they made friends with Thorne so quickly? But of course it was easy; he remembered how easy they had been with each other after mere days. The memory of how resentful Thorne had been to him after his accident came and kept him in his trance, his muscles stuck on his chair. Then the ghastly, withering memory of the two unanswered letters also pinned him down with gnawing embarrassment. Then his mind cleared and all he wanted to do was stand up and greet him, to hug him and to lose himself immediately in their own old chatter.

But he didn't get up. Every second that Thorne came closer meant that it was one second later than he should have got up to greet him and another second's nail into their friendship. A dread came over him that Thorne would see him and realise that Edward had prevaricated. He was only five yards away now, smiling at a story that one of the others was telling. There was no way he wouldn't see him; Edward felt as though he was out in the open in No Man's Land and lit up by a star shell. The activity in the square around them blurred. The only thing of any clarity was Thorne. Closer and closer he got. If he tried he could reach out over the little line of shrubs that enclosed the bar's tables and touch him on the forearm.

And then he passed. Immediately Edward wanted to shout, to chase after him, mortified that he had let him slip. He made to stand up, just as Emerson tapped his ankle with his boot under the table.

'Sorry, old chap, am I boring you?'

Edward looked back to him, flustered, and mumbled an apology.

'Sorry, no. Just . . . Just I thought I saw someone. Sorry. I'm sorry. I must go. I have to go.'

He looked back to pick out Thorne again but the trio had dissolved into the crowd. He got up and left, clattering awkwardly into the table as he did so, with Emerson sitting puzzled and affronted. He bowled out through the seating area, losing precious time navigating the tables with a dozen sorrys and excuse-mes. People were laughing at him.

'Someone's had too much!'

'Can't take his drink.'

Finally he was free and he strode into the square, breaking into a run. 'Theo. Theo!' he called. People turned to look at him, jeering and whispering in embarrassment. But Thorne was nowhere to be seen. Gone. He felt empty, sick at heart. A line from schooldays came back to him and bounced round his head. *We have left undone those things which we ought to have done; And we have done those things which we ought not to have done; And there is no health in us.* He played it again and again. *Left undone. Left undone. Left undone.*

For twenty more minutes he walked round the square and the alleys that shot off from it, searching for Thorne. At one point he began to cry. Crying from frustration, crying over the missed chance of seeing his best friend. Crying for the shame of having denied him and let him down. Worst of all, crying at the thought that he might never have the chance to see him again. He sat down in a doorway and composed himself. Deep breath. *Get a hold of yourself, man.* Slowly he came back from his hysteria.

Left undone.

Defeated, he returned to the bar where he found that Emerson had given up on him and their table was now taken by three Service Corps lieutenants. He turned back to his hotel.

He had completely blown it.

CHAPTER THIRTY-TWO

A few days later, and back in the office, Edward was finally making some progress with the report he was writing, having spent the first thirty minutes of the day away mulling once again his betrayal of Thorne, a crime that only grew in his mind as the days passed by. Jean the clerk knocked on the door, came in without waiting for an answer and said, 'Major Salter, Colonel Fitzgerald's office please,' followed by a smile that could melt icebergs.

Anderson didn't look up from his desk. 'Well, go on, trot along and see what new lunacy they have planned for you.'

At Fitz's office Edward knocked, waited for the invitation to enter and walked in. Fitz was head down at his desk and flicked his non-writing hand at the chair opposite him. 'Apologies, Salter,' he said, 'in the middle of this frantic spat and I have to get this reply off by ten thirty.' He had an extraordinary ability to write at pace and yet seemingly give all his attention to whomever he was talking to. 'Got some good news for you. Finally you're going to find your metier. This Russian trip. You're on it.'

A jolt, excitement mixed with fear, went through Edward.

Fitz went on. 'For God's sake keep it under your hat, though I dare say half of bloody London knows already. We're going to go from Orkney up past Norway and to Murmansk. Thence to Petersburg, or Petrograd, or whatever bloody name they call it now. All I can say is thank goodness it's in June and not January.'

He paused for a moment. 'Quite poignant for you really, Salter. Tried and failed to break into the belly of Russia via the Dardanelles and here you are going at it from the north. I just hope you have some more luck this time, for all our sakes. What do you reckon?'

Edward stomach shifted. 'Well, that sounds fantastic, sir, but what do I do once we're there?'

'Oh the usual. Just what you've been doing. Pick up peripheral noise. Try to see what's going on away from the visit. The embassy staff can't do that; they're watched the entire time by the Okhrana. K and I won't be able to do that, as we'll be constantly met by bigwigs trained to tell us exactly nothing of importance. But a major on the edge of our party? You've every excuse in the world to get lost and go for a wander. Get around, meet people. Tell us everything.'

Fitzgerald went on. 'Be back here a week on Thursday. We'll be going around then. In the meantime, get back out to France. Between you, me and that hatstand, when we get back from Russia there isn't going to be an awful lot of time before the big push. You didn't hear this from me, Salter, but can you let us know how it's all going around Albert?'

'Yes, sir. I know it already. Swung through there a couple of times.'

'Good. Just get us the atmospherics, what the line is like. What the boys are like. What the new ones are like. Meet me back here next Friday, second of June at midday.'

Edward's hands felt clammy and sweat filmed the back of his neck. It felt as though things were slipping away from his grasp and while he hoped that this feeling of helplessness didn't show, in truth Fitzgerald also had the air of a man who didn't look as though he was entirely in control either. After a short while he nodded and simply said, 'Yes, sir. Understood. A week on Friday. Midday.'

'Good man.' He carried on his writing and Edward turned to leave. At the door Fitzgerald added, 'And Salter?'

'Sir?'

'I mean it. Don't tell anyone.' An anxiety came over his usually cheerful voice. 'This place is as leaky as a sieve. And even if it wasn't, Downing Street is. So word's doubtless already out. But still, not a word to anyone. Understood? Not even to Anderson.'

Edward knew by now how to handle Fitzgerald and when he could banter with him; this was not one of those times. 'Of course not, sir. I'll see you in ten days.'

'Good man. Safe travels.' Edward left and a few seconds later a muffled shout boomed from the office. 'And keep your bloody head down.'

CHAPTER THIRTY-THREE

May in northern France. Marching, everywhere was marching. Every day saw the sun rise yet higher above the plateau between Paris and the Channel coast, the landscape formed by wave on wave of shallow, broad, flat-topped rises stretching into the distance and over the milky horizon. The bare valleys offered no shelter from the sun as it beat down on the chalk. Dust hung in low clouds on the ridgelines, thrown up by vast numbers of boots. The men soldiered on, sometimes cheerful, other times resentful and tired, the miles softening their boots' leather and deepening their creases, bare necks bronzing underneath the sun, in stark contrast to the alabaster-white torsos, visible when the columns stopped to bathe in the pools of a stream. Only the occasional rainstorm brought the land relief, briefly slickening its top to mud, only for it to be baked hard again just hours afterwards.

Edward scoured all around the rear areas, watching and talking. Troops on the approach to Albert sleeping outside a barn as lambs were being born within, drunk men pouring out of bars, a group of staff officers drinking dainty glasses of wine outside a tiny estaminet, red and white tablecloth fluttering in the breeze as their car sat underneath the rustling trees of a village square. Endless trickles of wounded and dead being brought back from the line on a London bus requisitioned for that purpose, its metal floor permanently stained by the blood which coagulated into an ooze in the corrugated grooves, thick, black and viscous. Great processions of artillery pieces led by magnificent horses, resplendent in their shiny black coats in the morning and in the evening white as ghosts with dust and chalk glued to their sweat. The guns and limbers clanking and jingling as a thousand hooves hammered into the ground and shook it for acres around. But more than any of these, Edward's abiding memory of those days in mid-May was the pale battalions of the millions, blurring past so that they became mouthless, faceless, the individuals smeared into those around them to become one great long line of soldiery.

Near the end of the trip, he had a couple of hours in Amiens. He didn't like being there, freighted as it was with the awful moment of missing Thorne. He was walking through the main square with the brigade major who was hosting his latest visit, a smart, somewhat aloof hussar called Shepherd. As he looked at the spread of soldiers around them he blurred the periphery of his vision in a bid to stop replaying the whole wretched scene, finally concentrating only on the ground in front of him. To escape from his addled mind, on the spur of the moment he asked Shepherd if he knew about what had happened with Haynes-Mattingly.

'Gosh yes. Frightful hullaballoo about all that. Division are engaged in all sorts of wrangling to get him out of there so he can be tried by us in a court martial. Hell of a process. Know him, d'you? I say, did K ask about all this?' he added at the end, suddenly looking fearful.

'No. I served with him on the Peninsula. At Gallipoli,' he added, seeing Shepherd's face vacant. 'We were company commanders together.'

'I see. Friend of yours?' The way Shepherd asked him seemed to imply that he thought Edward might not only have some sympathy for him but share his enthusiasms.

'God, no. Well, we started out as friends, but then he seemed to grow detached from reality. He was the one of all of us who just seemed to enjoy it more and more. I've seen people enjoy fighting, goodness knows when you're in the moment it's an extraordinary thrill—' he noted from Shepherd's face that he didn't know what he was talking about '—but I've never seen someone have such a, I don't know, a lust for it. We became ever more distant, really. We didn't really have a word to say to each other by the end, if I'm honest.'

'He's allowed visitors.' Shepherd left the follow-up question in the air unanswered.

Edward hadn't expected this, and very nearly replied yes, shaking off the past year and thinking back to when they had been on the boat out to Malta as platoon commanders. He remembered how funny Bruce could be, how he had made them all laugh, how his nonchalance had acted as a boost for them all especially in the frantic first days. But then he remembered everything else and imagined the scene in the room with the girl for the thousandth time. He replied firmly but cheerfully, as though declining an invitation to afternoon tea, 'Thank you, but no. Perhaps at another time. I think I had best be off.' He got into the car. They both knew there would never be another time.

In the car he thought again about Haynes-Mattingly and the time that he had dragged the wounded Williamson up to the parapet when they were attacking the blind crests only to see him shot in the head. What he had said next played again and again in his head: 'Waste of fucking flesh'. *How could you say that?* Again a guilt hit him, this time that Thorne should have been exposed to his evil, for that was what it had become, no matter the reasons for it, and that he, Edward, wasn't there to shield him from it. *He* should have been dealing with the wretched case, not Thorne. The thought of him at High Hedges when they had been reunited during leave and how his youth had surprised him when he had appeared dressed like a student. Why was that boy having to deal with something like this? What Miranda had said to him on the roof also came to him, how having Edward there was like seeing what it would be like to have an older brother. The swell of pride, of belonging, of the recognition of a deep, feral attachment that came from that memory was quickly gainsaid by a repeat of the coaxing, nagging knowledge that he had failed Thorne since and was still failing him. Some brother. Some friend.

CHAPTER THIRTY-FOUR

London was in turmoil, news still filtering back in about the great naval clash at Jutland. Rumours advanced in pockets of conversation all over the streets that first the navy's Grand Fleet, and then the German fleet, had been destroyed as Edward made his way from the boat train to the War Office. Inside the building the atmosphere was even more frenzied than he expected. He was relieved to see that Anderson was the only person in the capital unmoved by the chaos.

'What the hell's happening, Mark? Are the Germans about to invade?'

'Ha, not quite, old chap, though the bloody carry-on round here is pathetic.' He looked at his watch. 'I say, do you fancy a spot of lunch?'

Edward looked hesitant and Anderson reassured him, 'Oh, don't worry, K and Fitz won't be back for a while.'

'Why not. Six o'clock somewhere, isn't it?'

'That's the spirit. Want a debrief from you, if I may.'

They left the office and went down to the Embankment and underneath the back of Charing Cross station to Gordon's Wine Bar, eschewing the dark and dank interior for one of the outside tables, and ordered ham sandwiches and a bottle of wine.

Edward decided to broach a question he hadn't yet had the gall to ask. 'So what's he like then? K, I mean.'

Anderson leant back in his chair and blew out his cigarette

smoke exaggeratedly. 'There's a question. I mean, where do you begin?' He stayed in the position, looking into the air, like a school prefect who had just been asked something by a younger boy and was enjoying the feeling of omniscience.

'Well look. Here's a man who has had more ink spilled over him than I've ever poured bathwater. There's a million and one men in this man's army that can talk on him. Half the chaps in the War Office have served under him at one time or other. Sudan, Egypt, South Africa, India. I mean the man has traversed the globe in a way no one's ever done since Alexander the bloody Great. Look, I don't know. He's . . . strange. That's the word I would use. Not that that's a crime, mind you. The odder the better, as far as I'm concerned. But he is strange, that's for sure. Look, I don't really know K from Adam, to be honest, but there was this quite funny time earlier this year.'

He leant forward again, bringing the front legs of his chair down with a crash, and poured himself another glass of wine, relishing being a raconteur.

'You know the Beefsteak Club?'

Edward didn't, but nodded in a way that he thought would convey that he did.

Anderson saw through it. 'This lunch place just above Trafalgar Square, Irving Street. Bloody good fun. I've been a member for a year or so. There's just one long table and so you sit next to whomever's there when you arrive. Anyway, one Friday a few months ago I snuck out of work and went to go and meet a pal from the Coldstream there. The grub's decent and the vino flows and we were getting started when who should walk in but bloody K. The table's full of politicians and journalists and the whole room stiffens a bit. His face is like thunder, as though he's about to pack the whole bloody room off to Belgium for daring to have a good time, but then he breaks into this enormous grin, orders a large gin and sits down and gets stuck in like he's one of the chaps. Never seen him so relaxed. Stays there for two hours at least, listening to everyone's stories and chipping in now and again, spinning some lines about Sudan. Then he just gets up, fixes me with those sniper rifle eyes of his and says, "Have a good weekend, Marco—" never called me Marco before or since "—Don't do anything I wouldn't do. See you on Monday," and just buggers off. On the Monday morning he was in a foul mood, as though it had never happened. As I said, damned strange man, but I like him.'

Anderson stubbed out his old cigarette and lit a new one, making the moment an apt place to change the subject and said, 'So what do you reckon about the big push then?'

Edward exhaled and leant back, running his hands back through his hair. 'I don't know. I just don't know. I mean, the men are ready. Well, they're as ready as they'll ever be. It's just that, wherever they attack, they're going to face exactly the same problem as we did, as everyone is: attacking a well-established defence. I mean, good luck to them and the artillery part of the game is vastly more impressive than we had, which will help, but I still can't help thinking that if it's a decisive breakthrough they want then they're going to be disappointed.'

Anderson nodded, 'Well, that's exactly it. I don't think they do want one.'

'What do you mean?'

'Oh, don't worry, it's not some kind of conspiracy. They want a crucible. They want a British Verdun. They know the chance of some kind of rapier blow opening up the heart of the line and offering us a scalpel's route into Berlin is never going to happen, but what we can do is to inflict such a massive trauma on them that leaves a bruise that festers and suppurates into a gangrenous lump from which the patient will never recover.'

'Lovely image.'

'Thank you. Quite like it myself. Well, we'll see. My prediction is that it's going to be just like jolly jack tar at this Jutland insanity.' He tipped his head back towards a newspaper boy yelling hoarse updates from the battle. 'Inconclusive, confusing, draining. But probably, in the end, worthwhile.'

They lapsed into silence. The waiter appeared and they paid up.

'Shall we?' said Anderson.

As they walked back to the War Office, Anderson asked, 'So what are you going to tell K? Everything you've told me?'

'Yes, don't see why not. The brief from Fitz was to give him the unvarnished truth.'

'Good lad.'

'He'll be all right, won't he?'

'How do you mean?'

'I don't know. How he keeps on being marginalised, how he just seems yesterday's man.'

'That's the thing old man. Knives are out for him all over the place and the only person keeping him there is the PM. With old K he's invested so much personally but he now thinks that he's become an embarrassment for him. That's why he keeps on inventing these trips to get rid of him. You know when he came out to visit your rabble at Gallipoli the whole idea was that he'd catch the eastern bug again and stay out there for the duration, maybe take up the reins in Egypt for a second time. They were devastated when he came back. That's the whole thing about this Russia mission. When are you lot leaving for that one?'

Edward didn't know how to respond, remembering Fitzgerald's warning about not telling anyone. Surely though Anderson was OK. Still, he decided to play it straight, feeling awkward at having to behave like this with him. 'News to me. What's that about?'

'You going with K and Fitz,' Anderson pressed. 'Toss it up in St Petersburg for a bit. Sounds rather jolly.'

'Not heard a thing about it, I'm afraid. Does sound fun, though heaven knows why they'd take me.'

Anderson drew to a halt abruptly. 'Well said, old chap. Good to hear.' He reached inside the pocket of his service dress jacket and drew out an envelope, unmarked, buff and crisp. 'For you.' He nodded at it. 'Go on.'

Edward opened it and took out a cream letter, written in Fitzgerald's customary fastidiously small text. 'Salter. If you've read this you've passed the test. Anderson knows all about the Russian trip. Please come down to Broome Park tomorrow afternoon to debrief the field marshal and then we go on Sunday. Pack your bags; quick turnaround for you, I'm afraid. Fitzgerald.'

Anderson grinned and patted him on the back. '*Bon voyage*, old man. Pack your woollies if I were you.'

CHAPTER THIRTY-FIVE

Late afternoon the next day, the car left the War Office and made good speed down the empty Saturday Whitehall to cross Westminster Bridge, the river in its plump pomp, the breeze hurling little waves against the Embankment. Edward soon fell asleep and woke up in the dark in a different world. Looking at his watch it was only six o'clock, and as his eyes adjusted better he realised that they were driving through a deep wood, so dark that it had the effect of night. Gradually, light pierced the gaps in the fringes of the woodland and they emerged into the evening.

'Nearly there,' the driver, Coombe, called through. 'I tapped on the brake a couple of times to wake you up.'

Soon after, they turned into the driveway of Broome Park, a couple of sentries on the gate recognising Coombe and waving him straight through. Ahead up the drive lay the house and Edward drew in a breath when he saw it, huge and immaculate.

Coombe chuckled in the front. 'That's what everyone does when they first see it. Not a bad little place, is it?'

'It's . . . it's marvellous.' The car rolled up to the front of the house and braked softly. Edward climbed out and looked up at the edifice, the three-sided square improbably tall with one more floor than the proportions needed but somehow pulling it off. High, thin, mullioned windows streaked up and added to its sense of height. There was nobody about, Coombe having disappeared wordlessly. Edward, a little nonplussed, stood before the house and tried to drink in the details of the edifice.

He didn't feel as though he could just walk straight in through the front door, grandly jutting out of the recessed middle of the house in a cubed portico, flanked by Corinthian pilasters. Maybe there was another, less formal entrance round the side. He wondered if the field marshal was inside the house, imagining him at a vast desk in a wood-panelled room with an enormous map of the Western Front laid out before him, mementoes and souvenirs from his campaigns hung on the walls, tiger skins strewn on the floor. He walked round the eastern side, now in the shade as the sun tipped towards evening proper. The scrunch of gravel, tiny and grainy beneath his boots provided the only sound as he trod round the corner to find the ground before him fall away into a sunken rose garden, spots of pinks and reds and the occasional blue studding the heavy, golden air.

Then, from a corner, there was a flash of cream as a man stood up, his torso split into a Y by a pair of braces. Edward didn't want to disturb the sense of peace by calling out to him and so walked gingerly down the shallow steps into the garden. The gardener was kneeling over again now, straw sun hat on, stabbing away at the base of a rose bush with a trowel. Edward halted ten yards away and said, 'I don't suppose you could help me with some directions, could you? I wonder where I might find the field marshal.'

'Right in front of you, old chap,' said the gardener, who stood up and turned in a swift, lithe movement that seemed totally beyond his circus strongman's trunk. He took his hat off and used a red handkerchief from his pocket to wipe sweat from his huge brow. 'Tip I learned in the Franco-Prussian war. Always carry a handkerchief, but just make damned sure it's not a white one. Can cause all sorts of misunderstandings on the battlefield, that.'

Edward stiffened and saluted and then, trying to appear at ease with this bizarre encounter, added, 'Unless you wanted to surrender or negotiate, my Lord?'

Kitchener adopted a look of mock horror on his face. 'But why in hell's name would you be doing that? Here, Salter, you must be parched. I certainly am.' He nodded to a tray on the grass with a jug and glass on it. 'You have the glass,' he said, filling it with the cloudy liquid, so cold that the glass started sweating immediately. Kitchener then drew heavily from the jug itself like some kind of Falstaffian trencherman, while Edward sipped from his glass like a maiden aunt to find that it was orange cordial and extremely refreshing.

He took a moment to appraise the oddness of the situation, drinking cordial in the garden of this amazing, almost monstrous house with the most powerful man in the Empire, surrounded only by roses and the low humming of bees.

Kitchener brought his handkerchief to his brow again and then his huge forearms, bigger than Edward's biceps, folded it to tie round his neck. On the inside of his forearm there was a distinct tattoo, a fleur-de-lys about the size of a large coin. Edward must have looked surprised, as Kitchener smiled and said, 'Oh, that. Another relic from the Prussian war. Had a hell of a time there, tell you. Learned a lot though. Luckily they thought I was all right as I'd picked up the lingo at school in Switzerland. I got the insignia of the regiment who hosted me as a tribute to them. Put my initials underneath.' He paused. 'And here we are, decades later and armies at loggerheads in virtually the same part of Europe again. So much for progress, eh?' He smiled but his eyes were only half joking.

He changed the subject. 'You came to tell me how my armies are.'

'Yes, sir, full report's in here.' Edward motioned to his attaché case.

Kitchener reached forward and took the whole thing from

him, not waiting for him to open it to hand him the report and said, 'Christ, I'll leave all this with Fitz. He'll wade through the bumph. But come on, what's the thrust of it?'

In the gap that hung between them as Edward readied his answer, still trying to work out if he should say anything about his attaché case being snatched wholesale from him. He thought he heard something; perhaps the rumble of distant thunder, although the air was fresh. They had to be too far inland to hear them here, surely, but still he swore that from the far distance came a low growl, rolling away in the background. In his imagination guns in Belgium rained down misery, while a sea and a world away here the same noise provided merely a stirring, almost reassuring low bass hum.

'They'll be all right, sir. They're as ready as they'll ever be. They won't break, that's for sure.'

Kitchener didn't answer and Edward went on. 'Do you think you'll get out and see them when we get back from Russia? They'd love to see you.'

'Russia?' Kitchener looked surprised, his tone suggesting Edward was mad.

'Yes, sir. We go tomorrow, don't we?' Edward answered, confused, thinking the old man was going senile.

'No we bloody well do not. Who the hell said that you were coming?'

'Er, Fitz, er, Colonel Fitzgerald did, sir.'

As if on cue Fitz appeared at the edge of the sunken rose garden, wearing slacks and a dark-blue shirt like a writer, smiling a greeting at Edward and then stiffening as Kitchener turned his wrath onto him.

'Who the hell invited Salter on the Russian trip? No, Fitz, no. No, no, no. The world and his damned wife are coming on it, it seems. Every spy from here to Berlin will know about it. It's grown so many arms and legs, this trip, it's like we're bloody invading the place. No. No. No. No. I will not have it.' He threw down his trowel, stood up and stormed off, leaving Edward standing bright red, shocked.

Fitz hurried over. 'Goodness, I'm so sorry, old chap. He does know all about you coming; he was the one who suggested it. Sorry, he can be quite bloody impossible sometimes. Give me ten minutes. Let me see what I can do.' He hurried off.

Edward, plunged back into the quiet of the rose garden after the violence of Kitchener's rage, felt completely stung. He walked around the garden, butterflies and bees flitting in and around the petals and the spears of late sun that made it through the trees. Eventually he recovered his pulse rate and pace of his breath, the mucky sweat that had welled up on his brow now dry. He walked back to the front of the house and the car. With nothing better to do he climbed back into the back seat, feeling like a child who had been expelled from a birthday party. After a while Fitz came round the side of the house, looking acutely embarrassed. Edward got out and they faced each other awkwardly over the bonnet.

'Look, I'm sorry, old chap. He's having none of it, being quite impossible. I have no idea what's come over him. What did you say to him?'

'Nothing!' Edward held his hands up. 'I was just going over the state of things in France and then mentioned that I was coming on the Russia trip with you.'

Fitz locked his forehead into furrows. 'Well, there's nothing for it, I'm afraid. We're too close to going. If we were off on Wednesday or something then I could shift him. But he just won't budge. He's right, in a way the whole thing is a bit of a circus. But you'd have been a hell of a lot more use than some of the others. I'm sorry, Salter.'

Edward could see the genuine contrition in Fitz's face; he knew he had done his best.

'So what now?'

'Here's what you do. K will calm down, I'm sure of it. Pound to a pinch of salt when we're halfway to Murmansk, or whatever godforsaken town the navy are taking us to, he'll call me into his cabin looking like an old dog and mumble how he thought he was too hard on you. Whereupon he'll then ask how he can make it up to you. I know you think he should visit France before it all kicks off in July; get out there again, will you, and start scoping a visit for him? Then when we get back from Russia we can nip over. Will do him good to see some soldiers again. How does that sound?'

Edward had unconsciously cheered up a little as Fitz was speaking; no wonder, he thought, that he had such a prized reputation across Whitehall as a diplomat, or as Anderson called him 'a prize de-ruffler of feathers'.

'Yes. All right, that sounds a good plan.'

'Good man. Get back out there and start forming a visit. I hope we're back with you in the twenties of June. That's if we ever escape Russia, mind you. Right, I'd better go and digest your epic tome.' He took out the papers from the attaché case and then handed it back over to Edward. 'Sorry. He spends his entire time going round picking things up that aren't his and then forgetting that they're not. Gets him into a hell of a lot of awkward situations. Or, rather, gets me into them.'

Coombe appeared then at the door, surprised to see them both there. 'Ah, Coombe. Major Salter is leaving us. Be a sport and get him up to London, will you?'

Edward saluted and said, 'Thank you, Colonel. Safe trip. See you in a few weeks.'

'Thanks, old man.' Fitz opened the door and then shut it after him, leaning down and saying through the open window, 'And remember, keep your bloody head down.'

Edward smiled as Coombe then glided away, the tyres crunching pleasingly on the gravel. He looked back out the rear window as Fitz remained there waving at him until the car took a bend in the drive and the house disappeared.

CHAPTER THIRTY-SIX

Edward got the boat train on Monday morning, wondering where Kitchener, Fitz and the rest of their party would be by now; surely well north of Edinburgh. He was still adjusting to the disappointment of not being included on the trip, feeling sluggish and bored at the prospect of yet more visits to units and headquarters. The hurt he had felt at being so loudly and forthrightly barred by Kitchener still keened. He found that, not for the first time that summer, he missed the simplicity and uncomplicated routine of battalion life, where no matter how difficult, boring or absurd things became at least there was always someone nearby to share a joke with. He wondered how Fitz managed to put up with it.

He got a car down to Amiens where he spent the night in one of the divisional headquarters, sleeping soundly after an unexpectedly convivial night drinking with some majors on the staff there.

Amiens again though. This wretched town and its constant associations with Thorne. He knew that he would be on the line with the battalion near Arras to the north, so there was no chance of seeing him, but the very bricks of the place haunted him with his inaction and what he had done to their friendship, or rather what he hadn't done. A hundred times in his daydreams he had created various scripts for when they were reunited, cut differently according to the time of day, who else might be around, what the weather was like, whether they met in the rear or in the line, each scenario planned and choreographed down to the manner in which Edward would offer him a cigarette, or how he himself would display gratitude by raising his eyebrows upon being given a light by Thorne. How they would shake hands. Perhaps even embrace. He lost himself in these imaginings, allowing himself to fall back into the joy of the friendship unharried for a tiny moment by the knowledge that none of it was real. Soon, he vowed. Soon he would see to it.

The next day, he did his customary digging around but without the same thoroughness or zeal as he had before, still resentful of the chewing out that he had. That night he went to bed early, dog-tired but in the end unable to sleep for quite a while, the rumble of the guns in the background of the night now definite in comparison to their remoteness in the quiet of Kitchener's garden.

Wednesday dawned bright and he moved on in mid-morning, requisitioning a car and driver from the motor pool and heading north-eastwards in the direction of Albert. Even by the outskirts of Amiens it was clear that the car was having problems and despite the attentions of the driver, a chirpy, cheerful head waiter type from the Service Corps called Robinson, they could never manage more than a couple of miles before something else went wrong with it. The fourth time Robinson had to open the hood, it was clear that it had packed in completely. Edward cursed; they should have called it a day when the first noises had come from the engine. Now they had dragged the vehicle so far on that they were marooned.

Robinson, not to be deterred, shrugged and said, 'Oh well. Shanks's pony for me then. I'll get back to the depot and get a fix sent out. Shouldn't be more than three hours, I imagine. You wouldn't mind guarding the motor, would you, sir?' Edward felt a little awkward, thinking for a moment that he should be the one doing the hard work before realising that he had absolutely no idea what was wrong with the car and so would be unable to convey what was needed to get them moving again. Come to think of it, the idea of an afternoon on his own in the sun was not unappealing. 'All right then. Thanks Robinson. Good stuff.'

Robinson took his leave and set off back down the straight road. Edward lay down on the grass, contentedly looking up at the vault above him. He dozed off for a little while before he was woken by the steady beat of vibrations. Sitting up and adjusting his loosened jacket and tie he saw the first of what became dozens of columns that passed him that afternoon, troops taking the same route as them up to the area behind Albert in preparation for the push. Occasionally he would hear a jibe or jeer aimed his way by soldiers mocking his red tabs and broken-down situation and he couldn't help but smile back; he would have been doing exactly the same in their position.

All that long afternoon the road teemed with streams of marching men. Edward became transfixed; never had he seen such a sheer mass. It was almost grotesque, like watching a beehive being swarmed over for too long. He remembered the flies at Gallipoli and his stomach turned further.

At nine o'clock, just as the evening hinted at turning into night, he noticed something, a shift in attitude amongst those on the road, an alertness as they walked quicker and more stiffly, stepping out of the easy trudge that had been there during the day and with murmuring and chatter replacing songs. Then a truck appeared and an Engineer lieutenant jumped out, holding a newspaper. Robinson got out too with the truck driver and went straight to the engine. The officer, who looked in his late teens, approached Edward with some trepidation, blustering an apology for the delay in getting to him and then handed over the newspaper, a copy of that day's *Times*. 'This just arrived at our HQ, sir. One of the chaps came over on the boat train today with a few copies. They got him. The bastards got him.'

'Who?'

'Lord Kitchener. Killed by a mine in his ship, off to Russia for some bloody reason.'

'What?' Edward snatched the paper from him.

'It's page ten I think, sir.'

Edward rustled through, fingers and thumbs, unable to get to it and shaking. Eventually he found it. There it was, in all its starkness, the words tumbling from the page in fractured clauses: '*Lost in sunken cruiser; a mission to Russia; no lives saved; possibility of spying;* Hampshire *with Lord Kitchener and his staff on board was sunk to the west of the Orkneys, whether by a mine or a torpedo; only some bodies and a capsized boat have been found up to the present; the western coast of the islands presents to the Atlantic an inhospitable front of high, rugged cliffs; we shall ne'er look upon his like again; the villain hand of Death has struck at him; John Bull personified . . .*'

There was Fitz's name listed amongst the party, with civil servants, diplomats and other officers. Near the bottom of the page was a note on Fitz's own life. 'Possessed of great tact and charm, a level head and no little business capacity, he rapidly proved himself the ideal occupant of a delicate and difficult position.'

His time in the rose garden with Kitchener, now exactly four days past, felt as though it had been an hour ago. He could still smell the full air, warm with bees and butterflies. He could see the fleur-de-lys tattoo on Kitchener's forearm, the jug of cordial with its beads of condensation. And now that body was somewhere under the water of the North Atlantic and had been for two days already.

He could only imagine the panic currently going on in London, with the fallout from Jutland and the preparations for the push now undercut totally by this news. He thought of Fitz's empty office, normally the quiet centre of the vast spinning wheel when things like this happened, now unmanned.

'Are you all right, sir?' The sapper officer was asking him questions; he could hear them but they were disembodied, as though he was in another room. His legs started shaking and he sat down, unable to process anything any more. He didn't know what to do, just sitting there open mouthed.

Trying to concentrate, he folded the newspaper carefully, placed it on the grass and looked ahead into the distance. He put his hands up to rub his temples, moving them gradually round his forehead to his eye sockets and then to the bridge of his nose, where they met and stayed for he didn't know how long. Scores of images came to harrow his brain: the panic on the ship as it sank in the freezing water, the rough sea, the mass of men in the water. A fate that was to have been his but for Kitchener having his tantrum a few evenings ago.

He dry retched at the thought of his missed death, one so unlike that for which he had steeled himself on the Peninsula. He imagined Fitz's thin frame, his limbs like flower stems, trying in vain to survive in those waters. How bravely he would have faced his end. He thought of the field marshal, for so long imperious in his own universe, his puffed up majesty rendered so pathetic, so laughable in the face of the elemental. He thought of the reaction in London, in Whitehall, in Downing Street, across the country, in the line, across the Empire. The keystone was gone.

And if he was gone then where was he, Edward? He was now, technically, ownerless. Definitely jobless. Completely rudderless. All of a sudden then his brain cleared, the field in front of him opening up in a glorious second. He stood up, galvanised, and looked around. Only Robinson was there, the sapper having left without saying goodbye, obviously not wanting to disturb him in his state.

Robinson smiled. 'Where to, sir? Albert still?'

'No. Do you think we can get to Arras tonight?'

Robinson frowned as his brain chewed through its gears. 'Don't see why not, sir. If she doesn't pack in again, that is.'

'Good man. Let's go. And don't spare the horses.' They walked over to the car, got in and drove off, not seeing the faint breeze pick up the corners of the discarded newspaper and flutter the pages to billow out apart from each other and drift over the fields and into the evening, the car now far down the road.

He needed to get back to the battalion, feeling a primal urge to be amongst friends again, in the only place he could really now call home. Most of all, though, he needed to see Thorne. That base imperative, to clear the air with his best friend and to seize back what he had so awfully let slip away, charged his body with such energy that there was no chance of sleep as the car glided through summer's almost night, the waxing crescent moon setting the road before them as a silver-grey ribbon, the peace punctured occasionally by the ripple of guns flashing in the east. They passed countless grey shapes of men, stretched out sleeping on the ground, their bodies forming hillocks and blurred by their blankets giving each one the appearance of a newly dug grave. Robinson took the route unerringly and they arrived at the divisional HQ at four in the morning.

CHAPTER THIRTY-SEVEN

They were directed to the brigade in a village just to the north of Arras, where Edward told the exhausted Robinson to get some sleep. He himself, having been told where the battalion was by the brigade major, went forward to cover the mile by foot, the day waking up around him. He felt inordinately happy as he walked through the calm, settled greenery around him, heading towards the war as though strolling to work one morning.

The battalion was in reserve, having come back from the line two days previously, and HQ was in an old farmhouse. The house was still largely intact, save for the wall round its kitchen garden, which had been blown apart by a shell. The windows sat in the walls like missing teeth, with their panes punched out and mattresses put up behind them. There was more activity here than there had been at brigade although he did not recognise the men he saw running about. At the door to the farmhouse was a bowling ball of a lance corporal who made a half-hearted effort at a salute and, divining from Edward's red tabs that there was only one person he might reasonably want to see said, 'Commanding officer's inside, sir. Second on the right.'

Edward slowed to a walk through the door into the dank hall, trying to gather himself. He walked over the gnarled floorboards, their grainy surfaces long shorn of any polish. Through the gap in the door he could see the CO standing over a map board, running his hand through his hair. He felt a lump in his throat at seeing him again, such a sparrow-like, fragile man who had brought them all through Gallipoli and was now yet again at the front of some other fight. He took a few breaths before knocking.

'Come.'

Edward stepped straight in.

The CO looked up and surprised Edward by looking shocked at this interruption, before his eyes softened and he smiled and said gently, 'Salter. How nice to see you.' He flicked his eyes over to a copy of *The Times* folded on the edge of the map board. 'I was terribly worried you'd been caught up in this *Hampshire* business.'

'No, sir. Bloody lucky escape. I wasn't needed on the Russian expedition. I was quite put out at the time at being left out, I must say, but it appears now I've rather dodged a bullet.'

'I'll say. Not sure swimming off Orkney is something I'd recommend. Well, I'm sure they'll find someone else to take over the War Office.'

A pause hung after Edward had finished the polite acknowledging laugh and the CO shifted awkwardly and looked back to the map board. He had thought that he would be more welcoming. Something was wrong. He couldn't be resentful about Edward having been away, could he? Still with his back to him he spoke, and as he said it Edward's skin itched with dread at what he knew was coming, 'Take a seat will you, old chap?'

He motioned to a couple of ancient wooden chairs in front of a window that looked out onto the garden. Dry-mouthed, Edward took an age to sit down, hoping to delay even by a couple of seconds the news going into his ears. The CO took his glasses off, put them on the low table between them and leant back, scratching his head with both hands and then massaging his neck. He looked devastated.

'I'll cut to the chase. He'll live, but it's terribly bad news. Damnable business. Blinded, I'm afraid.'

Edward heard himself ask, 'How did it happen sir? When?

Where is he now?' knowing that his body was going through the mechanics of formality for him, like a wind-up toy, while his brain was succubated by a thousand thoughts, by despair and pain dancing around his skull like the reflection of water on the underside of a bridge. Part of him still managed to take in the CO's words as he went on. 'He was damned good as company commander, you know. Very, very good. As good as you were. Different to you, but good. We'd been in the line for a week and had a night left. It's been all right here; it was pretty rocky back in April but there's this slight sense that everyone, the enemy included, is preparing for this bloody Picardy operation and getting into a down-tools mindset. But we've been busy enough; a few raids, a few efforts to iron out salients.

'On the night of the fourth B Company sent out a wiring party, young Drayton leading it. Good chap, terribly young though. All went fine until one of the men, Stanton – remember him? Gloomy fellow, was in C Company on the Peninsula – got caught on the wire. Terrible job freeing him and the enemy hear what's going on; all hell breaks loose and they open up with everything.

'Our lot return fire and Thorne jumps out the trench to try and free Stanton just as they bring their infernal trench mortar to bear. He was hit just as he'd got out of the trench and was blown back into it. His helmet bore the brunt of the blast to his head but it took one eye out wholly and the other wasn't looking too healthy; I'd be amazed if he keeps it. His side was fairly whacked with shrapnel too. He was in a devil of a state. When he fell back into the trench he seemed to have crunched his hips too. I saw him when he was brought back down the line. He'd refused all morphine, brave boy, but I got the doc to dose him up in any case. We had to leave Stanton where he was, sadly. He was absolutely riddled. Standing up ten yards inside no man's land, caught on the wire. Poor chap. I imagine he's still there. We'll find out soon enough; we're going back up in a few days.'

He broke off and looked at Edward, who was able to almost

feel the older man's gaze on him. He wouldn't break. Not now. He had to rise to this. With his tongue he coated the inside of his mouth with saliva again, took a deep breath to puff out his chest and stood up. He didn't want to be passive any more.

The CO stood too and said, 'I'm sorry, Salter. I know how close you are.'

'Thank you, sir. It's just . . . it's just not how I imagined it would play out. Where can I see him? Is he still in France?'

'Just missed him, I'm afraid. Well, best thing for him. Doctor in London's a darned sight better than some ghastly field hospital here. We heard he made the boat train yesterday afternoon. We had his effects sent off last night too. Usual mix of letters and trinkets. A couple of books. So nothing much really for you to grasp. All that really remains of the wretched affair is young Stanton. I dare say you'll see him when we go up again in a few days.'

He left a breath of a pause and Edward knew exactly what he was about to say, and exactly how he was going to reply. 'Talking of which, Salter, we're going back with no B Company commander . . .'

Edward answered automatically. 'Yes, sir, I'll do it.'

'Good man, I knew you would. I should get rid of those smart red tabs if I were you though. Rather a nice target for Boche snipers.'

Edward hesitated. 'Hang on, sir, just thinking how we'll square it. Shouldn't we tell people—'

'One thing I've learned over the years, Salter,' the CO said, cutting him off, 'is that it's much easier to ask for forgiveness than it is for permission. I think once everyone catches up with where you are they'll realise it's quite an elegant solution to have you take over your old company in the absence both of its previous commander and your former boss. Not as if you need to be shown the ropes, is it?'

'No. I suppose not.'

'That's the spirit.'

They sat in silence for some minutes, neither having anything to prove to the other man. The house became busier as the battalion got ready for the day and Edward got ready to go. A young captain came in, rubbing sleep from his eyes and stopped, alarmed at Edward's appearance. The CO said, 'Ah, Deering. This is the new – well, old but new – B Company commander, Edward Salter. Don't worry about him; knows his way around. My adjutant, Salter. Look at him, fifteen if he's a day.'

Edward recognised the younger man as one of the officers that Thorne had been walking with in the square that evening in Amiens. Automatically he reached over and shook his hand, smiling politely and with a dry, knowing friendliness. Inside though he felt a terrible pain, stinging his nerve endings and making him want to writhe, remembering yet again how he hadn't stood up to greet Thorne. In that outward fraction of a second that seemed to last an hour in his brain he felt a pure hate towards Deering, a cancerous envy of him, as though his friendship with Thorne had somehow taken him away from Edward's. The CO went on.

'Orders here at midday. See you then.'

CHAPTER THIRTY-EIGHT

Edward quickly reacquainted himself with B Company, grateful that they were not due up to the line again for four more nights. He and Baffle met like brothers, the gulf between their ranks as nothing in the moments that they took to appraise each other after months apart. The rest of the company, the vast majority of whom didn't know who Edward was, looked on bemused at a red-tabbed major and the flinty, murderous senior NCO fall upon each other so fondly. They swapped some initial greetings, each delighted to see the other and then Edward asked him, 'Tell me what happened.'

Then a most unexpected thing. Baffle lost his bluff, untouchable demeanour and his face fell to look desperately sad. He began, or tried to begin, to tell Edward about the night that Thorne was hit but after half a dozen false starts Edward reached forward and squeezed his shoulder, scared that Baffle might break down in front of others. 'It's all right, Michael. It's all right. You don't have to.'

Clearly trying to regain his usual easy composure, Baffle managed to croak out, 'That's the first time you've called me Michael, sir. Didn't even know you knew I had a first name.'

Edward grinned and let go of him and they both stepped a little further apart, straightening up.

Clearly wanting to move on as quickly as possible from such a moment, Baffle snapped back into his old self. 'This

Lord Kitchener malarkey then. When we heard the news we thought you'd have been for it. Can't say I'd fancy a dip up there myself.'

Edward smiled ruefully, remembering his upset at being left off the trip as though it was another age, and he a different person. 'They didn't want me on it. No idea why. They just cancelled me going at the last minute.'

'Probably heard you were going to make the brews.' Baffle lit a cigarette and breathed out the first puff exaggeratedly, as though telling a story in a bar. 'Anyway, me and a few of the lads think there's a lot more to it than meets the eye, that thing.'

'What do you mean?'

'I don't know. Just fucking odd. Secretary of state for war gets shipped off to Russia and soon as look at you he's dead? Best-protected bloke in the Empire? No witnesses, all hands gone? Like I said, odd. Anyway, what a man. Bet he was proud to have sat in that sap with me.'

'The pinnacle of his storied career, I dare say.'

'He liked his knitting. Wasn't expecting that. Bet he wished he had packed some woollies when he went for his swim.'

Seeing movement in the corner of his eye, Edward turned and saw Preston come scampering over. He knew fully then that he was back amongst friends. A strange kind of homecoming.

That evening, comfortably back into battalion life and feeling as though his previous life as Kitchener's scout was years ago, he went into the bell tent he had as company commander. A canvas chair sat before some ammunition crates that had been lashed together into a desk and with a clinical detachment that surprised him he sat at it to write the letter that he knew he must. He wrote as an automaton, divorcing his mind from the words so that they went into his eyes and out of his mouth as he muttered them back to himself so that they never touched his brain. He had imagined that it would be hard to write but he found in the event the words flowed freely and with a crescendo that he knew was overblown but that he thought natural and the right tone to strike.

My dear Miranda,

I have just heard the news about Theo. There is nothing that I can say that can assuage your grief or indeed his pain.

We go up to the front shortly where I shall take his place on the parapet. I do not know if I shall return from it or indeed even want to return. Whether that gives me release from fear and proves a help I do not know. But he will be forever in my mind as shall you too and our extraordinary holiday from reality that we all shared in February. A sun-bright lighthouse beam before the eternity of pitch, dreamless nothingness with all those neutered, agonised souls thrust into the void along with all their unborn, unthought-of, silent-screaming children.

I remain yours faithfully and this with my most pained sympathy and, if I might say so, love.

Edward

He read the letter and reread it. The language was terribly overblown but he couldn't imagine writing it in any other way. Somehow the moment demanded it. He put it in the envelope, sealed it and gently kissed it, laying it on the desk and leaning back in his chair. After a few minutes he left the tent to give it to Voigt, the company clerk, to put in the post. As he walked back in the twilight, the evening well gone ten o'clock, a doubt ran through him now that the rush of writing it had died down. He was about to turn back to reread the letter again just to see if he had got the tone right – *neutered, agonised souls?* – but at that moment Deering appeared for a word about manning and he forgot about it.

The next morning, he woke, that previously faint doubt now

a nagging certainty that he had completely misjudged the tone, letting the explosion of events in his life since he had learned of what happened to Kitchener and Thorne poison him with self-obsessed nihilism. He pulled on his shirt and ran shoeless and half-dressed over the thick, dewy grass to the company tent to find Voigt, who looked surprised at his manic appearance.

'That letter, Voigt; has it gone?'

'Yes, sir. Went off at zero-two with the rest of the lads' stuff. Will be at brigade now, I wager. Maybe even division; they've got their post operation swept up, I'll give them that, if nothing else.' He started ruminating about the various inadequacies and inefficiencies of the administrative chain but Edward wasn't listening, wondering how he could pull off intercepting the letter somehow and trying to remember exactly what it was that he had written, hoping that it wasn't as bad as he feared.

Eventually, wandering back to his tent, he gave up and meekly decided to imagine the problem away.

They went up to the front on his fourth afternoon. Edward soon became accustomed to the surroundings; a trench was just a trench no matter if it was in Turkey or in France. He was struck by his lack of nerves, wondering if it was just ingrained experience and increased sangfroid or whether he just didn't really care any longer. Once he had established himself in his HQ dugout and worked through the stretch of line that the company was to hold he sought out Baffle.

'Can you show me where it happened?'

'Aye, sir, right enough.' Baffle sprang up from the firestep where he had been reading a magazine and led him fifty yards down the trench. Two young soldiers manning a trench periscope stiffened when they saw him and Edward tutted at them not to be so formal.

'You'll want to take a look over the lip, sir. That's where Stanton is. Poor bastard.'

Edward took the periscope, scanned over the top of the trench and started as he immediately landed on a contorted, already rotting face. Well, he was now back in it, he thought grimly. Stanton was well and truly enmeshed in the wire, limbs that must have so frantically tried to free themselves wrapped inextricably by the cruel strands, patches of dull red and black all over his torso, one leg shot away and the top side of his neck too. 'Jesus,' he blurted out.

Below him Baffle said, 'I think even Jesus looked a bit better than that, sir.'

Edward smiled despite himself and weighed up the worth of trying to go out to get the body back that night, as though he could somehow honour Thorne by finally achieving what he had set out to do. But another look sufficed to show that it would be such an effort to free it he knew he couldn't risk the same thing happening again. And that wasn't Stanton any more, whoever he had been. It was just some cloth and rotting matter. He stepped down from the firestep, handing the periscope back to the two privates.

Baffle pointed to a patch of earth on the trench floor. 'This is it, sir, he fell back around here.' He then left as Edward tried to take the scene in. He knelt and rubbed the earth with his fingers trying to imagine it supporting Thorne's broken body. He ploughed a layer up with his fingernails to see if there was any soaked-up blood in those grains. Nothing. He took his helmet off and knelt even closer, face right down to the ground, rubbing his nose against it and trying to get a scent of him. Nothing. Whatever had happened here the earth had absolved itself of it. Aware now that he must look very odd to his new soldiers he allowed himself a few more seconds, wishing he could find something to say, to whisper to the earth but drawing a blank. Eventually he stood, dusted himself down and continued down the trench.

That night he put himself down to lead out a standing patrol into No Man's Land to lie in wait and ambush any Germans repairing their own wire. The patrol would usually be led by one of the platoon commanders, but he wanted to be seen by the men to be getting back on the horse and to get to know the ground as soon as he could. He could feel himself slipping away from the cautious, measured soldier that he had been in Turkey.

An hour before H-Hour, the day was still refusing to be dragged completely away, sunlight from well over the horizon still bouncing off the undersides of cirrus clouds. The mood in the trench was just like that of a hundred nights on the Peninsula. The patrol – Edward, Baffle and ten men – lay slumped in their stretch of trench like boxers conserving energy before a fight.

Along the line came Voigt, letters in his hand and dishing them out along the way. The names rang out, each followed by grunts of thanks that grew louder as he came closer. 'Carter, Earle, Strutt, Glendale, Knight, Harthope, Lilburn . . . and you, sir.' He held the last letter out to Edward. 'Hope it's a good one.' He faded back into the gloom.

In his nook of trench Edward took out a lighter to read it by. But who could it be from? As far as anyone else was concerned he was still attached to the War Office. He frowned, wondering whether to read it now or after the patrol. He opened it.

Dear Major Salter,

I am writing this under instruction from my mistress; she received your letter yesterday. She asks that you do not write to her again. Nor are you to write to my young master. She is so overwhelmed by grief that I think – if I were to venture an opinion – that she does not want a connection with anyone who reminds her of my young master's former self. He himself is, I am most anguished to say, in no fit state to receive anyone nor to hear letters. Nevertheless, at least he is now being looked after in London, by the very best doctors. He will not want for care nor expertise. Of that you have my mistress's word.

She asks me, additionally, to send on her best regards and God speed. Both Miranda and Theodore were as happy as I have known them when you came to stay here. It was a rare light. I do hope that one day we might see you again. Please take care. Yours sincerely and with the deepest condolences for our mutual, but I think somehow most especially your, sorrow.

Rosemary Gavin

Unflinching, not bothering to reread it, he held the letter to his lighter and watched as the flame curled up the paper, embers floating across the trench to land on Bebb and Gresley, two young privates who were dozing but remained undisturbed by the brittle black flakes. Baffle whispered over, 'Bad news from the bank manager, sir?'

Edward smiled bitterly. 'Something like that. Come on, you lot, up you get.'

The trench came to life, dozing mounds now growing into humans as though the dead were rising. Baffle went down the line, checking kit, encouraging, cajoling, joking as Edward lit a cigarette and took in the atmosphere; metallic, sweaty, close with rifle oil and sweat. He then inspected the line himself and came to Baffle at the end. 'Very good, colour sergeant. You haven't lost it.'

The teeth smiled back, white against the night.

'You haven't got one of your specials, do you? From the Peninsula? I quite fancy one.'

If Baffle was surprised by this he didn't show it and took off his haversack to pass Edward from it an evil-looking club fashioned from the handle of a stick grenade with a dozen or so horseshoe nails sticking out of it. God knew where he had had it made.

'What are you planning, sir? Shouldn't have thought we'll see anyone.'

'I don't know, I think we might. I've got a funny feeling about this one. And if we do I want to really hurt someone.' He said it in such a manner that Baffle was too taken aback to reply and shrank back into the dark and the freighted, pregnant forever moments before they left.

Edward felt the club in his hand, nicely weighted and reassuring. This would do. He noticed the total absence of the nerves that he had had on the dozens of missions like this on the Peninsula. The only thing he wanted to do now was to come across some Germans in No Man's Land and drive the club again and again on and into the skull of the first one he met. The minutes ticked down, too quickly for the others, far too slowly for him. While they all stood still he was a ball of energy, rocking up and down on his toes and clicking his fingers. At the point where he saw there were only thirty seconds to go, he realised that he had finally found where his old self ran out and where his new one began: in that scar in the earth and on that flat night. The other side of a mirror; everything almost the same but in fact utterly, irredeemably different.

His watch ticked to midnight. 'Come on, chaps. Shall we?' He stepped up the trench ladder and, as one, the other dark shapes broke the blackness and went with him.

PART FOUR

CHAPTER THIRTY-NINE

November 1918

Edward stood looking at the expanse of Horse Guards Parade in front of him. It was the thirteenth of November, two days after the Armistice, and London was in the loosening grip of an exhausted euphoria. Detritus of celebrations was everywhere; litter lined the streets, Union flags lay strewn on the ground and body parts of effigies of the Kaiser lay torn and trampled, the straw of their innards mulching in the nooks of kerbs and studded with glinting shards of broken glass.

He was to meet Anderson at midday and was pleased to see that he had beaten him to the rendezvous. Big Ben struck out its twelve bongs and a few seconds afterwards Anderson hove into view from underneath the Horse Guards arch. Crutch now gone, you would never have known he was missing a leg. He walked with purpose, like a steamroller, his uniform always somehow a size too small for him. Edward saluted the newly minted brigadier and then tapped his watch and said, 'I thought you guardsmen were never late. Heavy night?'

'Ha. Bugger off. Bloody bell's probably wrong. Grand to see you again.' They shook hands with genuine warmth. Anderson looked older, but then it had been more than two years, Edward supposed, since their last meeting. As they took each other in, and exchanged small talk, he wondered how he himself had aged.

Anderson pointed at Edward's lieutenant colonel's crown and star on his sleeves. 'Look at these. Someone's grown up. They suit you.'

Edward smiled. 'Thanks. I still feel like a platoon commander, to be honest.'

'Don't we all, amigo. Institutionalised bluffing, this game. Well, come on, let's have a turn round the park.' He set out towards Birdcage Walk, springing off with strides so long Edward took some time to get the pace.

As they walked they went over the previous years and what Edward had been doing. How after retaking command of B Company he had taken over the battalion itself when the CO had been killed in early 1917. How he had been moved to the divisional staff in 1918 just in time for the great German spring offensive. The division had been mauled but recovered to fight all summer in the great Allied counterattack. In August they were withdrawn to England, since when they had sat out the final, wheezing gasps of the war in Aldershot with a curious and growing sense of detachment, news from France every day losing potency as the inevitability of eventual German defeat grew. Which is what brought him here, to a conference in the War Office.

'Well, bloody hell,' said Anderson. 'Well done, old man. Quite a diverting few years, I must say. What now?'

'Oh, you know, get the division squared for Christmas leave and then see where on earth they send us next.'

'Or how quickly they demobilise you, more like.'

'Quite.'

'What do you think you'll do?'

'Not a clue. I'm sure there'll be some demand somewhere for a slightly out-of-practice lawyer,' he said, attempting to be cheery, knowing that demobilisation did indeed await and with it a terrible sense of having to return to a life that he had always found rather like a waiting room.

Anderson raised a hand and gave Edward a huge smack on the back, his palm almost winding him as it landed squarely between his shoulder blades. 'Cheer up, misery guts. Well, would you like a job under me? I'm setting up this new outfit. Terribly hush-hush. Need a few chaps to bridge the gap between the political sphere and military intelligence. I'm recruiting at the moment. Luckily there's a load of bozos like you around the place desperate for a job to save them having to go back to whatever it was they were doing before this little lot all kicked off. If you wanted I'd be delighted to have you. New place, by the way. Still in the War Office, but a corridor in the basement. Less glamorous but does allow one a spot more autonomy.'

Edward knew exactly what answer he would give as soon as Anderson had begun his pitch but decided to at least give a show of pretending to mull it over.

'Well, that's jolly kind of you to think of me, sir.' He felt that the two ranks now between them demanded that he call Anderson sir.

'Oh, drop the sir stuff, for heaven's sake. When it's just you and me together, it's the same two idle pillocks hiding in that cupboard of an office trying to avoid K, all right?'

'Understood. Marco then?'

He grimaced. 'Only my mother and K of Chaos have ever called me that.'

'Sorry. Mark. Thank you. Thank you very much for thinking of me. Where would it be based?'

'Well, London officially, but it depends on what's going on. Your passport will see some action, that's for sure. I don't know if you've noticed but the whole bloody country thinks that we're about to enjoy a century of peace and love like some kind of Poussin painting and the lands will flow with milk and honey. But they're in for a hell of a shock once the hangover hits. Sure, the Western front's been put out but the rest of the continent's a tinder box.

'The only people who are alive to it, oddly, are the Cabinet. Milner, Curzon, Winston; they all get it, and they know we need eyes and ears everywhere. Germany's about to explode soon enough and who knows what kind of peace is going to be thrust upon them. The PM's going to get so bullied by Clemenceau into smashing them that lo and behold they'll get so angry it'll all kick off again in a decade's time. Just you wait and see.' He broke off and smiled self-consciously. 'Well, that's what I think, at any rate. Anyway, the point is I need people. Reporting directly to me and then I go to the SoS.'

'Can you give me a little time?'

'So that's yes then?'

'No, not necessarily. I just need some . . .'

'It's yes, isn't it?'

'OK. You've got me. But can you just let me get the division wound down?'

'Not a problem. I'll see you in January.'

'But my replacement . . .'

'Come on, old chap, you're a divisional staff officer. You're not exactly irreplaceable. I'll get someone in for you. There's any number of slack bods around.'

They finished the walk around the park, said goodbye and Anderson set off for the War Office over Horse Guards again. Edward stood and watched him as he went, returning salute after smart salute as dribs and drabs of hungover soldiers passed him.

CHAPTER FORTY

Edward spent the rest of the year in Aldershot, helping the staff wind down the division, amazed at how quickly after the Armistice the army reverted to a peacetime mentality. It was as if this was its preferred state and that managing operations in a lethal environment was somehow a rather vulgar distraction. He also noticed that for many of the soldiers the feeling of relief at having survived the war was tinged with a maudlin feeling born not so much of sadness for lost friends but for the end of the defining experience of their lives. It was as though there was a fear of never being able to regain the adrenal, feral sense of belonging that the war had given them.

Going back to his old career wasn't a future that Edward wanted, so he was delighted when, on the day before New Year's Eve, an official transfer order landed on his desk requesting him to report at the War Office three days thence. Compared to the ad hoc way in which his attachment to Kitchener's private office in the helter-skelter months of 1916 had been bartered, this seemed like the pinnacle of due process. He held the document up in the weak winter light and smiled to himself, alone in his chilly office, the condensation from his breath filming the window of his little part of the huge brick headquarters block. He felt as though the transfer order symbolised a lifeline for him through the next decade; he was going to be all right.

He went up to his room and packed his things. Uniforms and a few civilian outfits barely filled half of his trunk and he even left most of the dozen or so books that he had on the shelves for the next occupant. Finally, from his bedside drawer he took the sheaf of letters that he had gathered over the years and couldn't throw away, ones that he had written to Thorne and Miranda but had never dared to send. He thumbed them, twenty in all, each of whose contents he knew by heart now, chronicling the last few years with all their great, tidal events as well as the trivialities that were almost more seismic and meaningful in their own way. He had thought about getting someone to type them up for him; at least then something would be left of their friendship, or its memory at any rate, once he himself was gone. He placed the letters carefully between two jackets and closed the trunk. But it sat badly with him and he opened it again to retrieve them to put in the pocket of his service dress jacket. It bulged awkwardly but at least he would not lose them. He went downstairs, settled his mess bill with the deputy mess steward, handed back his key and made his way to London.

On the Thursday he arrived at the War Office again. No one seemed to be the same amongst the skeleton Christmas period staff; the whole place had changed completely since the time he was there with K and Fitz. He was shown by a stocky corporal down to the basement where Anderson was waiting, a fug of smoke coming from his room and running down the whole corridor. 'Ah, Salter. Delighted you decided to come.'

The meeting was not long. 'I want you to go to Constantinople and then onto Georgia. We need as much intelligence as possible on how we can shore up that brigand Denikin and his mob, help them fight these Bolshevik vermin.'

He waited to see how Edward would react. In truth he was a bit stunned by the mention of Constantinople. It felt a little like someone had mentioned the name of an old lover, or rather someone whom he had loved from afar, utterly unrequited.

'Constantinople. Now there's a name.' He smiled wryly.

'Chance to see what you never got to in fifteen. I want you to go there for a few days, a week maybe. Get the lie of the land; the world and his wife are there at the moment and no one knows what the hell is what. Us, the French, the Italians, apparently all the Greeks there are cock-a-hoop that it's going to become a Christian city again. All of limited interest to us, at least for now. But there's a huge number of White Russians in exile there. You know the type; relics from a Tolstoy novel with more moustaches than you can shake a stick at and all carrying ancestral cigarette cases that stopped a musket ball at Borodino. Dispossessed countesses with jewels sewn into the hems of their dresses, that sort of thing. Crawling with Bolshevik spies too, apparently. This is where you come in. Get talking to people. See what you can find out. Find out – if you can – what that lot – White and Red – really think of Denikin's chances. But don't kick the arse out of it. A week, whatever, then get yourself over to Georgia. The Black Sea is crawling with our ships – you should have no problem cabbying onto one. Link up with our chaps there and work out exactly what's what. We might be about to seriously commit there – Winston's mad keen – and I want your assessment. Our chaps out there, Poole and Blackwood, I suspect have succumbed to the local charms a little too much and I want a grown-up to give me a grown-up reading of it.' He paused. 'Keen?'

'Yes.' Edward chuckled. 'What can possibly go wrong?'

'Good man. Sanders will give you the full brief. Get the boat train for Paris tomorrow. From Paris get the night train to Marseille. There's a boat, the *Magpie*, that will take you to Constantinople. With luck you should be there by Monday. Didn't have anything planned, did you?'

Edward grinned in exasperation at Anderson's manner, his sometimes breathtaking arrogance and needy demandingness. He shrugged a no.

'Any questions?

'A thousand. None that I won't discover the answer to pretty quickly, I imagine.'

'That's the spirit.'

He opened the desk drawer and took out two packages wrapped in brown paper and slid them over the desk to him. The smaller one he pointed to and said, 'Some gold sovereigns. Should help you to open mouths. Account for them, please. The bean counters here go crazy for that kind of thing.'

Edward put it into his pocket and then picked up the larger package. From its weight he could tell exactly what it was and asked, 'How many rounds?'

'Just a dozen. Enough to get you out of trouble at any rate. I wouldn't have thought you'll need it. Either way, make sure it gets back too. Unless you're dead. In which case I shouldn't worry.'

CHAPTER FORTY-ONE

In Marseille, two days later, he stepped onto the unsteady gangway of HMS *Magpie*, a scruffy destroyer with a cheerful crew, and was met by its captain, an absurdly youthful man called Iain Mackaness – 'That's Iain with two "*i*"s, not the Nelsonian one' – who greeted him with a conspiratorial grin. 'All I've been told about you is that you missed your previous trip out due to illness. You look as fit as a fiddle, which means that actually you're probably on some kind of terribly important mission. Don't worry. No further questions.' He showed Edward to his bunk. It was cramped and stuffy, but it was clean and he had it to himself.

'What time will we go through the Dardanelles?' Edward asked Mackaness at lunch on the first day.

Interest piqued, Mackaness replied through a mouthful of beef stew. 'Dusk tomorrow. Did you ever serve there?'

'Yes. Helles and Suvla. May to December. I'd like to be able to see it.'

'I'll do better than that. We'll have a drink together when we go through the Narrows. I was on the *Lord Nelson* when we tried to force them that March. On the eighteenth. We pushed and pushed but we just couldn't get through. Tell you what though, it was one hell of a sight, the fleet as we pushed up. My first action. But we just couldn't do it. And so we had to hand over to you chaps.' He said the last sentence apologetically.

Edward explored the ship, spending the best part of that afternoon in the engine room marvelling, hypnotised, at the Vulcanian scenes as the stokers, lean, with perfect muscles and virtually naked save for their underpants and sandals, shovelled coal into the furnaces. He had never got to know the guts of a ship before and stood mesmerised by the pistons spinning the propeller shafts in an adagio of gyroscopic sounds that in the rest of the ship was whispered, but in the engine room soared and pulsed.

The following day he felt a growing sense of something that he couldn't define – excitement tinged with nostalgia sometimes also touched with the gummy metallic taste of blood in his mouth. The day was beautiful. In the ship's wake the perfect geometry of light-blue sky and dark-blue sea lay before him.

They passed to the south of Lemnos, and he lost himself a little, thinking of the time the battalion had had there before the Peninsula. Presently he went forward to look ahead at the bulk of the Turkish mainland, remembering when Thorne had breathlessly told him about the beacon chain in the *Agamemnon*. He looked down at the water, lost in a thousand memories of him, smiling subconsciously though still with the never-abating stomach-deep pit of loss. He thought also of Miranda for a moment but somehow that was even worse, the sting of missed opportunity more painful than the ache of lost happiness.

Thorne. Thorne. Thorne. For the last two and a half years he had replayed moments they had shared over and over in his head, tried so often to imagine him unwounded and still serving, by each other's side, and what he would do or say at a given moment. He sometimes imagined teasing him about an incipient widow's peak he might have started to develop, or comparing girlfriends they might have, or whole conversations on what the other would do now the war was over.

He had attempted to use Mrs Gavin as a go-between in the months after Thorne had been wounded. She had given little away and despite her kind, functional replies, she had resolutely refused to pass anything on to either Thorne or Miranda. Edward had known that he was placing her in an awkward position by pressing her for information. Before her replies had dried up completely she did impart that Thorne and Miranda were leaving for America where it was thought that a surgeon there, a friend of their father's, might be able to save the sight of the left eye, but nothing since. That had been October 1916. Edward had stopped writing after that.

There was a movement behind him. It was Mackaness. 'We're almost there,' he said quietly. 'Here, have a go on these.' He held out a pair of binoculars as he stepped away. 'Leave you to it. I'll be on the bridge. Once we pass the Narrows we'll crack into something.'

Edward thought about asking him whether they could stop off at Suvla so that he could go ashore and see the blind crests once more but stopped himself, laughing a little at how arrogant it would be to use the sailors for such a task. He knew Thorne would have thought the same and then laughed again at how Haynes-Mattingly definitely would have ordered them to. The thought of Haynes-Mattingly made him shiver despite the late afternoon sunshine. It took an effort to throw the thought of him out of his mind.

Then suddenly there it was. The Peninsula. Through the binoculars he picked out all the familiar features: Helles with its cliffs at its southern tip and the curve going up to Anzac with its bluffs and nullahs that ran down the hillside like a curtain's fold before dropping away into the void of the Suvla Plain to the left. He remembered how Thorne had said that he had seen it before the war from the Asian side and how unimpressed he had been by it. He wondered now, however, if the events of 1915 had imbued the place with a sense of menace, palpable even in the bright and breezy day.

He thought of all the skeletons now crumbling into the dust.

The buckles, shrapnel, wire and rifles already gone to rust, the flesh, blood and skin long since eaten or soaked into the earth. The chatter that had hung mingling in the air all over the beaches and hillsides now replaced by unfelt breezes and the bleats of sheep and goats. All for what? He smiled despite himself at how darkly funny Thorne would find it all were he here beside him.

Then the straits themselves were coming into view and slowly he started to lose Suvla behind the southern promontory of Cape Helles, and V Beach and Morto Bay appeared with their sand bright yellow in the light. There was the *River Clyde*, still beached like a whale, one part of the expedition that had never left. It looked sad and innocuous, like an old holiday craft washed up on a beach.

As the ship entered the strait he looked up at the eastern flank of the Peninsula, amazed at this different aspect of it. For months his view of it had been limited to the feet in front of his face, granular and forensic. This view from the sea made him feel godlike, able to cover the entire stretch of land with a hand held a few inches in front of his eyes. Within a couple of minutes they were level with Achi Baba, the great ghost that had haunted them on Helles, winking and shimmering all day above them. The straits narrowed, the towns at either side of the Narrows passed and then the ship veered to starboard and the rest of the channel opened up. Behind him Mackaness coughed, and he turned to see half a dozen of the crew were with him.

Seeing Edward's surprise at having been woken from his daze Mackaness explained, 'This bunch here all did time around here in 1915 too. Sykes and Williams with me on the eighteenth, the others over the rest of the year. I thought it would be fitting to mark us coming through what we couldn't do back then.' He held out a bottle of rum and poured each of the sailors a ration. He raised his mug. 'To absent friends,' he said. The men muttered in manners ranging from cheery surprise at sudden remembrance to mumbles of long-held pain and they drank together. Edward felt that something was required from him and said, 'Well, thank you, Iain, and thank you all. It was a hell of a thing we tried to do. Just a shame we never managed it, eh?' He paused. 'But here we are, all to the good in the end.'

Whether out of genuine agreement or of politeness they murmured their assent and then Mackaness stepped in. 'Right, chop-chop. You've had your fun, hooligans,' he said, and the group dispersed back to their stations. Mackaness stayed as the others withdrew and looked out over the bow with Edward.

Edward said, 'It's funny. What on earth we were thinking? But I suppose it was so early in the war, wasn't it? None of us really had the slightest clue.'

Mackaness's eyes narrowed. 'I don't know. I often think about it. If we had done it imagine what might have happened.'

'Like what?'

'I don't know; a whole host of things. But if we had taken the Turks out at that stage and freed up old Ivan's southern flank then maybe they would have done better in the East, maybe the Bolshies wouldn't have seized power, maybe the war would have been over in 1916. Who the hell knows? Maybe old K wouldn't have had to go on his insane mission to Russia. A thousand things.'

Edward let mention of Kitchener slip. He wanted to see what Mackaness, who was clearly eager to talk, would say next.

'Before this little lot started I was a bond trader in the City. Good fun, let me tell you. To be honest, I can't wait to get back there once this jaunt is over and I finally get out of this damned uniform. Anyway, first lesson I got taught was by this old chap, who'd been around since the South Sea Bubble almost. "The market never lies." I know, sounds as trite as you like. Like saying the first rule of warfare is not to get shot. But the thing is, the market doesn't lie. Just like the first rule of warfare is indeed not to get shot. Anyway, a cousin of mine's a journalist covering the markets in America. When we were pushing up the straits the price of grain on the Chicago stock exchange plummeted.'

He looked at Edward meaningfully, as though somehow this simple fact explained everything. 'You get my point?'

Edward held his hands up in a 'No, I don't' gesture and said, 'Apologies. I'm afraid I'm almost entirely financially illiterate.'

'The point is that those Chicago money men, at the centre of the grain-trading universe, thought that if we'd only pushed up on the nineteenth then we'd have got to Constantinople, Turkey would have collapsed, Russian grain exports would have been able to come through the straits again and flood the market, Russia doesn't collapse, we win the war that year.' He fell silent for a while.

Edward felt he had rather missed his calling as an actor; Mackaness certainly had a sense of the theatrical.

He went on. 'But we didn't go on the nineteenth, the straits stay shut, you pongoes get ripped to pieces on these slices of hill and no one gets anywhere. And now we have this bedlam to deal with.' He waved his arm forward as though with it he was sweeping over the entirety of Russia, from the Baltic all the way to the Pacific. 'Still, all the fun of the fair, I suppose.'

Edward decided to push about Kitchener. 'Do you know anything about old K's mission to Russia?'

'Do I? Damned right I do.' Edward tried to get the rum out of his head and listen in as he carried on. 'I'll never forget it. I was up there the day it happened, a lieutenant on *Owl*. Damned strange business, that day. It just felt like something was going to go wrong but we couldn't imagine what.

'The whole thing stank. Total shambles from start to finish. The entire bloody fleet didn't know what way was north. Just come from Jutland, still trying to work out who was still alive and then we get the call that K's coming up and he's off to Russia. Massive flap. *Hampshire* had to turn around at the double and get ready to go to sodding Archangel. It was a good boat and the captain was sound but it was a pig of a day. You ever been to Scapa Flow? It's a brute. That day was Arctic squalls ripping round the islands and then right through you and it was June for God's sake.

'*Hampshire* heads off into this filthy evening and then a couple of hours later the call goes out that there's a ship in distress. At first we didn't think it's much but we go. And it's horrible, horrible. The night seemed to fold into the sea. Then it becomes clear it's *Hampshire* we're looking for and we start a search operation. But it's pitch black – we only found three or so bodies, poor wretches, they can't have lasted more than five minutes in those seas. But it was far too dark to find them all – even though morning came early most of them were on the bottom by then, or smashed against the cliffs that side of Orkney. And everyone desperately looking for K. Eventually we get called back in. But the strangest thing, though, was that we were in the middle of this damned minefield and we think we're going to hit one any second, but none of us did. The next day they find a shedload of them all over where we were. So it just beggars belief that none of us hit one.'

He carried on, almost as though Edward wasn't there. 'You ever been in a ship that has sunk? Me neither. I used to have nightmares about it, all through the war. Still might hit a stray mine, I suppose, but at least there's no bloody torpedoes. I used to get terrible shakes thinking about being sunk at night by a torpedo. Used to dream of being trapped in an air pocket and not drowning but remaining dry as the ship plunges down to the bottom, just dying eventually from using up all the oxygen, surrounded by metal in some steel tomb. Would your body even decompose? Or do you just stay there like an Egyptian mummy until at some point the entire ship rusts and melts into the seabed? Must have happened to some poor bugger once. Probably hundreds over the years if you think about it.'

Edward looked aside at Mackaness, realising he was likely still having those nightmares. He was corrupted internally, he realised, like a vase with some fatal flaw in it. Even an innocuous knock would break it. In all probability he would carry on with a normal life and go from strength to strength, leave the navy, go back to his old job, do very well at it. Become a pillar of the community in some village whose manor house he was able to buy. But one tap in the wrong place or at the wrong time along the way would break him.

Edward decided to change the subject. He nodded up the straits. 'So what's it like, then?

'Constantinople?' Mackaness brightened. 'Just you wait. Chaos.'

CHAPTER FORTY-TWO

Chaos it was. He had never been somewhere where the whole situation – in the streets, in squares, in the excited chatter of bars and cafes, almost in the air itself – was so tangibly fluid. It felt like he was on the very fault line of an earthquake as the plates either side were on the brink of shifting. A cocktail of languages: public school English, French, Greek, Russian, Turkish, Italian, the English of the engine room and the NCOs' mess. Laughter, relief, excitement at the new year and the new start for the city mixed with fear of the same, resentment, snarls, screams and the blood running in the gutter after fights between Turk and Greek, Frenchman and Briton, rivals from companies of the same regiment fuelled by lax restrictions and strong drink. It was intoxicating.

The hard winter's snow swirling round the tight-packed houses and disappearing into the grey Bosphorus somehow brought London to Edward's mind. This pleased him for its unexpectedness, although he knew that it proved a disappointment for most of the other British officers in the city, all of whom wanted something altogether more exotic from it; more gold, more tiling, more smoke coiling up the sides of streets, more colourful clothing than the dark wool that everyone seemed to be wearing.

He took a room in a house on the same street as the Pera Palace hotel, the honeypot round which all British activity centred. Every room in the house was taken by other officers, some navy, mostly army leavened by a few journalists and opportunist chancers and adventurer types. Nobody was ever there. They all preferred to be in the hotel itself, hanging round in the lobby or drinking in the bar that was effectively now a very grand mess, its usual filling of cosmopolitan gossip now replaced by military shop talk, lines being spun, whispered indiscretions about things that had been sworn to secrecy only minutes previously and the braying of subalterns delighting that they had the run of this polyglot city.

In the Pera Palace bar on the third day he was chatting with – as Anderson had predicted – an exiled Russian who introduced herself as Isabella Moiseyeva but who, while she claimed to be a countess, didn't appear to have jewels sewn into the seams of her dress. She was a ripe, about to be overripe, peony of a woman, heroically clinging on to the vestiges of a good figure and unable to contain the surfeit of flesh that bubbled around the top of her low-cut dress. She seemed to be moving her chair ever closer to him by minuscule movements every minute or so. Trapped in the corner, he started to flush. His discomfort wasn't helped by the fact Mackaness was at the bar with a few naval friends of his and kept on catching his eye and raising a glass. Edward inwardly groaned as a waiter arrived at their table with a bottle of wine, knowing it was sent by Mackaness. The countess sighed with delight, reminiscing about the wine grown on her own family's estates, a memory that triggered a bilious denunciation of the Bolsheviks who, she was sure, would have ripped up the vines and were probably now growing turnips in their stead. Picking up precisely zero of value to Anderson, Edward didn't think his espionage career was getting off to the most professional of beginnings. Eventually he made his excuses.

As he was about to leave the building, a man from reception – running after him with such a prim, affected gait it was as though he was trying to hold a pencil between his buttocks – handed over a folded piece of paper.

On it was written, in immaculate handwriting:

I did not want to disturb you as you seemed rather busy. Would love to have a drink with you. Cafe opposite the southeast corner of the Spice Bazaar. Blue and white awning. 8 o'clock. A friend from Gallipoli.

A thrill went through him. 'Well, well, well. This is more like it.'

'What is it?' said Mackaness, appearing beside him.

He handed it over. Mackaness read it and screwed up his face, wrinkles forming at the top of his nose, as though reading a tip list for some racehorses that he didn't quite trust. 'What do you think?'

'I think I'll go.'

'Really? Damned odd. Why didn't the mystery man just come up and give you the note himself?'

'Don't know. Don't blame him. Probably didn't want to get caught up in my interminable conversation.'

'Well, it's no skin off my nose, chum, but do you want an escort?'

'An escort?'

'I can send a couple of the lads along with you. Just in case you run into trouble.'

'I'll be fine, I promise you.'

'Look, it's none of my business, but are you sure about this? You don't know this town at all. None of us do. I hope you've got a revolver at any rate.'

'I do, and I'll be absolutely bloody fine,' he said spikily, patting the weapon that sat inside his jacket, feeling a little annoyed that Mackaness was intruding on his operation. Then he relented, seeing how hurt Mackaness was by his tone. He knew the wine was making him too headstrong, and he softened. 'I'll be OK, Iain.'

Mackaness shrugged. 'Well, suit yourself. The offer's there.'

'Seriously, I'll be fine. But thanks anyway.'

He took another drink to smooth over the slight feeling of awkwardness. 'Right, I've got to get out of here before I get caught by the countess again. See you tomorrow?'

Mackaness took a sip of his gin. 'Shall do. Pink gins at midday. Take care tonight.'

Edward patted him on the shoulder and winked, feeling uncharacteristically cocky. He found he was rather enjoying himself. As he left, Mackaness threw one final plea for caution after him.

'Have you ever done any of this kind of thing before?'

'God knows. Making it up as I go along. But it's common sense, isn't it?'

He left the bar behind, crossed the street and went back to his room.

He read for the rest of the afternoon and early evening as darkness came quickly over the city. The reading didn't stick as he clock-watched, increasingly nervous about the meeting. Putting the book down, he fidgeted about the sparse room for a while. Eventually he could stand it no more and got himself ready to leave, far earlier than he needed to. He took a looping, circuitous route, getting to the bar ten minutes early. He stood a hundred yards distant from it, looking around to make sure he hadn't been followed. The street was empty. On the stroke of eight he crossed the street and went in, to be greeted by a simpering, fastidious doorman with dramatically combed over hair who drew a red curtain back and motioned for him to go through. The room beyond was shrouded in red. Crimson wallpaper and red velvet curtains blanketed the low hum of conversation from half a dozen groups. It took a while before his eyes adjusted to the dark, and then he froze upon seeing who awaited him in the far corner.

Lipin.

Smoke from a cigarillo coiled up to obscure him a little, but it was still unmistakeably Lipin.

He blinked, his brain trying to stutter into motion. Lipin, whose peripheral vision must have been triggered by his awkward stillness looked up and caught him before grinning. They both stayed there for what felt like ages. Then Lipin started laughing, stood up and walked over to him, putting his hand out to crush Edward's. 'Well, well, the guardian of the Gallipoli Peninsula.'

Edward gargled a nothing response.

'Excellent to see you again, my friend. Honestly, I did not think that any of you would get away from that hell. Come, let's drink.' He ushered Edward over to the table, where the frosty top half of a champagne bottle stuck out of an ice bucket. Next to it sat a bottle of whisky that Lipin had evidently been tending to before his arrival. Lipin poured him a whisky, a huge one. 'You start with this. I need to go and piss. And then champagne.' He left Edward sitting there feeling as though south was north and left was right.

He sat back and took a large gulp of the whisky so that it burned his throat and jolted his brain alive. He cast his mind back to that day on the Peninsula he had spent with Lipin. Up to now it had been an enjoyable curio in his memory of those never-ending and never-changing summer weeks. Lipin. Charming, funny, brave as a lion. He smiled as he remembered how they had been lumbered with the lumpen Borov for the trip and how he had feigned blisters to avoid going up to the line. But then he remembered the sudden burst of venom when Lipin had switched into Russian at the start of the visit. He still wasn't sure whether he had managed to hide his shock. He would find out soon enough, he reasoned.

Lipin returned and Edward appraised him as he glided through the room in his tall, faintly mincing fashion, immaculate in a grey suit and cream silk shirt, a dark-blue tie with small polka dots on it making him look like a swell in St James's as opposed to a . . . whatever it was that Lipin was doing here. Well, at least he can't be a Bolshevik in that get-up, thought Edward. As he sat down on the plush velvet chair he offered him a cigarillo, sliding out his case from a breast pocket and opening it with the same hand in one smooth, slick action. Edward accepted; he knew that he was so nervous that he was in danger of drinking too much and that smoking would help by giving his hands something to occupy them. The tobacco was very strong. Lipin turned his attention to the bottle of champagne, opened it with the barest whisper ('Like strangling a grandmother,' he added) and then poured it with studied reverence into a pair of coupes before them. They were beautiful, the glass engraved with ivy leaves and the champagne sparkling and golden, a dozen tiny tornadoes of bubbles rising up from the bottom.

Lipin's insouciance and immediate friendliness – and the drink – quickly helped Edward feel at ease and he was grateful for the smoke's gravelly warmth down his throat. Lipin said in toast, 'Come, my friend. We have much to celebrate, no?' They looked at each other and raised glasses. 'To the end of your war in the West,' Lipin said. 'Sadly, for us in the East it goes on.' Then he flung back his head to drink it in one, while Edward sipped on his like a curate. He wondered whether Lipin was already drunk. He was one of those inscrutable people who could be stone cold sober or ten glasses in and you would never know which.

They started to speak in torrents, their stories tumbling out. Edward told Lipin about the end of Gallipoli and the evacuation and then his time with Kitchener and the return to the battalion. For Lipin's part he had escaped Petrograd after the October Revolution and had been on Kornilov's staff when the civil war had started, loyally following him in the great Ice March to Kuban. He was in Constantinople now, he said, to get money from exiles that might be used to support the White effort. He had been in the city since December. Edward rather suspected that getting the monies out of exiles was slightly more direct work than Lipin implied it was, preferring to give the impression that it was like asking villagers for a contribution for a pew for the church.

'Do you want to know how I found you?' Lipin said, shifting the direction of conversation.

'Well, the city is full of Russians. I imagine you've got quite a good network.'

Lipin nodded, 'That is true. All sorts of Russians. Sadly not solely the correct ones. Whites, Bolsheviks, Cossacks, everyone. But no, no network of spies. Believe me, I wish I had one. Let me tell you. I was sitting in the Pera Palace bar meeting a friend earlier and heard someone talking about some vineyards being ripped up. I looked over my shoulder and saw you. I nearly jumped out of my skin; I was surprised you didn't notice. Instantly it felt as though we were back on that stretch of hell again. I wanted to come over and hug you. But,' he grinned slyly, 'I saw you had your eyes full of something else—' he used his hands to do an impression on his own chest of Moiseyeva's '—and I didn't want to disturb you.'

Edward felt his face redden. 'It wasn't what it looked like.'

'I tease you, my friend. When I left I wrote the note and asked that it be given to you. But do you know what really surprised me about hearing you?'

It hit Edward the second before Lipin continued, in Russian, 'I had had no idea you were such a good Russian speaker.'

Edward was silent and so Lipin continued. 'I am impressed. Do you know I had no idea that you spoke it. I tried my trick on you when we first met. It works for me every time. The amount of people I have caught out using it.' He laughed, like a schoolboy. 'It's funny, it usually helps me, how do you say, to break the ice. They realise they have been caught and we laugh about the charade a little. But you, it passed straight through you. And if I recall I said some very rude things about your family. My apologies; the circumstances demanded it.'

Edward raised his palms a little to show that no offence was taken.

Lipin laughed in a friendly manner and topped up both their drinks. Edward, cursing the alcohol he had already had too much of, couldn't help but feel the back of his neck prickle at Lipin's icy coolness and the way in which he could shift moods so quickly.

'So what brings you here? It can't be the weather.' Lipin changed the subject.

'Truth be told, I'm just stopping off here. I'm trying to find out exactly want Denikin's chances are.'

Lipin laughed and made a motion of spitting on the floor. 'That's a good one.'

'What do you mean?'

Lipin looked for a moment immensely sad, his eyes appearing dreadfully tired despite the brio with which he tried to bear himself. 'We are done for. But we don't know it yet. Or we know it but can't bring ourselves to admit it yet. It was over when Kornilov was killed. But we will keep on. We have to.'

'But surely you can defeat them? Denikin, Kolchak, the Czechs, the help we're sending?'

Lipin waved dismissively. 'You don't understand, my friend. We have no chance. If you hold Moscow and Petrograd, you hold Russia. The Reds have the centre. They have the factories. They have the people. But more than any of that they have a central idea. They have fire running through their blood and they understand the one truth: that Russia is built on the peasants. If you have the peasants, then you have the soul of the country.'

He took another sip from his champagne, its gold glowing against the crimson room. As if reading Edward's thoughts he smiled and said, 'And yes, I am well aware of the irony of me commenting on the peasantry while drinking champagne in Constantinople. But deep down all of us are peasants, children of the land. Only a lot of people forgot that over the past decades.' He laughed again for a little while, took another sip and went on.

'The Bolsheviks are like religious fanatics. We, on the other hand, are too divided. Too many groups. No control, no cohesion. Too many ideas. And your help, if you will forgive me saying so, is worthless. You have no interest in fighting this war properly. And I don't blame you. Your people are exhausted and so all your governments can do is send us arms. And anti-freeze. Which doesn't go into engines by the way – it gets sold as liquor.

'But when the Reds win – and they will win, sadly – what will emerge will be nowhere near as different as they think it's going to be. Russia can only be ruled by one man, you see. It's the only model that works for us. Whatever name they invent for the replacement for the Tsar he'll still be a tsar. You know your Flaubert?'

'Not especially. The vague plot of *Madame Bovary* but that's all, really.'

Lipin leant back and lit another of his cigarillos. He was very much a man who enjoyed holding court.

'"Inside every revolutionary there is a policeman." It's exactly the same with this lot. They will get rid of us, rip our structures to pieces, tear down our statues, and then they will replace them with structures and statues that they think are entirely different, but that everyone else will be able to see are just the same. Quite funny if you think about it.'

Edward listened as Lipin described the nature of the war against the Bolsheviks. How he had been posted to Kornilov's staff at the beginning of 1917 and had remained with him through the events of that year and beyond. What it had been like to be with Kornilov on the day he was killed, how they had buried him in a churchyard only for his body to have been dug up again by the Bolsheviks and then burned. What had happened to another of Kornilov's staff the day before he had been killed; the Frenchman, they called him, who had been one of the general's closest advisors.

'He was brought to us, killed by a shell. A tiny wound,

shrapnel going in just under his heart. He did not even look as though he was dead – anyone would have thought he was just sleeping. I have never seen someone so peaceful. He was a huge man, bear-like. Old, but with fire still in him. Said he had spent all his life fighting.

'He was a magnificent man. A brilliant, brilliant tactician. When he was killed they put his body on a cart and we bowed as it passed. I washed his body for burial myself, making sure he was clean. We buried him beside a lake at sunset. It was a beautiful evening and I wondered what had driven him to us; what had made him leave his own country to come and help our cause against the Red scum. Still, that is the nature of wars like ours, I suppose. They attract all sorts from all over the world. You have no idea of the danger you will face when these Reds win, my friend.'

Lipin broke off to see if there was any more champagne left in the ice bucket. None left, Edward decided to bring the evening to a close. Lipin looked exhausted. Just then he got a second wind, straightened himself up, blinked several times and shook his head side to side to get new blood flowing again. 'One thing. Before we part. What happened to your friend?'

Edward knew immediately what he was talking about but wanted to create some room as to how he could frame the conversation. 'My friend?'

But Lipin was way ahead of him and said impatiently, clearly irritated by the obfuscation. 'Come, your friend. I don't recall his name. My guide in your trench.'

Edward thought back to the visit and how well Lipin and Thorne had got along, how much of an affinity they had struck up so quickly. This was the first time he had had to break the news of it to someone else. He wondered if he was able to do it but then his tongue ambushed his brain by just coming out with the words.

'I'm afraid he was terribly wounded. Blinded by a mortar round. In nineteen sixteen. France. They got him when a wiring party was caught in the open.' He was surprised at how bloodlessly he was able to say it.

Even after the new vim with which he had reinflated himself, this news punctured Lipin back down. 'I'm so sorry. He seemed . . . he seemed . . . I don't know. He seemed invincible.'

'I know.'

'I knew one or two like that. The problem is that when they are shown not to be invincible it hits harder than hearing a hundred lesser men have fallen.'

It seemed it was finally time to go, Lipin making non-committal noises about meeting again, but Edward knew that they were hollow; likely he would never see him again. He wondered what someone like Lipin now did with his life; whether he would go back into the storm or whether he would make a new beginning for himself somewhere else. France? London? New York, most likely. Someone like that, with a chameleon soul, would always be able to drop anchor somewhere and make a decent fist of it until they decided it was time to move on.

Outside, Edward's eyes took some time adjusting to the street and the quiet after the hubbub of the bar. The doorman smiled ingratiatingly as they left, his toothy, insincere grin designed more to garner tips than to express gratitude at their having come. Edward reached into his pocket for a coin. As he handed it over he saw the doorman's face changed into a puzzled look of alarm.

Edward spun around and saw the shapes of two men, walking quickly. In practised, fluid movements they both drew pistols from their coats.

'Send my regards to the Tsar,' said one, in Russian, and emptied three bullets into Lipin at near point-blank range.

Edward's hand reached immediately for his holster and fumbled for his revolver as the other man turned to him and fired at his chest, the bullet ricocheting off the handle and streaking upwards in a shrill whirr, its breath brushing his face. A second bullet then crashed into his shoulder and he was flung back against the wall. As he fell he saw the same man pause, put the barrel at the head of the doorman and then execute him, his brains flying over Edward's face. Edward lay on the ground as the man stood over him, pointed his gun at his forehead and muttered in Russian, 'Nothing personal.'

Then the world erupted and the man's head ripped back, his throat bursting open and spinning back, loosing off his pistol but the bullet only hitting the ground, the muzzle flash illuminating the black maw beneath his mouth as more bullets then thudded into him. The second man, the one who had shot Lipin, looked up and fired off six rounds up the street before then also crumpling after being shot in the stomach, his screaming falling away to animal whimpers and clutching his gut on the floor, his shoes kicking against Edward's own shin. Footsteps started running down the street. English voices. Edward felt himself passing out, tripping in and out of consciousness. He wondered how much blood he was losing. His shirt felt damp and he wasn't sure of it was from his blood or from the drizzle. It seemed far too warm to be rain. Torches came on and shouts filled the street.

'Check him, Frank.'

'He's fucked mate. Guts hanging out.'

'Here's the other cunt. Jesus, the state of it. Silly prick.'

'Bloody hell, this one's still breathing.'

'What, Salter's mate? Can't be. Fuck, you're right. Come on, let's get him and Salter back. Charlie, keep an eye down there for any other idiots.'

'Aye, chief.' The voice sounded comically young, as though delivered by a boy selling newspapers.

Then someone looked over him. 'You all right, sir?' He recognised him as the stoker, Sykes. 'What the hell have you been doing?' Edward couldn't keep his eyes open, just wanting to sleep, only held back from it by the stabs of pain pulsing through him.

Words and phrases came to him as his brain, stuck in treacle, tried to piece together what was happening, what had happened.

'Let's get the hell out of here, lads.'

'How's the Turk?'

'Fucked mate. Head half gone.'

'Get those fuckers' pistols.'

'Shall we hide the bodies?

'Nah, too much work. This kind of thing must happen the whole time. Wild bloody West this town.'

'Let's go, let's go.'

'Let's just get fucking out of here.'

Attention turned to him. 'Sorry sir, going to hurt a little.' Sykes heaved him up onto his shoulders, blood leaving Edward's head and he vomited down Sykes's back, tasting the whisky and champagne as they came back up his throat and stinging it with the stomach acid. It made him retch again and more came out.

'Let's go, let's go.'

They started running, and he passed out.

CHAPTER FORTY-THREE

There was a knock on the door. Mackaness, not waiting for a response, put his head round and smiled. 'Hello, old chap. Good to have you with us. Bloody hell, you gave us a scare. Doc checked you out last night and loaded you up with dope, so you'll feel like a rhino's run through your head for a while. It's goodbye from me, I'm afraid. You're being transferred to *Vesta* and she's taking you to Malta tonight. Thought I'd pop in and bid farewell.'

Even in his drowsy, dreadfully heavy mind, Edward managed to croak out what he knew he had to. 'Thank you, thank you for sending the men.' He tried to say more but couldn't.

Mackaness waved a hand, evidently not wanting to dwell on the embarrassment that Edward felt at having been so blasé about setting off for the meeting alone. 'Bit of amusement for the chaps. A little cloak-and-dagger stuff to keep their minds sharp. Most fun they've had in ages. I have to say you're better off than your drinking partner. The sawbones did his best on him but he didn't make it, I'm afraid. He was going to die the moment he wore those slugs.'

'Where is he now?' Edward croaked.

'Some backstreet. He'll get picked up soon enough. Last thing we need is a dead Russian on our hands. Anyway, we took the liberty of searching his body for anything that might be useful.' He fended off Edward's inevitable next question, 'Don't worry, we left his watch on him, though doubtless that's now in the bazaar somewhere. We're not grave robbers. But Sykes did find this in his jacket. We reasoned that it could only be of use to us.' He took a black leather notebook out from his pocket and gave it a cursory thumb through.

'It's all Greek to me at any rate. But look at the back; he wasn't a half-bad draughtsman, your chum.' He tossed the book onto Edward's chest. Picking it up with his good arm, he opened the book and flicked through it – about a hundred pages' worth of diary entries, map drawings, lists of ammunition and provisions, descriptions of battles and meetings between White commanders. He would read them in full later.

He went to the back pages, which were covered in doodles and sketches, all done in pencil where the rest of the book had been in blue ink. There were patterns, some simple, many far more intricate. There were some likenesses – various comrades, he presumed, although there were also a few of women and children.

The final five pages were filled with what were marked as being tattoos that Lipin had noted on soldiers of his and had wanted to capture for posterity. A few of them were elaborate, wonderfully drawn skulls that were so precise that it was almost as if they were taken from the pages of a medical textbook. One skull had a snake intertwined through its eye sockets and mouth; another had its tongue sticking out and was impaled by a bayonet. Underneath, Lipin had annotated that many of the tattoos belonged to ex-convicts for whom they denoted gang membership or were riddled with symbolism and code. Of the whole macabre, strangely beautiful drawings, however, one in particular caught his eye, at the bottom of the penultimate page. A fleur-de-lys with three letters at its base – HHK – and written underneath it the caption: '*Tattoo on arm of French commander killed at Ekaterinodar, April 1918*'.

'What's the matter? You look as though you've seen a ghost,' said Mackaness.

Edward held the book in his grip as though he was having

a seizure, his morphine-addled brain trying to come to terms with what he was looking at. Somehow he managed to compose himself and reply, at the very moment orderlies came into the room with a stretcher to take him away to the ship to Malta.

'Nothing. Nothing. Just brought back a memory, that was all. Thank you, Iain. Thank you very, very much indeed.'

He was lifted down from the bed onto the stretcher and then picked up again, the blood leaving his head briefly and he smiled at Mackaness, who winked back as he then slipped again into unconsciousness, the last thing he remembered being to grip the book by his side as hard as he could.

PART FIVE

CHAPTER FORTY-FOUR

The ADC, an artillery captain with a bar to his MC, knocked at the door and Anderson barked, 'Come.'

Edward went in, saluted, and Anderson stood up and guffawed.

'Well, well, well. If it isn't the worst secret agent Britain has ever produced.' He sprung up from his desk, almost danced around it and, about to thump Edward on the back, stopped at the last minute. 'Better not. How is it?'

'It's all right. Still gives me some gyp in the evening but should be fine soon enough. Collar bone chipped and my shoulder blade's not very pretty, but hey-ho. Blood loss was the main thing.'

'This calls for something stronger than coffee, I think.' He opened the door and shouted down the corridor at the ADC. 'Jimmy, a bottle of red, please.'

Edward looked around the new office – huge, high and intricately plastered ceilings and with triple windows looking out onto the bustling street below. He raised his eyebrows pointedly as though accusing Anderson of having sold out somehow by deserting the basement office existence that he had professed to love so much.

Anderson laughed and said, 'I know. Swish digs, eh? Well, when Winston came in as SoS just after you left he decided to elevate us a little. No bad thing; our budget's been doubled too.'

Edward smiled inside at Anderson's eternally opportunist soul. He remembered back to early 1916, when he had held Churchill as a byword for treachery and incompetence; now it seemed he could do no wrong.

The ADC brought in a bottle of wine and two glasses and they settled into two deep rattan chairs next to the central window, the spring sun magnified by the glass and warming them like a pair of old men sitting in an orangery.

Edward talked him through what had happened in Constantinople, really just a recap of the report he had written the day after he had come round from the operation where he had been patched up and the ripped skin on his back stitched back together.

Vesta had taken him to Malta for the operation but just before he was due to go back to Britain, he had fallen seriously ill with an infection. He had remained at the hospital in Valletta for two months in an exhausting, unchanging fever that had left him hollowed out in a way that he had never been throughout the war. Skeletal, pale, he had regained himself a little by the time he eventually managed to sail back to Portsmouth and here he now was, pathetically weak, uniform hanging off him, but far better than he had been.

As he talked, Edward could feel that there was something not quite right with the conversation, a little different to the ease they had had before. Anderson, although sympathetic for his injury and concerned for his health, seemed to be annoyed that Edward hadn't really accomplished anything of note, although he didn't say so explicitly.

Anderson then waded in to confirm the suspicion. 'Bloody hell, old boy. You've had a hell of a time. Now look, I'm not quite sure you're necessarily cut out for this. Tell you what we'll do. You have a period of leave and we'll get you back to the field army, eh?' Edward bristled at this, annoyed that after all he had been through he was being dealt with so peremptorily.

He decided to play his cards. He had planned to do it a little later but wanted to cut Anderson off. As he was waffling on about arranging the transfer he came in with, 'There was one other thing that I think you ought to know.'

Anderson's brow darkening at the interruption – Edward could see how used he had already become to people dancing to his tune – he then raised his eyebrows as if to beckon the piece of information.

Edward took out Lipin's notebook from his pocket. 'It's this book, Mark. I managed to get my hands on it.' He handed it over and said, 'Look at the drawings in the last pages.'

He watched Anderson flick through them. 'Yes, yes, old boy. All very interesting, but a few sketches aren't going to suddenly show us the way to Trotsky's medicine cabinet.'

'Look at the bottom right-hand corner of that page. The fleur-de-lys.'

Anderson muttered, annoyed by the game, and said, 'All right, a fleur-de-lys and HHK. Well so what. H is Russian for N. Some bloke called Nikolai's initials.'

'What if they're not Cyrillic?'

Edward remained silent, watching the gears of Anderson's brain grind. 'Hang on, They were . . .'

'Yes. Exactly.'

'Well, what the hell does this have to do with anything?'

'The caption, written by this chap Lipin, says that this tattoo was on the body of a general who had been on Kornilov's staff, killed by a shell. Lipin used to sketch all sorts of things – you can see from the other jottings, tattoos seemed to be his thing. But the point is, this tattoo was on the body of this dead general whom everyone thought was from France.'

'OK?'

'Well, Mark, K had this exact tattoo. I saw it as clear as day just before he went off for Orkney, even told me he got it as a memento of his time in the Franco-Prussian war.'

'Hang on, So what you're saying is . . .'

'You know there were all those ridiculous stories about what had happened to him.'

'Yes, but they're the work of tragic cranks.'

'I don't know. I made friends with a naval bod who was involved in the recovery of the *Hampshire* crew. Cutting round the site of the sinking for hours in his destroyer. And no one hit a mine in what was reported as a large minefield.'

Anderson flicked his fingers dismissively. 'Draught of a destroyer's nowhere near as deep as a cruiser, old chap. I've no sea legs but even I know that. And what the hell do you do with the crew? Spirit them all to Russia and hide them forever? Come on.'

Edward held his hands up. 'I know, Mark. But I saw that tattoo.'

Anderson looked away and lost himself in thought. The drumming of his fingertips on the chair was the only sound for several minutes.

Then he said, 'And what was all that about you not going on the trip?'

'That's what I've been thinking about all these weeks. I just couldn't understand it; it made no sense. There I was for all the world going to Russia with him and he shoots me down at the last minute with this extraordinary tantrum.'

Anderson nodded and went on thinking, the space between them lapsing again into a freighted silence. Eventually, wearily, he stood up. He went over to the window and then tore, surprisingly gently, the page from the notebook. Walking over to the fire he hesitated at the last moment, as if remembering something, and then gently laid the paper on the little licking flames. A few seconds later it was gone. He walked back to the chair and said, 'Best place for it, old boy. Sleeping dogs best left to lie and all that.'

They looked at each other for a while until a tiny ghost of

a smile appeared at the corners of Anderson's mouth. 'Well, I have to say that really is some juice you managed to find. Just might be your thing after all, this lark. Right, what are you doing this weekend?'

'I think I'll just collapse on my bed.'

'Well, you've earned it. Take some leave. I don't want to see you here until after Easter. You've been flat out.'

'Are you sure?'

'Absolutely. See you back here after Easter Monday. What will it be, Tuesday the twenty-second of April? The Paris Conference isn't going to go away; there's an awful lot of barking mad water to go under that bridge of insanity before anything gets signed. The only thing that will likely ever get signed there is a whole lot of restaurant bills. What a bloody circus. There'll be more than enough for you to get your teeth into there. But between now and then – leave. I'll get it all squared with the admin bods.'

For the first time in years, Edward was being given some time to himself; four and a half glorious weeks spread before him. It felt wonderful. 'Are you sure?'

'Quite sure. You need a rest, my friend. I was too hasty sending you out there in any case. Damned lucky not to lose you. Well, that's a civil war for you, chum. Decidedly uncivil.' He took a final swig from his glass in a sign that he considered that the meeting was over. They stood, transitioned to friendly small talk and Edward made to leave.

Just as he was at the door, Anderson said, 'Oh, one thing.'

'Yes?'

'You need a codename. So you can get in touch with us on future operations. What do you want?'

'I get to choose?'

'Well, if you want to, or I can get one of the chaps downstairs to give you a name. But then don't blame me if you end up with something like Trench or Pavement.'

'I'd like to be Beacon, please.'

Anderson frowned, 'Suit yourself. Beacon it is. A light shining in the darkness. Yes, I rather like it. Well, see you in April, old boy.'

Edward mumbled thanks and left the room, walking in a haze through the building full of its chatter and hubbub as though there was no one else in it. Outside he adjusted his hat and felt the traces of spring on his face. He spent a moment trying to take it in, as though he could somehow coax more sunlight through his pores.

He knew exactly what he had to do. He was back in it. Now, finally, was the moment.

That evening, when he got back to his rooms, he sat down, appraised his pen for a while next to an open pad of paper and then picked it up and wrote.

Dear Miranda,

I would very much like to see you and Theo. An awful lot has happened. You may very well not want me to come but I think I might be able to do something that will help. Please reply saying yes or no and I will obey either instruction.

Separately, I enclose the letters – there are twenty in all – that I have written to you over the last few years but never had the courage to send. I know that you had instructed me not to write but I still should have done; instead I used that as an excuse to myself not to send them and so assuage my fear of engaging with you only to be rebutted. In truth I simply lacked the gumption to say what I should have done years ago. That is to say that my time with you at High Hedges allowed me to dream of a future after the war that offered a happiness whose attainment seemed all but impossible and even less likely with every day that passed. A dream, nevertheless, that granted me a hope without which I am not sure I would have retained the strength to carry on.

You said years ago that for me life is like a chess match that I wanted to win, but was also a feast that I never wanted to end. I'm not sure that was quite right. Instead, these last years for me have really been a chess match that I've desperately wanted to be over, so that I can start a feast, or at least try to find how to start one. I've never thought of being in love with anyone before and I am sure that what passed between us in those glorious days would not qualify as love to any neutral observer or experienced hand. To me, though, those days seemed to offer the prospect of the beginnings of the richest feast I could ever imagine. I want to declare this to you so at least I can finally escape any charges of cowardice in this matter. I do not expect you to reciprocate in any way whatsoever, merely to understand my feelings for you, however clumsily expressed.

I am going to post this right now and pray that I do not stay my hand.

With my best as ever and, indeed, my love,

Edward Salter

It felt cold and formal using his surname but he didn't think that the age-long separation warranted just 'Edward'. Then, not allowing himself room for hesitation, he put the letter in a large envelope with the bundle of unsent letters, and walked straight to the nearest post box, humming exaggeratedly as he did so, as though he was about to go to the dentist, to ward off any urge not to post them. But he got there and did it. Just before he dropped the envelope in, he brushed it against his lips, looking around furtively in case anyone saw him.

A week later, after a holiday in Suffolk, he arrived back at the mess in London late in the afternoon to find a reply in his pigeon hole. The nerves he had been expecting to feel as he picked it up failed to materialise. He did, though, blur his eyes just for a second and hoped what would follow would be a yes.

My dear Edward,

Yes. We are both looking forward to having you here. Please stay for a while. Also – and he is adamant on this – please come in your uniform. A train gets into Burridge at a quarter to three on Friday. I will meet you there.

Thank you for your letters. You are brave to have sent them.

Miranda (Thorne). I've never seen a more ridiculous inclusion of a surname in my life. You silly soul.

Any awkwardness at the line about him being brave to have sent the letters was gainsaid by the deep excitement and joy he now felt. A few days later, he was packing his valise, ensuring he included a thick woollen jumper and his boots from the Peninsula – old friends – and with plenty of time to spare, he set off for King's Cross.

CHAPTER FORTY-FIVE

He made the train with a couple of minutes to spare, although it ended up being delayed by half an hour due to some unspecified complication. Finally it left the station and he found himself oddly relieved at the frustration he felt at the lateness. It meant that he wasn't losing command of reality, that he was retaining a link with his pre-war self. His old fastidiousness remained. He was always quite distrustful of the proud and bluff assertions made by people back from the war that their experience had helped them to put things into perspective to such an extent that they would never again worry about small things. Knowing that he retained the same quirks and foibles meant that he was still Edward, no matter what had been thrown at him.

Similarly, he had an adjacent thought that it was foolish to adopt the position, which he had noticed was becoming quite prevalent, of refusing to ever talk about the war. It was the single most exciting thing that had ever happened to him, a spark that had lit underneath him. For him not to talk about it would have been as sure a sign of madness as going too far the other way and making memories of it his master. Everything in moderation, he thought.

So it was that for the first hour of the journey he sat in silence looking out the window, grubby with an early spring film of dust and the tiny brush marks of dead insects, watching the landscape flicking by. Increasingly nervous as to what awaited him, he started to fret over how he would feel when reunited with Miranda and Thorne. The prospect grew so intimidating that he resolved not to think about it. Just deal with it when it comes. You can't dread something you're in, he remembered to himself. He made an effort to think about the Peninsula, the start of everything. His eyes glazed over, lost in a thousand fractured images that blazed themselves onto them, flicking past in succession sometimes with the smooth pattern of a film from a projector, at other times sticking on one particular picture. The voyage to Imbros, for instance, replayed smoothly, as did the first move up to the line on Helles and, oddly, the Turkish night attack when they had been about to launch the trench raid, that he found he could replay in his mind's eye with perfect recall, down to the amount of breaths he took between shots of his revolver and the exact feeling of his thumb frantically chambering new rounds into it. The sting of the sweat in his eyes and the way that it crystallised on his forehead. Other images jarred. The moment a sandbag fell away from atop a man on a stretcher whose face had been blown off and the discovery from the sight of his chest rising that he was still alive. The Turk's eyes on the attack on the blind crests after he had shot him through the forehead; a begging look spliced with a cold shock. Thorne appearing to him out of the smoke after the attack and guiding him back to the lines.

Then the train was pulling into the station and he realised with a start that he had been dribbling, a line of drool spooling from his lip down onto his chest. He waited as the other disembarking passengers mixed and then melted away with those who had come to meet them until the train had gone and the platform was empty save for a lad sweeping it. The boy looked barely eighteen and as he passed him Edward was surprised to see a livid red scar on the back of his hand and a couple of fingers missing. The boy looked up at him – vaguely cross-eyed – and Edward smiled him a greeting that he hoped would convey in it an acknowledgement that they had both served, and then smiled to himself a second time at how ridiculous a notion that was. He could have got that injury anywhere from Jutland to Ypres to an accident in a factory or a farm. But he felt sure the boy had been in the army. He wondered for how long he would view people through the prism of imagined shared experience.

In his nervous state, the platform seemed empty, and for a second he started to wonder if Miranda had reneged on the plan. But then there she was. At the end of the platform, in the wide empty dustbowl studded with gravel and horse dung, she was parked up and was standing by the car, leaning back on the bonnet with arms folded, looking over at him quizzically. His mouth went dry.

He walked over to her for what felt like an age and drew himself up a few yards away, still conscious of the gulf in time and events between now and when he had last seen her. Neither of them spoke. It was better that way, he felt. Words would only obfuscate or confuse. Everything stood still for several steady beats. She looked thinner, he thought, more drawn. Still that quicksilver in her eyes though. He took his cap off and smiled. Then, to his horror he felt his eyes mist up and just as a whole tear started to form he realised the only way he could hide it was to go closer. He darted over to her and then almost picked her up, putting his head over her shoulder so she wouldn't see him crying. But then all was lost as the solitary tear became a stream, and he broke into great gulps of sobs and enveloped her, as she whispered into his ear the words that no one had ever said to him over the entire span of the war.

'It's all right. It's all right. It's all right, Edward. You're here. We're here. Everything is going to be all right.'

CHAPTER FORTY-SIX

There was no need for him to fill in his history, he realised. She knew it already. So as they drove to High Hedges she told him what had happened there in the last few years. After Thorne's injury they had stayed in America for a year, but in the end to no avail, returning in the autumn of 1917. His other injuries, ones that no one had concentrated on in the rush to see if his sight could be saved, had been neglected. His right arm was very weak and its nerves so damaged that he couldn't really do anything with it. His right lung had taken a beating too.

Edward was impressed by how bloodlessly she narrated all of this, winding it up with, 'He won't make old bones now, you know.' She smoked as she drove, calm and measured.

Then she added, as though she was talking about people she had barely met, 'You do know my parents are dead, don't you? Daddy last year and then Mummy in January. This wretched flu.'

Edward didn't say anything at first. Then, deliberately and trying to convey as much contrition as he could, said. 'The letter I sent you. When Theo was injured. I'm so sorry. It was entirely inappropriate. I can't believe I wrote such a thing. You must have thought that I had lost it.' Which, in several ways, he had.

She looked puzzled at first and then said, 'No. God no. It wasn't your letter at all. In fact I rather liked it. It was more that I just didn't want to engage with anything about the war. And neither did he. Nothing at all. And you were the first target that came my way. The letter must have been the first to arrive and you were so recent in my thoughts, the only one of his comrades that any of us had met so you were guilty by association. I did calm down. After a few months I thought about writing back but somehow couldn't. I did like it in fact. I read it almost every day, even now. Though it did make you sound as though you had swallowed a dictionary.'

The lost chance of friendship created by two and a half years of mutual stonewalling was too much for Edward to comprehend. They sat in silence for a while. It was just too sad for words.

She brightened. 'But now I have your other letters. At last. I wish you had sent them when you wrote them. But that's my fault, I know. I should have written to you. I haven't told Theo about them.' She shifted her tone and said slyly, 'Goodness me; I didn't know how much of an impression I had made.' She looked across at him and smiled at his immediate blushing. 'Look at you. Red as an apple. Don't worry, I'm only teasing.'

Then, 'How's the shoulder?' she asked, a hint of a smile breaking through.

He instinctively put a hand to his bullet wound and she said, 'I thought it was your right one?'

He grinned. 'Yes, that one was. Oh, that healed very quickly. No – I got my left one broken in January. In Constantinople. Got shot. Long story.'

'One war, two broken collarbones?'

'Yes. Terribly clumsy.'

They started to speak about more general things, touching on every subject that wasn't Thorne, and the stiffness between them gradually dialled down until he judged it was the right time to ask.

'How is he? As in, his character.'

'You'll see. The same, in so many respects, but obviously different. He's not bitter, I don't think, thank goodness, but there's a sort of apathy that I never expected. As though he just can't be bothered. I think I was expecting anger. You can reason with anger. But with listlessness it's just so frustrating; you can't shake a rag doll into life, you know.'

He let a moment of silence settle before then asking the next question.

'And how does he look?'

She brightened and said, 'Oh, much better. Much better. Goodness, it was dreadful at first. But the scars have got so much better.' She said this with a pride that made Edward want to choke. 'In some light it can be as though it never happened. Well, if you disregard the patch. But you'll notice it. Mostly round the right side of his forehead. A little on his cheeks. Makes him a bit more rakish, sometimes. I suppose the good thing is that if you are shocked by it he won't be able to tell. But I think he's still good looking at any rate.'

Then she chuckled a little. 'Well, I know he is; the nurses he had were all in love with him from the very first. I suppose you think me frightfully blasé. I know I am, but we saw so many others in the hospitals who were so much worse than he was. At first I was horrified but eventually one comes to get used to it.'

'And how are you?'

He had timed the question badly as at that point she slowed into Leighton, only a few hundred yards from the gates to High Hedges. She smiled but he knew her eyes were lying. 'Oh, you know. Keeping on, keeping on. Look, here we are. You won't recognise it like this. A million miles from that drab old February.'

They turned up the drive and he felt a calming surge at being back.

Then she changed tone from breezily conversational to quick formality. 'Now, he's not here at the moment. He's off helping Mr Claremont. He does an afternoon a week for him. Goodness knows what, but it gets him out. It's normally on Tuesdays but when he found out you were coming he asked for today as well. I think he wants you to see him up and about. So get inside and make yourself at home; you've got your old room. He should be back at four. There'll be tea for you both then.'

He suddenly felt afraid. 'Will you not be there too?'

The car pulled to a halt outside the front door. 'No,' she replied, 'some errands to run.' She tutted impatiently. 'Now chop-chop, out you get.'

He got out, took his valise from the boot and waved her off as she sped away. He knew she didn't have any errands. His stomach felt light as he wondered how the next hour would go.

Looking over the grand sweep of the parkland that sloped away before him, he tried to imagine the line that he and Miranda had taken on their fog-wrapped ride three years ago now. More than a thousand days, he realised, since then.

He went into the house. In the hall he looked down towards either wing. No one. He walked over the huge rugs towards the piano with a slow, heavy tread and paused, thinking for a moment before going up the stairs to his bedroom. It was exactly as it had been. He took his jacket and tie off, splashed some water over his face to brighten himself up and in the mirror examined how his shaving had held up and then re-knotted his tie with keen precision. He took his two medals from his valise and pinned them onto his jacket. Fully dressed, he looked at himself in the mirror. Not half bad, he thought.

He went downstairs and, at the first-floor landing, on an impulse, he went down the corridor to Thorne's room. He opened the door, feeling neither nervous nor as though he was trespassing. It seemed to him to be the most natural thing in the world. Come to check in on his friend's dugout.

He looked round the room, vast and double-windowed, not having had the chance to really appraise it during his previous stay. Thorne came flooding back to him. A jumble of kit stuffed into every nook, the walls were mounted with photographs, now unseen, of school sports teams. Around the sink were stuck dozens of cigarette cards of cricketers and soldiers. He smiled disbelievingly to see ones of Kitchener and Hamilton as part of a 'Heroes of the Transvaal War' series. On a rattan stand to the side of the sink were a pair of hairbrushes with Thorne's initials on them. Cricket caps, ties and novels were all ordered neatly on their shelves, the ragged, dignified teddy bear on the chaise longue making him smile. The room was fresh and clean, with bedsheets that had been well made. It made him as pleased as it did sad at the futility of it all.

He stood and went over to the left-hand window, the scene before the house beautiful in the bright afternoon light. The panes were so warped with glacial, decades-long movement of the glass that their lower halves sat imperfect and distorted their light, shifting and breaking the geometry of the garden. Edward tried to picture Thorne as a boy playing on the lawn and imagined if the glass somehow held that image still, a captured moment written in it to hang in eternity. He stayed like that for a while.

Leaving the room, he closed the door behind him and made his way back to the landing, down the stairs and to the piano. He rested his right thumb on middle C and ghosted a note, pressing the key down so slowly that it made no sound. Then his middle finger on E and his little finger on G, playing a C major broken chord's silent shadow. He couldn't bring himself to sound the notes, as though to do so would be an assault upon Thorne's privacy.

His watch said five minutes to four. He went outside to the gravel to await Thorne's arrival but instantly felt ridiculous. It was as though he was welcoming Thorne into his own home; would he be annoyed by this, not mind one bit or perhaps even find it funny? He wished that Miranda hadn't left them. Just at the point where he decided it would be better to go up to his room a nasal drone came faintly from behind the house. As it grew louder its source became apparent: a motorcycle swooped round the drive, driven by a boy who Edward recognised instantly as Tyson, the catalyst of his horse riding accident. And there, riding pillion, his fringe billowing backwards and gripping Tyson's waist, was Thorne.

There he was.

The boy stopped and looked at him. 'I know you. How's your arm, sir?'

'Oh, do be more polite, you impudent wretch,' admonished Thorne. 'Is our honoured visitor finally here? Off you go, Tyson, and thank you for the lift. Same time on Tuesday?'

The boy made to get off the motorcycle, presumably to help Thorne inside, but he forestalled him. 'No thank you. I can do it from here. Or my friend can help me.'

The boy shrugged in a suit-yourself gesture and drove away.

As the noise faded, Thorne stood up as straight as he seemed able to, shrunken and frail, extending a long white stick in front of him. 'Now where are you? Just say and I'll find you. My hearing's terribly good now.'

Edward couldn't speak.

'Don't hide, Wise Owl.'

Finally he managed to croak, 'I'm here. Ten yards to your front.'

'In your uniform, as requested?'

'Suited and booted.'

'Good. Now let's see if you pass muster.' He moved over to him with surprising speed and stopped when his stick touched Edward's boot. He transferred the stick to his right arm, which remained limply by his side as his left hand felt up Edward's chest to his neck and chin. 'More work shaving, chum; what did you shave with this morning, a brick? There's not an ounce of fat on you. Mrs Gavin will soon see that right.' Then his hand moved down to his jacket and his medals.

'Fourteen to fifteen Star, snap. Can't believe they didn't give us a bespoke one for the Peninsula. You know the French did? Unbelievable. Hello, what's this? Someone's been in the butter.

A bloody DSO, if I'm not mistaken. Or is it one of those funny French jobbies?'

'DSO. It wasn't anything. The battalion's award, really. They were . . .'

'. . . handing them out with the rations,' they said at the same time and then both started laughing.

All the while, Edward had been appraising him, shocked at his appearance. Whatever Miranda had promised, she had misrepresented how bad he looked. He wasn't horrendously disfigured as such, just not nearly the same as he had been. The right-hand side of his face had borne the brunt of the explosion, much of the skin warped and mottled, a coarse mess of lines and craters. That right eye was covered with a natty black silk patch and the left hung directionless as though a doll's. And he had lost his strength, it seemed, his frame no longer as immaculate nor as firm as it had been; he stooped and his clothes billowed around him. Thorne seemed to guess what he had been doing and asked him, 'So, what do you think? Same as I was?'

Edward struggled to answer but knew he had to say something. 'You look like a brigand. Quite a raffish one, at that.'

'Don't lie. I look like what I am. Some wizened old cripple. Well, tea?'

He broke away from their conversation and made towards the front door, feeling his way deftly as Edward followed him. At the door Edward tried to overtake him to open it for him but Thorne kept up his standoffish tone. 'I can bloody manage, all right?' Inside the hall he closed the door behind them and said, 'Right, drawing room to hear about your DSO. I want to know everything.'

Whatever Edward had expected after speaking to Miranda earlier it hadn't been this. He thought he would find him in one of three states; melancholia, tetchiness or determined, stoic pluck. But what was presented to him was a mix of all three, sometimes all manifesting in the same minute while at other times two of the trio would cede for an amount of time to let the third be master before then rushing back in. He was completely out of his depth and while outwardly managing to keep up a patient, forgiving humour he was desperate for support to arrive in the form of Miranda.

They talked about what Edward had been doing in the war, Thorne lightening to tales of the men. He was visibly delighted at hearing about Baffle and Preston in particular, both having survived without injury, somewhat miraculously. Thorne said cheerfully and without any of the front that had been so evident so far, 'Well we ought to have a reunion sometime soon. I've missed the chaps so much. I really have,' but then that only led to a question about the commanding officer and Edward had to break that dread news.

He moved on to the Constantinople mission but only deflated Thorne further with Lipin's death. Edward thought he detected some pause, a catch of breath, when he told Thorne about being shot himself, but it was so quick a moment he couldn't be sure. Throughout, however, their conversation was characterised by the lack of quick rejoinders, the snappy, barbed, fond stichomythia they used to have together.

Miranda did come back eventually and raised the mood somewhat. They went upstairs to get ready for supper, Edward changing out of his uniform into jacket and tie. He spent longer than he thought he would in his room, timid to come down and see Thorne again.

When he finally went downstairs, he heard Miranda's soft voice coming from the drawing room and hesitated about going in, caught in a quandary about not wanting to disturb them but also not to eavesdrop. But the noise was all hers without any reply and so he peeped through the gap in the door and saw Thorne lying on the sofa, his legs over hers as she sat reading a novel to him. He looked happy and content. After a minute or so he went in.

Dinner passed in the same stop-start fashion as before – no sooner had Edward thought he had broken through the screen of formality, suddenly the odd, starchy froideur snapped back into place. Miranda didn't seem to notice it; she must, he reasoned, be used to it by now. Conversation flowed but with none of the abandon that it had previously, when words would tumble out over each other in their excitement at coming together as a trio. Thorne had regressed, it seemed, into someone who trusted only slowly and it was as if Edward was having to forge their friendship from the very beginning again.

After dinner, they had a drink in the drawing room, with Edward – if there was one boon to be taken from the evening – happily surprised at how mobile Thorne was and how well he could navigate the house. He noticed that when Thorne asked for another glass of wine how Miranda would water it down half and half before handing it back to him. He wondered how much of a problem that had become. The evening wound up and they went to bed.

Edward lay awake for two hours, hoping that one of them would come to his room and help to break the ice so they could talk unguardedly and without the barricades that were still very much up. But no creak came along the corridor and presently he fell asleep, glad at least to be finally under the same roof as them both.

CHAPTER FORTY-SEVEN

The weekend passed largely in the nervy, strangulated tone with which it had begun. Tuesday morning they spent quietly, if enjoyably, in the greenhouse, planting bulbs in various pots. Edward looked at Thorne and thought of the moment in Amiens when he had seen him walking through the crowd but had stayed still, neither brave nor decisive enough to go over to him. That episode seemed to be some dreadful foreshadowing of the distance that still stretched between them.

After lunch, they took coffee in the drawing room, Thorne about to get ready to go off with Tyson and drive to Claremont's practice. Miranda left to write some letters in the adjacent study, and Thorne said quite suddenly, as he was deftly pouring himself a second cup, 'So, what's this great plan you have?'

'I'm sorry, plan?'

'Yes. You said in your postcard that you thought you might be able to help. So, can you? What's the theory? Because you sure as hell can't do anything about my eyes.'

Edward scrambled to get his thoughts together, ambushed by the belligerence of the demand. As calmly as he could he explained what he had thought he might be able to do. As he heard himself speak he realised with growing horror how half-cocked and wishy-washy it sounded, like a pupil made to read out an essay that he hadn't spent sufficient time on. 'You remember on the Peninsula, when poor old Sinden got it and you said that the thing that kept you going was walking back here from the railway station?'

Thorne didn't reply and so he went on, feeling resigned about the reaction that he sensed might follow. 'I thought it might be an idea for us both to go to the station and to do the walk, me guiding you. I've done a map recce of the route and am pretty sure how it goes. And then when we get back here you can play your chords on the piano.'

Silence, that stretched for an age.

'So you think I haven't yet fully come home do you?'

'No, that's not what I'm saying . . .'

'You have the temerity to come and see me and my sister, who has single-handedly, by the way, looked after me ever since I got my whole life blown out of me in that godforsaken stretch of line by an enemy who you avoided to swan off and go and fluff some bloody pillows? I've been here for two and a half years, I know my way round the house blind, quite literally bloody blind. I've buried both my parents here and you come and tell me I haven't properly come home yet?'

Edward was shaking, the only certainty he had being that he knew this was only going to get worse.

'And you think that us going for some kind of nature ramble is going to cure anything? Anything at all? And then what? You drop me off here and then sod off back to wherever the hell it is that you call home, your conscience clear and feeling smug that at least good old Theo is now finally back home? I'll be all right, won't I? It doesn't matter what my face looks like. It doesn't matter that the only thing I ever bloody see is the explosion lighting up the body of Stanton and for one split second I know he's dead and I'm wasting my time trying to get him and then my face erupts as what feels like a thousand pieces of metal fly into it. That is all I think of. All I bloody ever think of. And doing a walk – a FUCKING WALK – isn't going to change a damned thing. A damned thing.'

'Theo . . .'

'Kindly leave. KINDLY LEAVE.' He stood with arm outstretched, not to the door of the drawing room but through the fireplace in the direction of the gates to the house. 'Thank you for coming; I have genuinely enjoyed seeing you again but your stay should now come to an end.' There seemed in his tone to be a tiny hint of mollification, an acceptance at least of how violent he had been, but it did nothing to change its sentence.

Edward desperately tried to keep some coldness in his own tone, as if this would preserve his dignity. 'I understand, I'm very sorry. I'm very sorry. Please know that all I wanted was to help in some way, to right the wrong I have felt every single day since we were split up. But I will go. That's no problem. But please know that – from my point of view at least – our friendship will survive all of this. You might hate me, resent me, want never to see me again. But know that you are – and always will be – my greatest friend.'

He turned and started; Miranda was at the door, eyes wet with tears. For how long she had been standing there, he had no idea; she had probably heard the whole exchange. She put a hand out to hold his forearm and though he made to brush it away she held him firm with a surprising grip and whispered viciously, 'Please. Please. Give him a chance. Let me take you to the station at least.'

Something in him held on just enough. He didn't answer but nodded and held her eyes until finally she let go.

Upstairs, he packed quickly, wanting to be out as soon as possible.

Miranda had also wasted no time and was at the front door. Of Thorne there was no sign. Wordlessly they left, got into the car and went down the driveway, Edward refusing to look at the house as they pulled away in case Thorne was watching out of a window himself. But then of course, he wouldn't be watching anything. He lurched sick with sadness. At the gate Miranda braked quickly to avoid the motorcycle driven by Tyson, coming to pick Thorne up to take him to Claremont.

'What a hooligan. He's going to have a dreadful accident one of these days.'

They pulled out of the entrance. Edward couldn't think of a single thing to say.

After a while she broke the ice. 'You do know that no matter what has just happened between you two I should very much like to see you again. I'm just so sorry, for so many things. But I'm very, very glad that you came back to us.' He looked over at her as she broke into a full, sad smile.

He grinned back. 'It's the least I could try to do for him. The Magwitch to his Pip.'

'Sorry?'

'Sorry for what?' he replied, confused.

'What do you mean by Magwitch?'

'You know. *Great Expectations*. Pip's unexpected benefactor.'

'Oh.' Her face fell. 'He never told you, did he?'

'What do you mean?'

She hesitated. 'Why he was called Pip.'

'I suppose not,' Edward said, puzzled and feeling that the ground was being pulled out from beneath him for the second time that day. 'So why was he, if not that?'

Eventually, and after several hesitations, she said, 'He was called Pip because when Mummy was first pregnant with him the doctor came to visit to check everything was all right and said to her that at that stage of the pregnancy the baby was the size of a bat in her stomach. So from then on he was referred to as Pip – pipistrelle bat. When he was born Mummy and Daddy just continued the name. He was always quite embarrassed by it being used around others, so often pretended it was Pip from *Great Expectations*.'

Edward remembered the exact moment that Thorne had told him that and was transported back to that evening. It was just

after Thorne had said that he had no qualms about telling Edward
everything about himself. Clearly, however, not quite everything.
A desperate attempt to keep his whole self from being known
and – as he had put it – to remain still worth finding out about.

She went on. 'But he doesn't like to be called it any more, you
know. Because of the phrase "blind as a bat". From the moment
he came back. None of us were allowed to call him it.'

They arrived at the station and got out. The next train was
due in fifteen minutes. Gradually the platform filled around them
as they talked, Edward wishing that the train could be delayed.
His heart sank as the rails in front of them started singing a little
with their warning of the train about to appear and the crowd
accordingly shifted in response and started to get itself ready.
Round the shallow bend half a mile away the engine appeared
and he picked up his suitcase and prepared to say goodbye to her.

A drone filled their ears, and they both turned to look as
among the carriages and cars outside the station weaved Tyson's
motorbike, Thorne on the back.

Edward dropped his suitcase and lurched along the platform,
mumbling apologies as he went. He broke into a jog and came to
the parked motorcycle as Thorne tried to scramble off it, Tyson
holding him steady. 'It's all right, sir. We made it. He's here.'

In the background, the shrill hiss of the engine braked to a
halt and the platform broke into its chaos but none of it registered
with Edward. All he could see was Thorne as he was marched
over to him and put both his hands on his shoulders. He smiled
his star-shell-bright grin. 'You asked about a walk in this area,' he
said. 'I know quite a good one. Care for a companion?'

CHAPTER FORTY-EIGHT

The bustle around the station died down and Tyson rode away. Edward, Thorne and Miranda fumbled together, laughingly coming up with a plan, splitting up luggage, repacking and preparing for the two boys to do the walk. Eventually they were ready, kitted out in something approaching normal walking gear. Edward carried the large haversack that Thorne had brought with a groundsheet and some basic supplies, biscuits and sandwiches that he had hurriedly made with Mrs Gavin before the frantic ride to the station. 'I have no idea how fast he was going, but from the amount of honking from cars on the road I think it was pretty sharpish.'

It was five o'clock by the time they waved goodbye to Miranda, who was to drive home and await their arrival at some point the next day. Then the granite shroud of the station was fading behind them as they walked off into the evening.

The road took them a mile to the west and they worked out each other's stride, Thorne tapping away with his stick and needing only an occasional touch on his elbow from Edward to keep him straight. Their progress was slower than Edward's usual pace, but not by much. They walked into the setting sun with the gloaming enveloping them, winter's nip still fighting to its last as the new spring warmth ebbed back at day's end. Twenty yards from the wooden signpost that marked the footpath and their route off the road Edward grinned as Thorne said with a smiling, knowing arrogance, 'Now, unless I'm much mistaken then this is where we leave the road.' A clean slab of stone laid vertically into a frame set into the drystone wall made a stile, and Edward helped Thorne over it, feeling for a moment like a parent helping their small child.

A thin dark line of dried mud now marked the path before them, harder going as they had to go in single file, Edward leading and Thorne holding his left shoulder with his own left arm, necessitating shorter steps. It took some getting used to and often Thorne would catch Edward's heels. 'This is like that wretched first journey up to the line on the Peninsula,' he said, the first reference he had made to their joint history.

Step by step, they established a trusting, steady rhythm and made good progress northwards with the dusk, nearly complete now with the sun hidden behind a low bank of cloud sitting to their left. Their paces became softer in concert with the gathering gloom.

'It's getting dark, isn't it?' said Thorne.

'Yes. How did you know?'

'It's the noises. They change around now. Twenty minutes until pitch black, I bet.'

It was indeed twenty minutes. Realising that April's sky was threatening to break open into rain, Edward spied a mulberry tree on the edge of a copse, sitting beneath the umbrella of a taller sycamore that offered some shelter. Beneath the tree, cow parsley was already well grown and tangled with the lower branches of the mulberry. It made for a pleasing sense of security as they burrowed into it, and Edward took the groundsheet from his bag and spread it above them, the strong stems easily supporting it.

The shower did come but was mercifully short and failed to breach the shelter. They ate the sandwiches and biscuits and lay in the dark taking nips from the hip flask that Thorne had also brought. Unable to see anything, Edward felt that they had at last reached parity. If anything, Thorne was more the master of their surroundings than he was.

They chatted inconsequentially, Edward slowly allowing the day's stress to fade and his brain to declutter and make way for sleep as they lapsed into silence.

Then, after some time, Thorne said, 'I can tell you're not asleep. Your breathing's too busy. Why did you not reply to those letters I sent?'

Edward scrunched his eyes and dug his nails into his hands to prepare himself for this. 'It's something I've asked myself a thousand times,' he replied.

'I'll say. You and me both.'

This was it, Edward thought. The moment. Just get it out. It had to be the way. No artifice, no flannel. You can't dread what you're in. He started to speak and found the words easier than he thought he would, free and loose as though waiting to come out, like pus from a blister.

'When I left you, to go to K, I felt excited, sure, but also I felt as though I was deserting you. Deserting you all. Yes, my brain knew that I wasn't but my heart still thought it. And that guilt coupled with then having to translate what we had on the Peninsula, so easy, so clean, so . . . unspoken, into the written word just felt incredibly awkward, impossible. I don't know – I know this sounds so pathetic – but it was like being asked to turn something concrete into something abstract.'

'What, you mean like trying to teach a cricket ball?'

'Exactly, but in reverse, I suppose like trying to throw fortitude. And the longer it went on the harder it became to do.'

Thorne snorted in derision. 'Come on, we've all delayed a thank-you letter so long that you just give up on it, but that's a thank-you letter, not a friendship. Do you know how sad I was you didn't reply? How . . . just so bloody upset. I just couldn't understand what had happened.'

Edward realised he liked having this talk in the pitch black. For one, it felt like it was happening inside his brain, as though it was merely him imagining such a conversation, easier to engage with than one where he could see Thorne. And, of course, perhaps it was easier precisely because he now knew what it was for Thorne to talk to him, always in the dark. Free from any visual cues, free from the tricks and wiles of body language, from the false sympathy of a smile or the beguiling dampening or widening of the eyes. He went on, feeling not happiness, quite, but a release at last at being able to be so pure, so unbuttoned.

'I can't even begin to excuse it. I think perhaps a part of it was also that what happened on the Peninsula and at High Hedges was such a departure from what I had ever seen before – offering such an amazing prospect of what a future might offer – that I shrank back from trying to reignite it in case I wasn't able to.'

'But of course you would have,' Thorne said. 'The Peninsula will always be there between us. Everything that happened there. I remember you pushing me up onto the boat at the evacuation and knowing that for the rest of my life we were going to be joined by it. But I knew that already. Joined by that evening swimming on Helles. By all those nothing moments in dugouts or on the line. By a hundred other times.'

'I know . . .' Edward couldn't bear to hear the litany but Thorne ignored him and carried on.

'The blind crests when we were running back together. The time on Lemnos when you picked up the picture of Miranda. All that was going to be destroyed by you being in London and me being in France? Come on. When you didn't write I couldn't fathom it. And so then when it all happened to me in France with poor old bloody Stanton I was already so stung that you hadn't been in touch that I got this bitterness that you sure as hell wouldn't want to see me now, in this state, so told Miranda to tell you not to even try.'

Edward tried to reply but couldn't. No words could possibly be adequate. Then, though, mercifully and gallantly, it was as though something broke or melted or shifted inside Thorne's own head and he knew the storm, or the eye of it at least, had passed. 'When Miranda told me last week about those unsent letters of yours though, I did rethink.'

'She wasn't meant to . . .'

'Well, she did. She's my sister, old boy. More loyalty to me than to you, I'm afraid.'

Both were silent again. Edward didn't think there was anything more left to say. Then Thorne said, 'In case you hadn't noticed, I'm currently holding my hand above your chest. Do me a favour and shake it, will you? It's killing me holding it here.'

Edward searched for it, found it and shook it, flinching at how weak it was and thinking how painful it must have been for Thorne to have lifted it up. 'Thank you. I'm sorry. I'm so sorry.'

He wondered quickly whether now would be the time to mention Amiens? No. Even now, in this confessional, he couldn't bear to think of it, to bring it out into the open. That was an episode he would take to his grave.

Thorne said, 'And I am too. Thank you. I mean it. Thank you for coming back, my friend.'

They both left it there; nothing more needed to be said, and Edward could tell, as he himself slipped off to sleep, that from the sound of Thorne's own breathing he was fading too. But then just before his eyelids added an extra layer of darkness over his eyes he heard, one more time, 'My great friend.'

Then nothing.

Edward's thick jumper proved its mettle and he slept soundly, stirring only around midnight as a snuffling deer broke nearby branches around the edge of the tree. He was awake for a few minutes while memories of nights on the front came to him, staring out into a dark night or peeping fearfully over the parapet when a baleful alabaster shone over the Peninsula in a sniper's moon. He remembered nights on the line as they both had to try desperately to suppress their chuckles into yelps of breathing. He was sure that he let out a giggle into the night before nothingness then fell over him, dreamless and warm.

He woke with his thighs damp from dew and drew away the groundsheet to see the million droplets on the cow parsley sparkle gold and rainbow colours from the low sun breaching the underside of the tree. A ghostly network of spiders' webs hung above his head, made fuller by the dew, more ossified. He felt an awful pang, as Thorne stirred beside him, that he wasn't able to see any of it.

They wormed out from under the tree and creaked limbs back to life, shaking away the residue of sleep and rubbing their sandpaper chins, teeth chattering at the morning's chill. They got ready to go, the imprint of their bodies in the cow parsley already disappearing as the crushed stalks started to lean up again, and they rejoined the path and carried on.

The route took them over miles of gentle fields and woods, folds in the ground offering one of the most beautiful mornings Edward could remember; folds that, on a battlefield, would become must-take ridges and valleys raked by machine gun fire. Here though was a perfect land, unpoisoned by such snaky heads. The rising sun, still yet to gain its heat, uncovered spring's half-built hedgerows as nearby woodpeckers saluted their arrival. So infrequent was any sign of habitation, with only a couple of soft yellow stone farmhouses nestling nearly invisibly into their surroundings, that it seemed for a time that they were walking through a zero-humaned world.

They moved so softly, boots tracing their way noiselessly over the grass and the soft earth, that at every wood or new field animals failed to notice them and carried on their activities unalarmed. In one small clump of trees were a cock and hen pheasant, he strutting and boastful with his neck thrust out in grandiose stupidity and she following along behind him picking up the food and grubs that he, in his magnificent self-regard, missed on his morning *passeggiata*.

Edward stopped for a while to watch them, and then started to describe the scene to Thorne, but not going on as long as he thought he might, seeing writ across his face a sheer exultation in the day and being where they were. Not the sights, of course, but the scents and the touch of the air on his skin seemed to be elevating him to the same sense of contented rapture as Edward felt. The gap between them may not be quite as unbridgeable as he had feared, then. Perhaps.

They covered the twelve miles with a joyful ease of movement and at no point did Thorne stumble or trip. They came to Leighton at midday, looking as pure a picture of English mythic as Edward had seen. They walked through the village and past the pond next to the green, its rushes starting to come back to life again, and Edward's pulse quickened as they drew nearer to High Hedges.

Violent green downy new leaves on the beech hedges around the gates pushed themselves around the old, marcescent husks left from the previous year. Up the drive, the woods flanking it were carpeted with the daffodils now just on the wane from their pomp and some crows cawed boisterously. Then came the light grey stone of the stables, behind which the back of the house loomed with its prominent chimneys. The earthy, acid tang of horses hung somewhere in the air but there were none to be seen, Falcon and Eagle long gone, the stables themselves all closed, the chipped mounting block standing sadly at the side of the yard. Edward remembered the absurdity of his accident and how angry Thorne had been. For the thousandth time he wondered if it had made any difference. Would he have been allowed to take the job with Kitchener if he hadn't been injured? Could he have been with Thorne in France, to protect him, or to have been in his stead that night on the parapet? The thoughts hung pointless, unanswered, already eternal stabs underneath his heart.

The closer they drew to the house the further apart they began to walk, Thorne's almost microscopic knowledge of every inch of the land showing itself. Edward started to feel a sad anti-climax approaching, a dread that the end of the walk might herald the end of them re-establishing the cord that had held between them all the time on the Peninsula.

Miranda was waiting outside the door. Thorne seemed to sense her presence as he went forward and hugged her, as Edward stood aside for a moment, trying to arrange his thoughts. Thorne broke off the hug and went into the house. He strode without hesitation over to the piano, shiny and ebony and glinting in the light that flooded the hall. Miranda and Edward followed, Miranda reaching for Edward's hand, squeezing it tight and mouthing, 'Thank you'.

Thorne sat down on the seat, its yellow silk covering puckered and frayed. The keys lay before him slightly off-white.

His fingers rested there for a moment, and then he took a breath and played the chord. Just once, without the pedal, so that the three notes sounded clear and simple, dying after a finger left its key. He waited a little, pressed the pedal and then played the chord again and then a third time, the notes now falling into one another and the sound filling the hall. His hands began to move more quickly and he played other chords, his face in the friendly, open, trusting smile that Edward remembered so well from that first night in Valletta and had then seen so often since. Smiling at a sunrise, smiling at a joke, smiling after the action on the blind crests. Finally he stopped and brought his hands down to his sides, the three of them swimming in the cleanness of the silence around them.

Slowly he got up and walked unerringly over to Edward. He held out his hand and Edward took it, dismayed for a moment by the loss of its strength. Then Thorne pulled him closer and put his head over his shoulder in a tight embrace.

'Thank you, my friend. My guide. My Ariadne's thread. Thank you.'

'Welcome home, Theo.'

'It's been a hell of a journey, hasn't it?'

CHAPTER FORTY-NINE

That evening, Edward bathed, changed and went down to drinks where he found Miranda on the sofa. He was about to offer to make her a cocktail when she forestalled him.

'I have something for you. I was going to give it to you at the station for you to read on the train but he arrived in the nick of time. I thought that it might save your friendship with him but luckily he decided to do that himself. He doesn't know I have it; it arrived with all his things a few days after he came back home. Have a read.'

She handed over an envelope, no name on it and yellowed by the years since it had been written. Faint dust markings were on it and inside were two sheets of writing paper. He thought about waiting a few moments before reading it, as if he should brace himself for what he was about to see, but decided to just dive back into the rush of their friendship.

31st May 1916

My Dear Wise Owl,

I've been meaning to do this for you ever since that morning on Lemnos when we went to the top of that hill and I told you all about the beacon chain. The thing is, I needed a copy of the Agamemnon *to mark the places correctly but I didn't want to send for one on the Peninsula as otherwise you'd have found it and spent all the time mobbing me up about being like Brooke and those other blowhards. Anyway, I've now brought my copy from home out here, without you to bother me, and I've made this map of the beacon chain. What do you think? I've had to fill a few of the early ones in from guesswork – the text is unclear in parts – but I think it does a pretty decent job. What I'd like very much is for you and me to go and have a trip out to see if it actually could be done when this lot's all over. Keen? Very good; I knew you would be.*

Incidentally, the slip of paper that I forgot to bring with me when I left the line to go and be adjutant, and that you brought me the next day, was the first attempt at this. I was terrified you had seen it but something in the look on your face told me you hadn't. Well here it is, about nine months and a continent later. Completed it just today.

We miss you here. It's a hell of a show. It's not the Peninsula, at least not quite, but try telling that to the new lot. They're all right though. As said though; I miss you.

Must dash, wiring party's going out tonight and I need to square them away. Will write again soon. Take care my great friend,

Theo

He stayed focused on the second sheet, unable to look away from the map Thorne had drawn. It was of the Aegean, beautifully detailed and annotated with the mountains of the beacon chain shown in smart florid writing. In the bottom right-hand corner he had even drawn a sea monster next to the compass rose. All he could think of was how close he had been to being able to go through Thorne's personal effects and finding the letter when he had arrived back at battalion. What was it the CO had said? He had missed them by a day? Less? What would have happened if he had found the letter then? What would have been different – anything? Nothing? Everything?

25

Miranda was smiling kindly, her face restored to its bright fullness. 'Make any sense to you, does it?' she said. 'I'm glad someone understands it. All Greek to me.'

Her skin shone gold in the evening sunlight as she stood and walked over to the drinks trolley. 'Well, I don't know about you but I could murder a martini. You?'

AFTERWORD

Given that *The Fires of Gallipoli* throws the reader into the deep end of First World War history, some background may be helpful on both the Gallipoli campaign of 1915–16 and the death of Lord Kitchener in June 1916.

By the end of 1914, there was a stalemate in France and Belgium, the fluid fighting of the start of the war having crystallised into the trench-scored lines that would endure with remarkably little movement for the next four years. Winston Churchill and Kitchener proposed an attack from southeast Europe to help relieve pressure on Britain's Russian allies. They planned to capture Constantinople (now Istanbul) to knock the German ally Turkey out of the war. But Constantinople was guarded by the Sea of Marmara whose entrance is the Dardanelles straits, 40 miles long and varying in width from several miles to only a mile at places. The straits were defended by mines in the sea and artillery on the flanking shorelines.

In February and March 1915, the Royal Navy tried to force the straits, but after an all-out attack on 18 March was repulsed with heavy losses, it withdrew completely, the commanders not knowing that the Turkish batteries were now virtually out of ammunition and could not have withstood another day's onslaught. Instead it was decided that the Gallipoli Peninsula on the western side of the straits needed to be captured to allow the fleet safe passage through them. Therefore in April a land operation commanded by General Sir Ian Hamilton was launched to seize it but the British Empire and French forces were only ever able to hold a fraction of its mass as the year progressed, with savage fighting causing appalling casualties on both sides.

The military crisis quickly became a political one – claiming the jobs of Churchill and Hamilton and severely damaging Kitchener's reputation too – eventually only being solved by the final decision to withdraw completely from the Peninsula. Ever since visiting and researching this tragic and haunting battlefield, I have been fascinated by this what-if moment of the First World War.

It is somehow reassuring in our paranoid, fractious times to know that conspiracy theories are not a new phenomenon. When HMS *Hampshire* sank off Orkney on the evening of 5 June 1916 a raft of theories appeared: Kitchener had been killed by the British government wanting rid of him; he hadn't been killed at all but was in Russia helping the Tsar; *Hampshire* was sunk not by a mine but by a bomb planted by a German spy or Irish nationalists; and any number of other ideas that gainsaid the reality that *Hampshire* sailed into a thirty-four-strong minefield that had been laid on the western side of the archipelago a week previously by the German submarine *U-75*.

There were several unusual things about the sinking, not least *Hampshire*'s route out of Orkney. Normally ships bound for Russia would go up the eastern side of the islands using the land to shelter from the prevailing wind. The weather forecast at the time, however, was for an easterly wind, which meant that *Hampshire* took the less familiar route up the west. The forecast was wrong and the going was so dreadful that her two escorting destroyers had to turn back before they had seen *Hampshire* safely clear of the islands and so were not on hand to pick up survivors after the sinking. People had witnessed the explosion from the land but extremely poor communication and slow decision-making hampered the rescue. Only twelve of the 749 stricken sailors were saved.

I believe that it was a tragic accident exactly in line with the official verdict and that Kitchener drowned in the sinking but I liked the ghost of one of the conspiracy theories for a story. Also it *is* notable that none of the destroyers that helped in the subsequent search for survivors – described by Mackaness to Edward – hit a mine in what was such a well-laid field. Perhaps their draughts were indeed shallow enough to clear the submerged mines, as Anderson suggests.

The Fires of Gallipoli is draped over the skeleton of real events. I have taken liberties with real-life characters – Kitchener, Hamilton, Valentine Braithwaite, Henry Moseley, Clement Attlee – but tried to make their portraits as accurate as possible. Likewise for the real events: the dates, the geography and the tactical situations of the momentous events around the Dardanelles, in the seas round Orkney, in northern France in the build-up to the Somme offensive and in post-war Constantinople.

I hope that the reader holds most firmly in their memory, though, not the whys and wherefores of the history, but Edward, Theo and the joys, trials, troughs and surging crests of great friendship.

ACKNOWLEDGEMENTS

I am indebted to many people for this book's publication.

It has been good fun and extremely rewarding to work with the team at Elliott & Thompson. Katie Bond and Pippa Crane have worked on it tirelessly and with unfailing good humour and their vision for what *The Fires of Gallipoli* could become has been transformative and inspirational. It is impossible to overstate how much the book has benefited from editing by both Jill French and Celia Hayley; I am fortunate indeed to have had two such brilliant editors. Many thanks to Donna Hillyer for her incisive and sensitive copyedit, and also to Minna Fry and Robin Harvie. Alex Hippisley-Cox and Amy Greaves have masterminded the publicity and marketing and it has been very enjoyable to work with them. Thank you also to Anna Stelter and the Simon & Schuster sales team. I am grateful to Luke Bird, who designed the evocative and striking cover. Finally, an enormous thank you to Lorne Forsyth for believing in the manuscript when it was a shadow of what it is now.

Joyce Meader gave advice on embroidery and whether the Kitchener stitch, that Baffle talks about, could be attributed to the great man. Patrick Massey helped with the piano scenes. Xander Caldin read the first draft of the manuscript and I am grateful indeed for his counsel.

The book is dedicated to my late father; to him and my mother I owe the most extraordinary thank you, not only for such a happy upbringing but for instilling a love of reading and always encouraging my writing. To my sisters Poppy and Rosie my thanks and love as ever and I promise I will now stop going on about Gallipoli (honest).

To Alexandra, thank you for your love and support, and for Constance and Francis, who I hope will enjoy reading this one day.